What the critics are saying...

&

4 stars! "Wilde's **Hidden Enemies** takes the reader on a roller-coaster ride...This is a steamy anthology. All three authors serve up a hot read that will completely satisfy." ~ *Romantic Times*

4 Cups! "**Men To Die For** is an exciting anthology that I highly recommend to other avid readers of erotic romance. I am sure this terrific book will remain on my keeper shelf for many years to come. Ms. Wilde is a talented author with a knack for creating sexy heroes who really trip my trigger. I highly recommend this story to anyone who enjoys tales of love and the paranormal." ~ *Coffeetime Romance*

"Men To Die For delivers an extraordinary, zesty romance that is sure to build up your sexual tension to the highest power! I can say that these three authors have mastered the art of creating wildly hot stories featuring strong alpha-type men with equally self-determining women that quickly heated up the pages. This anthology is definitely a keeper! **Hidden Enemies** by Ravyn Wilde gets a 5 star O heat rating!" ~ *Just Erotic Romance Reviews*

"MEN TO DIE FOR encompasses three fabulous stories about the kind of men many women dream about. The military man, firefighter, P.I./shapeshifter are all idealistic candidates for hours of fantasizing. All of the stories have smart, sassy characters and interesting plots that pull the reader into the story as well as into the characters lives. This is definitely the ideal book to forget about your own troubles for a little while and embroil yourself in somebody else's." ~ *Romance Junkies*

"Men To Die For is certainly a temperature raising and a heart-pounding anthology that smolders from start to finish. Praising this book is so easy because I loved all the stories in this book. Each story varied and was able to capture my imagination from a romance suspense story, to one of a shape-shifting creature...all of them were great to read and I heartily recommend that you peruse this anthology too."~ *eCataromance*

"This book gives readers three tales of romance and seduction along with a little action, adventure and paranormal accents. All three tales includes strong willed men who are determined to find love and hold on to it. It also has women who go against the odds to find happiness. The love scenes are sensual and passionate and all three couples have a chemistry that readers will enjoy. Ravyn Wilde, Denise Agnew and Shelly Munro have created stories that will stick with readers long after they finish the book." ~ *The Romance Studio.*

"WOW! Denise A. Agnew did it again...a brilliant short story about emotionally wounded people who become insecure after tragic incidents happen and false decisions are made...Evan and Lillian are brilliantly written characters and Denise A. Agnew succeeded in bringing them and their feelings to life. The sex scenes are extraordinary. I seldom had the opportunity to read such magnificent, erotically written scenes. The author was successful in creating a sizzling atmosphere with a mere kiss. It's absolutely stunning and a must read." ~ *Cupid's Bow Reviews*

"Ms. Agnew is a talented and prolific author. I hope to read more of her terrific work in the future. I recommend this story to anyone who likes stories of sexy men in uniform." ~ *Coffee Time Romance*

MEN TO
Die FOR

DENISE A. AGNEW
SHELLEY MUNRO
RAVYN WILDE

ELLORA'S CAVE
ROMANTICA PUBLISHING

An Ellora's Cave Romantica Publication

www.ellorascave.com

Men to Die For

ISBN 9781419954382
ALL RIGHTS RESERVED.
Hidden Enemies Copyright © 2005 Ravyn Wilde
Meltdown Copyright © 2005 Denise A. Agnew
Make That Man Mine Copyright © 2005 Shelley Munro
Edited by Kelli Kwiatkowski, Sue-Ellen Gower and Mary Moran
Cover art by Willo

Electronic book Publication September 2005
Trade paperback Publication April 2007

Content Advisory:

S – ENSUOUS
E – ROTIC
X – TREME

Ellora's Cave Publishing offers three levels of Romantica™ reading entertainment: S (S-ensuous), E (E-rotic), and X (X-treme).

The following material contains graphic sexual content meant for mature readers. This story has been rated E–rotic.

S-*ensuous* love scenes are explicit and leave nothing to the imagination.

E-*rotic* love scenes are explicit, leave nothing to the imagination, and are high in volume per the overall word count. E-rated titles might contain material that some readers find objectionable—in other words, almost anything goes, sexually. E-rated titles are the most graphic titles we carry in terms of both sexual language and descriptiveness in these works of literature.

X-*treme* titles differ from E-rated titles only in plot premise and storyline execution. Stories designated with the letter X tend to contain difficult or controversial subject matter not for the faint of heart.

Contents

HIDDEN ENEMIES

Ravyn Wilde

છ

Dedication

ഔ

This book is dedicated to my girlfriends.

Those select few who take me out to let off steam by dancing on tabletops, are there for dinners to let me bitch and gambling trips where I can sit in front of the machines for hours. Thank you Joanne, Marjorie and Tracey.

There are days I couldn't go on without you.

Trademarks Acknowledgement

ഔ

Chapter One

Jenna pulled smoothly into the post office parking lot and stopped the car. Sitting quietly for a minute, she enjoyed the opportunity to really listen to the soothing patter of rain on the SUV's roof.

Peace.

Trying not to fidget, she closed her eyes and took a deep breath, focusing on the rare feeling of blessed tranquility at the end of this long day. Arriving at the office early, she'd worked frantically through lunch at her job as a financial analyst. Her chosen career meant obscenely good money, and a lot of stress. Add in the horror she'd been through during the last eighteen months, and any moment of calm deserved to be treasured.

So, was she at home with a glass of wine, in front of a roaring fire relaxing as she should be? No. Instead of toasting her toes she was parked in front of the post office to pick up her mail. Her soon-to-be ex-husband—*please God, let the final paperwork be in today's mail*—wanted to play juvenile games. Her mail had disappeared, been torn up, soaked through and opened until she had wised up and gotten a P.O. Box. No one saw her husband tampering with her mail, so she couldn't prove it, but she knew it was Rick.

Like she knew he was responsible for keying her car in the parking garage at the office, and knocking over her garbage can, strewing crap all over the front yard. And let's not forget the damage he caused when he'd saturated her lawn with gasoline, destroying large patches of grass she had to reseed.

The restraining order kept him from using her as his favorite punching bag, at least for now, but it seemed everything else was fair game for the jerk. For Jenna, living had become a waiting period in preparation for the day when the divorce was final...*please today*...the house had closed...*yeah, tomorrow*...and she could move on with her life.

Then she could use the money in her savings account and her half of the equity in the house to buy a little place of her own. Away from Rick.

She still hadn't decided if Dallas was big enough for the two of them, but it didn't matter if she had to leave. The last year and a half dealing with the problems Rick caused had isolated her. There was nothing holding her to this city.

A lull in the rainstorm caught Jenna's attention. Time to make a run for it.

Dressed comfortably in jeans and an old sweatshirt, Jenna could barely contain her satisfaction as she sat down at her kitchen table the next evening. She'd been working at home, packing for several hours before she allowed herself this little break.

Glancing around the now bare room, she sighed. She used to love this kitchen. After she'd painted it a pale blue and hung yellow and blue striped curtains in the large window over the sink, Rick had built corner shelves to display her favorite teapots. Now the walls looked dingy with the window and shelves naked. An open box sat in front of her, ready for the last of her kitchen things.

Refusing to be saddened by the sight, she took a sip from her glass of white wine and brought her attention back to the table. It was Friday, and in front of her were three pieces of paper guaranteeing a new beginning for her life. Amazing how important these papers were. There was the final divorce decree she'd received in the mail yesterday, the papers from today's house closing with the check for her half of the equity attached, and the largest commission check she'd ever made.

By no stretch of the imagination was she rich, but she had enough to start over. Her heart hurt when she thought of the past years.

Thirty-seven years old, she had married Rick Jessup five years ago. Almost four years of their marriage were good ones, full of love and laughter. The last year's quick descent into hell became a painful and vivid lesson in contrasts — the before and after pictures were not pretty.

Before the car accident that had somehow bruised Rick's brain, he'd been funny, attentive and very spontaneous. They'd fallen in love, married and lived a very normal life, the two of them working from home and spending the weekends taking little trips or doing chores around the house. Neither of them were partiers, they drank only occasionally and didn't use drugs.

After… Well, after was a different story.

Rick first turned moody, then secretive. Somehow compartmentalizing his life, at first he appeared to handle everything as usual, except for his relationship with Jenna. He focused on her in an alarming way. Always watching her, following her…he developed an insanely jealous streak she couldn't understand.

When she refused to stay home from a work conference in a neighboring city to placate his demands, he attacked her. Put his hands around her neck and almost choked her to death. Immediately he was contrite. Sorry. Willing to do anything, even see the psychologist she'd been trying to get him to make an appointment with.

The doctor diagnosed Traumatic Brain Injury Syndrome, TBIS, due to the injury he'd received to his frontal lobe during the car accident. At first, Jenna worked very hard to be supportive and understanding. But Rick refused any and all rehabilitation recommended by his doctors, and nothing she did made a difference. Their lives started to revolve around physically or emotionally abusive incidents, each followed by him begging to be forgiven.

Then Rick began self-medicating...taking drugs that exacerbated his descent into cruel and violent behavior.

Jenna started going to the psychologist on her own. When she discovered it was unlikely Rick would get any better without the treatment, and after he'd put her in the hospital...twice...she'd finally filed for divorce. The physical scars on her body and the emotional wounds left on her psyche were proof she hadn't done it fast enough.

Luckily she was her mother's daughter. Her mother had told Jenna all her life how a woman needed "mad money". Money that would be hers alone, money no one needed to know about, not even her husband. When Jenna turned sixteen, her mother helped her open a savings account under her mom's maiden name, with Jenna as a cosigner, and she'd been putting money in it since her first job. She had continued putting money in the account after she married Rick.

At first, Jenna felt guilty keeping the savings hidden. Rick spent everything they made on new cars, a large house and two weeks a year in Hawaii, so it didn't seem fair to keep the money a secret. Deciding to surprise him with a nest egg on their tenth anniversary helped alleviate those feelings.

Never again would she be so stupid. No matter what she did in the future, she would always keep her own hidden cache of money...not that she ever wanted another man in her life for more than maybe an occasional night of sex.

Jenna snorted inelegantly at that thought. Yeah right! She'd only been with one man before Rick, and none since. *Femme fatale* she was not. Stretching her memory, she couldn't even recall the last time she'd felt a sexual urge. Certainly not in the last six months since she'd filed for divorce. It had to have been a year—give or take a month—before that, as well. She hadn't wanted Rick after he started using her as an outlet for his rage. Loving Rick had been replaced first with confusion, then irritation and finally outright fear. It was hard to remember the man he used to be.

Glancing out the window to see night had fallen, Jenna figured she'd strolled down memory lane long enough. Gathering up the papers and checks, she stuck them back into her purse. It was time to make dinner and then walk through the house to make sure she hadn't missed anything. Everything should be packed up and ready for the movers tomorrow, sorted into three piles. One with boxes and furniture for Rick to pick up Sunday after she was long gone, another group of items for charity, and the last bunch included some things she would move to storage.

The most important things, like the few family heirlooms and the teapots Rick hadn't destroyed in one of his rages, along with her best clothes, were already loaded in her SUV. The rest would be put into storage until she figured out where she wanted to settle.

For the next week or so she would live in one of those residential hotels until she decided if she would stay in Dallas or not. The only thing holding her at this point was a job she loved.

Deep in thought, Jenna turned to set the cast-iron skillet on the burner. The pan had been her grandmothers, and was to go in the box on the counter and then into her car. She left it for last because she wanted pan-fried hash browns and scrambled eggs for dinner. The meal served the dual purpose of providing comfort food while using up the last few ingredients in her refrigerator.

Picking up a potato, she turned to get the grater, and saw Rick standing in the arch to the dining room. Tall and wiry, her ex-husband had short blond hair and moss-green eyes. He was dressed in jeans and a dark green pullover sweater that enhanced his eye color. The eyes that used to look at her with such love, now sparked with intense hatred.

Jenna squawked and dropped her potato. "Rick," she stuttered. Her heart was beating as fast as a hummingbird's and her hands started to shake.

"It was stupid to leave the french doors unlocked, Jenna," he said with a leer.

Jenna frowned. The doors in the dining room weren't unlocked. She'd checked them last night and hadn't used them since. If he'd broken in this evening, she would have heard him, so he must have come by earlier while she was still at work and set this up. Her entire body quaked in alarm and she took a deep breath, struggling to still the panic.

Trying to appear calm and nonconfrontational so she wouldn't upset him, Jenna softly questioned, "Why are you here, Rick?"

"Don't act so damn dumb, Jenna. I got something in the mail today that pissed me off. *You* piss me off. The divorce papers, Jenna. I fucking told you not to go through with it. I fucking told you you'd be sorry." His eyes were now completely focused on her. This close, she could see they were bloodshot and wild. The vein in his neck bulged. None of these things were good signs.

The physical signals and his tirade answered a few questions she wouldn't have dared to ask. Rick didn't swear unless he was high, he was in a violent mood...or he was threatening her. Knowing her neighbors weren't close enough to hear her scream meant she was on her own. Damn, Rick for putting her through this again! Her pulse leapt in fear and she could feel a trickle of sweat creeping down her lower back. *Just breathe*, she told herself, and started praying. *Help me. Oh, God, helpmehelpmehelpme.*

Rick took a step toward her.

Stifling a squeal of distress, Jenna took a step back and bumped into the stove. She was trapped. She started to rub her sweaty palms on the legs of her jeans, and then consciously curbed the nervous reaction. "You need to leave, Rick," she pleaded. She hated the whiny tone in her voice and knew nothing she said would help this situation. Her mind scrambled for a way out—landing on and discarding things she might say to diffuse the assault she knew was coming.

"What I need is to teach my wife a lesson. You don't understand, bitch. I've told you before but you don't listen.

You're too stupid to be on your own, and no one will ever want you but me," he spat out, as he again moved aggressively toward her.

Widening her eyes, she pushed back into the stove in an unconscious effort to get away. Her hands went behind her back as if she could brace herself for any blow he would throw. Her right hand settled over the handle of the iron skillet, a very solid weapon of defense. Maybe... Jenna knew she'd only get one chance.

"You are such a bitch, Jenna. You're a fucking lousy screw, and are so fucking brainless. You thought you would just sign me out of your life. And could get the cops to keep me from taking what's mine. You haven't learned your lesson, bitch. You can't leave me. You are mine! You need to realize you can't get away from me, *wife*." Rick snarled at her and came around the table in a lunge, his fist rising to hit her.

Without thinking, Jenna grabbed the skillet in both hands, like a baseball bat. With form worthy of a major league hitter, she swung the skillet with everything she had and connected with the side of Rick's head.

His fist glanced off her left cheek, hurting enough that she cried out...then she watched him crumple to the floor without a word. Yes! Sobering for one moment, she allowed herself to feel a measure of remorse for hitting him in the head. That couldn't be good for the TBIS.

His fault.

Pushing all her guilty thoughts away, Jenna swayed and quickly stepped around Rick's sprawled body to dash for the cell phone she'd left charging in her bedroom. Skidding to a stop, she muttered, "I am not Too Stupid to Live like all those dumb women in horror stories."

Spinning around, she grabbed the duct tape she'd been using to seal boxes from off the table. Carefully poking Rick's legs with her foot, she set the skillet beside her when he didn't move and in jerky motions, taped his wrists together, then his legs. Wrapping his legs several times, she wound the tape over itself to form a strong bond, leaving the end of the tape secured in back. No way could he move. For good measure, she snipped off a piece to put over his mouth.

When she was satisfied he wouldn't be able to free himself if he regained consciousness, she left the room to grab her phone. Calling 911 when she got back to the kitchen, she held the cell phone in one hand and the iron skillet in the other as she stood over the silent body of her ex-husband spread limp on the kitchen floor.

Several hours later, Jenna sat alone in a hotel bar with both hands wrapped around her Irish coffee. The cops managed to arrive within minutes of her call. They took her statement, checked to make sure she didn't need medical attention for her cheek, and then hauled Rick out of the house and booked him on assault, breaking and entering, and for violating the restraining order. After they took him to the hospital, he'd be in jail for a couple of days.

With the money he'd just received for his half of the house equity, he would probably be out on bail by Monday or Tuesday. As the police were leading him away in handcuffs, Jenna received a pretty clear signal from the look in his eyes and his muttered, "This isn't done, bitch," that he wouldn't stop trying to find her. And she knew next time he'd kill her.

After loading her now favorite skillet into a box, she'd called the new owners of the house and asked if they would like to look over the things she'd left behind to keep for themselves. The young couple had been thrilled at the chance, they were moving into the house with little furniture of their own. Now they could have hers. In exchange, they would meet the moving company in the morning and redirect them to take anything left over to charity.

Then she drove across town, not to one of the residential hotels like she'd planned, but to a luxury hotel. Even though Rick was behind bars tonight, she wanted the obvious safety of valet parking and the hotel security force. Needing the pampering of a jetted tub and room service, she also wanted to go to the hotel bar and surround herself with people while she tried to make plans.

She didn't want to be alone with her thoughts, yet there was no one she could call. So she sat in the bar and tried to drown Rick out.

As she sat drinking her heavily laced coffee, she kept hearing Rick's voice in her thoughts as he reiterated all the horrible things he'd said to her over the last year. She couldn't think about the steps she should be taking, she felt frozen—deer-caught-in-the-headlights frozen. Knowing that if she jumped in any direction, the lights would track her progress and the car would smack right into her. Only in her case, Rick was the car. In her mind, she railed at the unfairness of it. Why her? What was she going to do?

Her first thought was to run to her mother.

For a moment, Jenna considered that option carefully. Her mom had remarried a few years ago and moved to Spain with her new husband. Jenna knew Carlos had a little money, and their house was certainly big enough that she would have space of her own. Her mother and stepfather would accept her into their home with open arms and take over the burden of protecting her. It was tempting, so tempting to have someone else worry about keeping her safe.

But she couldn't do that to them, and she knew it would be impossible to work, leave the house without an escort or do anything else on her own. She'd be a sitting duck—her mom's would be the first place Rick would look for her. If Carlos or her mother were endangered, Jenna would never forgive herself. Nope, going to Spain was not an option.

She'd have to call her mother later to warn her Rick might be sniffing around, and let her know what her plans were. What plans? Her thoughts spiraled back to Rick.

Not able to shake the memory of him telling her she was ugly, horrible in bed and stupid, she tried another tack...taking inventory of the results of his beatings.

The bruises around her neck had faded long ago. Her broken arm had set fine. The scars on her back from being whipped bloody with a belt weren't pretty, but they no longer hurt. Her cheek did, though. It was bruised and sore from his deflected blow tonight, but invisible under makeup.

Finally she was able to drown the voice in her head, and she grinned in dark satisfaction. For once, she was sure he felt worse. His head had to hurt—the paramedic on the scene said he had a concussion. Poor baby.

Sobering, Jenna sat back. She'd been lucky this time. Even the cops told her to go away and hide for a while. They recommended she take a vacation for as long as she could afford, so Rick would have time to deal with "things."

Only she knew from talking with Rick's doctors he never would deal with anything. Would leaving Dallas make a difference? Would she be able to hide her tracks and settle somewhere else? If she couldn't, she didn't think he'd give up. Rick had enough money, enough brains and enough old connections with people who didn't know what he'd become, that he'd be able to look for her...and she was really afraid he would find her.

Somehow she needed to figure out how to disappear. Looking around the bar without really seeing anything, her mind raced in circles. Until a man walked through the door from the lobby and his powerful presence demanded her attention.

Oh, good Lord! Even looking at the hottie from this distance made her body start nagging, the pulsing shift of heat over her skin a sharp reminder that she'd been celibate for eighteen months. Well, ten...but she wasn't going to count or even think about Rick raping her eight months ago. That hadn't been sex in anyone's definition.

Just looking at this guy was orgasmic. She felt her heart speed up and her palms sweat for the second time this evening, to entirely different stimuli. Refusing to pay any attention to the flutter below her belly button, she knew this experience would be all look and no touch, so there wasn't any sense in getting her hopes up.

Six feet, two inches of unbelievably manly male...she knew his exact height because the door leading to the lobby had a growth chart of sorts along the wall—*that* distracted her for a second. *This is a classy place. What, they needed to know how tall the people buying drinks were? Are they robbed that much?* Maybe she didn't want to stay in the lounge much longer.

The man stopped and glanced around as he came in. You couldn't say he was beautiful, but he oozed sex and danger. Not the kind of danger she'd been living with lately, but the kind of danger that started between sweaty sheets and ended with fantasies that couldn't be fulfilled by anyone but him.

His hair was long and dark. Black? Brown? The lights were too dim for specifics at this distance. His eyes were, well...again, she couldn't tell the color, but they were what her mother referred to as "bedroom eyes," more lid than eyeball and even when they weren't looking at you, they screamed pillow talk.

Oh! And now he looked at her, and she felt herself blushing, melting. Snapping her eyes down, she returned her attention to her drink, breaking what to Jenna seemed like very hot eye contact. *Shake it off.* No one who looked like *that* would ever be interested in her. Even before Rick she hadn't been sexy or confident enough to attract anyone like him. She was just, well...just Jenna.

Besides, as tempting as he was— Oh lord. *Look at him walk.* Her gaze unconsciously locked on the man. She'd never understood what the romance novels meant when they said a man prowled. Well, now she got it.

But she didn't want it. Big and oozing testosterone, he was out of her league. Tempting and scary in a good way, with one look she could tell he'd be erotically wild and incredible in bed.

Jenna snorted to herself, allowing the heat and a secret smile to build. Whom was she kidding? If he crooked so much as a finger in her direction she would be all over him within seconds. As an award for living, she would take him as a gift. *Oh yeah!*

Cole Matheson settled at the bar and made sure he positioned himself, without appearing to do so, in such a way that he could watch the little blonde who'd caught his eye when he came in. Never having seen such an expression of longing on anyone's face, he smiled…she'd looked at him like he was cotton candy and sweet chocolate all rolled into one and she was dying to taste him. The thought of all those urges being let loose over his body made his groin tighten in expectation.

Yet when he made eye contact — sizzling eye contact — she'd obviously been flustered and diverted her attention.

Using his peripheral vision, he focused on her lush mouth, and it didn't surprise him when she smiled to herself and a look of suppressed desire flitted over her face. He *was* surprised when she didn't look around and try to find him, to reestablish contact. He'd been ready for her.

Shrugging his shoulders in disappointed acceptance, he turned to his drink and then went rigidly still when he realized what he was doing. When had he gotten lazy, expecting a woman to pursue him with little or no effort on his part? If a woman didn't chase him down, did he just ignore any attraction he might have for her? Reviewing the last few years of his life, he realized the answer was…yes.

Deciding it would be safer for all parties concerned if he didn't have a committed relationship was not the same thing as being totally uncaring about the women he had sex with. Right? Had he become so focused on keeping his feelings out of any connection, that he would lock himself away and not take any chances on meeting someone for something other than sex? Again the answer was, *yes*.

Cole thought about those questions and his answers for a moment and frowned. If he wanted to play tonight there were plenty of women in the bar who were blatantly sending I'm-yours-for-the-taking-come-get-me messages. No effort on his part would be required, he didn't have to try and seduce the shy one. Counting back, he realized it had been a very long time since he'd been with a woman he'd chosen, rather than the other way around.

Living in a small town restricted his sexual urges, the single women he knew wanted more than sex from him, so he kept his appetites under control unless he was traveling. He did not want or need a relationship. That hadn't changed. So what had?

He was traveling now, and he wanted to spend time getting to know *this* woman. Did he want sex? Hell yeah! But maybe he wanted to be the aggressor for once. His body flashed with heat and he realized that was his answer. Now the only question was…would he play fair?

No.

There had been many instances in his life when Cole wished his rather limited psychic abilities included being able to read someone's thoughts. Emotions could be misleading. Like the time Cole thought his best friend in fourth grade hated him because he was projecting hate very clearly while they were playing. Turned out his friend didn't hate him, but basketball.

Normally he kept the extrasensory side of his life separate from everyday things. He used his talents to keep himself and others alive, not for his own gain and certainly not to seduce women.

He didn't question why his normal self-imposed rules didn't apply to this situation. He dropped the mental wall he kept in place and read the first layer of the blonde's emotions, finding a jumble of impressions. He just couldn't get a clear enough picture of what he wanted to know.

He could feel her sadness and a lingering hint of fear as it flowed over him. Beyond that, the woman radiated conflicting needs — rediscovered lust battled with her longing to be held and a general confusion. Tempting her, he used his mind to send her images of the two of them, bodies naked and aroused. He opened his eyes to see if she felt…anything.

Eyes glued to her drink, she kept both hands wrapped around it in rigid concentration. But he watched with wicked glee as her skin flushed and she squirmed in her seat. *Gotcha!*

There was an underlying something about her that called to him. To both the man and the warrior. He could send more thoughts and desire through their mental bond, or he could give her a chance to refuse him.

As he glanced back at the woman with the long, curly blonde hair and hungry eyes, he realized he wanted her to choose him. Just for a few nights.

Chapter Two

ಐ

Jenna jerked in fright when a man slumped into the booth beside her—her heart nearly came out of her chest with its wild pounding and a small shriek passed her lips.

"Hiya sweetheart, lemmebuyyadrink," he slurred.

"No thank you," she said forcefully, while taking a deep breath, trying to regain control. She did not need this aggravation. Turning in her seat, she frowned at the drunk who was crowding her. Trying to move away, she became exasperated when he just leaned closer.

"Aaah c'mon, be a good girl and lemme buy you a drink," the man demanded.

The drunk reeked of alcohol and smoke. Wrinkling her nose in distaste, Jenna put her hand on the man's chest to keep him from coming closer. "No. Now please leave me—"

"The lady said no," grumbled a low voice.

Jenna looked up to see sex-on-the-hoof standing over t' table. The look in his eyes and his body posture should h' scared her. If that didn't do it, the scar running down the side of his face told her this man could be lethal.

Not to you, I'd never hurt you, an internal voice assured.

Oh, great. The combination of tonight's activities alcohol on an empty stomach worked to send her imagi into overdrive. First she'd envisaged detailed fantasies and this man—her mind supplying surprising detail of hi stripped and laid out before her—and now she was voices.

Jenna lost her train of thought as she cataloged her midshoulder-length dark brown hair and chocol

Gorgeous. The scar only added to the sensual appeal of her champion. Jenna forced herself to stop drooling and pulled her attention back to the unwelcome man beside her. "Yes, please leave," she reiterated.

"I didn't know she was waiting for someone," the drunk whined. After a quick glance at the tall and very muscular man, he stood up and shuffled away.

"Thank you," Jenna said, meeting his warm gaze.

Grinning, with a look in his eyes that could only be called mischievous, he bent over the table to whisper softly, "Ah, but see…now we have a problem."

The mysterious-as-sin tone rumbled through Jenna and sparked nerve endings long dead. His lips were only a few short inches from hers. Shifting a little in her seat, she cleared her throat. "Problem?" The husky whisper didn't sound like her voice. She knew better than to even attempt speaking in more than one-word sentences. This man fried every active brain cell she had and turned her to mush.

"Problem," he stated assuredly, and leaned back. "The drunk thinks I'm joining you. If I don't, he will be back. So we have a choice. I can sit with you until he passes out or leaves, or I can go get security and have him removed."

Jenna blinked. The man was right. Damn. She didn't want to attract attention. If Rick came looking they might remember her. But Lord, it would be pure torture to sit across from this man and look but not touch. Trying to keep the repressed hunger from her voice, Jenna responded, "Oh. Please. Join me." *Stupid, stupid girl*, she thought.

The man sat after catching the bartender's eye. Within econds of sitting down across from her, his beer had been rought over and a second Irish coffee had been ordered for nna. For one brief moment she debated the wisdom of ultiple drinks with no breakfast, lunch or dinner. No way uld she sit here with just water.

"My name is Cole," he all but purred, as he offered his hand.

"Jen— Uh, just Jen," she replied, kicking herself mentally. Registering in this hotel as Maxine Adair meant she should have said her name was Max. The pseudonym was her mother's maiden name, and the name she'd used on the nest egg account. Deceit had never been something she did well.

Slowly extending her arm to shake his hand, she was shocked at the warm sexual response of her entire body as their palms met and melded. Her shocked gaze flew to meet his, and the intense heat in those warm brown eyes surprised her even more. *He's interested in me*, she thought incredulously. Pulling her gaze and hand away, she searched frantically for something else to say. Thank heavens he spoke before she made a fool of herself.

"Sorry if I've interrupted anything."

He didn't look sorry in the least, and after one touch of his hand spiked the heat simmering between them, she wasn't sorry either.

"Interrupted? Oh." Jenna saw he was looking at the notes she'd been making. A sadly short checklist of things she needed to do if she wanted to stay alive. Quit her job, change her appearance, and figure out how to hide. "It's nothing," she said, as she moved the notebook back into her purse. "It's just a list of things to do in the next couple of days."

What was wrong with her that a simple look and the touch of Cole's hand made her feel as if her body had been dipped in some sort of skin aphrodisiac? Even her scalp tingled, and she could just imagine how it would feel if he grabbed her by the hair and pulled her head back to kiss her. Trying to rein in her heartbeat and pulsing body, she promised herself she wouldn't attack this man.

"Are you staying at the hotel?"

Jenna looked at him and said slowly, "I'm not sure I should answer that question. I seem to remember it was one of the top Don't Ever Do's in women's safety."

Cole laughed. "You're right. As someone who teaches a personal safety course, I agree it's definitely right up there with not walking alone in a dark parking lot. Forgive me."

"Is that what you do? Teach safety courses for a living?" Jenna asked.

Somehow, she found that hard to believe.

Smiling with easy charm, Cole could see Jenna making a concerted effort to relax with him. He could help her with that. Projecting warmth and security with his mind, he selected his words carefully. "Not all I do. I'm retired military. I write books and teach seminars to select units within the armed forces and law enforcement on discovery techniques. Sometimes I'm called out as a consultant on a tough case. I live in a small town and volunteer at the community center, teaching women how to keep themselves safe, or how to react if they get into a bad situation."

Making a conscious effort to relax his own body, Cole decided to back off on the sensual signals for now. Before he exploded and pulled her across the table. He wanted this woman, and to get her, he would use every look, every touch and every mental persuasion he possessed to ensure she wanted him as well. Wanted him enough to forget her natural reserve.

"Okay, that gives me about forty questions to ask," Jenna said, smiling. "Let's start with the military. What branch?"

"I was in the Army." Cole didn't explain he'd been in an elite terrorist-fighting unit within Special Forces...that information was definitely on a need-to-know basis. "And before you have to ask, I'll tell you that you've never seen one of my books. They're written for the seminars I teach and are definitely not light reading for a civilian. Now it's your turn, Jen. What do you do for a living?"

When Jen looked at him and crinkled her eyes in a smile, Cole's temperature rose several degrees. She wasn't blatantly sexual or model stunning, but she had the prettiest blue eyes— eyes you could drown in. And her hair was fantastic. It was long and curly and he had to physically keep himself from reaching out to see if it felt as soft as it looked. Hanging to the middle of her back, the shimmering blonde locks seemed to have a life of their own. He could imagine the satin fall drifting over his body as she moved her mouth over him.

Cole suppressed a groan and tried to turn his mind back to the conversation. Switching his focus away from erotic fantasies didn't seem to be working and his erection was getting out of hand.

"I'm a financial analyst. I figure out where to put other people's money." Her laugh seemed almost forced as she continued, "Which is definitely not as interesting as writing books and teaching seminars. Are you in Dallas teaching?"

"Yes ma'am. I'm here for the weekend. There was a quick social tonight, then I have classes tomorrow and Sunday. The seminar is down the street in another hotel, but I'm staying here. All the overblown testosterone in one place can drive a person crazy. I've learned from experience that it is less complicated if I stay a block or two away from the other men."

This time Jenna's giggle flowed naturally. "All those military types and cops get a little wild?"

Cole snorted. "Everyone thinks their branch, their division or their precinct is better. Between the drinking contests and the arm-wrestling matches and the outright brawls, believe me, this is much nicer. Hooyah! I'm finally past the age and inclination of trying to prove I'm the baddest, meanest, strongest man in the bar."

"I can certainly believe you don't need to prove your strength or warrior prowess."

Cole laughed with her and ignored her blush. He allowed her emotions to flow over him. Knowing she liked his looks—

and that she'd tamped down her urge to flee him because she enjoyed his company — went a long way toward making him feel he'd made the right decision tonight. Normally, the emotions he read weren't this clear. He got overall impressions rather than detailed thoughts. But Jen was projecting very clearly.

He read her intent to savor every moment she spent with him instead of running in the opposite direction.

The waitress came by and Cole ordered them another round. For a while they discussed little things. Safe things. The weather, the difference between city life and the small town Cole lived in. He shared several funny anecdotes, but never told her even which state the town was in.

Then Cole asked her a question that seemed to upset her. "Are you married?"

Jenna looked up at him and he sucked in a breath. In Jenna's mind, he'd felt the shadows of a deep sadness and fatigue, but now he could read the pain on her face. The light hit her just right, also allowing him to document the outline of the bruise on her face. Cole's protective instincts jumped to the fore.

"No. I'm not married. Are you?"

Starting to ask her what had happened, Cole noted Jen's now-defensive posture, and changed his mind, deciding to table this discussion for the time being. After all, he didn't live here and he couldn't provide much help if she needed it. Beyond alerting a friend on the Dallas police force, there was little he could do for her. Besides help her to forget for a time. "No, I'm not married either. I can see you're tired, maybe we ought to call it a night. Are you going to be here until Sunday? I've enjoyed talking to you, Jen. Would you like to have dinner with me tomorrow night?" Dinner wasn't all he wanted, but he'd allow things to slow down for her sake.

Jenna started at his question. Just a little tipsy, she tried to get her mind around the fact that this fascinating man had asked to spend more time with her. She was really enjoying being able to forget her long list of problems, and the previous events of her evening. It was a huge relief to have her thoughts full of her body's intrinsic reaction to the alpha male before her. And the wonderful things she could do with him.

Tilting her head to the side, she considered his offer. Well, the room *was* booked until Monday. She would be a fool to turn away the first man she'd been interested in for such a long time. She wasn't stupid. She knew this wasn't a 'til-death-do-you-part type of proposition. Hadn't she experienced enough of *that* for a lifetime? "I would love to, Cole. And I think it *is* time for me to go up to my room. I guess that answers the question of whether or not I'm staying at the hotel."

Cole's smile should be registered as a lethal weapon. His dark brown eyes crinkled and shone with inner promise. She really did want to get to know this man better, and she wasn't entirely sure she could wait for tomorrow night.

"Let me walk you to the elevators. It's getting late, and it's time for me to turn in as well."

Jenna nodded in agreement and they walked to the elevators together. Cole had touched her lightly at the small of her back to guide her through the doors, and Jen worked hard to stifle a gasp at the intense pleasure spreading through her body at the contact. They agreed to meet in the lobby at six o'clock the next evening for dinner.

When the elevator opened they stepped in together. Cole pushed the button for the eleventh floor, then the sixteenth at Jen's request. Being this close to him and alone in a small space increased her body's awareness of his size and scent. Yummy — all-man smell.

She felt flushed and needy from head to toe, each breath bringing the spicy clean fragrance of Cole into her lungs. She stood ramrod straight with her legs pressed tightly together, trying to stem the pulsing between her thighs. Thank God she was wearing a long skirt so he couldn't see her clenching — a telltale sign of her internal conflict.

When the elevator stopped and the doors opened, Jenna watched Cole reach out and press the stop button to keep the elevator stationary as he turned toward her to wish her good night. In slow motion, he moved closer and reached out to pull her into his arms. She knew he was giving her time to pull back or protest. But she couldn't. She would be lying to herself if she said she didn't want this.

Cole's lips moved in a silent caress over Jen's. Intending a short but enticing embrace, when he captured her mouth with his and her lips trembled in surrender, he lost his good intentions. As he angled his head to take control, the warning bells going off in some distant part of his subconscious rang too faint to make him release her. Mentally he coaxed, *open for me, Jen*.

Without hesitation she responded to him, her lips parting. The kiss that may have started soft and sweet rapidly progressed to hungry and demanding. Exhaling in a ragged rush, her legs buckled and she sank into him, knotting her slender hands in his shirt to keep herself upright. Cole wrapped his arms around her waist and held her to him. No way would this kiss be short.

Her mouth was hot, the flavor of her so honeyed and intoxicating it made him ache. Cupping his left hand over the back of her head to deepen the kiss, he swallowed her moan, the sound a muted cry of delight that further inflamed him.

He wanted this woman as he'd not wanted anything in a very long time. It wasn't a decision. It wasn't even really a thought. He only knew he had to have her, the sensation riding high on a devastating wave of urgency that stained his vision with red.

She moaned again, moving even closer to kiss him back with such abandon, he lost it. *Sweet. Oh God, so sweet.* He couldn't believe this. All his life, he'd prided himself on being cautious and never losing control. Now, suddenly, he had no control at all, and being cautious was the farthest thing from his mind. Forgetting where they were, he devoured her, and slipped a hand under her sweater to touch her skin. The warm, satiny expanse made him hunger for more. Growling low in his throat, he turned to press her against the wall of the elevator.

Jenna's head was swimming with pleasure. Her breathing became shallow and rapid and between pants, her teeth nipped hungrily at his lips. She ran her hands over his body, molding his shoulders, learning the shape of his arms as every press of her fingertips conveyed a frantic need that seemed to match his. Lifting her arms to entwine about Cole's neck, she pulled him closer to her.

Cole's hands settled at her hips and he pressed into her aching body. His tongue swept into her mouth and thrilled her with its rhythm. Any reservations she'd had were immediately overwhelmed by the potent sensuality of this man and the writhing demands of her own body.

Holding her motionless with a push of his hips between her legs, Cole cupped her breasts in his hands. The idea of being held captive and confined for his pleasure increased her fall into carnal insanity.

She'd worn a broomstick skirt and sweater this evening. And she thanked God for the choice when she felt the hard ridge of his arousal through the thin fabric, and when his hands moved up under her sweater, gaining unrestricted access to her skin. Her breasts were small enough to allow her to go without a bra if she chose, and tonight was thankfully one of those times. Whimpering in ecstasy when he thumbed her nipples, she tilted her pelvis against him with every pass. She felt the answering constriction of her vaginal muscles and her feminine juices oozed slowly from her body.

"Ah Jen, this is killing me, baby," Cole moaned. Straightening away from her and dropping his hands back to her hips, he glanced out the open elevator doors, reminding Jenna they might have an audience, but she was beyond the point of caring. Then he looked down and she lost herself in his dazed, passion-glazed eyes. "Come to my room Jen, let me love you," he demanded hoarsely.

Instead of playing fair, he lightly brushed one hand up under her sweater and feathered a caress over her peaked nipple.

Jenna gasped. Never had she felt such intense desire. One of Rick's biggest complaints had been her need for extended foreplay. Squashing the thought of her ex, she struggled to think of a reason why she shouldn't be doing this. But her own body and Cole's fingers pulling softly on her taut nipple didn't allow her to think. "Yes!" she gasped. "Please, yes!"

Cole didn't give her a chance to change her mind. His room was one door down from the elevator. He had her in the room and her sweater off before she could regain her familiar reserve. Bending her back over his arm, Cole curved his body over hers and dropped his head to take a very responsive nipple into his mouth.

Gasping, Jenna wallowed in his concentrated interest. Cole fed on her breasts, licking and sucking with a passionate attentiveness. He knew just what he was doing, too. It seemed as if he could read her mind—before she could think that she wanted a firm, drawing pull, he was doing just that. When she wanted a soft graze of his teeth or she a laving swipe of his tongue, he obliged her without any sign or sound from her. She was beyond speech or movement anyway. She'd never been so totally aware of her own body or so happy to be driven completely out of her mind. Moaning helplessly, she felt herself going limp in his arms, surrendering to whatever he wanted to do to her.

Her moans turned into a shriek when he bent to lift her in his arms. His mouth found hers and he kissed her again. No tender, friendly kiss, but a powerful, challenging provocation. His mouth a ravishing dare, alluring in the blaze it suggested and tantalizing in its sensual promise. His lips were hard, hungry and mercilessly persistent. It only took a few heartbeats for Jenna to react. Winding her arms about his neck, she kissed him back. Eagerly. With all the heat and pain in her soul. Desire ripped through her—hot, strong and fierce.

She wanted him, now. She could hardly miss the fact that he wanted her. For tonight, she would forget everything else in her life and live only for this soul-riveting slide into heat.

"More." Jenna said, as he broke the kiss to lay her down on the bed. With a quick movement, Cole pulled off her boots and the broomstick skirt, leaving Jenna in a red lace thong.

Cole's quick intake of breath was gratifying, but she wanted him with her. As she started to sit up, he lay down beside her. He'd pulled off his shirt and shoes, but left his jeans on.

"Too many clothes," Jenna managed, before Cole seized her mouth again.

He mumbled against her lips, "Let me enjoy you first," and then proceeded to drive her insane.

Cole strove to control his body. He knew if he took his jeans off, his only action would be to bury himself hip-deep in Jenna. He wanted more than a quick fuck. He wanted her taste and her cries long before he took his own satisfaction.

Shifting beside her, he wrapped one hand in her hair to hold her mouth to his, and smoothed the other down her arm to her chest. Running his hand over her velvet skin, he cupped the perfect weight of her breast, then took the beaded tip between his fingers to pluck at her.

She was quick to respond to his every movement, and he opened his mind, allowing him to read even her slightest reaction. In response to her unvoiced demands, he slowly slid his hand down, over and around her hip to the juncture of her thighs.

Jenna shifted easily for him, parting her legs, and Cole reached his hand between her thighs to rub through the small scrap of red lace she still wore, finding her soaked and ready for him. Moving his hand back to her hip, he slipped his fingers under the tiny strap of material and pulled it down her legs. Jen helped him by catching the fabric with her toes and dragging it the rest of the way down.

He began a leisurely exploration of her body, slipping his fingers across her moist heat and bending his head so his mouth could reach her breast. Using his thumb to strum her clit in time with his tongue laving her nipple, his long forefinger slid deep. Stroked. Riding the frantic bucking of her hips with his hand, he never lost rhythm. Her wild cries filled the room.

He inhaled the sweet musk of her skin, the erotic scent of her arousal filling him as he suckled her breast. He was in pain, the jean material an unrelenting restriction over his rigid cock, and he ached to be buried deep within her. *Not yet*.

For long, delicious minutes he played with her pussy and his mouth stayed busy at her breasts. Pulling, laving and sucking hard while his fingers created magic, delving into her heat. First one finger, then two, were stretching and stroking into her tight passage. Fisting both hands in his long hair, she jerked against him, her cries of passion telling him how much she loved what he was doing to her.

Jen whimpered when Cole drew away from her and stood up beside the bed. Struggling to open her eyes, she looked at him through the erotic haze blurring her vision. God, he was fine. Seeing him standing before her—his dark hair tangled from her demanding hands, the fierce glint of fire in his eyes, the well-formed muscles that glistened with sweat and jeans riding low on his hips—sent a burst of lust to scramble her brain.

Watching in lust-filled fascination as he stripped his clothes off and sheathed his magnificent erection in a condom, she wanted to touch him. She started to sit up, but before she could lift her head he was pressing her back into the mattress and moving quickly down her body. His hands skimming over her flesh to her hips, he pulled her legs farther apart and lifted her to him, bringing her to the heat of his mouth.

Cole made her feel as if she was a banquet spread before him, feasting on her, moving his tongue up and over her clit. Pushing his tongue into her in hard thrusts, he set her hips back down on the mattress. Scooting down between her legs so he could free his hands, he added the torment of thick fingers moving in and out of her while his tongue continued to lap over her clit. She felt the sensations building, the tight clench of her stomach and the rush of blood as the climax slammed into her, a fast punch leaving her senseless. Staggering from the blow, she sobbed out his name and trembled with the aftershocks.

Nearly blinded by his need, Cole reared over Jenna and gripped her hands. He knew he couldn't last another second without burying his cock within her clenching depths. Positioning the tip of his swollen shaft at her entrance, he paused to glance down at the beautiful woman in his bed. "Jen," he demanded huskily. "Look at me." When she raised her lashes to look with astonished wonder into his eyes, he flexed his hips forward, breaching her entrance a scant inch. In satisfaction, he watched her eyes widen, her pupils dilate even further.

Jenna's heightened pleasure inundated his mind with a tidal wave of sensation and Cole surged forward. Still rippling in small spasms from her last orgasm, her tight sheath pulsed and he could feel those tiny contractions as he buried his cock in the wet suctioning heat of her body. He stopped all movement, wanting to prolong the pleasure and reassert his dwindling self-restraint.

Shifting underneath him, Jenna wrapped her long legs around his hips and drove him deeper. He drew out of her slowly and then plunged back in. Cole could feel each press of his body as it raked against the hard nub of her clit, and he shared her growing desperation for more.

Cole groaned. "That's it," he said, tightening his grip on her butt and angling her so he could reach even deeper with his long hard cock. "Let it go."

Picking up speed, he dug his hips in and out with powerful, dizzying strokes. Jenna could only anchor her calves around his muscled legs and hold on for the ride as a storm of pleasure battered the two of them.

"God, you feel so good," Cole gritted. "So wet, so tight." Shoving deep, he stiffened and their voices mingled in a shared scream as his long, hot orgasm violently exploded through their joined bodies.

Chapter Three

ဆ

Cole's internal alarm clock went off early the next morning. He'd intended it to. Even after the amazing night he'd spent touching and tasting every inch of Jen's body, he had an overwhelming impulse to see her bathed in sunlight. With careful precision he stood up to slide the hotel drapery to the side, enough so the sun's rays would highlight her body but not shine in her eyes.

Jen had fallen asleep on her side facing the window and him. Cole was meticulous when he'd risen, draping the sheet on her arm so the absence of covering wouldn't wake her, yet her front would be exposed to his view.

And the view was as incredible as he'd imagined. Her skin was the color of tea with a whole lot of cream, as if she'd tanned just enough to give herself some color. She had a few widely spaced freckles, one or two on her perfectly globed breasts, a half dozen scattered across her belly and upper thighs.

Angel kisses. Cole remembered his grandmother calling his freckles angel kisses and placing a kiss on his cheeks for each one, the summer he'd turned ten. At the time he'd been embarrassed to have his grandmother kissing on him like that. Now he owed her big time for the idea. He promised himself that tonight he'd treat each freckle and cute little mole on Jen's body to his grandmother's treatment.

Her face in sleep was relaxed, and almost pixie perfect. She had a cute pointed nose, with high cheekbones setting off her oval face, and eyelashes that were long and thick and light brown to match her eyebrows. Her closed eyelids covered bright, brilliant and flashing blue eyes he remembered getting lost in last night.

The sight of all her curly, golden blonde hair spread across his pillow hit him like a fist to the gut when he realized he was wishing it was his pillow at home, not the hotel's. He'd go home in a few days to a pillow that wouldn't smell like her clean vanilla and musk scent. For a moment he seriously considered taking the pillowcase home, and he stood there in shock.

Cole took a deep breath and looked down. The turn of his thoughts would not scare him away from this stolen moment.

The ring of color on her nipples was a pale, pale pink and they were the size of half-dollars, the puckered tips a darker, almost raspberry color. The very visceral memory of his mouth sucking and laving those nipples had his morning erection standing at stiff attention.

He let his eyes drift lower to catalog the small pooch of her stomach and the trim strip of light blonde hair covering the center of her pussy. Jen was definitely a true blonde.

Considering teasing and stroking her into a state of semi-wakefulness, Cole glanced at the clock and closed his eyes. If he got back in that bed it wouldn't be quick, and he didn't have the luxury of enough time to do his libido justice this morning. All those physical impulses would have to wait until this evening.

Gently he rearranged Jen's covers and headed for the shower.

Jenna stretched lazily and opened one eye. She didn't have to think to remember where she was, her body's aching tenderness evoked pleasant memories of who and what she'd been doing the previous night, and again several times very early this morning. Hearing the sound of the shower running, she assumed Cole was getting ready to leave for his seminar.

Propping herself up on the bed pillows, she allowed her mind to drift over the last few hours and her sexual marathon. Totally out of character, she'd slept with a man she'd known only a few very short hours, and didn't feel the smallest twinge of remorse. In fact, her attitude about the entire experience bordered on the antithesis of regret—it approached blatant reverence.

When she remembered the heights Cole had taken her to, the things they'd done to one another and the pleasure they shared…several times…she wanted to purr and strut like a sated cat.

Her bubbling self-satisfaction morphed quickly into curiosity when Jenna noticed several books stacked on the dresser beside Cole's suitcase. They were all the same and that reminded her vaguely of something Cole said last night. He'd written a book she wouldn't understand or be interested in. Hah! Everything about him interested her.

Hopping stark-naked from the bed, she charged across the room, searching for her clothes. Since she wouldn't bother with a shower until she went back to her room, and her hair was beyond help, it took her all of one minute to dress. Grabbing one of the books, she settled down in the chair by the open drapes.

Cole hadn't told Jenna his last name, but it was written in bold black letters across his book. Cole Matheson. The title, *Hidden Enemies*, intrigued her. The book sounded like a murder mystery. Opening the book to the table of contents, she scanned the contents and her stomach dropped to the floor and rolled over.

Hiding in Plain Sight.

False Identities—from Copy Machines to the Internet

Where's the Money?—Techniques that are Almost Impossible to Trace

And it went on. Quickly skimming the first few pages proved to Jenna that she was holding the answer to all her problems in her shaking hands. Cole had written a fugitive's bible. It might be intended to help law enforcement and the military track criminals and terrorists, but in her fast read she'd already managed to pick up a few helpful hints. She went back to the beginning and started over.

Absorbed in Cole's book, Jenna briefly glanced up when the door to the bathroom opened, her attention riveted when Cole sauntered boldly into the room dressed in only a small, white towel that barely managed to reach around his hips. She'd traced and thought she'd memorized every inch of his body last night. But she decided to really get the best effect he needed to be naked and standing a few feet away. In the sunlight, his hair wasn't just brown—it was streaked with fiery highlights of red and blond. His long hair was brushed back from his face, allowing her to appreciate the dark slash of his eyebrows accenting a rugged and chiseled face. The long thin scar on the left side ran from the apple of his cheek to his chin, and gave him a bad boy look instead of detracting from his male beauty.

His massive shoulders were thrown back in perfect military posture, his smooth, tan chest accented by the dark discs of his large areolas. "Wow."

"You're drooling."

"Ummm, how much time before—"

"Not enough for that, sweetheart. I wouldn't want to rush. We'll have to hold those thoughts for tonight. Speaking of tonight, where would you like to go for dinner?"

"Room service." Jenna blinked. *Did I just say that?*

"Room service sounds perfect to me. So, what do you think of my book? Pretty dry reading, huh?"

The change in conversation topics confused her. What book? Fighting to pull her attention away from the impressive body in front of her, Jen looked at the book sitting in her lap. *Oh, got it.*

Dry reading? Not for her. Each word on every single page could mean the difference between life and death. Hers. But she would have to be careful here, too effusive and he would wonder at her motivations.

"The book is great, it's amazing to me that it can be so easy for people to start another life and just disappear if they have the techniques. I guess that's the hard part, most people don't have a clue what to do or there'd be a lot more deadbeat fathers, and uh, abused wives who are just fed up with their life, going...well, underground."

"Unfortunately, many of the really bad criminals do know this stuff and if someone wants to figure it out, more often than not they find a way to do so. In the military and with law enforcement, we struggle to keep up with new technologies but we are usually a step or two behind. Catching someone who has disappeared behind a new identity can be tough, often it takes them making a mistake...getting caught on camera or leaving behind traceable fingerprints. Of course if they haven't been fingerprinted before, that makes it more difficult."

Jenna drew her eyebrows together in a frown. "It hasn't been that long since I traveled outside the U.S., but it seems to me if we know that terrorists and other criminals use false identification, and they might have fingerprints on file...why doesn't the government take everyone's fingerprints and compare them with a database when they enter the United States?"

"Good question. One mired in politics and economics. Does fingerprinting take away personal freedoms or do we have enough money for the equipment, will it do any good, because it would take quite a bit of time for each search? You'd almost have to have people come in and be fingerprinted a day or two in advance of crossing the border."

Jenna really had a hard time paying attention to the conversation. As Cole spoke, he moved around the room, putting on black briefs — showing a great ass when he dropped the towel — dress slacks and a white shirt, before fiddling with a tie. Gorgeous.

"So, would you mind if I keep your book to read today? I find it pretty interesting stuff." She crossed her fingers.

Cole turned away from the mirror where he was still working on his tie and smiled. "I can't, Jen. The books have been deemed a security risk, even those taking the seminars have to sign a confidentiality agreement stating they will be held responsible for keeping access to all course materials restricted at all times. Failing to do so can lead to a prison sentence even for me. Reading it here is one thing, but I can't let you take one out of the room. Sorry."

Damn. "No problem," she said, as she closed the book and stood. Grinning wickedly she added, "I don't think, however, that I'll do much reading tonight. You can have your book back." Crossing the room, she handed him the book and wrapped her arms around his neck to pull him to her for a kiss.

Her mind whirled, assaulted by the incredible sensation of Cole's lips on hers, while ideas spun in her head of how she would have to somehow steal one of the books from his room tonight. She hated using him like this, but couldn't see a way around the dilemma if she wanted to get away from Rick. Jenna's mind shut down and she melted into the kiss.

Jenna soaked in a hot bubble bath to prepare for her date with Cole. Well, maybe not a date…room service and sex. Laid out on her bed was a little black dress she hoped would make it difficult for him to concentrate on dinner.

Hating what she would have to do tonight, finding a way to steal a copy of *Hidden Enemies* from Cole, she still said a little prayer of thanks that the fates had somehow thrown them together. Inadvertently through his book, he'd already helped her.

Thanks to him, she'd been able to take the first steps in setting up her disappearance. When she read his book this morning, she'd concentrated on the first chapter, Hiding in Plain Sight. Today she'd driven around until she found a few long and short term parking garages, followed the signs to the levels designated for those vehicles parked for extended periods of time, and been very lucky after cruising a few different locations to discover a vehicle the same make and model as hers.

Going past the blue SUV, she parked on another level and came back with the screwdriver she'd purchased that morning in anticipation of her illegal activity, and snatched the front license plate off the matching car. She'd been trembling so badly from fear of getting caught that it had taken an excruciatingly long time and several attempts to complete the simple task.

When she left Dallas behind her, she'd take her plates off and put the stolen license plate on the rear of her SUV. If Rick somehow managed to track her and stumbled across the vehicle, he'd hopefully believe it was the wrong one.

If nothing else it would buy her enough time to drive to a state that required the seller to take the license plates when the car was sold. Another tidbit she'd found in *Hidden Enemies,* some states made leaving the plates with the car mandatory when it sold, so the new owner could just amend the existing registration. This would make the car easier to track and put the new owners in danger. Texas was one of those states. The book even listed the states, in order of how strict their laws were for vehicle registration.

That list would give her an idea of where to go next—the only states she could remember were North Dakota, Nevada and she thought she recalled Utah.

Jenna planned on using Cole's book to get herself a couple of new identities, sell the car with her old identity, destroy her old license plate, and buy another vehicle with a new identity. Only she hadn't been able to read far enough in the book to know exactly how to do that.

For one tiny moment, she let tears trickle from her eyes when she contemplated the future. She didn't want to break the law and turn herself into a fugitive. Hating what her life would become, knowing she had no choice, she allowed the pain and uncertainty to wash over her.

Most of all, she didn't want to steal from Cole. In the very short time she'd known him, she liked and respected him…a lot. Intentionally going to his room tonight, not just to treasure every minute with him, but to take a book that was a national security risk…oh yeah, getting caught wouldn't just mean he would hate her, she'd be thrown in jail. Yet it couldn't change what she would have to do. Wishing circumstances were different was an exercise in futility.

Jenna washed her face and took a deep breath. Hell, in payment she'd give him the best sex of his life. Her subconscious delighted in asking her if that made her a whore.

No…just desperate.

An hour latter, Jenna stood outside Cole's room poised to knock on his door. It was six o'clock on the dot. A minute earlier and she would appear too anxious, any later and she wouldn't be giving their time together the reverence she felt it deserved. Dressing tonight for Cole's pleasure, she'd slathered her body with her best lotion, and put just a light hint of her favorite fragrance behind her ears and at pulse points lower on her body. The black shift fit her like a second skin, the thigh-high black stockings were silk and the heels were CFM stilettos.

Come Fuck Me.

If that didn't do it, she was hoping her lack of underwear would.

Chapter Four

ಬಂ

Looking around the room, Cole felt a little foolish. On the way back to his hotel from the seminar he'd stopped in a little store on the street to buy condoms. Once in the store, he'd had the notion to make the sterile hotel room a little more romantic for Jen. So he had bought several candles whose vanilla-musk aroma reminded him of Jen's sweet scent, a romantic CD to play in the hotels CD/DVD player, and a couple of silk scarves to drape over the lamps.

Glancing at the strong cane headboard, he allowed himself a quick moment to fantasize about using those scarves in an entirely different manner. He'd even prepared for that—just in case the opportunity presented itself, he had a few little goodies hidden away in the nightstand drawer.

He'd bought a vase filled with wildflowers, then gone to the hotel bar and picked up a bottle of wine, an ice bucket and glasses.

Back in his hotel room, he took a shower, set the stage for seduction and dressed in a pair of dark brown silk dress pants and shirt, leaving his feet bare. He'd left the collar of the shirt open a few buttons, not wanting to have to deal with a tie later.

Now he worried that he'd done too much. Should he douse the candles and stash away the scarves? It wasn't as if he was courting her. This night—and hopefully tomorrow night— would be the only times he saw Jen. Their relationship was about sex, not romance.

Before he could make up his mind, her knock sounded at the door.

There were many words to describe the woman standing in the hallway outside his room. But the only thing ringing through

Cole's brain at the moment was a very juvenile sentiment—
hubba-hubba.

Framed in the doorway, her hair was a tumbled mass of
golden curls and her body was displayed lovingly in a tight
black sheath, with sheer black stockings highlighting what
seemed like miles of legs. Cole quickly rearranged his priorities.
Food was now way down on the list. Hell, anything that didn't
include his hands and body in contact with hers didn't even
exist.

Taking her hand to slowly pull her into the room, he
slammed the door and turned his back against it. "Jesus Jen.
You're going to give this old man a heart attack. Baby, you look
absolutely incredible."

"Hello to you too, Cole. And I must say you're looking
pretty nice yourself." Over her shoulder she glanced down the
short hall and into the room that had been transformed with the
soft light of candles and a gorgeous vase of flowers. Her voice
was watery when she tried to thank him. "The room looks
lovely, Cole." Leaning into him, she slid her hands up the
smooth silk of the shirt covering his chest.

When she smiled, his attention caught on her full lips. She'd
used a pink gloss that reminded him of the color of her nipples.

Bending forward, intent on capturing her lush mouth, he
whispered against her skin, "I hope you're not very hungry, Jen.
I've thought about this all day and now you've just destroyed
the little bit of control I'd managed to muster. So if you want to
eat any time soon, you'd better stop me now." He let his hands
rest against her hips, not allowing his urges to get the better of
him and dragging her closer.

She didn't answer him with words. Instead she finished the
journey with her hands by wrapping them around his neck and
tugging him the rest of the way forward. The kiss started out
gentle, a sweet fall into almost innocent pleasure. Parting her
lips with his tongue, he pushed into the sweet recess of her
mouth. Shuddering, he pulled her tight against him and felt
himself grow harder than stone.

Once he'd tasted her, sweet innocence gave way to intense hunger. Raising his hands, he burrowed his fingers into her wild mane of hair and positioned her for his sensual assault. Feasting on her mouth, he plunged his tongue in and out, taking her breath…her little moans of growing need. When his hands drifted down to her zipper, he groaned in protest as she pulled her lips away from his.

"Please. Let me."

Cole thought she meant to undress herself and he started to object, when her hands moved down his shirt, quickly undoing buttons, and she set her mouth against his chest, proceeding to lick and lave her way to his nipple. Teasing the little nub, she sucked it into her mouth while her hands moved to his belt. Rasping in air as her fingers played over the taut fabric covering his swollen shaft, he wasn't quick enough to stop her when she dropped to her knees in front of him.

"Jen, no sweetheart." Biting the words out between clenched teeth, he reached down to haul her back up. Her words stopped him.

"I've thought of this all day, I didn't get a chance last night." She'd already unfastened the front of his pants, thankfully with careful concern as he'd gone commando, leaving nothing underneath the silk pants but his skin. Her soft sigh thrilled him as she folded back the fabric and unleashed his straining erection to cup him in her warm hands.

"Good Lord you're magnificent," her voice was husky, enthralled. He looked down to watch as she encircled him between her thumb and fingers. They didn't touch. His cock was long and thick, and it appeared Jen was set to worship.

"Damn Jen!" he gasped, and threw his arms out, trying to steady himself by clutching at the walls in the short hall. She used the tip of her tongue, darting it out between her glossy pink lips to lick the slit already leaking pre-come. A lightning jolt of sensation seared though his body. Unable to tear his gaze away from her, he watched as she used both hands to grip him, then lowered her head and parted her lips to suck him into the heated moisture of her mouth.

Without any effort on his part he could feel a hint of what she felt. The twin sensations, her fingers around his cock and how it made him feel almost brought him to his knees.

And he was her, her hand wrapped around the base of his shaft, feeling the silky smooth length and the pounding of his pulse in the vein against her flesh. "Jesus," he gasped.

Oh, fuck me! The sight of those pink lips moving back and forth over his turgid shaft sent such a surge of lust through his body, he felt his cock grow impossibly harder. Powerless to stop, he rocked his hips forward and lowered one hand from its death grip on the wall to tunnel into the soft curls of her hair. With each forward motion the tendrils raked over the skin of his thighs. He didn't remember her pulling his pants down around his ankles.

She suckled him, licked and laved, trying to take as much of his cock as she could into her soft heat. Grasping him with her hands, she pumped the length she couldn't take into her mouth, and bobbed her head over his groin. He could feel his balls draw up, tighten painfully in readiness for the explosive release he knew was coming. She drew back and licked a wet trail up the throbbing vein on the underside of his length, and lapped at his balls.

When she cupped his sac with one hand and stroked her fist up and down his length with the other, his body shook with trembling need. When she took the head of his cock back into her mouth, his sex jerked. Throbbed. And with his connection to her he could feel her enjoyment of his thick shaft, the hot salty taste. When she hummed in delight, his body went rigid. *Too fast.*

"Stop, Jesus, Jen you've got to stop. I don't want it this way." Pulling back on her hair, Cole made sure she obeyed him. Kicking off his pants and throwing off his shirt, he pulled her to her feet and turned her backside to him in one swift motion. Ignoring her squeal, hearing not a protest but excitement in her high tones, he marched her further into the room and stopped in front of the bed to lift her dress up around her waist. Jen, too, had gone commando.

Groaning at the sight of the pale globes of her ass, highlighted by the black thigh-high stockings and her killer heels, he clenched his teeth and barked out another order. "Bend over and spread your legs."

Tossing her hair to one side she looked back at him and grinned, then quickly complied.

Pushing his groin into the welcoming cradle of her ass, he skimmed his hands up and over the fabric of her dress bunched securely at her waist. He brushed her hair completely to one side and slid the zipper of her dress down, far enough so he could open the back and reach around to cup her breasts when he was ready.

Jen hadn't worn a bra either. The thought of her coming to him, riding the elevator and walking down the hall to his room with nothing but the short dress, nylons and high heels, excited him even more.

With the fingers of one hand he traced her backbone, frowning for a moment at the sight of dozens of thin white scars, some so faded he could barely make out their outline. *What the hell?* Jen arched into his touch, and moaning, she pressed back against him. *Now was definitely not the time to question her.*

Forgetting everything but the feel of her skin, he slipped his fingers down the crease of her ass and delved into the liquid heat between her pussy lips. "You're so wet, so slick and ready for me. I want to taste you here, but not yet. Now I need to fuck you, Jen. Quick and hard, because that hot little mouth of yours has just about sent me over the edge."

"Cole!" Squirming, she tried to push back against him, but he put one hand on her ass to hold her captive to his ministrations.

Taking his cock in the other hand, circling the base with his fingers like a cock ring to keep him from exploding immediately, he used the head to stroke through her wetness and manipulate her clit. Rocking his hips back and forth, he kept a tight hold on her ass and listened to the sweet sound of her panting whimpers.

"Pleaseohplease, damn it, Cole!"

Finding her weeping center, he slid a bare inch of his shaft into the tight opening. He allowed himself several minutes to tease them both this way. In, out. In, out. Repeatedly he delved in just enough to make them both crazy for more.

He couldn't stand it. His head felt as if it would explode any second if he didn't take her now. Hard. Fast. In scant seconds he'd grabbed a condom from the nightstand and covered himself. He fit his cock back into her channel, set both hands on her hips, and slowly pushed inside in to the hilt.

Her gasping cries mingled with his growl. He started pumping his cock inside of her, loving the way her muscles hugged his shaft. Speed and power intensified, the room ringing with their feral cries. So hot. Tight. Jesus. He slammed into her, moving one hand around to cup her breast and let his fingers pinch her nipple until the combination made her drop her head to her arms and she keened in sharp enjoyment.

With sweat beading his forehead, he stared down, transfixed by the sight of his cock wrapped in latex, wet and shining with her cream as it appeared and disappeared into her core.

Opening his mind, tearing down all the walls he kept in place, he let her emotions pour through him. At that moment, something happened that had never occurred before—a bond formed, snapping into place and his...her...*their* pleasure amplified beyond experience and he became Jen—felt her body's reactions interlaced with his own. He knew she felt the same thing, and the connection drove him wild.

Drawing back, he plunged into her. Digging his hips in and up, he removed the hand at her breast and shifted it to her clit.

Slapping his balls against her sex, he spread her juices and fondled her clit in rapid strokes.

As he moved within her, he drew her with him down the path to crushing release. All that mattered was her body meeting his, the primal connection merging their emotions, allowing them to cross individual barriers. As one, he felt her response layered over his, each time he stroked into her there were twin realities—his cock pushing through her tight pussy, and her muscles clenching and releasing around his invading shaft. And he knew she felt it too. Even though she didn't understand what was happening, he could feel her welcome the flood of erotic sensation. Together they reached for completion.

Maddening, challenging, intoxicating completion.

The force of her orgasm caught him, he felt it…clutching his body and shooting through his very essence.

Arching in the throes of unstoppable bliss, he kept hammering into her and she came a second time. He heard her gasping for air, sobbing his name in wonder. He felt his own release coming. Throwing his head back and hissing in almost pain, the veins on his neck standing out and throbbing, his climax built in the base of his spine and burst through his entire being. Every muscle taut and jerking with the explosive release. He felt as if he'd been drained of life as he collapsed, careful to fall to her side and rolling her into his arms.

The room remained silent for several minutes.

"Wow!"

Laughing, Cole kissed Jen's forehead. Like him, she was covered in sweat. "I think you've said that before," he teased.

"Yeah, but this time… Wow. Unbelievably, wow."

"Yes, well. I'm not even close to being finished with you. So don't think you're going to get to sleep yet. Why don't you grab a shower and put on one of the robes in the bathroom, I'll call room service for nourishment and we'll see if we can do better than wow."

"I *am* hungry, and I'm not picky. Just get lots of whatever if I'm going to need my strength. And for your information, I don't think it gets better than wow." Climbing off the bed, she pulled her dress off and tossed it onto the nearby chair. With half-closed eyes, Cole soaked in the view of her standing there with wild, sex-tangled hair, with nothing on but nylons and stiletto heels. Her face was still a little flushed from the multiple orgasms and her nipples remained puckered as if still begging for his kisses.

Groaning, he buried his face in the pillow and waved her away, only lifting enough to warn her to run or there would be no dinner.

Jenna demolished the food on her plate, eating the steak, baked potato, mixed veggies and *crème brûlée*. She had showered and fed, and she could feel her time with Cole sifting through her fingers. He'd asked her to meet him for dinner again tomorrow night, and she'd been happy to agree.

Watching him lick the chocolate pudding he'd chosen for desert from his spoon, she could feel her heartbeat pound. Memories from the night before, of what he could do with that nimble tongue shot through her mind and body with primitive need. Fixating on his mouth, she sat there silent. Staring. Never had she imagined she could crave someone like this, beyond thought, beyond all other requirements.

Oh, she'd spent about two seconds looking for Cole's book while he was in the shower. It hadn't been in plain sight, and she'd dismissed it with relief. *Not yet.*

"Jen."

Slowly switching her riveted attention from his darting, skillful tongue as it lapped the last trace of chocolate from the silverware, she raised her gaze to meet his. When he stood and held out his hand, she went to him, humming low in her throat as he skimmed the robe off her shoulders and traced her curves with his hands, re-igniting a fierce hunger within her. A deep sexual craving for more of this man ran through her, a desperate longing she had only a short time to fulfill.

In a sensual daze she let him move her to the bed and position her on her back. When he asked her if he could please tie her arms to the cane bedposts with a couple of the scarves so he could tease her to distraction, she sucked in a deep breath. Recognizing how the words and the idea of being at his mercy excited her, she murmured her acquiescence.

It took only moments to secure her to the bed, her arms stretched over her head and fastened so she could move only slightly. Then Cole settled beside her and touched her, softly moving his hands over her face, her neck and lower to her chest. He circled her nipples with the tips of his fingers, teasing them into tight crowns.

"I love your nipples. They're so soft...so damn sweet."

Leaning over, he used his oh-so-talented tongue. At first, he just used the tip, teasing over her, swirling then flicking her pebbled crest back and forth. Moaning, she arched her back and offered her breast to him. "Please," she moaned, and tugged on her bonds, wanting to bury her hands in his hair and hold him hard against her.

Finally closing his mouth over her, he suckled the nipple deep and pulled hard while she thrashed her head back and forth on the bed. Damn, that felt wonderful! He released her and sat back, fiddled in the drawer of the nightstand and turned back to her with several tubes in his hands.

Breathless from his avid attention she asked weakly, "What's that?"

"Ummm, several things I thought we might enjoy. This first is a nipple cream, the directions promise to bring increased blood supply to your nipples and make them extra responsive. I have a similar one for your sweet pussy, to make it more sensitive, and it claims to increase the odds for multiple orgasms." He grinned wickedly. "And for me...a potion that is supposed to make me hard, keep me hard and *delay* ejaculation.

Do you get what I'm going for here? You bound, unable to escape me, and hours of pleasure."

"Oh, dear God."

Laughing, he opened the first tube. "I kept thinking of you today, of how you looked, tasted. How you made such sweet little cries when I touched you just right. When I was lecturing, I thought of you naked. So when I walked by this little shop and saw the display geared to driving a woman wild, I succumbed to the temptation. That's what I want…to drive you fucking wild."

"Cole!"

Grinning wickedly, he squeezed the tube, coating his fingertips with the emollient. "The instructions say this cream is water resistant, which means I'll be able to suck and lick you all night. Once I put this on you're suppose to feel the effect for a long time."

Reaching out, he coated one breast to see if she could tell the difference. And she could. At first it was a rush of warmth, a pleasant tingling as blood rushed to where he'd rubbed in the lotion and the sensitivity built. When he could see it worked, he slathered her other breast and then changed tubes to work another ointment into her pussy.

She could feel his generously covered fingers rubbing the cool lubrication around her folds, over her clit and into her channel. He even slid his fingers down and rimmed her anus, pushing in slightly until she bucked off the bed. And then he did it again, making sure she was well coated.

"Cole!" By this time Jen could barely stand it. Her cunt was on fire—not really burning, it throbbed with heat. Making her ache to be touched, petted and stroked. "Please, Cole. Please touch me. Fuck me."

She didn't know what was worse. Having him ignore her, or having him touch and play with her body until she screamed.

Under heavy-lidded eyes she watched him sit back from her to grab the final tube. She moaned when he poured the white lotion into his hands and took hold of his cock. In shocked rapture she followed his motions with her eyes as he coated himself, rubbing every inch of his shaft and balls. He pumped up and down a few times as he studied her.

Jen squirmed to get loose. "I could do that for you," she panted.

"Ah, but then you'd be free. I love having you at my mercy, my own little sex toy. This is supposed to deaden me, make me hard but keep me from feeling it so much." Grabbing a little foil packet from the bedside table, he opened it and rolled a condom down his thrusting erection as Jenna watched intently, mesmerized by the sensuality of his movements. "And now I can see to your pleasure."

Bending over her once again, he sealed his mouth to hers. When he slid his tongue between her lips, she opened for him and he stroked over her teeth and across the roof of her mouth— overwhelming her with his spicy essence. Moving his hands down her shoulders and arms to cup her breasts, he massaged them restlessly, tweaking and pulling her nipples until she squirmed madly in her silken shackles.

Leaving her mouth, he moved his lips slowly down to torment her with a warm wet slide, laving a path from her neck to her chest. She could feel her nipples stabbing out, pulsing in eagerness for his attention. The first lick across their sensitized tips sent her hips charging from the mattress.

With his hand flat against her torso, he kept her still, using his mouth on her breasts until she was sobbing, begging him for more. Starting a tortuous glide with his hand, he moved over her belly, her mound, until he cupped her. She could feel her hot cream pool as he groaned around her breast and dipped his fingers into the wetness running from her pussy. The little bit of pressure sent her over the edge and she screamed through her climax.

"Damn, it's working," Cole murmured against her skin, as he released her nipple and moved to position his body between her thighs. His hair fell across her body as he moved, caressing and teasing every inch of her exposed flesh. Pressing his mouth to her belly, he moved lower and lower until he was just above her sex.

His gaze caught and held hers. He blew softly across her damp curls, causing her to arch her back. Closing her eyes, she felt him grab her ankles and push them up as he parted her thighs wider, opening her further. The first stab of his tongue across her clit had her begging again.

"Please, Cole. Ohgodohgod fuck me."

Cole stared at the naked mound of her sex, topped with a small, trim stripe of light blonde curls. "You're so soft, smooth…sweet." He leaned in to breathe the scent of her, slid his tongue up the glistening wet seam and watched her thrash her head back and forth as she started keening her enjoyment.

Moving his hands up her thighs, he used his thumbs to part her flesh and pushed his tongue into the deep, dark depths of her pussy.

"Cole…" She bucked, struggled to get away, or get closer.

Growling, he shifted his hands to grasp the cheeks of her ass and lift her against his mouth. Catching her clit in his teeth, he tugged it gently, and then plunged his tongue inside her weeping channel once more.

Jen shrieked and he smiled, flickering his tongue over her in a rapid cadence. Loving the sound of her mewling cries and the way she begged him to fuck her. Twice more he made her come with his mouth, and then he surged up and over her, plunging his cock into the still vibrating softness of her sex—he wanted to drive them both crazy.

The deadening cream did its job. For a very long time he rocked himself into her, feeling as if he might explode, but yet unable to quite reach the peak. He dug himself in and out of Jen's tight pussy, using his hands and his mouth to nip the skin at her neck, her shoulder, to find and devour her mouth and to tease her very sensitive nipples. Each time he suckled and laved those nipples he could feel her vaginal muscles clench tightly and her cream would drench his cock and balls as she screamed through another orgasm. The wash of her emotions and sharing her erotic torture finally pushed him beyond thought or care.

A storm of need built inside him. Molten, ferocious need. He pushed himself deep within her, grasping her hips to tilt her to accept all of him. He sank further into her, angling so that he rubbed against her clit with each deep thrust as she wrapped her legs around his waist and clutched his shoulders with desperate fingers.

His mouth captured hers and she sobbed, her entire body trembling under his driving assault. Shuddering as the wet, silky walls clutched at this cock, he slapped his balls against her ass. He pulled out and slammed in again—harder and harder as the sounds of sex and her keening cries echoing in the small room drove him insane.

"Fuck," he gasped, now crouching low over her. "So fucking wonderful." He pulled out, driving into her again with bruising force, over and over until a mutual climax soared through them, and her pussy clamped forcefully on his plunging cock and he started to come, jerking uncontrollable as hot thick steams flooded the condom. He bit his cheek to keep from roaring his release loud enough to wake the entire floor of hotel guests.

When he was eventually able to lift his chest off Jen, he looked down. She'd fallen asleep, tied to his bed with a blissful smile on her lips. Hissing low, he pressed his fingers to the base of his cock, over the end of the condom and gently pulled out of her body. After taking care of the mess, he untied her bonds and used a washrag to cleanse her breasts and nipples of the cream and his attentions, then rolled her into his arms and covered them for the night.

In the few minutes before they slept, he wondered about the clarity of the bond between them. He'd never experienced anything like it when he'd had sex before. Sure, he got the faint brush of his partner's excitement, enough to know if he'd hit the right spots. But he'd never once felt as if he were in both bodies, enjoying two sets of sensations. The experience had been overwhelming…and addicting.

The next morning, Cole bent over her to place a soft kiss on Jen's forehead, murmuring, "See you tonight, sweetheart. Just rest here as long as you want." Smiling at her mumbled response, he felt a wave of satisfaction. He'd worn her out. Lying there boneless and limp from the night's activities, hair wild and spread over his pillow, naked and warm beneath his sheets…she was the perfect picture of a sated woman.

Knowing he'd see that picture running through his head all day, he turned and walked resolutely toward the door. Reminding himself that he'd see her tonight, he let the door close with a soft click.

Chapter Five

&

Click.

Jenna snuggled further under the covers and breathed in the spicy scent of Cole and sex. Every inch of her had been satisfied beyond her wildest imaginings. She'd been right the first time she'd seen him—Cole was a very sexual creature.

But there was so much more to him than erotic fantasies. Smiling in sweet remembrance of the candles and flowers, she let herself relive a few of the very romantic moments of the night before. Tender words and soft enticing caresses mingled with hard driving desire…Cole had managed all three within the space of one night. Several times.

The affection he'd shown her when he kissed her forehead and reminded her of their date tonight brought tears to her eyes. Cocooned in his bed and still only half awake, she thought he was the perfect man—considerate, caring and a phenomenal lover. He'd realized she was tired from their activities, so instead of waking her to go back to her room, he'd tucked her in and let her sleep.

A few short minutes later, Jen remembered the click she'd heard and sat straight up in bed and glanced around in horror. He'd left her alone in his room!

Last night she'd been more than happy to postpone looking for Cole's book. The books hadn't been by his suitcase and she didn't have a chance to search for them as Cole only used the bathroom for brief seconds. Each time he'd left her alone she'd been too exhausted to move. She knew once she had a copy of *Hidden Enemies* in her possession, she'd have to leave immediately, unable to risk him discovering its absence.

And now he'd given her the opportunity. *Argh!*

She thought she'd have another night with him, but obviously it wasn't meant to be. Damn, damn, damn, damn. Jenna gave in to her rage, flopping back on the bed and pounding her heels and fists into the mattress in a temper tantrum that would impress a two-year-old child.

Finishing her outburst and drying her tears, she woodenly got off the bed and put her clothes on. Feeling like the lowest slug, she started looking for the book. Not in the suitcase, not in any of the drawers, and not on the shelf in the closet. For one moment she started to panic. Had he taken the extra books to the seminar?

Then she noticed the hanging suit bag slumped in a corner of the closet. Cole's suits and shirts were all on hangers, but something was in the black bag on the floor. Kneeling, she spread the bag out and unzipped it. Yes!

After she'd lightened his load by one book and one set of seminar handouts, she repositioned the carrier on the floor, just as she'd found it. Standing slowly to look around the room, Jenna understood this was it. She couldn't take the chance that he wouldn't come back to the room tonight and repack his things. It was what *she* would do in his place…get everything ready to go so she could spend every minute left with Cole.

Her mind shut down and she walked around the room, desperate to hold something of him to her, something besides the stolen book. She gathered up a single candle, a beautiful chocolate brown silk scarf that reminded her of the color of his eyes, and then she took the pillow he'd slept on. She debated taking the shirt he'd worn last night. It would be wonderful to wrap it around her body when she was feeling overwhelmed and sad, so she could remember this time. Instead, she pulled a T-shirt out of his suitcase, one fragrant with his unique aroma, and then she sat down to write the hardest note of her life.

When she left, she paused with the door open and debated leaving the Do Not Disturb sign on the door. She could turn it over so the maids would clean the room, eradicating all traces of their short time together. The sheets would be changed, erasing her scent. The scarves folded and set in a neat pile beside the remnants of candles, and the ice bucket and glasses returned to the hotel.

Selfishly she realized she didn't want him to come back to the sterile room, all hint of what they'd shared reduced to little more than a note of farewell. Shutting the door, she ran her finger down the sign and left it swinging on the knob as she turned and walked toward the elevator. There was no going back.

Running his fingers through his disheveled hair, Cole couldn't believe Jen was gone. There was nothing left of her in this hotel but the light sent of vanilla musk in his room and the mussed impression of her in his bed.

When he'd opened the door this evening, it hadn't surprised him to see the room had not been cleaned. He thought she might have been tired when she left his room, and just forgot to switch the sign on the door to indicate it was available for cleaning.

Then he noticed she'd taken a few little things, like a candle and scarf, the pillow from his side of the bed—and he'd seen the note.

Cole… Words can never express what the last few days have meant to me. I'll always treasure my memories of this time with you. I'm so sorry I have to miss our date tonight. Something came up and I have to leave earlier than I'd planned. Jen.

He'd held that note in his hand, reading it through several times yet unable to believe she'd really left. So he called the desk and asked for Jen on the sixteenth floor. And was told there was no one registered by that name staying anywhere in the hotel.

He'd never asked her last name. He couldn't believe his lapse. What? He could fuck her but wasn't interested enough to know more about her? Only that wasn't it. Finding himself caring too much when he didn't want to, he hadn't asked many questions. Tried to keep not his body, but his emotions separate from her. Like *that* worked.

Using his subtle form of mind persuasion and a detailed description, he managed to find out she'd registered in the hotel as Maxine Adair, but checked out early this morning. Shortly after he'd gone to the seminar. Jen hadn't stayed for their final night. Taking a few lovers mementoes, she'd split, and he had to wonder if maybe it was for the best. He already missed her, and knew one more night would have only made it worse.

He'd already been taught a very clear lesson that no woman would want him peeking into her head to read her emotions, nor would she want kids with a *psycho* like him. His ex-fiancée, Mary Ann, very definitely convinced him of his undesirably as a mate the day he'd confided in her. And he wouldn't be able to hide his abilities for long from someone so intimately connected with him—a long-term relationship was out of the question. This was the first time in a very long while that his commitment to remaining single bothered him.

Deciding to stop worrying about it, he started to pack.

A few minutes later his curses filled the room. "What the holy fuck?" Jen had taken one of his books and a copy of the course materials for the seminar.

Why, for another sexual souvenir? Or had he been taken in, fooled into believing the little blonde had been attracted to him, when all the time she was really after information. For one moment Cole was caught in a red haze of anger when he considered what that would mean—that she'd stalked him, known from the beginning who he was and used him to get access to one of his books.

Then he recalled the tiny white lines on her back that he'd seen but hadn't questioned last night, and the bruise on her cheek the night he'd met her. The sad and sometimes panicked emotions he'd felt flowing out from her at times. Wondered if perhaps she had taken his book for purely selfish reasons, without knowing from the beginning what she could gain from him.

The planes of his face changed into hard lines. It didn't matter. Jen had stolen something from him that could endanger lives if it fell into the wrong hands. He wanted it back. Before the feeling had a chance to grow, Cole strangled the brief surge of emotion building within him when he considered seeing her again, and went to work.

She had no idea who she was dealing with.

This particular side to his talent had been discovered by accident—hell, all his abilities were uncovered by accident. But this one had been a shock he'd welcomed gladly. Several years ago, he and his best friend and sometime partner, Mike, were undercover in a drug cartel in Colombia. Mike was in deep shit, living in the ringleader's home in the jungle, cut off from all communication when Cole came across information that Mike's cover had been blown to hell.

A messenger with proof of his friend's identity was already headed into the jungle, bringing Mike certain death. And Cole had no way to stop what would happen.

Frantic with fear, paralyzed with the knowledge that there was no way to warn Mike or stop what would happen, Cole had wailed at the injustice of it in his mind. Over and over he'd mentally called out to his friend in building agony and pain, wishing somehow he could stop the inevitable.

No one had been more shocked than Cole when Mike had broken the silence and called that day, supremely pissed off. As soon as Cole picked up the phone he'd gotten an earful.

"What the fuck is going on, Cole! I know you have a bunch of shit psychic skills, but do you have to practice some new fucking mojo on me while I'm here? All of a sudden I can't concentrate on anything but getting in touch with you. Knock it off!"

Cole hadn't even bothered to explain. He'd told his friend to get the hell out of Dodge *now*.

Mike had gotten out alive. One of the few people who knew even a little of what Cole could do, Mike had helped to test and hone Cole's powers. They'd discovered that Cole could send out a focused command to direct another person's actions. Sometimes it worked very quickly, like if the person was standing right before him. Or it could take days, weeks even, if the person was a great distance away. All he needed to make sure the call went to the right person was something they'd touched, preferably something they owned, but it could be something they'd just been in contact with for several hours.

The day he'd unknowingly reached out to Mike in that jungle, Cole had been clutching one of Mike's dirty shirts that had been left in the hotel room in Bogotá when the man they'd been trying to make contact with invited Mike to his home. Thank God the shirt had been left behind, and Cole had grabbed onto it when he'd paced the confines of their room, sick at heart over what would happen to his friend.

Now all he had to do was find something to hold the connection to Jen. Looking around the room, he quickly rejected the scarves and the hotel robe, they hadn't touched her skin long enough to be of use. She hadn't worn any jewelry that she might have left behind, nor had she left anything from her purse, no piece of clothing or makeup.

Scanning the room in frustration, his eyes locked on the pillow she'd used for the last two nights. That should work. He couldn't use the pillow itself—there was no telling how many ties would be formed considering all the people who might have slept on it. But the pillowcase was another story. The case would have been laundered before being placed in his room, so all other connections should have been severed. And a housekeeper wouldn't have touched it long enough for any small piece of their spirit to linger.

Walking over to the bed, he picked up the pillow and stripped off the case. Holding only the square of fabric in his hands, he closed his eyes, concentrating for a moment on what he wanted to project. The simplest commands worked best over any distance, and he flung his mental power into the night.

Come to Secret Haven. You won't rest well or feel comfortable until you've reached the sweet peace of Secret Haven. In his mind he pictured his home, and sent the mental image with the summons.

When his pager went off, calling him to the aid of his country, he shrugged. It didn't matter that Homeland Security needed his services now, and he wouldn't be in Secret Haven to intercept her. It might take her a couple of weeks or months, but she'd show up there eventually…and be unable to leave until he released her.

Chapter Six

ဢ

Jenna knew it was time to face reality. After driving through the fourth little town of the day, fully intending to stop and check it out as a possible home, she found herself thirty minutes past the tiny community. She was going crazy. The area appeared to meet all of her newly determined objectives as a place to start over, but she'd sped on by, never taking her foot off the gas pedal. This was getting ridiculous.

That night she lay on the bed in her sterile hotel room, so tired from the mental war with herself she couldn't think. When she finally fell asleep it was only to dream of a small, secret haven where she could finally stop her travels and set down roots. The longing her fantasy home generated was almost palpable. Feeling as if she could reach out and touch the image, her hallucination changed to one of Cole. Standing naked before her, his eyes flashing anger as he handcuffed her and threw her into a jail that appeared beside his completely exposed body.

Waking up drenched in a cold sweat, it didn't take a genius to figure out what the dream was telling her. She hated how much she missed him. Two nights of sex shouldn't have left her with this visceral craving. But she had a giant loop running in her mind of the incredible passion and romance they'd shared the last night they were together.

Get over it, Jenna. She'd been carrying on the same conversation with herself for almost six weeks.

It seemed like years had passed since she left Dallas. Now hundreds of miles and several states away from Texas, she'd managed to follow the information in *Hidden Enemies* to acquire three sets of untraceable identities. Spending several terror-filled weeks in one city enabled her to arrange the basis for a new life.

Her first stop had been an expensive beauty parlor, where she'd exchanged her long, curly blonde hair for straight, shoulder-length brown tresses. She'd gone right to a photo shop to get pictures taken with her new hairstyle, for the first set of false identification.

Over the following weeks she'd used a dark wig and had other pictures taken for second and third sets of IDs. Then rented short-term shared office space so she'd have an untraceable place to get her mail and logon to the Internet. Bought a prepaid cell phone and set up a couple of different email accounts, then crossed her fingers when she contacted the first of several illegal websites promising her untraceable documents.

She went everywhere looking over her shoulder until the first package arrived. When she used those documents to get a driver's license and bank account, she'd been nothing but raw nerves.

After she sold her old blue SUV, she bought a different model in black and stashed her money in bank accounts — under the different names on her IDs — where she could access her funds with a cash card.

Her skin crawled every time she stepped out the door of another cheap hotel room — she moved often and paid cash. When everything was fixed to her satisfaction, she'd left Jenna Jessup behind.

And Jennie Jackson had been born with new hair, new style and new habits.

Now all she needed to do was settle down and start over. But no large city — a midsize town or small hamlet felt right. Waking up every morning intending to get a paper and explore the area's possibilities for a job or maybe a small business to buy, she'd become overwhelmed by a sharp feeling of unease each time, and scrambled for her vehicle, unable to breathe in anything but short pants until she was back on the road headed someplace else.

Knowing she was looking for the vision of serene perfection in her dreams, she couldn't help but doubt her sanity. There was no place like her secret haven. Promising her subconscious that somewhere on the drive through Colorado's mountains she'd stop and check out at least one community, she headed out.

Jen pulled over and sat in her vehicle on the side of the road, staring at the billboard in front of her in bewilderment. The sign advertised a summer festival in a town called *Secret Haven* All she had to do was turn right at the next crossroad and drive twenty-five miles into the valley. Unbelievable.

This coincidence bothered her a great deal, and yet when she thought she would ignore the sign, her stomach clenched and she felt nauseous.

So she turned right down a curvy mountain road lined with tall pine trees and dappled in sunlight. The air was clean and fresh, she could hear birds chirping merrily through her open window. For the first time in weeks she felt optimistic about her future. Driving around a sharp corner, she caught her breath. This was just too spooky — in front of her was an idyllic little town nestled in a valley. It looked exactly as it had in her dreams.

Descending the hill, she meandered through the town. It was quaint, a little old-fashioned and the drive from one end of town to another took three minutes. There were two options for lodging. A Victorian bed and breakfast at one end of town, and an outmoded motor lodge made up of multicolored cabins at the other. A sign for the cabins advertised kitchenettes and weekly or monthly rates. She decided to check out the cabins first.

The elderly man running the front desk happily gave her a key to a turquoise-colored cabin tucked back in the corner of the property. Surrounded on two sides by woods, the little bungalow faced into the forest. Parking across from the office at the back of the cabin, she walked around the small building to find a front deck big enough for a couple of patio chairs. The door was situated in the middle of the wall, with a window on both sides.

Unlocking the door, Jenna stepped inside and smiled. Rustic simplicity at its finest, the rectangular room served as a combination living room with a kitchen and dining area. The left side of the room had a large window looking out into the woods, with a small brown couch positioned underneath and little tables at either end. A green, overstuffed chair sat in one corner and there was a small desk under the window that looked out toward the deck.

On the right side of the room there was a window over the sink looking across the parking lot. Through it, she could see the other cabins and the motel office, and she would be able to keep track of other people coming and going. Next to the sink was a stove and in the corner a refrigerator. Sitting under the larger window looking out toward the deck were a small table and two chairs. Across the small space were two additional doors, the right one leading to a good-size bathroom with a large tub and enclosed shower. The left door opened into a small bedroom.

Stepping into the bedroom, she noted the window on the left wall had the same view as the one from the living room, looking out at the dense foliage of the forest. There was a dresser below the window, and a double bed shoved up against the far wall with a nightstand beside it. A small closet in the wall between the bedroom and the living room would give her plenty of room to hang the few dresses and suits she'd brought with her.

The space certainly didn't have the feel of the cookie-cutter hotel rooms she'd been staying in. It seemed perfect, allowing her a little space to spread out and the ability to cook her own meals. Maybe she could finally relax, enjoy the surrounding countryside and explore Secret Haven to decide if this really was the place to start her life over. The location would allow her privacy, and was close enough to town to walk if she wanted.

Going back out to the kitchen, she opened up the cupboards to find them stocked with the bare essentials, including a few dishes and a small array of pots and pans. If she needed, she could unpack a few things from her SUV, otherwise she would be set.

Arranging to take the cabin for a few weeks, she took her suitcase inside and made a grocery list. She was looking forward to being in one place for at least a short while.

The bell over the door of the small bookstore jingled merrily. Jenna stepped inside and looked around with a smile. Bookshelves filled every nook and cranny of the small building, except for the space along one wall where there was a counter with a cash register, and a tiny alcove with several comfy chairs for reading. In the corner was a small table with a coffee pot and cookies on a tray.

"Hello, dearie. Can I help you find something?" The shaky voice came from a short, gray-haired lady who walked out from behind one of the shelves.

Jen smiled. The woman was so darn cute in her bright purple pantsuit and green tennis shoes, with her hair in a bun seemingly held up by the several pencils she'd wound into the mass. "I thought I'd just browse a bit, and see if I might leave an application for any job you might have available."

This was the tough part. Jenna had decided that it wouldn't work to have a history of employment that couldn't be verified. Her skills were valid, but for obvious reasons she couldn't rely on her work history. So she'd come up with the story of running her husband's business, which was sold after the divorce. She could offer to show a prospective employer that she knew how to use a computer and any number of software programs. Everything else would be dependent on her sparkling personality. *Yeah, right.* She'd completely forgotten how to smile these days.

"Oh, I'm sorry, hon. I'm the only employee and I own the place, such as it is. In fact, I am really thinking of selling the store. My sister wants me to travel with her, take a few cruises and enjoy our retirement. Keeping up with this place is beginning to wear me down...I'm just a little old lady, you know." The woman giggled and winked as if imparting a great secret.

All Jen heard was — *thinking of selling the store.*

"Ummm. I'm new to the area, just got here today and am checking it out. I might be interested in buying a small business here...if you are seriously thinking about selling, could we talk about it? This might be just what I'm looking for."

Forty-eight hours later, Jenna was the proud and bemused owner of Simple Pleasures. Not the original name of the store she'd bought, but somehow Millicent's Books just didn't seem to work for her. She now owned the building, and everything inside.

Snorting almost hysterically, she thought how looks could be deceiving. She couldn't believe how sharp Millicent had been. She knew to the penny what her inventory was worth, her accounts payable and receivable were detailed to the nth degree, and she'd had an appraisal on the building less than a month ago. Jenna had been shocked when Millicent Marker brought out a contract stating what she'd take as down payment, and that she was willing to carry the financing for a specified percentage — payable to her for ten years, or if she died before the contract expired, to her niece.

Thinking of selling the building, my ass. The razor-sharp woman had known exactly what she wanted.

The older woman hid the heart and soul of a hurricane, and had been a force to be reckoned with. In dazed disbelief, Jen rattled the keys to the bookstore in her hands. At least she had been able to negotiate a month of Millicent's time, so that she could learn at least a little of what it would take to run the place. Since she'd never owned a bookstore before, she needed to figure out the simple things — like where the hell did you order books from?

Once Millicent started on her, Jen didn't have time to even make a conscious decision on whether or not she wanted to stay in Secret Haven. The terms for the store were perfect, the down payment hadn't made a huge dent in her savings, and she didn't have to go to a bank for financing. Fate seemed to want her here.

Never having given much thought to words like karma and destiny, she realized now she had a healthy belief in both. Enough to make her believe there were many things in this life that she had no experience with. And didn't that just make Jenna very nervous.

Cole sat in Pete's Diner, letting the idle gossip of small-town life wash over him. He was very glad to be home. Having gone straight from Dallas to Washington, D.C., he was tired of dealing with bureaucrats. Add to that the sharp surge of adrenaline he'd expended over the last two months tracking and finding a terrorist cell, and he was left on edge.

Pete slid into the booth across from Cole. "Have ya seen the cute little chicky who bought Millicent's bookstore, Cole? If I was a younger man and not happily married to my Maggie, I'd be smashing my TV and hanging out in her shop just for the view. Course, she's changed the name. Can't be calling it Millicent's Books if'n her name is Jennie, now can she? Calling it Simple Pleasures now. She's sure cute as a bug with those big blue eyes of hers."

Staring blankly at Pete, Cole's thoughts whirled madly in his head. Jennie? Jen? Maybe. Without bothering to comment, he threw a couple dollars on the table and headed out the door. Fatigue forgotten, his body was now primed for a fight. Well, primed for something.

Glancing over the changes to the old building, in the back of his mind he logged the new paint, new sign and the big urns of flowers flanking the entrance. When he opened the door, the same bell Millie had used jingled his arrival. There was no one at the counter.

There were two ways in and out of the building. He'd just come in the front, and he'd have to make sure she didn't see him first and go out the back. Ducking behind the nearest bookshelf, he waited until he could hear footsteps coming very close.

Stepping out into the aisle, he was amazed at the transformation of the woman he'd known as Jen. His body reacted strongly and he forgot for a moment the need to keep her from bolting in favor of just looking at her. Gone was the long and very curly blonde hair, in its place a sleek, sophisticated light brown hairstyle. Cole hated it.

As soon as he saw her, he reached for her emotions with his mind.

Shock he could see in the widening of her eyes, and hear in her sharp gasp. Happy—oh-so happy—was followed immediately by a jolt of fear. Before he had a chance to say a word, she turned and ran toward the back of the store. When she slammed a door between the public area and what had once been Millicent's office, he realized other changes had been made. There used to be a curtain hanging between the two rooms—not a door Jenna could obviously lock. Now she could run out the back exit without him able to follow.

By the time he retraced his steps to the front of the building, he could see her halfway to the south end of town. Still running. Which meant she hadn't driven a car to work, and now she was scrambling to get to her vehicle before Cole could reach her.

She didn't have a chance.

Cole forged after her, watching intently as she ducked around the corner of a rental cabin, and followed on her heels. Slipping silently inside, he caught up with her in the bedroom and slid to a stop at the view of Jen on her knees in front of the closet, pulling out a stuffed suitcase. He couldn't stop his body's reaction to her position on the floor and the display of tight jeans hugging her ass. The mounting awareness and excitement in his blood punctuated the extent he'd been fooling himself into believing this wasn't about finding Jen, but getting back the stolen book.

Whirling around as soon as she heard him, she blanched and shrieked, "Don't hurt me please!" The slump of her shoulders as she cowered in the corner on the floor, along with the dejected look in her eyes, told him she'd given up even before the wave of sad emotions hit him. Sad and fearful—she was afraid of him.

"Jen—"

Before Cole could say anything, she interrupted, "I know, I know. I promise I'll go willingly and you won't have to handcuff me. Here's your book back." Reaching into the bag beside her, she unzipped the top and took out a very well-worn copy of *Hidden Enemies*. When she tossed it to him, he looked down to see it flagged with sticky notes, and thumbing through, saw several highlighted passages. Obviously she'd not only read the manuscript, but studied it in detail.

"So. It was all a ruse. Meeting me in the bar, having sex. All you wanted was my book," he said in disgust. "Who'd you sell the information to, Jen? Aren't you even a little sorry for the lives you might have put at risk with your stint of espionage?"

"What are you talking about? I haven't sold any information from this book—I used it for myself. I didn't have any idea you existed until I met you that night. And ditto for the book. I saw it our first morning together, when you were in the shower. After we'd already had sex."

When she tried to stand he moved toward her, and she reacted immediately by throwing her hands up in front of her face, crying, "Please, don't hit me!"

Cole stopped and studied her, frowning in disbelief at her actions. She expected him to hit her, and her body language told him that she'd been beaten before. He started putting things together, knowing that part of him had wondered about this possibility from the beginning...he didn't like the scenarios playing out in his mind.

Keeping his voice soft and nonthreatening, he worked at reassuring her. "I won't hurt you, Jen. Here, let's go sit at your table and talk about a few things. I want explanations, and maybe you won't flinch every time I move if we're sitting down." Glancing around the room, he verified there was no way she could get out unless she could shimmy through one of the window louvers. These old cabins didn't have windows that opened, just little glass panes that could be unwound for airflow. Turning on his heels, he walked back out to the front of the cabin and sat in one of the kitchen chairs, his back to the door and his view toward the bedroom.

Keeping his eyes on the bedroom door, he grimaced when Jen walked out. This was not at all the way he thought the scenario would go. He expected her to scream and cuss him out, tell him she'd been using him and then he would have to haul her to jail. But no. She'd admitted taking the book, but said it was for her own use. If he added her reaction to the small lines he'd seen on her back and the bruised cheek he'd noticed when he'd met her, he couldn't help but think his other supposition was the one on the mark. She'd been abused and was trying to hide.

Gentling his voice, he pushed a chair toward her with his foot. "Sit down, Jen. I really am not going to hurt you. Let's start from the beginning and see if I can't figure out a way to help."

The spark of hope emanating from Jen at his offer of help made his stomach clench. Her sadness quickly overran any optimism.

"Let me get my cell phone," she said sadly. "I think you'd have an easier time believing the circumstances if you heard some of this from a reliable source. I don't want you wondering if I'm lying." Stepping back into the bedroom, he saw her get a cell phone out of the nightstand. "This has a speakerphone, and it's a prepaid phone I picked up in New Mexico, so it's not traceable to Colorado. Is it okay if I use this?"

He nodded. There was no doubt now that she had used his book for herself, as she was parroting information from the Hidden in Plain Sight chapter. Jen dialed a number and turned on the speaker. Cole could hear the phone ring and then a woman's voice, "Dallas Police Department, how can I direct your call."

"Captain Matt Jones, please." As they waited to be transferred, Cole glanced around the cabin. Obviously she'd felt comfortable enough in Secret Haven to unpack a few things and settle in. Plus, she'd bought a business. Wondering how long she'd been here and what had happened to her, he tapped his fingers lightly on the table in impatience.

"Matt Jones." The gruff voice filled the room.

"Hi, Matt. It's Jenna Jessup," she said, glancing at Cole.

He raised his eyebrows in acknowledgement. So, Jen was a nickname, and by using Jennie, she'd again followed a tenet espoused in his book. To keep it simple, and try and use something you won't forget to answer to.

"Jenna, you okay? Safe?"

"I'm okay. I just…well. I wanted to see how things were going. I haven't talked to you for a few weeks."

"Not going well. Rick didn't show up for his court appearance. We verified he was in Spain during the time your mother and stepfather's house was broken into…and Jenna, he went to Financial Fidelity a few nights ago and surprised your old boss, Victor. I'm sorry to tell you honey, but he put Victor in the hospital with several broken bones and a concussion."

"Oh, my God!" Jenna gasped, and lowered her head into her hands. She started shaking.

"Don't get too upset, Jen. Victor is already on the mend and has been released from the hospital. I'll tell him you called and are okay. He calls and asks me about you every day since Rick assaulted him, but don't be contacting him. Send me what you want to say by email or just tell me and I'll make sure he gets it. Just keep on doing what you're doing now. I haven't even been able to trace you the couple of times I've tried, when I wanted to make sure Rick wouldn't have any luck. Stay hidden, Jen. Rick told Victor he was going to find you and kill you as soon he got the chance. We've got an all-points bulletin out on Rick and we're trying to pick him up, but we have to find him first."

Cole caught Jen's gaze, watched her eyes grow wide and felt her confusion when he entered the conversation. "Captain Jones, this is Cole Matheson. I'm a friend of Jen's. I have worked with Lieutenant John Garrison of the Dallas police force. Do you know John?"

Matt's voice was filled with unspoken questions when he replied. "Yes."

"I often consult with different agencies in searching for and locating criminals. Because of my association with Jen, I'd like to volunteer my services. Please talk to John and verify my credentials, he knows how to get in touch with me and can get copies of files and information to me without violating Jen's whereabouts. Can you tell me where Rick was last sighted?"

"I'll tell you he was last sighted in New Mexico. But if you don't mind, I'll talk to John first before disclosing anything else. I am assuming since you let Cole hear this conversation, Jenna, that you're okay with him getting involved?"

Jenna nodded, realized immediately that Matt couldn't see her and said, "Yes. I met Cole in Dallas. He actually teaches seminars on finding terrorists and criminals for the military and police, Matt. I…I trust him."

"Okay, that information just jiggled a memory. I've heard of you, Cole. Good things. I'll talk to John ASAP and take him copies of Rick's file. I'd be happy to have any help in this—"

Jenna interrupted the conversation. "I called Victor once on the cell phone I got in New Mexico, do you think that's why Rick was seen there?"

Both men were silent for a moment. Finally Cole said, "Did Victor say anything about writing down Jenna's number, or her calling him?"

"He didn't. I'll call him as soon as we get off the phone and ask a couple of questions."

"Good. I'll go over Jenna's movements up through today and verify if Rick might have something to trace her this far. I'll also make sure she's kept safe on this end. Let's find the bastard before he gets to her."

"I'll be in touch through John. Be careful, Jen." With that, Matt disconnected and Jenna reached over to close her cell phone. Cole could see her struggle with questions and could feel her emotions in turmoil.

Slowly, Cole reached out and touched her hand. "Why didn't you tell me you were in trouble?"

Jenna's laugh was not a happy sound. Almost hysterically, she replied, "What, tell a man I met in a bar, a man who I had sex with just a few hours after meeting him—with nothing but a physical attraction between us—that my crazy ex-husband was trying to kill me? Yeah, right. Are you going to have me arrested for stealing your book?"

Cole drew his hand back and shook his head. He really couldn't blame her for asking. "No, Jen. I'm not going to have you arrested. What I *am* going to do is see if I can't find this bastard and turn him over to the police, so you might have some peace and the chance to live your life without hiding."

The backlash of emotions pouring from Jenna overwhelmed Cole. Helplessly, he watched as she put her head down on her arms and sobbed. Emotional pain, fear mixed with a relief he hoped she felt because she was no longer in this alone and not because she thought he would take her to jail, filled the small room. Knowing she wouldn't want him to touch her, he tamped done the need to take her in his arms and hold her while she cried. Instead, he used his phone to call Millicent, asked the older woman if she wouldn't mind closing up Jen's shop for the night, and got up to make coffee.

When she pulled herself together, he wanted to hear the story from the beginning...and see how well she'd concealed her trail.

Chapter Seven

ဆ

Rubbing his chest, Cole realized his heart hurt. It felt as if bands of agony were wrapped around the organ and squeezing. For several hours he'd listened to Jenna explain the last year of her marriage to Rick, including each time he'd abused or harassed her. Watching as she'd gone through the entire range of emotions, he'd been with her. At first she was embarrassed that she had to share her sordid story with him. He'd been rather blunt when he assured her she wasn't responsible for the things that had been done to her.

Then he sensed confusion when she explained her ex-husband's change in personality.

When her throat clogged with fear, he had to hold onto the sides of the kitchen chair to keep from lashing out. Not at her, but at the conflicting needs within him to either hold and comfort the woman before him...or pound something with his fists in reaction to her torment. Jenna didn't want him to hold her. She'd decided he would only be doing it out of pity. The tether he tried to keep on his control almost snapped with her remark.

Unlike her capitulation under his assertion that she had nothing to be embarrassed about, she wouldn't listen to his insistence that there was nothing about her to be pitied. The woman he saw before him was strong...courageous. When she turned his comments away with a wave of her hand, he turned his irritation back to Rick.

He especially wanted to use his own belt to mark Rick the way he'd lashed Jen's back. Or put his fingers around the bastard's neck and show him how it felt to be choked. Recompense for the rape would be more difficult to arrange. But there were men in prison who owed him favors. Every inch of his body had been shaking with the need to seek revenge for her.

That need had quickly turned first to amazement, and then awe, when he listened to Jenna relate the series of steps she took after leaving Dallas. Pride filled him when he realized that his book had enabled her to care for herself so well...to take the measures necessary to start a new life. He realized there were abused women and others out there who could benefit from the secrets detailed in his book, he just didn't see any way to share those secrets without criminals misusing the information.

After he did his best to help Jenna, maybe he would talk to some of his buddies. He knew he could put together a group that would donate time and energy volunteering to help people in similar situations. They could get the word out that their services were free...a consultation and a little detective work, along with suggestions for staying safe. And if lives were at stake...well, he certainly knew how to help them hide.

Jenna's flight across country was proof of that. He couldn't see anything left hanging out there that could possibly lead Rick to her. Later tonight he'd check, do some database scans and, since he knew where and when to look, he might find a little trail he could snuff out. But he didn't think the man would find Jenna on his own. Which meant anyone who knew her—parents, associates, even the police—could be in very real danger.

Cole didn't think Rick would stop trying to make her pay for whatever he imagined she'd done to him. His visit to Victor had proven that. So if they couldn't catch Rick, they would somehow have to draw him in. And Cole was very opposed to the idea of using Jen as bait.

Right now, his top concern would be to keep her safe. She'd pleaded a headache and went to bed early. Cole would give her this time and allow her to keep some distance between them. Until she woke up.

He would use those hours on her behalf. Already the Chief of Police for Secret Haven had agreed to go to Cole's home and pick up his laptop. Cole would fill Robert in once he showed up with the computer, and ensure the few state and local police in the area were alerted to possible threats. Cole knew this town, knew a few comments to the right people would have a network of wannabe spies calling him at all hours of the day or night to report strangers, cars parked in suspicious spots...any little unexplained noise or movement made by strangers coming into their town.

Before this was over, Jenna would be well acquainted with small-town life. He could just imagine how the little ladies from his senior self-defense class would react. They'd park their butts on every bench along Main Street, and take shifts for the coveted furniture within Simple Pleasures. He didn't expect them to actually have to defend Jenna—the thought of all those women using the skills he'd taught them would scare the bejesus out of anyone. No, their mission would be to provide warm bodies. Rick had shown himself to be a coward. He wouldn't try anything unless he found Jen alone.

So while Cole tracked him down, he would ensure she was never unaccompanied.

Jenna was not a happy camper this morning. She'd gone to bed early the night before with a headache, only to toss and turn and dream of Cole in his new role as both saint and savior. It hadn't taken long for those dreams to change into carnal fantasies.

She'd heard him talking to someone in low tones in her living room. And she remembered agreeing to his offer of protection, saying she would be grateful if he handled her problem with Rick. Swearing an oath to follow directions implicitly, she was too exhausted at the time to really think her promise through, or wonder who else he'd spoken to...both in person and on the phone. Today she was feeling a little nervous about that promise.

Coming out of the bedroom, she found him working at his laptop, discarded coffee cup and snack foods littering the table.

"Sleep well? Good. You need to hurry and take a shower and dress for work. I'll have something ready for you to eat and then I can drop you off at Simple Pleasures before I go take care of a few things."

Jenna stomped into the shower, upset that Cole was ordering her around like a child. She had also somehow come up with the idea that he wouldn't want her out of his sight. That he would take her home with him and...*well,* maybe act out some of her fantasies from the night before. To say she was a little disappointed would be an understatement. Obviously she'd been wrong to think he might have forgiven her theft of his book.

Pasting on a cheerful smile, she exited the shower dressed and groomed to the nines.

"I don't like the new hairstyle," Cole muttered, as he looked her up and down, brow furrowed in distaste when he looked at her hair. "How long will it take to get the brown dye out and the curls to come back? Can you get it colored and permed?"

Creep.

Refusing to acknowledge his comment, she glared at him. "I thought you said something about breakfast?" Waving her hand at the clean tabletop and obvious lack of food cooking in the kitchen, she picked up her purse to join him at the door.

Shuffling her out the door and into his car, he locked the cabin and pocketed her keys. "Someone will be bringing both your breakfast and lunch to the store. I'll pick you up at closing. I know you've got a big pot for coffee at the bookstore, I remember seeing it yesterday. Do you have plenty of plastic cups and supplies for today?

Jerk.

Having Cole order her day was not sitting well with Jenna. Fuming throughout the drive at his lack of concern for her safety while she was at work, she jumped out of his car when they arrived at her shop, slamming the door behind her.

Five minutes later the bell over the entrance to Simple Pleasures pealed and she looked up to find a gang of kamikaze blue-haired women entering her store, armed with plates of baked goods and large bags with knitting needles poking out. As a group, their claim to fame was graduating from one of Cole's defense classes. They took pride in informing her they were now her personal squad of aged guardians.

Every hour on the dot, groups of three women would switch places, and she realized someone had worked out a very complicated schedule. The three ladies sitting on the bench outside her store would move to the couch by the counter. The three ladies previously on the couch would start to browse her shelves. The ladies rearranging her stock—who were supposed to be "browsing" her shelves—would move into the office. The three ladies relieved of office duty would go home to rest, cook and compare notes. And three new women would fill the bench in front of the store.

The constant grandmotherly reassurances as to their suitability for this mission started to wear on her last nerve by the beginning of the second shift.

There were three things keeping her from shooing the elderly guards out onto the street and locking the door behind them. They brought incredible muffins and salads and all kinds of other food with them. They were cleaning her store shelves from top to bottom and rearranging the books in alphabetical order by genre and author. And she'd had the biggest sale day yet. Each time the browsers went off shift, they stopped at the cash register first. She'd tried to give them each a book for their help, and when that failed, tried to give them a discount, but they wouldn't allow it.

They kept saying things like, "This is the most fun we've had in years, dearie." And "Oh, no…I couldn't. We're your protectors. We can't be taking advantage of you."

What really scared her was the amount of books she'd sold from the martial arts section of the store, and self-help titles like *The Idiot's Guide to Disguise*. Cole had a lot to answer for.

Imbecile.

At three o'clock the gender of her guards changed, and this time doddering old men replaced all the women. Heaven help her, they polished off every goodie the ladies brought and looked around for more. They set up a checkerboard in her front window and drank decaf coffee by the gallons. Then they proceeded to mess up her well-ordered shelves.

Snake.

The only thing that saved these men was their unfailing charm. They amused her with little nicknames, calling her chickpea and turtledove, wagging their eyebrows when she bent over to pick up a book they'd dropped. Several times. The men's choice of purchased reading material ran to spy novels and old war histories. More than one of them commented on how they'd read up tonight and come back better prepared for tomorrow's mission.

Lord help her.

By the end of the day she was ready to beat Cole with a big stick.

As Cole pulled in front of the store in his big, black SUV, the last of her guardians filed out. Each one took the time to pat her hand and comfort her with the promise of their presence for as long as she needed them.

Starting to run through her litany of insults for Cole's benefit, she suddenly realized that since the first time she found herself afraid of Rick, this was the only day she could remember having not looked over her shoulder twenty times or jumped at the smallest noise. Her guardians had done a fine job of getting her to forget her troubles, and they'd provided company and companionship. Two things she'd lacked while on the run.

So instead of calling Cole an entire stream of nasty names when he walked in the door, she walked over and kissed him on the cheek. "Thank you."

Surprised, he still managed to pull her into his arms and find her mouth with his. "Ummm, I'm not sure what that was for but I certainly appreciate the thought."

A little stunned by the remembered heat of his body, she murmured, "For sending in the GeeGOSH."

"GeeGOSH?"

"Yesss," she rubbed against him and offered her mouth for another kiss, since he seemed to be inclined to humor her. After she'd recovered enough breath to speak, she explained, "Geriatric Guardians of Secret Haven—GeeGOSH."

It took Cole fifteen full minutes to stop laughing. During that time he managed to help her clear the register and make a deposit, set up the coffee pot so it was ready to go the next day and close down the shop. He then loaded her into his vehicle and started through town.

She hadn't changed Millicent's summer hours for the store. Being open from ten in the morning to seven at night made for a long day, but it meant there was still daylight outside when she closed. She looked around the little community and enjoyed seeing a slice of old-fashioned America. The large building façades with benches in front of each store, and either pots of flowers or large trees in strips of grass lining the sidewalks, gave the little community a very cozy feel.

When they passed the hardware store she realized Cole wasn't taking her back to her cabin. "Where are we going?"

"My house, I moved your things while you were at work."

"Moved my things? What things?"

"Everything. You know, your clothes and whatever Bill said didn't belong to the motor lodge. He said you could come by tomorrow morning and do a walk-through to make sure we didn't forget anything. I also put your SUV in my garage."

Jenna was stunned. "Why?"

When Cole just shrugged and turned the vehicle she felt like screaming.

"Jen, the cabin is a security nightmare. A three-year-old could break through the door, and located halfway into the forest with all those windows…forget it. For the duration you're bunking with me. If it makes you feel any better, I put your stuff in the spare bedroom."

Clenching her fists in her lap, she decided she was too mature to just lunge across the seat and rip his eyes out. Who did he think he was treating her like this? Out of the corner of her eye she saw him glance at her and smirk. Maybe she wasn't as mature as she thought.

"Don't get so pissy, Jen. You promised me you would let me handle this in the way I thought was best. Moving in with me is one of those steps. My home has a security system and is easily defendable." Pulling into a long driveway, he parked in front of the house and waited for her reaction to both his pushy, take-charge manner and his home. He didn't need psychic abilities to read her emotions. She was angry with him. Tough. There was no way he would take risks with her safety—and he wasn't willing to examine his own need to have her close and protected.

With blind eyes she stared out the window of the SUV, thinking. Just this morning she'd been hoping he would keep her with him, take her home…make love to her. Why had she done an about-face and become irritated with him for doing what she'd wanted earlier? Because her emotions around Cole were too extreme. She wanted to go in that house and have him spread her out on the nearest flat surface. *He'd put her things in the spare bedroom.*

She'd spent months trying to relegate her thoughts of Cole to a little box in her mind labeled Weekend Fling. Then he'd stepped into her bookstore, a vibrant resident of the town she'd accidentally made her own.

Accidentally made her own. Oh, no.

Remembering the weeks of dreams, of *seeing* Secret Haven, yearning for it, unable to even imagine putting down roots somewhere else, and picturing the settlement in her mind…exactly as it had looked when she drove over the last hill before finding it displayed in perfect—no! That was crazy. *Wasn't it?*

Unable to deal with the path her inner thoughts were trying to move toward, she focused outside the car and gasped in surprise. "Holy… This is your house?"

Rather smugly, Cole smiled. "Yeah. Like it?"

Nestled in an area overgrown with evergreen trees, the structure was an amazing blend of big, light, pine-colored knotty logs and glass. The two-story roof pitched at a sharp V and the front wall was nothing but windows. She could see into the house—high, open-beamed ceilings and a large rock fireplace captured her attention. There was a loft at the far end overhanging the great room and a large wraparound porch in the front. Groupings of oversized, rough-hewn wood furniture and planter boxes of multicolored flowers completed the picture of a peaceful and luxurious mountain retreat.

"It's incredible, but I thought you said windows were a security risk?"

"The lower windows are bulletproof. You'll be safe here, Jenna, I promise you that." Cole really wasn't paying attention to her words. He was caught in the expressions on her face, watching as conflicting emotions played over her features. He'd missed her. Thought about her often and hated himself for doing it. Now the urge to protect and keep her safe twisted inside him. Along with the overwhelming urge to run as far as he could in the opposite direction so he wouldn't have to see the disgust in her eyes when she found out he had psychic abilities. He wasn't sure he could live through Jen rejecting him.

He'd brought her to Secret Haven and hadn't thought about the ramifications. So now he had choices. Be a friend, her protector and keep his hands off her…or her lover for as long as she would have him. The sharp slice of pain at the thought of her turning him away told him time wouldn't matter. When it was over he would hurt like hell.

Jenna sat at the table after eating the Greek pasta salad Cole had made for dinner. Dinner conversation had been light, with her amusing him with lively anecdotes from her day with Secret Haven's senior bodyguards. She loved making him laugh, seeing the light of amusement in his warm brown eyes, and how the little wrinkles that gave his face character showed when he smiled. The thin slash of scar on his left cheek was barely visible, not detracting from his looks but giving him an added layer of intrigue and appeal. Like he needed more.

There wasn't anything about this man that she didn't find attractive. Several times during the meal she had to restrain herself from reaching out and touching him. She had no idea how she would get through even one night under the same roof without screaming in frustration at their new "let's be friends" relationship. She didn't want to be friends, damn it.

"Would you like to go sit on the back porch and have a glass of wine? Deer often come into the little meadow behind the house to feed as the sun is setting."

Glancing up, she didn't realize yearning shown through her eyes and flowed from her in waves. Cole drew in a deep breath and let the sweet heat of her longing cut through him. The fear and indecision that previously mingled with her desire was gone. In their place was a sad resignation—he hoped it meant she thought he wanted her in the guest room instead of his bed.

Before she answered, he offered another choice. "Or I could run you a bubble bath in the large tub upstairs...hold you in my arms in the warm water and run my hands over every inch of your skin." Her eyes grew wide and a little glazed, he could see her chest expand with an indrawn breath. She jumped up in agitation and went to look out the sliding glass door into the falling night.

"Cole? I don't understand, I thought…well, you put me in the guest room," she questioned brokenly, her emotions tumultuous with hesitation and growing hope.

Standing up, he moved beside her, putting a hand on her shoulder to turn her to him. Reaching out to run his finger down her cheek, he stared intently into her sapphire blue eyes. "You torment me, Jen. Every day since we met I've replayed the nights in my head and worried how much I wanted more of you." His voice was low, intense. "Every moment has been long, slow torture where I've imagined your body stretched over me, beneath me…while we make love in every possible way. But this is more than you bargained for. We're not in Dallas and you can't just walk out of my hotel room and leave. I have to give you a choice."

Her gaze caught and held his. As always with Jen, he wished he could get more than the emotions, knowing she had questions and concerns she wouldn't voice.

"A choice?"

"Yes, to sleep in the guest room, or in my bed. If you choose my bed tonight, there's no going back. As long as you're under my roof…you'll sleep with me."

"And after? What are we doing, Cole? Neither of us wanted a relationship, but if we're having sex…living in the same town…what happens when the threat of Rick has been removed?"

"I don't know. There are things you don't know about me, things you may not like. I can't give you guarantees. You're right. I didn't want a relationship when this started and I don't sleep with any women who live in Secret Haven. But I look at you, I touch you," he ran his finger over her collarbone, teasing along the neck of her tank top, "and I don't care what I did in the past or what I wanted. I see you straining, panting and hungry beneath me, begging for my touch."

"Jesus, Cole." Sighing at his erotic words, she leaned into his body.

He stopped her, locking his eyes on hers and asked, "Are you sure, Jen? Be very sure this is what you want."

"Never any question," she mumbled, lifting her arms to wrap them around his neck and pull him to her.

Kissing Cole was like watching fireworks while having a massage and drinking a cinnamon-spice mocha coffee. She got lost in the lights flashing behind her eyes and the sonic boom reverberating in each cell of her body while trying to capture his taste and not misplace the sensation of his hands roaming her flesh. Immersed in sensual overload, she gave a little squeal of shock when he pulled away from her and immediately scooped her up in his arms.

"I'm taking that as a yes, and I think it's time to go drive each other crazy. Last chance to say no, darlin'."

"You're not going to hear that word from my lips. I believe you promised me a bubble bath, Cole."

Chuckling at her sultry tone, he climbed the stairs with ease, not setting her down until he'd reached the master bath. As he ran water in the tub, she looked around the large, sumptuous room. There were huge windows on two walls letting in the setting sun, the soft light casting a rosy glow on the pale cream walls and highlighting the antique brass fixtures and the enormous white porcelain bathtub. The bathroom boasted a separate double-headed shower and dual sinks set off by dark green and brown ceramic tiles. He had plants set in the deep windowsills, and lush emerald and chocolate towels echoed the color pattern she'd glimpsed as he'd passed through the bedroom.

By the time she turned back to him, he'd lit a few candles and stripped off his shirt. Moving to her, he set his hands on her hips, fingering the hem of her navy blue tank top. "Let me undress you."

Inch by agonizing inch, he raised the top over her head while his fingers skimmed over her skin. She reveled in his intake of breath when he uncovered her navy lace bra. Pulling the top over her head, he bent to kiss the curve of her neck.

"So sweet," he murmured against her skin.

Before Jenna could move into the touch she craved, he dropped to his knees in front of her and kissed her belly. "Let's get these jeans off you."

Unsnapping the front, he slowly, carefully unzipped her and then spread the two sides apart and slid his hands on either side of her hips, skimming the pants down her legs. "Put your hand on my shoulder and step out of these," he commanded.

She had removed her shoes earlier, not wanting to walk on Cole's beautiful hardwood floors with anything but her bare feet. So discarding her pants was a simple chore. When they were tossed to the side, he kept his hands on her hips and leaned forward to nuzzle the scrap of dark blue lace that barely covered her. Using his lips he nipped at her, following the trail of lace as he looped his thumbs into the sides of the fabric, pulling it down her thighs.

When he had exposed every inch of her flesh from the waist down, he pressed his mouth to the V of her thighs and used the tip of his tongue to part her folds and stroke the tip of her clit. He held her thighs together, not allowing her to spread herself for him, so each stroke was a long, slow push to separate her flesh and find the prize. When her knees started to give out, he pulled back to grin up the length of her body.

"Sit on the ledge of the tub, Jenna. There's room for you to brace yourself with your hands." Weakly sitting down on the cold porcelain of the oversized bathtub, she waited for Cole as he quickly shut off the water and knelt before her. Putting his hands on her tightly clenched knees, he purposefully pushed them apart and moved between them. He leaned over to kiss her lightly on the mouth, one hand at the back of her neck. Tangling his fingers in her hair, he tugged her head back, baring her neck to his lips, so he could slant a trail of wet heat from her collarbone to her breasts. She still had her bra on and he dipped and swirled around the edge until she thought she would scream. She couldn't raise her hands to tug him to where she wanted — she needed her arms for balance on the bathtub ledge, and they'd both go tumbling into the water if she didn't keep them in place.

Finally he lapped across the pouting tip of one nipple, dampening the lace and teasing unmercifully the flesh beneath. He sucked both fabric and flesh into his mouth, rolling her nipple with his tongue. The wet lace abraded her, adding to her arousal. She bowed her back, pressing her body into his tormenting mouth.

As he played with one breast, he moved a hand up to release the bra's catch at her back, then pushed the material up to expose her chest and free her for his pleasure. Using both hands, he pushed the mounds together and suckled each nipple in turn. Shuddering in reaction, her hips moved restlessly on her perch.

Releasing his hold on her breasts, Cole scooted back enough to lick a path down Jenna's stomach to her core. Using his hands to spread her folds, he licked from bottom to top, wiggling his tongue for a brief second into her weeping channel before flicking her clit in earnest. She felt each pass, each tormenting lick stoke the trembling fires in her body. Layer upon layer of sensation built and she strained to reach the top. He worked her body, using tongue and teeth and hands to drive her insane.

Plunging his tongue into her pussy, he shook his head from side to side so his nose batted her clit, one hand coming up to pinch and pull her nipple, and before long the enclosed room rang with her mewling cries. With her eyes tightly closed, her head thrown back and her arms barely able to support her quaking body, she begged him. "Pleaseohgod...don't stop...dontstopohplease!" It was too much. Too much. Her lungs burned, and her blood rushed to her head and her breasts and her cunt, the inflamed sensation adding to the extreme sensitivity of her skin.

She felt the press of his finger as he pushed first one, then two inside her to pump and grind as he suckled her nubbin, before lightly biting. She screamed through her climax, and rearing up to clutch his shoulders, she held on and sobbed as he raised his head but continued to finger-fuck her, each invasion working to build her toward a higher pinnacle.

"Cole!"

"Tell me what you want, baby, and I'll give it to you."

"Cole, please!"

"What do you want, Jen? Want me to stop?"

"No! God! I want you. Please Cole, please."

Cole stood up and quickly stripped off his jeans, covering his engorged cock with a condom. He stepped into the tub and helped Jen to stand in the hot water as well. Sitting down first, he positioned Jen with her back to his front and slowly lowered her to his lap, guiding the tip of his cock into the wet opening of her core and up into her swollen and still-pulsing softness. He pulled her back against him, helping her bend her knees and plant her feet on the outside of his thighs. He could feel the internal flutters of her muscles as they contracted and released in the final throes of her climax and his relentless penetration.

She tilted her head back and to one side and rested on his shoulder. Into the soft flesh at her nape he whispered, teasing her with his breath, "We're going to sit like this for as long as we can. Not moving. We can touch with our hands and you can squeeze your inner muscles, but I want you sitting here, with my cock filling you, while you consider how much you want me to slam in and out of your sweet heat. I want to drive you wild — or have you drive me wild. Who do you think can win this battle, sweetheart?"

Groaning low in her throat, Jen reached down between her legs to stroke where their bodies joined together. She pressed along the root of his shaft, the few inches left outside of her body, and ran her fingers over the throbbing vein on the underside of his cock. His inhalation of breath spurred her to reach a little farther, so she could gently fondle his ball sac and roll the tight spheres in her hand.

Cole brought up his hands, slick with soap, to stroke and play with Jen's breasts. He loved the feel of her in his hands, the slippery mounds and taut nipples he could twist between his fingers and flick with his thumbs. The rhythmic clenching of her cunt around his throbbing cock as she milked him supplemented the enticing feel of her sweet hand, and drove him insane. Latching his mouth on the sensitive skin at the juncture of her neck and shoulder, he moaned into her neck.

Their frenzied fight to break the other's control began in earnest. Dropping the thin mental wall he kept between them, he felt once again the flood of her emotional arousal, the connection so unique he felt a part of her. The combined pleasures beat at him and he rocked his hips, unable to still the need to claim that tight cunt as his own. To make her scream again in shared capitulation.

Against her ear, he said roughly, "I'm going to fuck you hard and deep, until you scream my name and beg me to stop and I feel your body tremble around mine in exhaustion. Then I'm going to let you slide into sleep, and I'll wake you to passion again, with my mouth and my hands and my body."

"Cole, God. Cole, please fuck me now, I can't—" She squirmed in his lap. Sitting up to lean forward, she brought her knees down and tried to rise above him. He clamped a hand on her belly and surged forward. Rising to his knees, he propped her over the rounded edge of the tub. After grabbing a nearby towel and folding it for her to drape over the cold rim, Cole brought both hands to the sweetly rounded mounds of her ass and set her rocking back and forth on his length.

God, the incredible feel of her suctioning inner walls drawing along his shaft as he pulled out, enveloping each time he moved back into her. He pushed deep inside, then moved almost all the way out, staring down at the sight of his cock, wet with her cream and poised to press its way back into her pussy.

He drove in hard, loving the sound of the surprised gasp he'd forced from her. The tight, constricting glove of her sex clung to him as he pulled out and slammed back in, the silky vibrations driving him insane. Again and again he repeated the motion. Harder and harder, increasing speed to the panting chant of her cries. His name.

"Cole. Cole. Cole. Cole!"

The muscles of her pussy started to shudder, and knowing she was starting to come, he dug in and lifted her hips, increasing the angle so his balls slapped against the sensitive bud of her clit. He threw his head back, feeling the lightning sizzle at the base of his spine and his own rush to completion. Balls drawing tight against his body, he felt her shake and struggle to force him further into her. Pumping deeper and deeper into the hot recesses of her body, he brought his hand around and pinched her clit. With bruising force he dug his hips in until she shrieked long and high, the climax thundering through her and racking her entire body with tremors, her pussy clamping powerfully on his plunging cock.

He held still as he started to come, his cock jerking as his seed filled the condom with hot, thick streams that seemed pulled from the bottoms of his feet.

When he could move—could think—Cole pulled out and leaned over to kiss the small of her back, then rinsed and dried them both before carrying her to bed. God, he'd missed this.

Chapter Eight

ଈ୬

The next morning, Cole drove Jenna into town just before she was due to open the bookstore. He couldn't help grinning smugly at her sleepy yawn...he'd definitely kept to his promise the night before, waking her again and again, unable to resist the lure of her body resting beside him. Dropping her off in front of Simple Pleasures, he laughed at her look of astonishment. Standing in front of her store was a group of people twice the size she'd had on hand yesterday. As in all small towns, the word had spread that one of their own needed assistance. It didn't matter that Jen hadn't lived here for long, what mattered was that everyone wanted to help.

He could leave her in their hands, knowing she'd never have a moment alone the entire day.

"You are so dead, Cole."

"Ah, come on, Jen. No one would dare try and get to you through this mob. I can work on tracking Rick and not have to worry that he'll pop in before I'm ready for him."

"How about I go to some nice, quiet room and spend the day on the computer, while you go in there and referee?"

Shaking his head, he gave her a quick kiss that several of the seniors noticed before letting her slide out of the car. "I'll pick you up at seven o'clock and take you for a nice dinner down at Pete's." When she slammed the door he snorted, and, waving at the crowd, drove away.

At 7:30 they walked hand in hand down Main Street heading for the diner. Cole laughing heartily at Jen's amusing take on the townspeople who'd "babysat" her all day. While he laughed, he kept a close eye on their surroundings, hyper-aware even though he didn't think they had anything to worry about from Rick.

All day he'd been unable to shake the edgy vigilance of his body, chalking it up to the fact he hadn't dispelled all the tension from his last job before he'd been thrown back together with Jen. Normally he could relax here in Secret Haven, and not be on his guard so much.

A quick flash of emotion, one of murky hatred, had him whipping around toward the alley between the hardware store and the antique shop. Catching a brief glimpse of a dark-haired man and the flash of light on metal, Cole pushed Jen behind him and into the recessed door of the building they were just passing.

"What? Cole!"

The sharp snap of gunshots cut through the summer night. Cole used his body as a shield, pushing Jen further into the corner. He felt the sting of hot metal in his left shoulder and saw the gunman bolt as people came out into the street to check out the sound of gunfire. "Get back," he shouted. Running while crouched and dragging Jen at his side, he shoved her into the hands of Pete at the café. "Make sure she hasn't been hit, call Robert, and for God's sake stay inside and lock the doors." Then he took off running toward the alley.

Whoever had shot at them had made a mistake — Cole knew where each street, each alley and byway led in this town. Without slowing down, he ran past the first side street — there was no cover and no exit for anyone to hide down the first lane. But several other outlets zigzagged, and could provide a place to stop and take a shot at anyone coming. Thankful that he'd started wearing his gun in a shoulder holster under his light jacket, Cole eased around a few blind spots with it firmly in hand. He'd taken the precaution in case he needed the firearm to protect Jenna from Rick.

The shooter had to have planned an escape route. Must have stashed a getaway car, and the only places that could work would be at the end of the alley, just in front of the National

Forest, or on one of the old logging roads through the woods, depending on how bad he didn't want the car to be seen. Parks and federal land reserves surrounded Secret Haven. Once you left the confines of town there were a million places to hide. He had to catch sight of the man soon.

Cole knew Jenna's ex-husband had sported short blond hair when she'd left Dallas. This man had dark brown hair down to his shoulders. His facial hair — the eyebrows and stubble on the man's face — had been dark as well.

If they weren't dealing with a crazy ex-husband, it could only be someone from Cole's past, and none of the options were good. He came to a stop at the end of the last building and crouched behind a convenient row of garbage cans to peer around the corner. If the fugitive was out there he wouldn't be able to see Cole, and there were several alley endings the man would have to keep an eye on.

Nothing. No car, no fugitive. Nothing. He waited for a moment, concentrating on emotions in the area. Behind him were the jumbled reactions of the townspeople. Easy to discern, they were excited, scared — and furious. Probably because someone had dared to fire shots on their peaceful streets.

A faint taint of hatred and disgust came from the other side of the road. *Gotcha. Now the question is, scumbag, are you crouched in hiding and just waiting for me to show my pretty face, or are you hightailing it to the getaway car?* Listening, he heard the sound of someone behind him and a short, three-note whistle. Without taking his eyes from the bushes across the way, he signaled behind his back with his left hand. *Son of a bitch that hurt!*

"What do we have, Cole?" Robert's voice was pitched not to carry any farther than needed.

"Shooter, small caliber. Somewhere in the bushes, waiting for me to make a move."

Robert used the radio fastened to his shoulder to alert his deputies to block the road in front of them, and to start setting up roadblocks for the exits to the logging roads. "Do you want someone to drop down behind him?"

"I don't think so, Rob. We don't know if the shooter is friendless. This doesn't feel like an angry ex-husband. There is a very real chance my cover's been blown somewhere along the way. I don't want any of your boys butting heads against something we don't understand yet."

Just as the words left his mouth, the man across the road ran out of patience and jumped up from behind a thick hedge of bushes to run up the hill. Cole grabbed Robert, not allowing him to charge after the man—he'd seen this play before. When nothing happened, the man stopped, turned around and threw up his hands, cursing in Arabic. Within seconds, another man stepped out of the trees and they started to argue. Cole gave them a minute. When no one else appeared, he nodded at Robert and they both fired off warning shots.

"Put down your guns and raise your hands in the air, now!" Cole's voice boomed across the area, and he watched as the startled men swung toward the sound of his voice.

In what seemed like slow motion, one of the men complied, dropping his gun and sticking both hands in the air. The remaining gunman turned quickly to shoot his comrade before turning his weapon on himself.

Damn.

It was hours later when Cole made it back to Pete's Diner. He'd checked in to make sure Jenna hadn't been injured and to tell everyone they'd caught the shooter and found the getaway car, and there didn't appear to be any risk in going home. It didn't surprise him to walk through the door and find Jenna surrounded by many of her GeeGOSH ladies, with a secondary circle made up of the men. She sat in a booth sandwiched between two blue-haired ladies, her hands wrapped tightly around the cup of coffee in front of her. It reminded him of the night they'd met, when she'd been sitting in the hotel bar in Dallas in a similar pose. This time he had to wade through several bodies to get to her.

When she saw Cole, her eyes widened and filled with tears. He swooped down to extract her from her cheering section and pulled her toward the door, explaining to everyone that Robert was on his way to Pete's, intending to fill them all in on any details he could share. He squired Jenna out to his SUV waiting at the curb.

"Oh God, Cole, I'm so sorry," she sobbed, throwing herself into his arms before he could get her into the truck.

Wincing, he wrapped his right arm around her and hugged. "Hey, doll. Nothing to be sorry for." When she continued to sob he added, "It wasn't Rick, Jen."

That stopped the tears. Drawing back, she looked him in the eye and questioned, "It wasn't Rick?"

"Nope. Let me wait to explain until we get home and get comfortable."

Jenna was quiet on the ride home. The emotions Cole read from her were mixed—lots of relief, some sadness and a little hero worship. At least, that's what he labeled the bit of awe she projected. Once they were in the door, they agreed to take separate showers before meeting in front of the fireplace for a glass of wine, where Cole would fill Jenna in. The summer night air was brisk, not really cold enough for a fire…they just agreed the flames would be comforting.

Standing in front of the bathroom mirror, he managed to get the jacket off by taking his right hand out of its sleeve first and letting it fall off his left arm. The blue T-shirt was going to be a bigger problem.

"Cole, do you have some shampoo I can borrow? You must have left mine in the shower at the cab— Oh my God!"

He'd heard her coming but hadn't managed to duck behind the door to hide his shoulder. "It's not as bad as it looks, Jen."

"How would you know, you haven't been able to get your shirt off to see *what* it looks like! You should have gone to the hospital!"

Cole winced. Jenna's voice wasn't shrill, but it definitely rose in volume. And he hated hospitals. "I hate hospitals."

"Tough. If I get this shirt off you and it's more than a scratch, you're going to let me drive you to one anyway. Where are your scissors?"

After she'd cut the material away, and gently cleaned the area with antiseptic and sterile gauze he kept in his first-aid kit, she frowned at the deep furrow. "At least the bullet's not in your arm. But I think you need stitches, Cole."

"I don't want stitches…tell you what, if I take a shower and let you bandage it for me tonight with antiseptic cream, I promise we'll stop at the clinic in town in the morning. Will that work? I'm tired, Jen. I don't think I can deal with getting a needle threaded through my skin tonight." Sinking to a very low level, he slumped his shoulders and gave her his best sad eyes.

She just shook her head and rolled her eyes. "You big baby. I'll agree on one condition — give me the name of your doctor at the clinic and I'll call him or her and describe the injury, and see if there are any objections to you coming in tomorrow instead of going to the hospital tonight."

Feeling like he had no choice, Cole let Jenna run roughshod over him. Half an hour later he was settled in front of the fire. Evidently the injury could wait until morning. She settled onto the hearth to listen to his story, the glow from the fire outlining her body through the fabric of her cotton dress. This would be a long night. The doctor had recommended resting…no physical activity. Cole could read the steely resolve of Jenna's emotions and knew he wasn't going to have a chance in hell.

"So who was this guy and why did he shoot at us?"

"Both men came from Washington, D.C., where I went after Dallas to help locate a terrorist cell. When the cell was raided, these men escaped capture. We'd identified them as brothers of the leader and they were being searched for. Somehow the two managed to evade capture and they followed me home. I'm not sure how. With both of them dead, I doubt Robert will ever be able to figure it out. But I'm sure they chose to follow me because I was in charge of the raid, and very visible.

"So how did you know the man was in the alley? I didn't see anything, and you were looking at me until you whipped your head around."

"I saw his reflection in the glass beside you."

Jenna raised her eyebrows at him. "Bullshit, Cole. The store's windows are set higher up on the wall. One of the GeeGOSH ladies told me it was because that store used to be a lawyer's office, and even a hundred years ago, when the building was built, they didn't install windows on the ground floor, ensuring privacy for clients."

Looking at her, Cole knew she would believe him if he said he didn't know what made him turn around. But if he wanted her to accept him for who he was, he couldn't lie to her. With his brain screaming *fool*, he took a deep breath and explained, "You're right. I didn't see the man in the window. Since I was a small child I've been able to read people's emotions. It's a psychic ability that allows me to know what someone is feeling. I picked up a burst of intense hostility from the guy who tried to shoot me right before he showed himself." Waiting for Jenna's reaction to his disclosure was one of the hardest things he'd ever done.

"Psychic? Really?"

Nodding, he held her gaze in serious acknowledgement.

"So you felt the hatred rolling off this guy? That is so cool! I'll bet that came in handy when you were in the Army. And you can read my emotions? What about thoughts?" Jenna's words bubbled out in excitement.

When he shook his head, she went on, "No? But it's still cool. Is that why...well, sex between us is phenomenal, Cole. Sometimes I feel a sort of connection with you. Like a faint sharing of what you would be feeling. Is that normal?"

Stunned at her reaction, he replied, "It's not normal, not even for me, but yes...I've felt the same thing. Jenna, I don't know what made me this way. My mother had some psychic abilities, as well. I don't know the extent of them because she died when I was young, but if I were to have children, they could also have some type of strange power."

"Wow! Psychic babies."

"You're not disgusted by that thought? What if, well...what if we had children someday? Wouldn't the thought of me being the father scare you?" Cole picked up a pillow to hide the shaking of his hands. He couldn't believe for a moment that all of this didn't bother her.

A wicked light sparked in Jenna's bright blue eyes. "Is this a marriage proposal, Cole? Come on, why would it disgust or scare me?"

Before he could reply, he saw in the expression on her face that she'd figured out the answer to her own question.

"*Some woman dumped you because she found out about your psychic abilities?* Get real! What a wussy woman." Jen got up from the fire and walked over to sit at his side. Careful not to jar his injured shoulder, she cupped a hand to his face and leaned in to kiss him. "If you love me, Cole, if you wanted me for your wife and the mother of your children, I'd be honored to accept the role. I think maybe it's a little too soon to make that decision, but I'm already more than half in love with you."

"I forced you to come to Secret Haven, Jen. Do you still think it's not disgusting?" He was sick—sick because he knew he had to tell her everything and he didn't want to. More than half in love himself, he knew he wanted this woman beside him for the rest of his life. And he'd just said the words that would make that impossible.

"What do you mean you forced me to come here?"

"Besides reading emotions, I discovered a few years ago that I could project thoughts, making people carry out my commands. If they are standing right in front of me, they do it immediately. Turn away, give me information I'm seeking...whatever. If they are a long distance away, I have to have something they've been in extended contact with. Like the pillow you slept on in my room in Dallas. Holding it, I sent a command — *Don't rest until you find Secret Haven.*"

Jenna's face went blank and lost all color. "Could you send a mental picture of what Secret Haven looks like?"

Heart sinking, seeing the beginnings of what would soon show on her carefully concealed face, he nodded. Looking away from her to stare at the far wall, he waited for her to declare she never wanted to see him again.

"You're not reading my emotions right now, are you Cole?"

"No. I'm able to build a kind of mental wall and only read them when I want," he said, tone flat, every muscle in his body prepared for the blow he knew was coming.

"Drop the wall, Cole. Read me now."

He didn't want to feel what she felt right now, but she'd earned the right to command this. Slowly dropping his mental shield, he was snowed under with emotional stimuli. Acceptance. Love. Hope. And humor.

"Jen?"

"It's been a long day, Cole. What do you think about going upstairs and playing sex-starved patient and Nurse Nancy? Even though you've already had a shower, I think maybe you would benefit from a sponge bath...or maybe we'll make that a tongue bath. As long as you promise to stay flat on your back and not move one inch."

Oh yeah. He could do that.

Fifteen minutes later, Cole was clenching the sheet with his one good hand and begging her to climb up over him to finish what she'd started. With her mouth closed over his aching cock, her hair hanging in a curtain around her head, she was driving him crazy. Bobbing down and drawing back, teasing the slit at the end, swirling and sucking and humming until he thought his head would explode. Both of them.

One hand wrapped around the base of his shaft, she followed the up and down motion of her mouth with her tight fist, the other hand cupping his sac, stroking the heavy weight of his balls. Looking down his body, he watched her mouth move over him, shifting his view to include her ass sticking up in the air.

Bending forward farther to take as much of his length in as she could manage, Jenna took him deep, flicking her tongue along the underside of the bulbous crown as she drew back. Bracing his legs, he pushed his hips upward and focused his gaze on the wet sheen of her pink lips sliding over his flesh, and she raised her lowered lids to stare up at him. The pleasure glowing in her eyes excited him even more.

Gripping his thighs, she held him spread-eagle and open before her as she increased the stroke of her lips, moving him deeper and tightening her hold. Squeezing him, forcing his arousal to spike higher with each pass.

Now desperate for release, he punched his hips upward, all sense of control gone. When he closed his eyes in blissful agony, the sounds of her mouth pulling on his cock only made the immeasurable aching demand grow worse.

The rise of his orgasm was sharp. He was coming. He tried to call out, to warn her and give her time to pull back, but the words couldn't pass the strangled cries in his throat. Convulsing when the climax burst over him, he released his seed into the hot recesses of her mouth.

Shuddering, his body tensed as she drew slowly back along his length and licked her tongue once more around the rim, and his head fell back against the pillows as he groaned.

Chapter Nine

ॐ

Walking out of the clinic the next morning beside Jenna, Cole felt like shit. His entire upper body was sore and his stomach rumbled in agony. He'd really tried to control his nerves as Jen stood beside him the entire time he was being poked and prodded and sewn back together. Well, not sewn, but bandaged with those little butterfly thingies. The hospital smell and just the thought of needles made him sick to his stomach. It had been almost impossible to put a shirt on this morning. In the end, Jenna had slit the arm of one of his button-up shirts, and he slid his injured arm in first. Now his arm was wrapped and tied to his side, to prevent him from moving it and ripping the healing skin. He had his good arm and both shoulders in the shirt. The empty shirt sleeve wrapped around and tucked in the bandage kept him from appearing half naked in public.

One of the town's old-timers stood in front of the entrance with a video camera turned on them. Great. Preserving the moment to be shown at the VFW hall, no doubt. "Don't forget to get my good side, Marcus," he called out to the old man, and grinned. He hoped he wouldn't have to rehash yesterday too many times, counting on Robert to spread the story they'd agreed upon and keep Cole's name out of the press.

Rick sat in the bar in New Mexico and fumed. There was no trace of her. For weeks he'd been tailing her—when he'd beaten her old boss and found a New Mexico phone number with the initial J beside it, he'd been so sure it was her…Jenna. He'd found out what city the prefix belonged to and searched for her high and low. No luck.

And now he was on the run. It was all that bitch's fault. He'd grown his hair longer, when he hated long hair. Put some dark dye in it. It looked like shit. Grown a beard too, damn itchy thing. Jenna's fault. All of it. Couldn't look like himself because the bitch couldn't take orders.

He was running out of money too. Tried to access his bank account with his cash card yesterday and found out that the damn cops had frozen it. Probably his credit cards too. Cunt.

Absently watching the TV at the end of the bar, he froze when a video came on of a man and woman leaving what had to be a hospital. The man's chest was wrapped in bandages, and the woman—the woman had shoulder-length, straight brown hair and was dressed in jeans and a T-shirt. She didn't have makeup on. Even without the trappings—the blonde curly hair he liked to grab a handful of and yank when she didn't do as she was told—he knew. It was Jenna. His wife.

Eyes glued to the set, he was satisfied to see the words at the bottom of the screen. Secret Haven, Colorado. Rick stood and threw some money on the table.

For two days, Jenna had Millicent run the bookstore so she could stay home and take care of Cole. When he started snarling at her, she knew it was time to go back to work. Sweet, loving care only went so far. Deciding to go in a little early and look at the few days' receipts, do a little straightening of shelves and get the coffee started for the hordes, she went downstairs to shower and change, and left Cole sleeping after writing a note and propping it on the kitchen table.

Rick sat in Pete's Diner, listening to the small town gossip about some man named Cole, and Jennie Jackson. He wanted to stand up and tell these stupid old farts to shut up. Her name wasn't Jennie Jackson, it was *Jenna Jessup* and she was his wife. Feeling for the knife strapped to his side, he grinned—his soon-to-be-dead wife.

An SUV pulled into the parking space in front of Simple Pleasures. Rick sat up straighter when he noticed the New Mexico plates. When the woman with brown hair got out and unlocked the door to the bookstore, he wanted to rub his hands together in anticipation. About time.

The bell on the front door jingled loudly and Jenna frowned. Who could be here this early? She could kick herself for not locking the door behind her. She walked out of the little office and saw a man with dark brown hair peering out the window back into the street.

"I'm sorry, we're not open yet. If you'll come back in about twenty minutes— Rick!" The man had dark, stringy hair and beard stubble he'd dyed poorly. But there was no mistaking the mean look in those green eyes. "What are you doing here?" Jenna had to speak around the bile that tried to come up her throat at the sight of him, knowing it was a stupid question, but not knowing what else to do. Ask questions. Stall. Maybe someone would come to her— Oh no. She didn't want any of the older folks coming in here. *Oh please, dear Lord, keep them away*.

"Stupid bitch. I'm here to kill you and you know it. I'll teach you to run from me."

Jenna tried to tune his tirade out. It was always SSDD with Rick—Same Shit, Different Day. Instead of listening to the oft-repeated words, she concentrated on his body language…and watched his eyes. Every muscle tense, she was ready to throw her arms up and protect herself as best as she could, or roll into a fetal ball at his feet to give him the smallest target. She didn't take her eyes off him. Waited for what she was afraid would be his final moves.

Without appearing to, she inched behind the counter a little, thinking maybe she could take the phone off the hook and dial 911. Maybe the operator would hear something, or maybe they'd just send someone out if they didn't. This time she didn't have a cast-iron skillet lying around to smack him over the head with.

She could see her worst nightmare making a beeline for the store. Two of her GeeGOSH ladies carrying platters of baked goods would be coming in the door…now.

The jingling bell and the merry voices of the women forced Rick to whirl around. Jen used the distraction to reach under the counter and lift the handset off the cradle of the phone. She quickly punched in 911, and then set the handset on the shelf. She was standing in roughly the same place when Rick turned back to her.

"Hi ladies. You're here early this morning. I hope you've brought enough baked goods for the entire self-defense club meeting upstairs. Feel free to go on up. When the others come in, I'll send them up." She was taking a risk. Margaret and Marie were sisters, and Jen had spent a lovely half hour debating politics with the two women. They were both sharp, but would they understand what she was saying?

With only a slight hesitation, Margaret stepped into the breach. "Yes, dear. The other ladies will be here soon. We have more goodies in the car. I'll just lay these on the counter here and go get some more—"

"No!" Rick shouted, and lunged at Jenna, grabbing her by the shoulder and spinning her around, locking his arm around her neck. He had a knife in the other hand.

Marie dropped her plate of baked goods in shock, while Margaret shook her head. "You really don't want to hurt Jennie. She's such a sweet girl."

"Shut up, you old broad. And both of you come away from the door!"

Cole dressed himself in sweatpants and a shirt Jen had cut the sleeve out of. He started downstairs to find her when the phone rang. Grabbing the cordless off the nightstand with his right hand, he peered over the loft wall, looking for her.

"Cole, we have a problem."

Cole ran out the door and jumped in his SUV. Robert called to tell him he'd just found out Marcus had sold a homemade video to some national TV station several days ago. Cole and Jenna's picture had been spread all over the countryside, along with a report describing Secret Haven as the site of a terrorist attack! Cole and Jenna hadn't been watching TV, and Robert had been caught up in dealing with federal officials. He'd just seen a replay today.

Cole had no way of knowing if Rick had seen the video. It scared him to think about Jenna taking it upon herself to get out of his hair today and go to work early—without a safety buffer of bodies showing up for at least a half hour. He headed down the driveway at breakneck speed, cursing when his cell phone rang.

"What?"

"We got a 911 call from Jenna's bookstore. No one on the line, and then the operator heard a man shouting obscenities. I've already called Millicent. She still has a key to the back door, and she'll meet us in the alley."

Let me be there in time, please let me be there in time. His heart in his throat, Cole prayed.

Rick still held Jen around the neck with one arm, the hand with the knife gesturing wildly as he ranted. As Jenna watched, Margaret seemed to shift a little. She saw the older lady's shocked expression change to wary hope and her eyes grow wide, focusing for a quick moment on something behind Jenna's back. Jenna hoped the cavalry had arrived.

Meeting Jen's eyes, Margaret nodded slightly and screamed, "Drop to the floor!" as she spun the silver platter of cookies at Rick like a Frisbee.

Everything happened so fast, yet Jenna saw it all in slow motion. She picked both feet off the ground, breaking Rick's hold. Thrown off balance, he stumbled to the side, away from her. As she fell to the floor with a thud she saw the platter flying at Rick's head. He batted it away with the hand holding the knife, giving Jenna time to scramble on her hands and knees to safety behind the counter. By the time she'd stuck her head back out, she caught the sight of Cole making a running leap, tackling Rick around the legs. The chief of police, standing with gun pointed, shouted, "You're under arrest!"

The knife skidded across the floor when Rick fell with Cole on top of him. Cole was rearing back to stand when Rick rolled and tried to strike out with his fist.

Stupid man.

Cole pummeled him to the accompaniment of his own cheering section. Jenna just bet that Margaret and Marie watched late-night wrestling. When it was obvious that Rick wouldn't be getting up under his own steam, she looked at the two sisters and smiled. Margaret's hair had come out of the tight bun she wore, and both ladies had flushed faces and beaming smiles.

While Robert took care of handcuffing and carting Rick away, Jenna rushed over to help her warrior. His arm was bleeding again.

Cole looked at her and smiled a big cheesy grin. "That was fun."

"Ummm. My hero." She reached up to kiss him before laying her head on his chest for a quiet moment of thanksgiving. "You know you're going to have to go back to see the doctor?"

Six days later, Jen was lying in Cole's arms, the early morning light streaming thought the bedroom window. He'd just told her something she couldn't believe.

"You're telling me that Rick died of an aneurysm in jail?"

"I'm sorry, Jen. The doctor's said there would be an autopsy, but they think with past and present head injuries and the amount and variety of drugs he used, the combination caused a blood vessel to burst in his brain."

Jenna was silent, absorbing what Cole told her after he got off the phone with Robert. How did she feel? Sad. Sad that Rick's life had ended this way. Tried to imagine what would have happened if… Well…there were no ifs. And she felt relief—and immediate guilt. "Do you think it makes me a bad person that I'm almost thankful Rick won't be able to go to trial and possibly get released in a few years?"

"Hell, no. It makes you human. His prison sentence wouldn't have been light, not with attempted murder and several accounts of assault and battery." He sighed. "But we know his defense could have pleaded insanity, and there's always early parole. No, Jen. I'm glad we don't have to worry about him anymore, even though I'm sorry that his life came down to this. I was already thinking of how we could disappear if he ever got released. You know you can go back to being Jenna Jessup now?"

"Ugh. I suppose I really have to, don't I."

"Yeah. The law frowns on people who've created a false identity."

"Well…I guess that means I should turn in all of them, huh?"

"All of them?"

"I got three sets—different names, different hair. You know." She could feel his chest rumble beneath her ear as he tried to repress his laughter.

"Remind me to hide that book from you, will you? I have an idea on how you can change your name legally if you want to."

Jenna frowned. This time she could feel his body tense. "You mean like go back to my maiden name, Jenna Thompson?"

"Thompson, huh? Doesn't really work for me. How about Jenna Matheson?"

Now it was Jenna's turn to tense up. *Was he asking her to marry him?*

"Cole?"

"Marry me, Jenna. I only have one small request."

Lifting her head, she turned to lay her hands over his heart, resting her chin on her folded hands. She wondered if he would ask her something about having psychic babies. "What's the request?"

"Can we go into town tomorrow and have someone at Bella's hair salon make you a curly-haired blonde again?"

The love and laughter flowed over him, and he had his answer.

Also by Ravyn Wilde

➩

By the Book
Ellora's Cavemen: Dreams of the Oasis IV *(anthology)*
Ellora's Cavemen: Legendary Tails IV *(anthology)*
Ellora's Cavemen: Tales From the Temple I *(anthology)*
Let Them Eat Cake
Uncontrolled Magic
Undying Magic
Unholy Magic
Zylar's Moons 1: Zylan Captive
Zylar's Moons 2: Selven Refuge
Zylar's Moons 3: Zylan Rebellion

About the Author

➩

Ravyn Wilde was born in Oregon and has spent several years in New Guinea and Singapore. She is married, has three children and is currently living in Utah. Ravyn is happiest when she has a book in one hand and a drink in the other—preferably sprawled on a beach! Readers may write to Ravyn at RavynWilde@msn.com.

MELTDOWN

Denise A. Agnew

ဆာ

Dedication

&

As always, to the keeper of my heart, Terry.

To my sister Gayle, who witnessed a man-made earthquake that occurred in the 1960s in Colorado, and experienced a rumble in Durango, Colorado.

To my sister Loretta, for continuing to write.

And to Karen Morris, who is always there when I need firefighting information.

Author's Note

According to the USGS, Colorado is listed as a region of minor earthquake activity.

Yet, there have been sizable earthquakes there in the past.

It would surprise most to know that, of the fifty states, Colorado is number fourteen in earthquake activity. Induced seismicity is a reality.

In 1961, a 12,000-foot well was drilled at the Rocky Mountain Arsenal for disposing of waste fluids from the Arsenal operations. A strange series of earthquakes occurred shortly thereafter.

Chapter One

"When an inner situation is not made conscious, it appears outside as fate."
— Carl Jung

ဆာ

Lil O'Hara awoke Monday morning to a rendition of shake, rattle and roll.

A low growling, deep from the bowels of the Earth, came from all around her. Her eyes flicked open. Her bed vibrated, which would have been dandy if her head didn't throb already.

"What the—?" she mumbled as the shuddering and rumbling halted.

She lay in bed trying to make sense of what happened. It took only ten seconds.

Earthquake. Another earthquake.

Stumbling from bed, she headed for the window. She yanked back the thick blue moiré curtain and gazed at the street two stories below. She was half-expecting to see people running from her Victorian-era apartment building and screaming.

"That's what they usually do about right now," she said as she scratched her head. "In the movies anyway." A few people rushed to their cars as if they could find shelter there. "Or maybe they can't wait to get to work." She grinned. "Poor bastards."

Instead of being one of those overworked drones, her week of vacation started now. She hoped it would mean rest and relaxation. She sighed, a little concerned. This old warehouse in Denver had been converted to apartments many years ago, and while it seemed well-built, she wondered if the earthquakes had taken a toll on the structure's stability.

She wandered to the bedside table and turned on the radio. A confident male voice came over the airwaves.

"Morning everyone, this is Jason Maverick. Well, if that wasn't a good wake-up, I don't know what is. My guess is you didn't miss the latest in a series of tremors to strike Denver and outlying areas this week. There have been some earthquakes in Denver's distant past, so it isn't entirely inconceivable that a big one could be on the way. According to our sources, these tremors are foreshocks of a possibly larger event to come."

The reporter droned on, his data for the most part correct. Impressed, she decided someone had given him the scoop on the hows and whys of Earth Science.

She rubbed her forehead and closed her eyes. *Damn these headaches.*

Although used to feeling these weird headaches at a time like this, it wasn't a talent she appreciated or wanted. As her English cousin in London said on more than one occasion, "Fat lot of good it does you."

Right. She was damned right.

June sunrise hurt her eyes even though her bedroom window faced west, and she closed the drapes. She shuffled into the connecting bathroom and gazed up at the weak light making its way through the small window over the tub. When she checked in the mirror, she groaned. A ruffled mess of shoulder-length hair and puffy eyes did jack for her ego. She squinted and fingered the almost-ready-for-charity short, flaming pink nightshirt. The obnoxious color itself almost caused pain.

"Just think," she said to her mirror image, "you don't have to put up with the earthquake bunk this week. Nada. Nope. No way. You have a whole week of laziness scheduled."

Like a disapproving lightning bolt from the heavens, pain rocketed through her forehead and she gasped. She held one trembling hand to her forehead and tried breathing deeply.

"Not again. Please not again."

The building shivered beneath her feet. This tremor lasted a few seconds, then died.

She inhaled as the ache subsided. "Thank goodness."

After washing her face and taking a shower, she stood in the bathroom and towel dried her hair.

One week of peace, reading and reflection would rejuvenate her. Nothing exciting, nothing more dramatic than maybe renting a few new movies and eating popcorn.

Okay, so maybe one more sighting of her hunky new next-door neighbor would be nice.

Hell, it would be fantastic.

She'd spied him from a distance two weeks ago when he moved into the warehouse. At first, she'd wondered at his strange hours. Then Cynthia Carlsbad across the hall said she'd heard he was a firefighter working at Station One down the street.

Considering Cynthia loved men in dangerous occupations, she figured the blonde, petite woman would jump him at next opportunity.

After fixing and eating a quick breakfast of scrambled eggs and toast, Lillian realized her garbage needed emptying before it spilled over. She glanced at her watch. The mall would open soon, and she could grab a novel she'd ordered from her favorite bookstore.

A good book. That's all I need.

Well, a hot man wouldn't hurt, either.

She strapped on her fanny pack and gathered up the trash bag as she left her apartment.

"Dream on, Lil," she muttered. "You've got about as much chance of dating hunk firefighter as you do of convincing your boss to give you a raise."

She treaded down the hallway to the staircase, intent on taking her garbage to the dumpster. She took the stairwell quickly, and almost reached the bottom floor when another dull pain rolled through her head.

A rumble echoed through the building, and as she took one more step, she lost her balance. Her left foot shot out from under her. Before she could do more than gasp in alarm and paw at the banister, she fell.

Hunk-of-a-neighbor came around the corner heading upstairs. "Whoa!"

Lil reached out for him at the same time he reached for her. Her left wrist wrenched and her right ankle twisted as she scrambled for a hold. A tiny cry of pain escaped her lips. He dropped his duffle bag. His left arm came around her waist while with his other hand he grabbed the banister. The trash bag bounced down the stairs.

The earthquake halted.

Hunk managed to keep them both upright. She gripped his shoulders and stared up into melting caramel brown eyes fringed by the darkest, most gorgeous eyelashes. At five-seven and medium build, she never felt petite around most men. This guy towered over her with his solid, big body.

Her fingers slipped over his white T-shirt down to his biceps. *Oh, my. Yeah.* Granite sinew shifted under her touch. Thick black hair waved close to his head and highlighted a face more rugged than handsome. A small scar above one brow and another near the corner of his wide, carved mouth caught her attention. His nose held an aristocratic tilt. His virile intensity spiraled off the charts.

A frown pinched his brows and as he shifted, his hard thighs snuggled against her. Her entire body reacted to his embrace, her throat dry and her belly fluttering with instant attraction.

Sparklers of pain ran through her wrist and ankle, and she gasped involuntarily.

"You all right?" His voice rumbled up from his chest, a deep and husky sound that sent another shiver through her frame.

Lil detected the slightest accent, something not exactly mainstream American. She couldn't place it.

She gave a wobbly smile. "I think I have some mild damage. Nothing to worry about."

He didn't look convinced. "Where are you hurt?"

She lifted her left hand from his shoulder and wiggled her fingers. "A wrenched right ankle and a twisted wrist. They'll be fine in a few minutes."

"Sit down and let me see."

He eased her into a sitting position on a step and sat down next to her. His large body crowded her, and she inhaled his musky, delicious scent.

He gripped her hand with big, gentle fingers, his work-callused skin brushing against her small digits and narrow palm. He felt around her wrist and explored like a doctor. Tingles raced through her skin under his careful exploration.

"Any more pain?" he asked, keeping a light grip on her wrist.

"It aches a little."

"At least it's not broken. It should feel better by tomorrow, but if not, see your doctor. Let's see your ankle."

Embarrassment heated her face. "I'm sure it's fine."

His gaze snapped to hers, then he released her hand. "I don't like to take chances. Turn to the side so I can check the ankle."

She did as told, turning on the step and swinging her foot toward him.

He lifted her ankle over his thigh. "I'm taking off your shoe for just a minute."

Nervous flutters danced in her stomach, and she smiled, feeling goofy and out of her element. Damn, she couldn't remember the last time a man made her feel this gauche.

She cleared her throat. "Sure, I'll bet you say that to all the girls."

He blinked and swung his gaze toward her, his lips parting. He looked a little startled.

"I mean, you know —" She stalled, mortified.

Oh, god. Shut up, Lil. You're a ditz. Heat flamed her face again.

His mouth tipped into a wide grin, his eyes sparkling as a chuckle came from his throat. "I arrange earthquakes all the time so beautiful women can fall into my arms, and I can touch their ankles."

Beautiful, eh? Everything feminine and naturally vain flared to life. Her heart picked up speed, and she felt a little breathless.

"Actually, no," she said. "I arranged the earthquake. I'm a seismologist."

His dark eyebrows quirked up and he removed her shoe. He felt around her ankle. Despite his professional attitude and touch, her heartbeat started a more frantic tattoo.

"Oh, yeah? Is that like being the weatherman when these earthquakes started?" he asked.

She smiled. "Exactly. We don't get any respect. I'm teasing, really. I'm an administrative assistant in the Earth Sciences department at the local branch offices of Denver University."

"You know a lot about quakes, though?"

She nodded. "It makes sense when I'm working in the department to know the details."

Another heart-stopping grin transformed his mouth. His eyes turned intent, searching. "So, why are we having all these quakes?"

She shrugged, not wanting to talk about work. "Plate tectonics. The usual."

"It's not usual for here."

She shook her head. "It's not as strange as you think. We have microquakes more frequently than people know."

"Microquakes?"

"Earthquakes smaller than humans can usually feel."

Here I am on vacation, and I still can't get away from work.

His fingers pressed around her ankle, and she wished she didn't have on the white athletic sock. Feeling those fingers against her bare flesh again would be exquisite.

"I think I know you," she said into the silence. "You're my next-door neighbor. The firefighter."

He stopped examining her ankle, his gaze curious. "Which apartment are you in?"

"Six."

"How did you know I'm a firefighter?"

"Cynthia across the hall. And your T-shirt."

He actually blushed and looked down at the front of his T-shirt at the emblem that declared him a member of the fire department and Station One. "Oh, yeah."

"Gotcha."

A heart-wrenching grin crooked one corner of his mouth. "Cynthia cornered me in the hall a couple of times. One time she cut her finger, and rather than put a dressing on it, she knocked on my door."

Her eyebrows went up. "Oh?"

"I made the mistake of telling her I was a firefighter and a paramedic."

"So every time she has a boo-boo now, you'll be the one she runs to?"

"You got it." He winked. "She called me a couple of times last week at the fire station and asked about ingestion of drain cleaner."

"What?"

"Don't worry. She wasn't trying to commit suicide or murder. She's a mystery writer and needed some information for her current novel."

"Oh. Well, that's a relief."

"Rotate your ankle for me."

"Really, I think it—"

She gasped as pain pierced through the ankle. "Ow!"

He frowned. "How badly does it hurt?"

"Like the devil."

As he peeled the sock down, more pain darted through her entire foot. She bit her lower lip and held back an expletive.

"We'd better get you to the hospital. Your ankle is already swelling and there's a little bruising along the side."

"Ouch. I didn't think it was that bad. Couldn't I put ice on it and leave it at that?"

He threw her a stern glance. "You need an x-ray. I don't think it's broken, but to be safe you should get it checked out."

She wanted to whine and grumble, but managed a smile instead. "Not exactly the vacation I imagined."

"You're leaving on vacation?"

"No. But I was planning on having a week at home relaxing."

He stood slowly. "Now you'll have a relaxing vacation with your foot propped up."

She moaned. "Terrific."

"Hold on to your shoe and sock. I'm carrying you down to my car."

"It's nice of you, but you don't have to take me to the hospital. I can get an appointment with my doctor sometime this week."

"Nope. If your ankle is broken it needs immediate attention. Up you go." He reached for her arm and eased her upward until she stood on her uninjured leg.

Before she could protest, he swept her up in his arms.

"Whoa," she said with a soft laugh. "This isn't exactly a fireman's hold."

"Grab my duffle bag, would you?"

He dipped from the knees, and she reached for the bag. She kept it in her grip as they proceeded.

She hadn't been carried by a man in…she couldn't remember the last time. Firefighters carried full-grown men over their shoulders if the need arose. Her weight would seem like nothing. She couldn't deny excitement stirring inside her. It felt good to have a man's concern and protection, even though she loved her independence.

For a guilty, shining moment, she enjoyed feeling cherished and special. Not a feeling that came along often. Not ever.

Once in the parking lot, he walked toward a blue Ford Taurus. She squinted in the bright sun, the headache throbbing in her temple.

He set her on her feet by the car and fished his keys out of his jeans. New denim conformed to a tight ass and over clearly muscled thighs. Arousal darted like a wild thing over her erogenous zones.

"Before I get into your car, I think I should least introduce myself." She held out her hand. "Lillian O'Hara. Lil for short."

He shook hands, his big palm encompassing hers. "Lillian. I like that. Sounds old-fashioned."

"You like old-fashioned girls?"

"I like independent, modern women."

She nodded, satisfied. "And you are?"

"Evan Murdoch. I work at Station One, four blocks away."

As her hand slipped from his, she said, "Pleased to meet you, Evan."

After she got into the car, she buckled her seatbelt. He climbed in the driver's side and she sensed his intense scrutiny.

"Something wrong?" she asked when he continued to stare.

"Yeah." He reached out and put his hand on her forehead.

"What are you doing?"

"You're flushed. You've got a fever."

She smiled as he took his hand away. "Oh, that's all."

"That's all? You're sick *and* you're hurt? Nasty combination."

"No, I'm not sick. It's a by-product of…"

When she didn't finish, he almost glared at her. He looked fierce as a warrior, a hardness gleaming in his eyes.

"Byproduct of what?" he asked as he started the car and backed out of his parking space.

"Well, I don't tell many people this because of the reaction I get."

"Reaction?"

"People think I'm full of it. My boss laughed his ass off the first time he heard about it. I don't know what possessed me to tell him."

Keep it up, silly. You're letting the cat out of the proverbial bag.

His sinfully sexy mouth curved as he directed the car onto the street and headed for the hospital. "I'm open-minded. Try me."

An unrelated vision of her trying him on for size zipped through her active imagination. What would he feel like deep inside her? Heat stirred low and tight between her legs.

She cleared her throat and banished the fantasy. "Right before a quake, I get this painful headache."

His eyebrows went up, but he didn't look at her as he negotiated traffic. "Wow. That's interesting."

Interesting. That one word could mean many things. Interesting, you're a fruitcake, or interesting, tell me more. She went for telling him more.

"Most of the people at work say I'm a human seismograph. That I can predict quakes. Problem is I never have enough warning to make it useful."

"How many minutes before a quake do you get a headache?"

"If I'm lucky, thirty seconds. Enough time to shout earthquake and hide under a desk or stand in a doorway. It's a talent not much good to anyone."

He came to an easy glide at a stoplight. He drove with patience, a man aware of safety. "So why haven't scientists tried to bottle your talent and figure out how you do it?"

Skepticism tinted his voice, and the inevitable letdown started. *Lil, girl, someday you'll learn.*

"Because my boss has seen me predict quakes and it never makes a difference to him."

They went silent for a couple of minutes. She caught him eyeballing her left hand and the Celtic silver scrollwork ring. The intricate design held a single one-carat, round brilliant diamond in the center.

"Do you need to call someone to meet you at the hospital?" he asked. "Your husband?"

For the first time since she'd inherited the ring from her grandmother, she regretted wearing it on her left hand. "No. I'm not married."

Did she see relief in his eyes? No, not at all. That would be too much to ask. Evan showed genuine concern and did his job. She shouldn't make this into anything more personal. He didn't wear a wedding ring, but in his occupation, many men didn't.

Oh, what the hell. Ask him.

"Are you married?" she asked.

A slow smile developed on his gorgeous mouth. "No. Not even once. You ever been married?"

"Once, a long time ago. When I was in college."

Again, they lapsed into silence while Evan negotiated morning traffic. The small quakes this morning hadn't caused much damage other than two traffic signals malfunctioning.

"You think there's going to be a bigger quake?" he asked. "The so-called experts the news media has interviewed over the last few weeks say it's nothing to worry about."

"It isn't. People watch too many disaster movies."

He chuckled. The low, hearty sound sent trailers of arousal into her stomach.

She reached up and felt her forehead. Sure enough, the fever she generated with these headaches still clung to her skin.

I've gotta face it. Mr. Sex on Fire has fried my jets.

Evan's concerned gaze skated over her features. "You're more flushed than you were earlier."

Well, red-hot firefighters could do that to a woman.

For a horrifying second she wondered if she'd said it out loud.

"Are you sure you're not sick?" he asked.

"Trust me, this happens every time a quake occurs. I'll be over it in an hour or less."

"Hmm." He didn't sound the least convinced.

She unzipped the fanny pack at her waist and extracted a tissue. She dabbed at her neck and hairline. "I've experienced enough quakes to know what constitutes a fever brought on by disease and a quake fever."

He shook his head. "Well, it's damned weird."

Should she take that as an insult or statement of fact? She wished she'd never confessed. She should have learned from experience. Evan engendered calm and trustworthiness, so she'd taken the plunge. Mistake, again. Old tapes played inside her.

Her ex-husband Doug smirking at her. Doug saying her earthquake headaches were bunk. Doug telling her she should keep her mouth shut about the headaches.

She sighed. Yep, she should keep her mouth shut about it.

Evan shifted his grip from the top of the steering wheel to the bottom. Big and capable, his hands held strong, beautiful lines for a man in his profession. Mile-wide shoulders, flat stomach, cut biceps, and the dark hair peppering his forearms added to the package. His watch, one of those two-hundred-million fathoms deep things, circled a strong wrist. His thigh muscles moved under faded jeans, and between those strong thighs he sported an unmistakable, large bulge. Lord, what would he look like aroused—

Get a grip. You're salivating over this man like a carnivore ready to consume a tasty meal.

Liquid heat spread from her stomach to her face. Man, oh, man. He defined gorgeous. Not in a suit and tie, suave way. In a primitive Me-Tarzan, You-Jane way that reminded Lil of her womanhood.

Less then five minutes later, they arrived at the emergency room entrance. He told her to stay there, and within moments, he returned with a wheelchair. He helped her into the wheelchair and rolled her inside the hospital. When she reached the counter, he helped her pass her insurance card and paperwork back and forth.

"You don't have to do this," she said as he handed her a pen. "I mean, you don't have to wait."

A sincere smile came over that sinful mouth. "No, I don't have to. I want to. You'll need transportation back home when you're done here. Hang out here a minute. I'll move the car." He pushed her over to a section out of the way, then headed to the car. While she waited, she contemplated her good luck at meeting him. He returned quicker than she expected.

Voices, the sound of children babbling, and the irritating chatter from a TV news channel assaulted her ears when he rolled her into the waiting area. Her guilt increased as she surveyed the overflow of people. A man she didn't know planned on waiting with her in a noisy, crowded emergency room.

"I can get a friend to pick me up when I'm done here," she said.

He winked, and a sensual gleam entered his eyes. "Give it up, Lil. I'm not leaving you."

"Don't you have to go fight fires or something?"

"I'm on vacation."

After he wheeled her into position next to an empty chair, he sat next to her. He sprawled with his legs open and his hands clasped together over his stomach, every inch the relaxed male animal. His casualness covered leashed energy. She could feel it inside him like a quake, ready to rock and roll if the occasion demanded. It made sense. A firefighter needed a significant level of courage to jump in when others retreated. He appeared ready for the long haul.

Time passed easily because Evan kept her entertained with jokes and general conversation. She asked him about his job, and when he talked about firefighting, she saw the pride he took in his work. Their conversation covered a wide range, until it came time for her to go inside for an exam.

"I'll be here," Evan said as they wheeled her away.

As the nurse rolled her toward an exam room, Lil allowed a heady contentment to enfold her. Ankle trashed or not, she looked forward to learning more about the calm, quiet firefighter waiting for her.

* * * * *

Evan watched a nurse bring Lil out a considerable time later. His heart did a funny little flip, and he fixated on her beautiful face.

She confirmed that she only had a sprained ankle.

After a trip to orthopedics to grab crutches, they headed out to the car. He glanced down at her head and smiled.

When he'd first seen her in the stairwell, he'd tapped into electricity, almost knocked down by her prettiness along with the shuddering quake. She looked fragile with her delicate nose, rosebud lips and wide-eyed moss green stare. Cherry wood brown—that was all he could think to call it—hair fell a few inches below her shoulders in cascading waves that begged a man to touch. It didn't help that she wore a pair of low-rise jeans with a snug-fitting red top that outlined rounded breasts. Heat rushed to his groin when he recalled how damned good she'd felt pressed against him, long-legged and curvy. Her quirky humor and vulnerability intrigued him. He wrestled with a desire to know her better, and the notion he shouldn't become more interested. Memories of Lani threatened to slap him across the face and hold him back.

Damn, damn. He had to move forward.

Caution stalled him. What did he know about her? She made some strange assertions earlier about her headaches and fevers. He didn't tangle with a woman who lied. He'd explored that craggy emotional roller coaster too many times with Lani. If Lil played games with him, he'd pick it up fast and extricate.

Once he assisted her into the car and deposited the crutches in the back, he drove back to the apartment complex.

Her stomach growled. She laughed and put her hand over her stomach. "Oops. Sorry. All that emergency room activity must have burned some calories."

"No apologies necessary. It's almost eleven o'clock."

"Damn," she whispered.

"What's wrong?"

"I was going to the grocery store today." She chewed her lower lip, and the sight of her tongue swiping over her rose lips made his cock ache. "I'll have to think of a backup plan."

An idea blindsided him. "Have lunch with me."

"Oh." Her breathy syllable, followed by blank stare, made him wonder if she planned a solid rejection.

"Oh? As in no?"

"Um…no. I mean, yes. I'd love to have lunch with you. Where?"

"I'd say someplace public, but I don't know if you want to try your first day on crutches maneuvering into a restaurant. How about my place?"

"Your place. Why, Mr. Murdoch, I don't know you from Adam." Her dry tone sounded serious.

When they came to a stoplight, he glanced at her. A ready smile slipped over her lips and disappeared, as if she tried to resist a laugh.

"If you can't trust a firefighter, who can you trust?" he asked half-seriously.

"I've imposed on you long enough."

He shrugged. "Like I said, I don't have plans."

Not long after, they pulled into the apartment complex and parked.

Lil opened her door, but he said, "Don't try to get out. Let me help."

"I'll use the crutches."

"I'll carry you. You'll have enough opportunity to use them later."

Lil's hormones went online like a supercomputer. Lunch with this gorgeous guy? Excitement skittered up and down her spine, despite the heavy throb in her ankle. Wicked thoughts darted into her mind as he assisted her from the car.

"Easy." He caught her against his chest when she tottered on one leg.

Caught against hard, uncompromising muscle, she looked up into eyes filled unexpectedly with smoldering intensity. Thick lashes couldn't cover the sleepy nuance in those eyes. She inhaled his scent, a heady combination of sandalwood and a musk that called to her feminine instincts. He hadn't shaved, and the dark shadow over his jaw and upper lip gave him a rough-and-tumble, disreputable air. Her nipples tightened and tingled against her bra. Her pussy heated, and moisture dampened her folds. Breathing became a little more difficult when he didn't look away. Without thinking, her hands slid down his shoulders and brushed over his pectorals. He shivered a little, his lips parting and those smoky eyes darkening into flagrant passion.

She'd freed a caged beast, and she knew it.

A second later his hands on her waist tightened and his mouth came down on hers.

Chapter Two

ഇ

Evan's lips brushed Lil's with an exquisite taste. A mere touch, light pressure, a warm embrace of mouth against mouth. Desire stirred strongly inside her. Their mouths meshed and time filled with acute physical sensation. Excitement shimmered low in her belly as his muscular form cradled her gently. Power rippled in his stalwart body, yet he treated her like delicate porcelain. He drew back, his body still pressed close to hers. His eyes held an intoxicating heat. He kissed with restraint, but his gaze screamed hunger.

What just happened? One minute they acted as companionable strangers, the next, a tentative kiss turned everything on its head.

Bit by bit, the searing quality in his eyes turned to teasing. "I'm sorry." He shook his head. "No, I'm not."

Wary, she asked, "Which is it?"

He brushed his index finger over her cheek. She quivered under the intimate touch. "Maybe I shouldn't have kissed you, but I'm not sorry I did. It felt too good."

His kiss left her yearning and yet afraid. Fearing the hot connection between them couldn't be real in such a short time.

He swept her up into his arms. "I'll come down and get your crutches in a moment."

All the way to the apartment, she fought back a desire to analyze why he'd kissed her and to ask him for answers.

When he set her down beside the doorway to his apartment and unlocked the door, she asked, "Why did you kiss me?"

He lifted her into his arms once more and walked through the door. He kicked the door shut. Gently he set her down on her feet and kept his hands around her waist to support her. She felt his heart beating strong and true against her fingertips.

He cupped her face with one hand. Interest and genuine caring filled his eyes. "Because I'm attracted to you way down in my gut, in my instincts. I want to get to know you better."

"You believe in following instinct?"

"Yeah."

"That's reassuring. Very few men I know follow their intuition."

"Maybe more of them do than you think. They don't talk about it much." His grin sent a pulsating heat throughout her body. "I'll be back."

Oh, yes. Danger lurked around the corner with every moment she stayed near him.

She sank onto his couch while he went downstairs. She slipped her fingers over the dark green leather and paisley chenille, both masculine and old world. An easy chair sat to the side with chunky, dark wood coffee and side tables to match. Dark green and burgundy rugs lay strategically around the room. The apartment smelled like him, a musk and male scent, incredibly arousing. A painting of ruins in the Andes hung over his fireplace, and a few photos graced the mantle. Green roman shades diffused hot summer sun. Observing his apartment made her forget the throbbing in her ankle.

New pain throbbed in her temples. She closed her eyes as weakness passed through her at the same time a low rumble pulsated under her feet. She clutched at the seat cushion. The couch vibrated, dishes in the kitchen cupboards rattled, the chrome chandelier above the dining set swayed.

Not again.

She covered her eyes, riding through the pain and the quake. Please don't let this be a big one. As the rattling increased, she realized it was bigger than the other two today.

Gritting her teeth as pain charged through her leg, she dropped to her knees and crawled toward the dining table. She slid under it. With a shuddering last rumble, the quake ceased.

Footsteps ran down the hall, and Evan swiftly opened the door and entered with the crutches and his duffle bag. "Lil?"

"Here." She edged out from under the table on her hands and knees and smiled. "That one was damned unnerving."

He dropped the duffle bag and leaned the crutches against the wall. Frowning, he crossed to her quickly and helped her to her feet. He examined her face with concern as he trailed one finger over her jawline.

"You okay? Your skin is hot again."

"The headache's gone already. The fever will go away in a minute."

"Did the doctor say anything about the fever?"

"I didn't have one when he saw me."

Puzzlement etched lines between his brows. "Humph."

She chose to ignore his continual skepticism and patted his chest. "Believe or not."

He shook his head. "I was in the stairwell when it started. I'm not taking the elevator until these damn quakes stop."

"Good idea." Her stomach growled again. "Oops."

A smiled erased the trepidation on his face. "Have a seat at the table, and we'll eat. What would you like to drink?"

"Whatever you're having."

He drew two bottles of sparkling water from the refrigerator and gave her one. They chatted companionably as he made them toasted cheese and ham sandwiches. She traced her fingers over the navy placemat in front of her. Low-gauge nervousness hummed inside her. She knew he wouldn't hurt her—his protectiveness was obvious—yet she couldn't settle down.

"So where are you from?" she asked.

He flipped a sandwich with a spatula then turned toward her. "Pueblo. How about you?"

"I was born in San Francisco. We moved to Denver when I was six."

"Ah, so that explains your interest in earthquakes. You were in rock and roll central."

She shrugged. "It wasn't bad. Now, if I wanted to be in earthquake land I should live in Alaska. Alaska has many more earthquakes then California, but most people don't know that."

"Out of sight, out of mind."

He wandered around the kitchen and she admired the easy way he moved. He walked with masculine assurance, a crackling palpable energy. Leashed power rippled in his muscles. Firefighting no doubt put sinew on him, but he must work out to obtain that solid, streamlined body.

She watched him maneuver around the kitchen. "San Francisco isn't my real reason for interest in quakes."

He leaned against the counter next to the stove. "The headaches?"

"Yes. I've had them since I was a little kid."

"What did your parents think?"

She frowned. "Mom was a geophysicist and Dad, a vulcanologist. They believed in hard science."

One of his dark brows quirked up. "Aha. Another reason why you're interested in quakes."

She smiled. "It's in my blood."

He flipped the sandwiches again then reached for plates in the cupboard. He retrieved utensils and set the table.

"I told Mom and Dad about my headaches when I was seven years old. I'd noticed the headaches and fever corresponded with quakes. They told me it was all in my imagination." She waited as he placed a napkin and utensils in front of her before asking a tentative question. "You can't tell me you believed the headache and fever story when I told you?"

His eyes twinkled with warmth as he gripped the back of a chair. "It made me pause."

She shrugged. "You barely know me. I don't expect you to believe me."

He wandered back to the kitchen. "You're an honest woman."

"How do you know?"

"I've got a sixth sense about people."

He placed the sandwiches on a plate and rustled around in the pantry. He brought the plates and a bag of baked tortilla chips to the table. Lil's stomach growled in appreciation as she drew in the aroma of their sandwiches. The only thing more mouthwatering was the firefighter in front of her.

Once they'd settled down to eat, she continued. "Do you believe in ESP?"

He crunched a chip before answering. "I've had some strange things happen in my life that can't be explained any other way."

"You'll have to tell me about them some time."

Oh, Lil. You're making this sound like hanging with him will continue after today.

They ate in silence for a while, and he ate like men often did. Fast.

"So you have a few days off?" she asked.

A dark cloud marred his features. "Yeah. More than a few days."

She sensed an undercurrent. "Is everything all right?"

A cool edge came into his tone. "Everything is fine. I needed some R&R and took it."

After taking a sip of her water, she said, "I'm sorry. It's none of my business. Your job must take a lot out of you."

He drew in a deep breath, as if cleansing his memories. He brightened a little. "I love my job. I wouldn't trade it for anything." His voice held passion and conviction. "It's all I've ever wanted to do."

For a moment, as she saw the love he possessed for his career, she wondered if he'd ever loved a woman the same way. Their gazes clashed. Searing longing heated her from the inside out, a glowing and primitive sensation. Wistful, she chewed her sandwich. Along with respect, envy sideswiped her.

"You're brave, you know that?" she asked.

He smiled. "Not brave. Well-trained."

"Any man or woman who can do what you do is a hero in my mind."

With a fierce look, he pinned her to the spot. "Whatever I am, it's sure as hell not a hero."

He pushed back from the table and the chair squeaked across the flooring. He took his plate to the sink.

Okay, so she'd hit a sore spot. "I didn't realize telling you that I think you're courageous would make you angry."

He put his plate in the dishwasher, then returned to her. Restless energy came off him in waves. "I'm sorry, Lil. The last few days at work were pretty bad. We had a couple of arson fires and a few of our guys were hurt."

A wounded look stole over his rugged features, and he sat down at the table again.

"Oh," she said gently, "Are they... Were their injuries very serious?"

"One suffered a few burns and a concussion. Another got a broken arm. The rest had smoke inhalation problems."

"So you needed a few days to chill after that?"

His mouth twisted in a sardonic grin. "Not exactly."

She'd done it again. Stuck her nose where it didn't belong. "Sorry. It isn't my business."

She reached over and squeezed his forearm. Crisp hair tickled her fingers and muscle bunched under her touch. He sucked in a slow breath, and time seemed to still. His smoky gaze trapped her, and raw chemistry arced between them. Warmth pooled in her lower stomach, and her breath hitched.

She released his arm, wondering if she should apologize for touching him. He didn't comment, and embarrassment wended its inevitable way through her. Doug's cool response to her impromptu touches often haunted her. She had to work at remembering that all men didn't react the same way Doug had.

"How was lunch?" he asked, the superheated awareness between them easing.

Maybe she'd imagined that electric moment of bone-deep attraction. Tightness seemed to have left his body, and the intensity ebbed from his expression.

"Delicious. You make a mean toasted cheese and ham."

He grinned. "Thanks."

Get a move on, Lil. Don't overstay the welcome. "I should get back to my apartment."

A teasing grin touched his mouth. "Eat and run?"

I'd rather spend more time with you. But, no. She wouldn't say that.

She pushed back her plate and wiped her hands on the napkin. "I don't want to outstay my welcome. You took me to the hospital, you fed me lunch."

"It was my pleasure."

He didn't try and dissuade her. She didn't know whether to feel good or bad about it.

Take this slow. Whatever it is.

"I'll help you back to the apartment," he said. "After you practice on the crutches."

She groaned. "Oh, boy. That sounds like fun."

Before too long her armpits started to protest, and so did her arms. She grunted as she took one step, then another. "I hate these things."

"A necessary evil." He walked behind her, as if he expected Lil to fall.

"I'm fine. You don't have to —"

She overbalanced. A little surprised squeak slipped from her as she toppled and lost the crutches.

Strong arms slipped around her waist and drew her back against a powerful, hard body. "Easy, there. Are you trying to injure something else?"

She inhaled sharply as his embrace tightened around her. "Yeah. Right."

Lil tingled from head to toe as his body cradled her. His hips nestled hers. Again, that energy crackled between them. His hands smoothed over her rib cage, and her breasts ached. If he looked down from his vantage point, he would see her nipples pressing against her shirt. Heat filled her face.

His warm breath touched her ear as he said softly and slowly, "You need more practice. Here. Like this."

His fingers brushed the undersides of her breasts, and she gasped. One hand slid down her belly and rested there. Spicy warm musk, all man, tantalized her senses. Her hands settled over his in a caress. Arousal twisted low in her stomach. He breathed close to her ear, and hunger for him roiled inside her. It felt beyond good to have his strength and assurance wrapped around her.

"Sit down and I'll show you what I mean," he said.

As his arms slipped away, she wanted to moan a protest. His touch felt so good. He helped her to sit down, and then he demonstrated how to best use the crutches.

She grinned. "It's easier for you because your arms are stronger."

Not much later, he helped her to her apartment, watching as she negotiated the hall with the crutches.

After she opened her door and went inside, she turned toward him. "I don't know how to thank you, Evan. For everything."

"I have an idea," he said with a gentle smile.

He cupped her face in both hands and brushed an exquisite, almost chaste kiss over her mouth. Involuntarily, she reached up and placed her hands over his to hold him in place. Exhilarated by the longing inside for more of his warm mouth, she responded.

"God, you are so…" His voice faded as his lips drew closer again.

That interesting inflection in his voice tantalized her beyond bearing. Husky and passionate, his tone held emotion. She melted under his gaze and the prevailing need in his voice.

Her breath sucked in. "I'm so…what?"

"Stubborn. Isn't there someone who can stay with you? You're going to have a hard time getting around with that ankle."

"No. I can't ask any of my friends. They have families and obligations." She added a smile. "I'm not helpless."

He returned her amused look. "Of course you're not. I'm worried."

She couldn't recall the last time a man admitted to caring about her welfare. "Thank you."

Damn, this man drove her to think things she shouldn't, to want things she shouldn't. He was so giving, she grew suspicious. A man like this didn't come along every day.

"No boyfriend to stay with you?" he asked.

"No."

A wicked grin touched his mouth, then disappeared when her eyes narrowed.

He winked. "I had to know."

"Why?"

His mouth seemed so close, his heat enveloping her in sharp awareness of him as a sexy man. Tension drew muscles tight across her shoulders.

"Because I wanted to know if a boyfriend was going to come walking in here any minute and kick my ass."

A smile quirked her mouth. "No, afraid not."

"I'm surprised there isn't a husband or boyfriend looking out for you." He tilted his head to the side a little. "Look, I'm not explaining myself very well. I've got a protective streak a mile wide. I have a hard time not imagining a guy wanting to protect you."

A sweet, glowing tingle raced from her stomach straight down to the folds between her legs. His gaze assessed, eating away her defenses as he scrutinized. Exposed, emotions opened up. He'd hit her between the eyes, all right. Humility, one of those values her mother taught her, reared up.

"I'm confident enough in my work," she said suddenly. "Not always with the dating scene."

His slow, easy grin captured her breath and held it prisoner.

He reached up to cup her face. "I can't understand why. You've got a great sense of humor, and I've never met anyone who could predict earthquakes."

"Thank you, but there are plenty of people who think I'm boring and not the least funny."

His thumb brushed against her cheek. His eyes took on a half-mast, slumberous quality that made her shiver with need. "You're way too hard on yourself. And anyone who finds you boring is nuts."

Seconds later his lips touched hers. Feather-soft, his kiss didn't demand. It brushed affection, an almost innocent taste to his embrace.

Hot, urgent need sent her into motion. Her grip tightened on his shoulders, her anchor in the storm that carried her into forbidden territory. His kiss eased away.

Her eyes opened slowly, and as he released her, he smiled.

His eyes twinkled. "Wow."

"Yeah," she said softly, stunned by the power behind his kiss.

He stepped away. "I'll leave you my number." He reached for a small notepad on the telephone table by her door. He wrote the number quickly and ripped off the top sheet. "If you need anything at all, just give me a call, okay?" He placed the number on the table, then held the pen above the pad. "Can I call you?"

"Sure." She spoke before she thought, and he wrote down her number.

He tucked the number into his jeans pocket and headed for the door. "Take it easy for the rest of the day. I'll see myself out."

He departed, closing the door behind him.

She stood grounded to the spot for a good three minutes. Her mind whirled with the speed of emotions building inside and the events of the day. Things like this, interesting and adventurous, didn't happen to her.

You don't want them to happen. Remember?

Chapter Three

ഇ

The phone rang, and Lil jumped. Out of the silence, the noise startled her more than usual. She grabbed the cordless phone off the coffee table on the second ring and answered a little breathlessly.

"Lil?" The deep, pleasant voice didn't trigger recognition.

"Yes?"

"Hey, it's Evan."

"Evan, hi." Surprised and yet pleased, she asked, "Everything all right?"

"That's what I was going to ask you. How's the ankle?"

"Actually, it feels pretty good. It aches, but nothing too severe."

"You get a headache from that last quake?"

"Are you kidding? Of course."

His low chuckle, warm and soft, tingled over her skin. "Hey, I know this is short notice, but are you busy tomorrow?"

"No. My vacation plan consisted of lots of free time."

"This sounds like a weird invitation maybe, but how would you like to hang out with me by the pool tomorrow? Read. Sit around. Talk? If someone doesn't get there first, we can snatch that gazebo. Keep from getting too much sun."

Appreciative, she grinned. "That sounds like fun."

"I'll stop by for you at ten o'clock."

"Sounds great."

"I'll let you go then."

"Good night."

When she clicked off the phone, her heart pounded a faster pace. Aware of the satisfied smile on her lips, she lay back on the couch and absorbed the feeling. One of the hunkiest guys she'd met in her life asked her to sit around the pool with him tomorrow. She sighed. Maybe this vacation wouldn't become a waste after all.

* * * * *

Lil tugged at the halter strap on the turquoise tankini top. Her breasts looked larger in this torso conforming, v-neck top. The cover up skirt over the bikini bottom stayed snug below her belly button. No, she couldn't complain about her figure, but that elastic bandage around her ankle and foot looked funny. Thankfully, her Velcro sandal fit fine over the bandage and didn't bother her ankle.

The doorbell rang, and she hurried to slip the matching coverall T-shirt over her suit. She left her bedroom with her beach bag, stumping along with an awkward gait. When she glanced out the peephole, she almost swallowed her tongue. Even through the distortion caused by the peephole, Evan's gorgeous body clad only in swim trunks and sandals blitzed her libido.

"My God," she whispered. "What a hunk."

She shivered as longing snaked through her loins. Why did this man call to her so deeply and why did his rough-and-tumble good looks intoxicate her on every feminine level? *Patience, girl.* It takes time to get to know a man. *Don't rush it. You rushed with Doug and look what happened there.*

She unlocked and opened the door slowly, an eager smile ready. "You're early."

Evan's wide grin held mischief. "I'm chronically early. Sorry."

"No problem. Much better than being late. I'm ready."

He frowned. "Where're your crutches?"

"My ankle feels pretty good this morning."

Concern flashed in his eyes. "You're not walking on it?"

She stepped back and let him inside. She closed the door and shrugged. "I'm moving around okay." She demonstrated by walking with a limp. "Besides, I really hate those crutches."

His frown changed into a scorching smile that illuminated his face and made him so damned handsome she ached.

"You could make the ankle worse," he said.

"I'll risk it."

He set the large cooler and a stack of white towels on the kitchen counter, and put his hands on his hips.

She appreciated his hard, carved arms, broad shoulders, and defined pectorals. Dark hair fanned over his chest and spilled downward to his muscled stomach. A very nicely developed six-pack. The hair narrowed until it disappeared into the navy blue swim trunks that hung below his belly button. As he approached, his long, sinewy legs ate up ground. In a few short steps, he stood at an intimate distance in front of her.

"I'll carry you," he said.

She tore her gaze from his to-die-for body and glanced self-consciously at her feet. "That's not necessary."

"I'll come back up for the towels and the cooler."

When she stayed silent and defiant, his lopsided grin disappeared and altered to a soul-deep attention that filled her with exhilarating hunger. Lord, he needed to box and sell the potent way he looked at a woman. She didn't look into his eyes, a little afraid of what she'd see there. Intoxicating and vital, Evan represented strong, confident manhood at its most intimidating.

"Come on," he said softly. "You need to take it easy on the ankle. I know you hate the crutches, so I'll carry you."

What red-blooded woman wouldn't want this man to carry her? "Okay. You're right. It's just that the crutches are killing my armpits."

"I understand. Let's go."

He lifted her with ease, and she slipped one arm around his shoulders. Her fingers touched the back of his neck, and the short hair tickled her fingers. Overpowering awareness rippled through her arm and straight to the deepest feminine recess. His skin felt smooth, his muscles steel hard as he carried her. His heat and strength made her a little breathless.

As they left the apartment, she held her beach bag filled with sunscreen, her floppy big-brimmed hat, and a romance novel.

"You like carrying me?" she asked, satisfied.

His masculine grunt confirmed it. "Are you kidding? Any man who wouldn't enjoy holding you has to be nuts."

If he didn't stop saying things like that, she might combust right there. Before she could think of a response, they'd arrived outside. He walked toward the pool, his stride confident, his unstressed breathing proving his fitness.

Sun already beat down on the large rectangle swimming pool.

After easing her onto a chaise under the small gazebo-like structure, he took her keys and went back to the apartment. She watched his back muscles shift as he walked away.

"Damn," she whispered. She searched in her bag for her sunglasses and plopped them on her nose. "No man has a right to be that delicious."

Lil slipped out of her cover-up and revealed her tankini. Lying back on the chaise, she closed her eyes and tried to relax. How could she find ease of mind when Evan disturbed her equilibrium? She took deep breaths. She remembered the last time Doug had seen her in a bikini. He'd commented that she needed to drop some weight. She'd been within the acceptable weight for her height, but his constant criticism had whittled away at her self-image. She'd started a weight-lifting and exercise regimen, and he still hadn't been satisfied. She'd improved her figure and kept in shape now, egged on by Doug's critical voice haunting her memories.

Evan forced himself to walk toward the pool a few minutes later. He felt a little guilty using Lil like this. She couldn't guess his crazy reason for inviting her to the pool. Then he saw her spread out on the chaise, one long, shapely leg tilted upward at the knee, and he forgot to breathe. His groin tightened. Long, lithe, and yet curved, her body drew him like a starving lion to a feast. Her breasts weren't large, but the push-up effect of her swimsuit top made them sit up plump and tantalizing. Her hair fluffed around her face, and her sunglasses shaded her eyes from his view. He wanted to lie with her on the chaise, hold her close, taste her lips and fuck her until neither one of them could stand upright. Yeah, he could admit it.

Sure, he'd allowed his id to overrule his ego when he'd carried her. Cradling her in his arms, showing her his strength...okay, he'd admit it to himself at least. He did want her to take it easy on the ankle, but wrapping his arms around her and showing off his hard-earned muscles appealed to him. He hadn't acted this goofy around a woman since he was sixteen.

Thirty years old and acting like a teenager. Get a hold on your libido, man, or you'll scare her.

Guilt served to dampen his desire. What about Lani? She hadn't been gone that long, had she?

Thoughts of Lil intruded over his ruminating. When she'd touched the back of his neck his cock had almost reared to full attention. His heart had picked up speed, and he'd filled with self-gratification. Last night she'd dominated his dreams, her open expression, her lips beckoning to him. Christ, he'd awakened from a wet dream so powerful he'd gripped his cock and powered to a semen-spewing finish.

She smiled as he approached. Man, if she knew how she turned him on, she'd run screaming. Or maybe he'd get lucky and she'd want him as much as he wanted her.

He dragged a chaise closer to hers and put the cooler and towels down next to it. "Comfortable?"

She sighed. "This is heaven. What have you got in that cooler?"

"Some soft drinks, water."

"That was so nice of you. I didn't think to bring anything."

He shrugged and settled down on the chaise. "Don't worry about it. Next time is on you."

Her rose-colored lips parted on a small smile, and her pink tongue licked over her bottom lip. His stomach muscles tightened.

"It's a deal," she said softly.

He didn't lay back, preferring to sit on the edge and watch her. "Your skin is so pale. You're Irish, right?"

"Part Irish. I'm a mix of Irish, English and French. My ancestors came over in the 1700s."

"Can't say that about me." He opened the soft-sided cooler and plucked out bottled water. "Want anything to drink?"

"No. I'm good for now. What's your ancestry?"

"English and Welsh. I'm a first-generation American. My father was a lawyer in England and met my mother at a society party on a trip to Wales."

She titled up her sunglasses and peered at him, curiosity lighting her eyes. "So you were born in Wales?"

"Yep. I was raised in Wales until I was thirteen."

A wide smile curved her generous mouth. "Oh, that explains it."

"What?" he asked with hint of apprehension.

"I've got a good ear for accents. You have a little of that Welsh lilt in your voice."

"I'm impressed you can pick it up. I didn't think it was still strong enough after all these years."

"It's in the tone. Did you take theater classes in school?"

He raised his eyebrows. "Now I'm really impressed. How did you know?"

"It's in your face. You've got expressive eyes. That sort of Richard Burton-Tom Jones-Anthony Hopkins passion going for you."

He laughed, and she looked at the ground, a bashful grin on her face.

"I'm sorry," she said.

"Why? I'm flattered. Richard Burton, eh?"

"Well, you don't look a thing like him, but you have that passion, as I said."

His ego thoroughly stroked, he sat up a little straighter.

"Where did you live in Wales?" she asked.

"Cardiff."

"Why did your family come to the United States?" she asked.

He didn't expect the question, though he should have. His reaction bothered him. He didn't want to tell her.

She tilted her head to the side. "Did I ask something I shouldn't have?"

Hell, he could be honest with her. Anything less wouldn't be fair. "No. It's okay. My mother died and after that my dad didn't want to live there anymore."

"I'm so sorry. Was it hard to leave Wales?"

He nodded as memories he hadn't thought about in a long time rushed back. "Yeah, it was. All my friends and extended family were there. I missed my maternal grandparents, and my other grandparents were in England."

"Do you get to go back often?"

He picked up his water bottle and took a drink. "Too expensive to go back often, but I visited two years ago. My grandparents are getting old, so I try and take a long vacation when I can."

"How long is your vacation this time?"

Another great question that he could hedge or he could be honest. He chose honesty. "A month."

Her eyes widened. "I didn't think firefighters had that much time off."

"They don't normally…not all at one time, anyway. I put myself on administrative leave."

He stopped right there, not wanting to fall into the realm of too much information. If she wanted to know more, she'd ask.

Evan's disclosure made Lil hesitate. Administrative leave could mean more than one thing. An injury on the job, or a problem needing a solution. She reined back. He would tell her if he felt comfortable. Delving too far into a person's history too fast could seem intrusive.

His gaze perused her from head to toe with admiring assessment. A slow tingle built inside her. She couldn't deny his lingering looks said he liked what he saw. Here she'd been a little apprehensive about showing off her body. She'd heard somewhere that men weren't half as critical about the female form as women were, and she'd taken that to heart more often lately.

She'd noticed a fine tension in him when she'd asked why he'd immigrated, and it made her want to know more. Intuition said more lay behind his statements.

"What drove you to become a firefighter?" she asked when silence stretched.

He lay back on the chaise and stared up at the white gazebo ceiling. She ogled his powerful body before staring up at the ceiling, too. The blankness served as a great, mindless backdrop to conversation.

"That's an easy question. I never wanted to do anything else. My father discouraged me, but I managed to push onward."

She sat up and swung her feet off the chaise. "Was he discouraging you because it's dangerous?"

He sniffed. "Among other things."

"Such as?"

"Family problems."

Uh-oh. A red flag buzzword. She wouldn't push.

Evan put his arms up over his head and stretched. Rippling muscles in his arms flexed and bunched, and her mouth went dry. She'd always liked it when a man put his arms above his head like that and showed his build to his advantage.

"Your turn if we're playing twenty questions." His tone turned laconic. "Have you always been interested in earthquakes?"

"Since I was about two. I was a curious child."

He turned his gaze on her, those eyes penetrating. "You still are, right?"

She laughed. "Maybe too much for my own good. Was I too nosy earlier?"

He frowned. "Do you realize you've apologized twice for asking me questions?"

She absorbed his observation and tried to decide whether to take it as simple statement of fact or criticism.

"You're right. Inquisitiveness is my forte, but I've been criticized frequently for it."

"I don't mind. I think it shows you're damned smart and personable at the same time. People who never ask questions always make me suspicious."

His gaze held hers until she turned her attention to the dazzling diamond points on the water caused by the bright sun.

A few moments later he asked, "You always wanted to work in Geology?"

"It was either that or start chasing tornados. I was always drawn to dangerous occupations." She propped her elbow on her leg and rested her chin in her hand.

"Geology is dangerous?"

"It can be."

She half expected him to probe for explanation, but he didn't. Thank goodness. She'd almost let the nastiest time in her life back into reality with living, breathing color. Wiping her hands over her face, she heaved a sigh. When she brought her eyes back to his, Evan's slow, sensuous smile about did her in. He sat up, too.

"I think I'll go for a swim," she said as she stood.

She dared to peel off the little swim skirt and reveal the bikini bottoms. His attention snapped to her breasts, waist, hips, and did a foray down her legs.

She dropped the swim skirt on the chaise and put her sunglasses on top of the swim skirt. "Want to jump in with me?"

Discomfort flashed through his eyes. "No, thanks. You go ahead."

Concerned, but deciding not press, she walked barefooted to the side of the pool and slipped over the side into the shallow end.

"I need to take swim lessons," she said as she took slow, unsteady laps.

He stood quickly and walked to the pool. That Welsh intensity came on full force. "What do you mean? You look like you can swim to me."

"I want to learn how to hold my breath longer, to become stronger." She gripped the edge of the pool. "I also have some trouble floating sometimes."

He inhaled slowly, deeply. He stared at the water, a haunted quality darkening his eyes. She edged nearer to him, following the pool edge. "I used to do all sorts of things when I was a teen. I learned to mountain climb, and I was good at it. I tried going out for girl's softball and basketball twice in high school and couldn't make the teams either times. I've tried many things and failed many times. If you're afraid to swim—"

"I'm not afraid." His gaze snapped to hers, his voice edgy.

He jumped into the pool suddenly, splashing her. She laughed as he went under, then speared his way up from the depths with a gasp. Water glistened over his hair, face and body, and accented his to-die-for muscles. He swam toward her with powerful strokes.

"I thought you didn't want to swim?" she asked.

"You need more swimming lessons, you're going to get them."

He sounded almost angry. His brows drew down and the determination in his eyes startled her silent.

For the next hour, he guided her through floating, and she relearned details of swimming she thought she'd forgotten. His touch lingered over her back, her hips, her shoulders as he instructed her. Her breath came a little faster, heartbeat more rapid as she enjoyed their closeness.

Evan's arms came around her waist at one point, and when she looked up into his dark eyes, she saw need burning inside them. "When you look at me like that, Lil, it makes you hard to resist."

"What way is that?"

A wicked gleam entered his eyes. "Wild and sexy as hell."

She grinned. "You're sure you're not describing some other woman you know?"

"Oh, believe me," he said huskily, "I don't know any other women like you. Seeing you in this water made me do something I haven't in several months."

"What's that?"

"Swim. I haven't been in a pool for months."

"That's not unusual, right? After all, Colorado winters can be long."

"For me it's strange. I kicked ass in swimming in high school, and I was on my college team." His words took on weight. His hands palmed her back, and she shivered delicately.

She allowed her fingers to trace up over his shoulders. "You're a fish, then. What changed?"

He shook his head slowly. "I developed a mild phobia of water. I couldn't let you swim around this pool without some more instruction."

She couldn't resist. She laughed and let inhibitions loosen. "I think you wanted to have an excuse to touch me, because you've been touching me a lot in the last few minutes."

His gaze heated with searing longing, and it built her hunger into a firestorm.

"Yeah, that was part of it," he said. "I wanted to see if you could entice me into the water, and you could."

His arms tightened, and as she looked into Evan's smoldering, deep eyes, she sensed a scalding connection that couldn't be controlled.

"So I was bait to get you into the water?" she asked.

"Oh, yeah. Damned tempting bait."

Flutters of arousal darted through her belly. With heated concentration in his gaze, he took her breath away. "My ego has shot up into the stratosphere, Evan."

"Good." His voice caressed her ears, a rough intonation that added to her excitement. "You really don't realize how sexy you are."

Evan's unwavering, honest gaze cemented his belief in her mind. "Thank you. I don't think I've ever inspired anyone to do anything."

His fingers slipped into her hair and his mouth grazed her forehead. His touch felt so sweet, so good. His lips pressed her forehead again, searing and possessive. Fire tingled deep in her pussy, arousal becoming an ache so irresistible she wanted to grab him and demand a kiss. Then, as he dipped his head, she got her wish.

Chapter Four

ജ

Evan's mouth brushed hers, a beautiful taste so like the others he'd given her. Tantalizing, teasing and making her mad with longing. She couldn't stand it. She plunged both hands into his hair and anchored him tighter to her body. Her breasts mashed against his chest, and the nipples went pebble-hard with arousal. His kiss exploded into ravenous need, his lips twisting to find a deeper fit. Her lips parted and his tongue dipped inside, then again. Again, with a thrusting cadence more sexual than a mere plunge of tongue into mouth. Repeatedly, he fucked her moist depths, dominating and giving until Lil trembled on the verge of begging for satisfaction.

Her hips moved, and he lifted her until her legs came up around his waist and her pussy ground against his undeniable hard-on. She gasped into his mouth as her clit rubbed over his cock. God, he felt huge, and her pussy pulsated, ached with desire.

Tormented, she allowed his kiss to nourish her soul, scalding her with an impression she'd never forget of wide shoulders, muscled arms, flat stomach and steel-hard cock rubbing her needy clit. Flooded by desire, she met his kisses with enthusiasm. Primitive, a woman in the depths of fierce cravings, she urged his touch to grow more forceful.

His hands coasted over her butt, squeezing as he rotated his hips, grinding and thrusting in a blatantly sexual pace.

She ached, wanting fulfillment in a way she hadn't experienced in a long time. When she tried to recall when she'd last experienced this mind-bending an attraction to a man, she realized she'd never felt this close, this connected. Even her ex-husband Doug hadn't turned her on this much. Passion-drugged, Lil responded to Evan's touch with spine-melting enthusiasm, her heart thumping. Evan continued to cup her ass possessively, pressing his cock against her pussy.

He drew back, his eyes dark and heated. Dazed by the inferno between them, she wondered if she dreamed this wild fantasy come true. An amazing, attractive man held her in his arms and kissed the breath from her. Right in this moment, she couldn't ask for anything more.

His breathing came hard, a little ragged. "We'd better chill." He brushed his wet fingers over her cheek, then down her neck in a gentle caress. "It's not that I want to stop, but I'm afraid some kids might come out here and uh…" He glanced down at the obvious erection tenting the front of his swim trunks.

She smiled. "You're right. We got a little…"

"Carried away?"

She nodded.

"You have any plans for the rest of the day?" he asked.

She wanted to explore this teasing, electric connection she felt with him. "I don't have any special plans. At least, nothing more exciting than laundry."

He grinned. "Wow."

She laughed. "Very exciting stuff. What do you usually do on a day off?"

"Depends. I do a lot of reading. I sometimes hike with my friend Mic from the department. Mic has tomorrow off, and I'm helping him with this old car he's trying to restore."

"You're good with cars?"

"I wasn't, but Mic's teaching me."

"I love Model As and others from the turn of the twentieth century."

Curiosity entered his eyes. "I don't know too many women who are into cars."

She shrugged and smiled. "Call me unusual."

His cocky, sensual grin made her body heat even more. Part of her wished he'd stop looking at her like that. Every time he did, she felt vulnerable and out of control.

"I'd say you're pretty damned special," he said matter-of-factly.

Gratification mixed with disbelief. "Thank you. But you hardly know me. I could be a banshee in disguise."

He grunted. "I don't believe it. And I want to get to know you better. I'd say we could go dancing tonight, but with your ankle that's out of the question."

Dancing. Oh, boy. Now that would have been a little much for her libido. Visions of slow dancing dashed through her head. "That's okay. I can't dance."

"If I can teach you how to swim a little better, I can teach you how to dance." He cupped her face in his hands, his touch gentle. She wanted to close her eyes and absorb the heat, the intoxicating blend of tenderness and longing. "What can you teach me, Lil?"

She palmed his chest and his nipples hardened under her touch. Her heartbeat quickened, and she sank into his gaze. He kissed her once more, this time slow and sensuous, his tongue brushing over her lips before dipping inside to stroke. She moaned softly, and he let her go.

"God, Lil, you're damned sexy. I'm having a hell of a time keeping my hands off you."

She stayed cautious, choosing to take his potent male compliments with the proverbial grain of salt. "Thanks. You're not so bad yourself."

He winked. "Come on, let's get dressed and decide what we want to do."

That isn't exactly what I want to do. Getting dressed when his incredible, half-naked body is so near to mine.

Suddenly a sharp stab of pain pierced her skull. She moaned and started to sink as she clasped her head with both hands. She went under and water immediately filled her nose and mouth. Lil choked on the intrusion and for one nasty minute panic caused her to thrash. Water rushed in her ears, and she reached upward, trying to find the surface. Hard hands grasped her around the waist and drew her upward with a yank. Water sloshed all around her like churning in a washing machine. As she burst into fresh air, instinct made her gasp and cough.

Evan's arms stayed anchored around her waist as he held her up. Extreme worry filled his eyes. "Easy. Take it easy. Breathe bit by bit."

Anxiety overflowed his voice, and she opened her eyes as another coughing fit burst from her lungs. His gaze watched her carefully, as if he expected complications. She smiled to reassure him. She tried to speak but couldn't make more than a strangling noise. Water continued to slap back and forth against the sides of the pool.

"Earth…quake?" she managed to gasp out the question.

"A small one. Come on, let's get you out of here." He helped her swim to the side.

She pushed upward on the side of the pool at the same time he pushed up, his hands big and warm against the back of her thighs. They sat on the edge of the pool. Evan's face looked pale, his eyes deeply worried and filled with a strange torment she didn't expect. Intimidated by the scalding sensations she'd experienced in his arms and the painful headache, she looked away.

"You scared the crap out of me," he said. "Are you all right? Does your head still hurt?"

Dazed by the unrestrained caliber of his attention, by the overwhelming sensation of his body hard and vital against hers, she reassured him. "I'm fine now."

Doubt still darkened his eyes, and she knew he didn't believe her.

* * * * *

I'm in deep shit.

As Evan stepped out of his shower, he pondered what to do. He'd taken Lil back to her apartment to shower, half wishing he'd insisted on redoing her ankle bandage. Her headaches worried him, and the incident in the pool brought back sharp, agonizing memories of Lani. When Lil had gone under the water, he'd reacted on instinct as a firefighter and paramedic. At the same time, a terrible fear made his muscles tight and his breathing harder. Panicking hadn't been an option, but it had built in his throat, threatening to destroy him.

On the other side, his body hummed from the way she'd kissed him, barely recovered from the roiling hunger Lil inspired. He wanted her with a wrenching desire.

Pain often accompanied memories of Lani. Now though, Lil's gorgeous body and warm smile replaced some of the hurt. Guilt wended through him. Lil's delicate, almost vulnerable air jacked up the warrior inside him. Even with Lani he hadn't felt this need to protect, to keep her safe. When she'd been in his arms, Lil had inspired gut-wrenching excitement, and a molten desire to lay her down and fuck like a beast. His cock twitched.

"Shit," he murmured. "Get control."

His friends at the firehouse would laugh their asses off if they saw him now, panting over a woman. He cracked the occasional ribald joke with the rest of them, but he didn't make a habit of it, and never in front of the female paramedic on duty.

Evan drew on blue shorts, a white tank top and athletic shoes. Not long after, the doorbell rang and he opened the door to Lil. She'd dressed in a form-fitting, red sleeveless top and denim shorts. Her hair was a little damp.

Shit, she looked even more fuckable than she did earlier. "Come in."

She entered, holding a bottle of red wine. "I thought we'd have this later if we like. It's been gathering dust in my pantry waiting for the right occasion." Her cheeks went pink. "I mean…"

He took the bottle of wine and looked at the label. "Thanks." He quirked a smile. "I don't know much about wine. Other than knowing I like Chianti the best."

He reached out and impulsively brushed a strand of hair away from her mouth. He touched the edge of her lips, and heat blossomed in his stomach. Damn, he needed to rein back this crazy lust, before he blurted out in living color that he wanted to nail her. Now. On the floor. On the couch. In the kitchen. Anywhere he could get her.

She turned a brighter pink, and he glanced at the wine label again.

"I make a mean plate of spaghetti. The guys at the firehouse like it, anyway. The wine will be perfect."

She frowned, limping her way to the couch. "I didn't mean for you to fix dinner for me tonight, too."

"I like to cook for other people." He grinned. "I don't get to do it that often, except for the firehouse. But they're no gauge of good food. Most of them would eat aardvark on a cracker if you gave it to them."

Lil's eyes went bright with laughter, then she cracked up. His heart wrenched, just as it did every time she smiled. He joined her, releasing tightness in his midsection. She restrained another belly laugh, and he became entangled in her warm gaze. He loved it when she opened up, became more unrestrained. He remembered her kiss, and how she'd opened then too. Warm and wet. His gut clenched as he imagined sliding into something else warm, wet and tight. Her sweet, hot pussy.

Clearing his throat, he turned away and went into the kitchen, trying to shake the over-the-top response.

He put the wine away and returned to the living area. He settled on the couch but far enough away he hoped she wouldn't feel crowded.

"What do you want to do for the rest of the day?" he asked.

Her hypnotizing gaze swept his way. "Here's an idea. Do you like board games?"

He blinked. "I haven't played board games in ages. I'm pretty competitive."

A wicked smile touched her mouth. "So am I. I have an old, old Battleship. I also have Monopoly and Clue."

"Sounds like fun."

She gave him her keys, and a few moments later, he retrieved them from her closet. Evan made sure they had iced tea and a clear dining table for the games.

They played Clue and, to Evan's consternation, Lil outmaneuvered him at every turn.

"This is a game of chance for the most part," she said when he grumbled. "And I'm very good at them."

He reached for his iced tea and took a swig. "I'm better at games of skill."

One of her dark eyebrows tweaked upward. She swept her long hair back with one hand. "Then we'd better play something after Battleship that you can win."

"I'll get you back for that one."

"How?"

Her soft question exposed something raw inside him. Raw, dark and willing to take a chance. "When you least expect it, you'll find out."

She rolled the dice and got a four. After moving her piece, she said, "You're a mysterious man. I sense all these depths in you. Sort of tortured and wounded."

Dumbfounded, he stared at her.

"Did I hit too close to the truth?" she asked.

A rough laugh, devoid of humor, left his throat. "I don't know what to say."

Once more, her cheeks went pink, and he saw mortification fill her eyes. "I did it again. Sorry."

Impulsively, he reached across the board and clasped her hand. "You're damned nosy all right. But I like you anyway.

You do strange things to me. I want to be with you, I want to learn more about you." He couldn't help the jagged tone in his voice. He caressed the top of her hand and saw her shiver. "And you scare the crap outta me."

Her eyes widened, her doe-like expression drawing him to her on a deeper level. "Me? Because I'm good at games of chance?"

"Yeah, in a way. Because I've screwed up on so many levels lately when it comes to instinct."

She turned her hand over, and their fingers came together in an undemanding grip. "Tell me how."

He drew a deep breath, tightness in his throat he didn't understand. "My work, number one."

"But firefighting is logic and strength."

"It's more than that. With a good firefighter anyway."

She leaned slightly forward, and her grip on his hand tightened. The heat of her palm seared him. Her gaze intensified, as if she wanted to read him inside and out.

"Fire is unpredictable." Her fingers caressed his. "But you used to anticipate its moves, its heart."

Longing punched him the gut the same time as dawning appreciation. He nudged aside the board, too absorbed in what she might say next. "Exactly. How did you know?"

She shook her head. "Like I said, my instincts are good. They tell me a lot if I pay attention to them."

"Mine used to be, but now they're broken."

A pained expression entered her eyes. "What happened?"

He swallowed hard. How much could he tell her? She placed her other hand over his and pressed gently. Man, how he wanted to explain. Her touch started a trembling inside he couldn't escape.

When he didn't speak, she said, "Fire is alive, and on some level predictable. Instinct helps you when fire jumps the boundaries, doesn't it?"

He shook his head. "Right again. Damn, you're something."

She chuckled. "Well, as long that something isn't bad."

He squeezed her hand. "It's wonderful. What else do you know about fire?"

"Only that it's dangerous, and I'm glad there are men like you willing to take it on."

Admiration filled him at the same time as awareness of her womanly rose scent. She intoxicated him at the same time her insight called to him with nourishing connection.

She released his hand. "I suppose I should finish beating you."

"I think I've figured out how to get you back." He held her gaze, refusing to let her hide. "Later, we'll play a different game."

"Monopoly?"

"Nope."

"Poker?"

"No."

She sighed. "What is it?"

"I'm not telling."

Evan watched her curiosity grow. Her eyes drew him, made him want to lose himself in her depths the way he had at the pool. Hunger, pent-up and primitive, stirred in his groin. Shit, he couldn't even play board games with her and keep his libido under control.

Later, after they'd eaten spaghetti and consumed Chianti, he'd pry a few answers out of her.

As they ended Clue and she won the game, her bright laughter echoed in his ears and kept him half-hard. He leaned back in his chair and allowed his body to relax. He hadn't been this uptight in a long time. Rubbing the back of his neck, he reached for the dice and hesitated. "Tell me something." He leaned on the table, his gaze searching hers. "You said you liked old cars, right?"

She pondered the board game as if it might be an intricate chess game rather than a battle of wits and chance. "That's right."

"Mic has a Model A in his backyard. Do you think you'd like to see it?"

"Absolutely." Her smile brightened with enthusiasm. "Sounds great."

"Come with me tomorrow and you can see it. Mic is a character. He might talk you to death. Then there's always watching two men muck around with cars."

She winked. "Sounds sexy." Lil waggled her eyebrows. "All that grease and rippling muscles."

He tilted his head to the side, amused as hell. "Mic will be glad to hear that. He's not shy when it comes to women." He shook his head. "Then again, maybe I shouldn't let you get to close too him."

"Is he a shameless flirt?"

"You could say that."

"And you don't want him to flirt with me?"

Smoldering and purposeful, his eyes filled with a new light. Her heartbeat increased rapid-fire, her reaction to his fierce stare generating heat inside her.

"I'll admit it," Evan said.

A breathless trembling ensnared her. She didn't know what to say.

"You're speechless," he said.

"For once."

"Now tell me more about your life."

She swallowed hard. Turnabout was fair play, but could she do it? "Okay, what do you want to know? My favorite color? My favorite food?"

He started putting game pieces back in the box. "I want to know something substantial."

"I can tell you one thing."

"Only one?"

She smiled. "You're in direct contrast to me. You're brave, and I'm sometimes too cautious for my own good."

He closed the game box and stacked it on top of the other boxes. "Think so?"

"Without a doubt. You seem like the kind of man who tries to reach all his goals and never quits."

Surprise ran through his eyes, and her interest rose like a tide. "That's the way I was in the past. Not so much now."

"I don't believe that."

"Believe it."

She nodded. "Well, I've tried some things over and over and never succeeded."

He turned the sweating iced tea glass around and around in his hand. "Such as?"

She wandered idly toward the kitchen. "Like I told you before, I tried out for everything I could in school. Tennis, softball, band, choir. You name it. I failed at all of them. It's a pattern for me."

He frowned, and she wondered if she sounded whiny and pitiful. God, she hoped not.

Evan left the table and followed her into the kitchen. "That's rough, but come on, there has to be something you've had a lot of success with."

She poured another glass of iced tea and placed the pitcher back in the refrigerator. "No, believe me. There hasn't been as much success as I like. I'm trying to relearn how to live. Risk seems too…dangerous right now."

He put his glass in the sink and invaded her personal space. "So you want an unchallenging life?"

"It's been plenty challenging up to this point." A little resentment welled up, old feelings of helplessness invading her secret, safe thoughts.

Understanding entered his haunting eyes. "Is that why you're not a vulcanologist or seismologist even though you love the science?"

His statement punched her in the gut. "Yes."

"Would you call yourself a pessimist?"

"Half and half. I used to be a total pessimist. With maturity comes understanding."

"Or more pessimism."

"Like you?"

He came closer, and as she leaned back against the counter, he did, too. "I'm not sure what I am right now."

Maybe that is his problem. Something is eating away at him. She wanted to discover his heart, the essence of this man's soul. Concerned, she searched his face. His gaze held the battle-hardened expression of a warrior.

Standing in the kitchen, she felt an intimate thread run between them, and she wanted to pursue it. Fear held her in check.

"You don't fight bullets, Evan," she said without thought. "But you do have battles every day. Did something bad happen on the job?"

Emotion flickered in the depths of his deep eyes. She waited for him to speak.

"It's a long story," he said.

"I'm not going anywhere."

He crossed his arms. His biceps bulged with power, and her gaze snagged on the hair peeking above the neckline of his shirt. Potent attraction pulsed and throbbed in her body, demanding action. She licked her lips and saw his attention find her lower lip.

His vulnerability disturbed her in a way she couldn't define, made her restless and craving more of his scalding, empowering kisses. His nearness sent thrills straight through her.

"You didn't warn me that you're good at picking a man's brains," he said.

She started to limp across the room toward the dining table again.

"You've been walking on that ankle too much today," he said.

He reached for her iced tea and put it down on the counter. Before she could escape, he swept her up into his arms and marched toward the couch.

Her gasp of indignation was ignored. She clutched at his back. "Put me down. What is this? Retaliation for winning?"

He grinned. "No, but that gives me an idea."

He sank down on the couch with her planted firmly on his lap.

Chapter Five

ଚ

Lil stiffened in his grip, far too aware of his hard thighs beneath her butt, strong arms and chest cradling her, and the way his broad shoulders felt under her touch. Her breath rushed with excitement and anticipation. Her awareness heightened, senses razor-sharp. Tingling darted into the moistening folds between her legs.

"Why are we here?" she asked lightly.

His gentle smile and warm eyes caressed her. "Because you're driving me nuts. Let's see your ankle."

He took the elastic bandage off her ankle, his touch gentle. His fingers slid up her calf, and delighted shivers trickled up her spine.

"That looks nasty." She wrinkled her nose as her bruised ankle came into view.

He frowned. "For the next few days you need to keep off of it. I shouldn't have let you walk on it."

His exquisitely gentle touch almost overwhelmed her indignation. "What? You shouldn't have let me walk on it? I'm an adult, Evan. I do what I want."

He looked down at the ankle as he rewrapped it. He sighed. "Sorry. I didn't mean it that way."

"What way did you mean it?"

He finished wrapping her ankle and secured it. Intimacy enfolded them as he looked into her eyes and held steady. His gazed shimmered with an invigorating longing. She wanted to stay near him, and she didn't move away.

"You said once you're very protective of women. Have you always been that way?" she asked.

His hand slid up her right thigh, his touch light and almost tickling. She trembled. Evan's lips parted, and she sensed he wanted to explain and couldn't quite speak. She yearned to discern more, died to know what he felt. She couldn't recall wanting a man to open up this way. Where had he been all her life? Right here, right now, a gift presented itself if she could only reach it.

"Yep, I've always been protective with women, but I haven't always succeeded."

She tossed him a cheeky grin. "One man can't save the entire world, even if the movies say he can."

He cracked a quick smile, appreciation warming his eyes before his expression sank back into thoughtfulness. "Ain't that the truth? Try telling most men, and they won't listen. I didn't."

Layers upon layers exposed to her, and the more she discovered, sitting here in his arms, the more she wanted to learn. "Did you play with cars as a kid, or did you dream about being a knight in armor saving the damsel in the castle?"

Light flashed in his eyes. "Maybe you should drop this seismology stuff and become a psychologist or therapist. You've got a way of pulling information out of a guy."

She shook her head. "No. I don't want information out of just any guy. Only you."

"I was the knight trying to save the damsel. I thought it was heroic. I like to help people in general. It's in my blood. But the only woman I'm interested in protecting this minute is you."

Heat flared through her lower belly. Evan's look stirred her femininity and reminded her strongly of his masculinity.

He slipped a finger down her cheek. "I care about you. I know we haven't known each other long, but I feel…a connection."

Happiness mixed with the unrelenting arousal within her. "Like a thread between us."

He nodded.

When his hand cupped her thigh intimately, she didn't flinch, his touch too exquisite to ignore. He slipped his hand down her thigh until his thumb caressed the inside with a tender caress.

She gasped. His brow arched as amusement and heat battled for supremacy in his eyes. A breath longer under his touch and she'd combust. One more feathery caress in an intimate place and she'd forget her own name. As he kept her pinned with his stare, Lil's breathing quickened. God, the man screamed sex personified. She drew in a shaky breath. He smelled delicious, earthy, hot and manly. Though they'd kissed, she felt he'd take his time making love—Evan believed foreplay should be long, slow and torturous. Then again, she saw fire in his eyes. He could be pushed to the edge and lose control. She wanted to see both sides of him.

His breath warmed the sensitive shell of her ear. He kissed the lobe, and she shivered delicately. "You're driving me nuts. I can't keep my hands off you."

Fear almost drove her to move away and deny what she experienced in his arms. Desire drove Lil to lean into him and allow his lips access to her neck where he planted soft kisses. His palms skimmed low until they rested above her butt.

"This is dangerous," she said.

He muffled a laugh into her neck, and his breath teased her skin. "Do you want to see where this takes us?"

God, she loved the feel of his arms around her. "Yes."

Danger surrounded Evan like an aura. Strength and honor combined in one man generated a strong pull toward him in her heart. Urgency grew as he explored with his consuming gaze. She wanted more than games with this man. Would he turn away if he knew the cowardly part of her that existed?

With tenderness, he traced her jawline with kisses. When he reached her mouth, he took control. Heat engulfed her as his lips plundered hers. Her fingers searched through his hair, enjoying the thick, silky texture. As she explored his shoulders, eager to feel bunching muscles beneath her touch, he groaned into her mouth and shifted. His hips moved, and his cock pressed hard against her buttocks. A shiver rippled through her as she recognized his quick response. He'd turned massively hard. Aroused far faster then she would have imagined.

Fire blossomed in her stomach. For the moment, she forgot all worries and fears as his caresses took her on a journey of discovery. Tentativeness abandoned, he tasted with hot enjoyment, his tongue pumping suggestively. The slow, repeated rasp of his tongue over hers startled her with soul-stirring excitement. She responded, hardly capable of breathing as their kiss went wild. He drew back with a rasp of breath, but returned at another angle. Repeatedly he kissed her, at times driving deep, tangling his tongue with hers in a duel aggressive and yet giving. They burned together and twisted in each other's arms, and Lil never experienced anything like it before. His lips returned to hers, making love with a cadence and pressure that swept her heavenward. She drew her mouth away to gain breath, and as her head tipped back, he kissed a burning path down her neck, his tongue teasing the sensitive skin. Writhing against the sweet sensation, she moaned.

"God, Lil," he whispered against her throat.

His lips returned to hers, and searing need made her twist, seeking more. Each new kiss brought more pleasure then the last. His fingers slipped under her T-shirt and cupped over her stomach. She shivered and squirmed against the wonderful caress of flesh over flesh. He kept his mouth fastened over hers, as with an almost cautious movement, Evan cupped her left breast. *Oh, yes. God, yes.* A second later, the warm heat slipped over her nipple, his fingers brushing and teasing. She arched into his touch, taking his mouth as he'd taken hers, ravenous for a completion and unwilling to leave his arms without one. His fingers plucked her taut nipple through the thin covering of her bra, and she arched into the tormenting contact as a streamer of pleasure shot through her.

He drew back from her kiss and looked down on the prize he'd captured. "So beautiful. Has anyone ever told you how beautiful your breasts are?"

She quivered, his praise unexpected and sweet. "No."

He flicked open the front clasp on her bra, and she stiffened in anticipation. His words rasped hot and sexy. "Yes. God yes."

She didn't know where this would end, but she wanted it with a searing drive that pushed her toward fulfillment.

He shaped her breasts and tugged at her nipples, alternating back and forth until she twisted and moaned in his arms. Evan tipped her backwards onto the couch and leaned over her, and she closed her eyes against his hungry gaze. As he lowered his head and licked one nipple with the tip of his tongue, she wriggled against the pleasure. Fear and passion fought for supremacy. A pulsating ache throbbed between her legs, molten and demanding.

He murmured against her flesh, "Jesus, you're pretty."

His words acted as an aphrodisiac. She slipped her fingers into his hair and held him to her breasts. He tongued and licked one hardened nipple while tormenting the other with dauntless caresses. Each tug, each sweep of his tongue drove her closer to the inferno. Passion-drugged, she clutched at his shoulders and enjoyed the steadily rising tide. Much more and she'd explode. He twisted to the side enough so his fingers could slide under the waistband of her shorts. She let him, unworried about consequences, about thinking beyond the heat singing in her veins.

His mouth covered hers in a plundering kiss. He eased his fingers down until he skimmed over the hair on her mound. Tiny tingles trembled through her, her folds moistening, slick with arousal. She gasped as he skimmed over exquisitely sensitive flesh. She gasped into his mouth. Relentless, his gave her his touch, his fervor. His tongue took her, his fingers circled and rubbed, taunting Lil. She ached so deeply, moving and trembling against his unwavering demands. When he brushed his touch over her clit, she moaned and tore her mouth from his.

She couldn't speak, only whimper, edging toward fulfillment as his fingers strummed over her clit. As her excitement heightened, she opened her eyes and saw him watching her with hungry eyes. Passion raged there, wrenching and electric. Satisfaction contorted within her, pushed to the apex. She cupped his face and brought his lips crushing down on hers. He kissed her passionately and gave her more. Flames licked at her body and stole her breath. Lil wriggled, pleasure gathering deep in the folds between her legs. Rippling currents sparked, flared. Burst.

Fire leapt and consumed her. Shaking, panting into his mouth, she screamed her joy.

* * * * *

Evan's cock ached and throbbed. *What I wouldn't give right now to be inside her.* He would give a lot, but as he looked down on her parted lips and flushed cheeks, he hesitated. He couldn't take this to the next level. Somewhere deep inside he knew timing meant everything with Lil. She didn't take sex lightly— he felt her hesitation to take the next step. The fact she'd opened herself intimately meant she trusted him. Gratified, he smiled.

Her breath came quickly, not quite slowed from climactic heights. God, he'd loved seeing her come as he'd teased her clit into full bloom. He could almost taste her hard little nub. Eating her pussy would taste delicious, and nothing would please him more. He took a deep breath and rubbed her creamy essence over her clit. She shivered and gasped. As her eyes searched his, he saw gentleness and a desire to give. Musky sex scented the air and excited his senses. He tasted her lips, a drugging, deep kiss she returned with enthusiasm. Tongue against tongue, they returned to a rhythm that threatened to shatter his control. On the edge, he cupped her face with one hand and devoured her mouth with one hot kiss after another. She moaned softly as she drew him closer…closer yet.

When he released Lil, he drew her upwards so that she sat in his lap again. "Are you all right?"

She smiled and ran her hand through his hair. "I'd say way better than all right. That was..."

"Mind-blowing? You looked beautiful."

She blushed. "You watched me?"

He winked. "Yeah. Watching you come turned me harder than granite."

She shifted on his lap, and he flinched as her buttocks brushed over his hard-on.

A know-it-all expression flitted through her slumberous eyes. "What about you? Don't you want to come, too?"

He kissed her forehead then buried his face in the intoxicating scent of her hair. "You feel wonderful, you smell great. Holding you is enough for me."

When he drew back, her gaze caressed him like a touch and warmed his weary soul. A man could get wrapped up in her strengths and her vulnerability. Her mouth beckoned to him, begging for another taste.

"There aren't too many men who would want to stop right here," she said.

He pushed his fingers through her hair. He nuzzled her ear and whispered, "I think we need more time. I don't want to push us into something we're not ready for."

She nodded. "I understand."

He kissed her earlobe. "For instance, I want to know what you like."

"What I like?"

Keeping his voice low, he said, "Do you like to be taken from behind? Do you like to ride on top?" His tongue traced the side of her neck, then he planted a searing kiss on the sensitive area between her neck and shoulder.

She hummed. "Mmmm. All of it sounds...great."

Despite the excitement zinging through his veins, he couldn't stop asking, "Do you like it when a man talks dirty to you?"

He pulled back to catch her expression. A sinful smile curved the plump curve of her mouth. "I hate to admit it, but a man has never talked dirty to me before. Not even my ex-husband."

"You're kidding?"

"No."

"Why?"

She frowned. "I guess he thought it was…too much. Or maybe he thought it would scare me. I didn't ask him."

He pressed a kiss to her forehead. "Would it? Scare you, I mean."

Her brow creased as she thought about it. "No. I'd like to try it."

"I promise to remember that."

Tight, hot pulses throbbed deep in his groin when she slipped her palm over his shoulder. Resisting her would kill him yet.

She closed her eyes as he kneaded the back of her neck with one hand. "You're a unique guy, Evan Murdoch."

Satisfaction and primal male want warred with restraint. His cock ached and his hips arched into her buttocks. A low, rough growl left his throat.

"As much as I want you, I want to savor this. Waiting can make it better," he said.

"Like waiting to taste a fine wine."

"Precisely."

Wonder crossed her delicate features. He sensed innocence mixed with womanly knowledge.

She leaned her head back and sighed. "I can't believe this is happening. It feels so good."

When she opened her eyes and looked at him, he grinned. "Are you one of those women who analyzes relationships?"

She looked wary. "Yes. Why?"

Be honest with her. "I had a girlfriend a few years back who wanted me to read her mind. She analyzed and over-thought our relationship until she convinced herself she knew everything about me." His arms tightened around her, one hand tracing over her hip. "She didn't ask me what I thought or felt. She just assumed."

"Ah, the old assume. It makes an ass of you and me." Lil brushed her fingers over his jaw, and he reveled in the intimate gesture. "Passive-aggressive behavior isn't for me. I've got friends who are always angry with their boyfriends or husbands because they expect the men to know what they want."

Relief made him reveal more to her. "My last girlfriend, Lani, was like that. She would never tell me what she wanted for her birthday or holidays, so it was always a crap shoot. Then she'd pout when I got it wrong."

She shook her head and a silky fall of hair fell over her brow. "That's crazy."

"Believe me, it made me nuts."

"How long were you with her?"

"A year and two months."

She looked down and stared at his chest, then rubbed her hand over his pec. "I'm not sure I could last for a year with someone who did that."

Could he tell her now? Explain that one night of anger had ended in tragedy? No. He couldn't ruin the quiet, the peace that surrounded them. Suddenly, he needed to make something clear. After Lani, he didn't want the same guilt and agony that often dogged him on the darkest nights.

"Promise me something, Lil."

"Okay. What is it?"

"Never be afraid to tell me what you want. Tell me the truth even when it hurts."

She traced the slight dimple in his chin. "All right. I promise. I'd like the same honesty from you."

"It's a deal."

God, her touch undid him one step at a time. Had he felt this way with Lani? *Never.*

She yawned. "You've exhausted me."

He slipped her off his lap until she sat on the couch. "We were going to watch some movies. Are you still up for that?"

"Sure."

Through the rest of the evening they cuddled, the occasional deep kiss interrupting their viewing. He never pushed too far and the contentment he found wrapped around him.

When they made love, it would be the right time.

Chapter Six

ॐ

Lil couldn't ignore her nervousness as she sat next to Evan in his car late the next morning. He drove toward his friend Mic Petrocelli's home, and as the car ate up the short miles, tension grew in her neck and spine. Since she'd left Evan with a quick kiss last night and gone to her lonely bed, she'd marveled at their fast-growing relationship. Burgeoning feelings for Evan outpaced her logical mind and went straight for her heart. Yesterday Evan's unselfish lovemaking, his obvious desire to give her pleasure and deny his own, had endeared him on a new plateau of her heart.

It alarmed her and yet thrilled deep inside that she'd been ready to make love with him last night. If he'd continued to caress her after her mind-melting orgasm, she would have made love with him. Regardless, she'd never felt the same passion, the same reckless abandon and staggering pleasure in another man's arms. The way she felt with Evan outstripped even her first feelings for Doug. She warned herself to slow down and allow a natural relationship to form.

An easy rock station played a sultry song on the radio, the male singer's voice sensual and silky in her ears. She couldn't help singing along, overcoming self-consciousness.

Don't keep me hanging on to a fantasy,

I need you to be there in my soul,

I want you, I need you forevermore.

I want you, don't keep me hanging on to a fantasy,

Stealing seconds from your nights,

I need you to be there in my soul…

Forever.

She trailed off as the singer took the melody into difficult vocal terrain.

Evan glanced her way as he came to a stop sign. "You've got a beautiful singing voice."

"Thank you." Pleasure washed over her.

"I think you said the other day you didn't make choir in high school?"

She tipped her head back on the seat. "I could sing, just not well enough for the Madrigal group. I ended up in regular choir, which was okay in the end. My voice didn't have the strength for the a capella singing required in Madrigals."

He nodded. "Then you can't count that as a failure."

She smiled and gazed at his profile. From this angle, he looked even more handsome, more rugged. "I looked at it that way at the time." She twisted her hands together. "Look, I don't want to give you the impression that I'm one of those women who obsesses over the past. I had a friend like that once and she drove me crazy. She wouldn't stop referring to X-Y-Z incident or X-Y-Z boyfriend from all those years ago. I wanted to scream at her to get over it. Finally, I cut off my relationship with her." She went on. "I messed it up. I should have told her why I was cutting off our friendship. Instead, I stopped e-mailing. Not very mature of me, but there you have it."

As traffic moved forward at a snail's pace, he said, "Do you always expect yourself to be perfect? Never make mistakes?"

"Oh, I definitely make mistakes."

"We all do. But do you beat yourself up when you do make one?"

"I guess it depends on the severity of the mistake. Can you forgive yourself for all your errors?"

A muscle in his jaw twitched and his expression hardened. He looked all business. "No. I can't forgive myself for all of them. I guess it keeps me humble. Reminds me not to play it too safe. Life is a gamble, a trial, an adventure. My past mistakes remind me when I get too confident, that if I hold on tight, I might lose sight of what's precious."

Humble. Yes, she saw his humility time after time. Despite his to-die-for body and matching personality, Evan didn't seem to have one arrogant molecule. What would be priceless to him? His remaining family? His car? His job?

"What do you do on holidays? Anything special?" she asked.

"Depends on the holiday. I spend time with my dad usually."

"Is it a good time?"

He smiled. "I have no complaints. What about you?"

She unzipped her purse and reached for lipstick. She spread on some pale pink before answering. "There's no one. I sometimes spend it with friends."

Again, he swung that intense gaze her way for a second before returning it to the road. "Are you saying you sometimes spend Christmas alone?"

She sighed. "Not often, but I have a couple of times."

His brow creased, but he didn't say anything. A deep ache formed in her center at the reminder she didn't have anyone she could be with every Christmas.

"My father might be at Mic's today," Evan said over the gentle hum of the radio. "I thought I'd warn you ahead of time."

Sensing an undercurrent, she almost didn't query Evan. Instead, she decided she'd take another in a long string of chances.

"Your father visiting requires a warning?"

He smiled sardonically. "Some women I've introduced him to found him overwhelming."

"In a good way or a bad way?"

"He's charismatic. He can be charming or abrasive."

"A bit of a chameleon?"

"Yep. He cuts just short of smarmy. He's on girlfriend number six in the last fifteen years. Doesn't sound like much unless you consider they all moved in with him."

"He took your mother's death very hard."

She felt Evan's scrutiny, lightning fast but hard. "You sound like my Aunt Eugenie. She thinks Dad keeps the endless row of girlfriends going because he's trying to fill Mom's place and it never quite works." He shrugged. "I'm not sure I believe it. A man can't always replace the woman he loved with all his heart."

Lil processed what he said, aware of the nuances. Could Evan be talking more about himself than his father? The idea this man may have deeply loved a woman at one time stirred her soul in an indefinable way that disturbed her deep down.

"Is your dad retired?"

"He's been teaching business law courses at a community college for the last four years as an adjunct professor. It keeps him happy and busy. I think he's bringing his current girlfriend with him today."

"What's he going to think of me showing up with you at Mic's?"

Evan tossed an impertinent grin her way. "He'll think you're my latest girlfriend."

Complicated. "And what will you tell him?"

"I've known you a couple of days, but I wouldn't dare call you only a friend."

Her heartbeat sped up, her thoughts turning to the last wild kiss she'd experienced with him yesterday and the mind-altering embraces they'd shared. "Is that okay with you?"

"Yeah. Don't worry about my dad. He's not going to try and steal you away from me if he's got his current girlfriend with him."

Her eyes widened as she stared at his profile. "Don't tell me. His last few girlfriends…none of them were yours to start with?"

A grim smile painted his mouth as he took a corner. "One. About ten years ago I had a girlfriend who was five years older than I was. She decided Dad's sophistication and maturity turned her on."

She contemplated how he must feel about his father's influence on his girlfriends. "The kiss of death for your relationship with her, I take it."

"That's a good way of putting it."

He slowed the car to a crawl as they pulled up to a house. The lazy blue mock-Victorian home sat among other homes of a similar theme, none of them older then ten years.

"Welcome to Mic's place."

Evan and Lil piled out of the car. Lil took a deep breath and hoped the afternoon would run like clockwork. He insisted on carrying her from the car to the door, then he set her down on the porch and rang the doorbell.

Mic greeted them at the door, a ready smile in place. Tall and well-built, with coal-black short hair, startling green eyes and a rugged features, Mic would easily cage female favor. Despite a grease smear on his jaw and rumpled T-shirt and jeans, this man could break hearts in ten counties.

Mic shook her hand vigorously and winked. "Pleased to meet you. Come on in." Mic's slight Southern drawl purred low and deep. A frown erased Mic's cocky expression. "Heard about your ankle. How is it doin'?"

"It's fine. Evan insists on carrying me around, but it's not that bad." She flushed, realizing a half second later how it may have sounded. "I mean, I was having a hard time with the crutches."

"Uh-huh. So that's how it is." He turned a conspiratorial eye on Evan, then slapped him on the back. "Evan's good at helping damsels in distress, aren't you?"

Evan clasped Lil's upper arm gently. "Yeah, right."

"Well, if you're going to haul her around for the rest of day, start with the garage. I've put a good chair out there in the shade."

A few moments later, Evan carried her out to the backyard where a large detached garage sat with the door open. A car from the 1930s sat in garage, hood open and waiting for repairs. Next to it sat the Model A. Evan carried her around so she could see the interiors of both cars, then he carefully ensconced her in a cushiony old navy recliner under a nearby tree. She'd remembered sunscreen and a huge floppy blue hat. Her ragged jeans and T-shirt had seen better days, but she didn't want to dress up when she might be getting dirty. Mic went into the kitchen and brought out a glass of lemonade for her.

The men stripped off their T-shirts. She offered to loop them over the back of her recliner. As Evan and Mic set to work, a few naughty thoughts ran through her head. *Oh, yes. A woman could get used to the view.*

After all, how many women sat cosseted in a recliner with sinfully tart lemonade and full view of two stunning men? Her gazed snagged on Evan, and her breath caught. *God, what a gorgeous piece of male flesh.* His shoulders seemed a mile wide, and his muscular arms flexed with each move. Yes, she'd enjoyed his physique when they went swimming, but seeing him like this spurred her attraction into high gear. His jeans rode low on his hips, but they molded to his ass and thighs in a way that made her mouth water. He'd also strapped on a tool belt heavy with screwdrivers, tape measure and wrench. She sighed.

A heated flush filled her face. Lil wanted to moan. He looked so damned delicious she thought she would melt on the spot from lustful thoughts. She'd like to take his tape measure and—

Oh, God. The flame in her face went higher. His cock must be at least eight inches when aroused. The idea she might get to find out someday soon made her heart beat triple time. She licked her lips. Yep, she was certifiably in lust.

Not only did she have the luck of watching Evan, but Mic definitely tipped the scales into appetizing. With his intense eyes and carefree smile, he projected confidence and good humor. A strong nose and carved lips made him handsome rather than boyishly cute. A little shorter then Evan, he had sinewy arms, smooth muscled chest and six-pack stomach. His jeans also conformed to his butt and thighs without being too tight. Without guilt, she compared the two men. Mic's sculpted body most certainly defined artwork, but more than hot attraction filled her whenever she saw Evan. Something profound and abiding threatened to overwhelm her whenever she looked at him. The more she discovered, the more she wanted to know Evan. Having tender feelings for him so soon should alarm her, but it felt natural.

After about thirty minutes of watching them tinker with the car, Lil thought she'd expire from watching muscles bunch, flex and stretch. Evan turned his back to her when he walked in front of the car, and her attention latched onto that glorious ass again.

"My God," she whispered.

"Lil?" Evan turned around, his gaze snapping to hers. "You all right?"

She kept a straight face. "Watching you guys is such a chore."

Mic stopped working and grinned. "I think she's flirting with us."

Evan grunted and went back to work.

Mic's cheeky expression made her laugh.

Lil heard a car drive up at the front of the house and Mic headed across the yard with a loping stride. "I'll see if that's your dad, Evan."

"So were you flirting with us?" Evan asked as he wiped his hands on a rag.

"Yes, I was. It was fun."

Sweat dappled the chest hair between his pectorals, and she longed to reach out and feel heated male skin.

He grinned and approached. He leaned down and planted his hands on the arms of her chair. His lips took hers in a warm, hot dance. Each slow, tantalizing rub of his tongue over hers made her yearn for more. Drugged with heated, renewed need, she reached up and cupped his face with both her hands. His lips moved strongly, sensually, tasting her with erotic intensity. When he released her, she felt dazed. One startling, emotion-filled moment later, he gazed heatedly into her eyes. She saw desire there, a soul-fulfilling desire to stamp his essence upon her. She felt owned, as if this man told her she belonged to him. His kiss implored that she accept his genuine expression of heart and soul. She couldn't deny the primal part of her that responded to his stamp of ownership. Since humans had crawled from the cave, there remained a primitive longing too difficult to ignore or deny.

He backed away and turned his attention to the men and one woman walking toward them from around the side of the house.

"Hey, Son." A tall older man wearing sunglasses walked toward them, his smile genuine. "Good to see you."

Evan greeted him with a handshake, though his smile appeared a bit strained. Behind his father stood a petite young woman around thirty, with platinum blonde hair hanging straight and shiny to her waist. Her tight, designer label, red T-shirt molded to her large breasts. Her trim body wore jeans so tight they looked painted onto her beautiful curves. Lil didn't like wearing jeans that tight. Talk about uncomfortable. The woman's spike heels made her taller, but the men still dwarfed her by a mile. She smiled at Lil, the grin genuine and warm. Lil decided to reserve judgment despite the woman's Barbie doll appearance.

A round of introductions started, and Lil learned the small blonde was Chandra Gibbons. Chandra's solid handshake and rich feminine voice didn't sound the least girly.

Arthur Murdoch kissed Lil's hand in an old-world gesture. "Pleased to meet you."

His voice, a rich English baritone, held good humor.

"Very pleased to meet you," Lil said. "Evan has told me a lot about you."

Evan's father released her hand. "I don't know if that's a good thing or not."

Up this close, Lil appreciated the middle-aged man's good looks. Sandy light brown hair still tossed over his head in thick curls, and his azure blue eyes held keen intelligence and warmth. About Evan's height, he looked strong under the western-style shirt and brand-new jeans. Sophistication cloaked in a little country. Hmm.

Mic retrieved another comfortable chair for Chandra. Then, to Lil's surprise, Evan's father stripped off his shirt and started working with the other two men. Lil gaped at Evan's father. Corded muscles lined his torso, and other than a sprinkling of gray in his chest hair and at his sideburns, the man might as well have been Evan's brother rather than his father.

Chandra leaned toward Lil and whispered, "Arthur is gorgeous. I can't believe he's in his fifties."

Lil couldn't keep back a smile. "Well, you're right. He is in great shape for a man his age. How long have you known Mr. Murdoch?"

"Oh, several months. We just moved in together. I'm a psychology professor at the college."

"That's wonderful." Lil picked up her lemonade and took a long sip.

Lil glanced at the men, glad their chairs were far enough away the men couldn't hear them easily. Lil pushed her floppy hat down farther on her head. "You seem very happy."

"I am. He's a great man." Chandra's pale, smooth hand clasped a cola can. "So, you're Evan's girlfriend?"

Words stuck in Lil's throat. *Well, we're almost lovers. I lust after him.* "We're... We met two days ago."

Right. Leave it at that. She couldn't sound that possessive and didn't want to.

How could she, when Lil didn't know what to make of her relationship with Evan after such a short time?

Lil discovered Chandra had a great sense of humor and they chatted like old friends. Impressed with the other woman's intelligence and forthright attitude, she wished she hadn't judged on first impressions.

"This is a real hardship, isn't it?" Chandra asked.

"What is?"

"Sitting around useless while watching three stunning men."

Lil couldn't hold back a wide, appreciative smile as her attention centered on Evan's muscles moving in his strong back. She again perused his hard, muscled ass.

Lil chuckled. "Oh yeah, a real pain in the butt."

They burst out in laughter. The men looked up from their work.

"What's up?" Evan asked. "Wanna let us in on the joke?"

Chandra shook her head. "Nope."

"Women," Mic muttered as he grabbed a screwdriver from his toolbox.

Arthur lifted one imperious brow, but said nothing.

"Do you think we're distracting them?" Lil asked Chandra.

The blonde crossed one leg over the other. The bejeweled high-heeled sandals she wore twinkled in the sun. "I'd say so. But it's kind of fun."

Lil decided she'd ignore the men for a while, and talked with Chandra about psychology. Soon Lil decided she enjoyed this woman's company immensely. Maybe today would be a winner.

* * * * *

Evan's dad jumped into the part of father figure the minute he walked into the garage. Evan's annoyance skyrocketed. He kept a straight face the first three times Arthur decided he would launch into overbearing.

"Hand me that wrench," Arthur said on the tail of another command.

Evan didn't want to deal with it.

Evan slapped the tool into his father's hand. "Dad, can you cool it a little? You're treating Mic and me like we're three."

His father didn't glance up from his work. Metal clinked against metal. "You do need the time off, don't you, Evan?"

Evan glared. "What?"

"That job of yours really eats a hole in you doesn't it?" The volume of his father's voice rose.

"Everybody's job does," Mic said in obvious defense.

Arthur sighed. "It's the same old story. Firefighting is a dangerous, stressful occupation."

"What has that got to do with my vacation?"

Arthur banged his thumb with something and cursed under his breath.

"If your job hadn't created problems for you, you wouldn't need that many weeks to recover, now would you?" Arthur reached over and snatched a tool from his son's belt. "We all know it isn't honestly a vacation."

Mic laughed. "You're telling us something we don't know?"

"You've had a week off already, right?" Evan's father asked.

Evan glanced over at the women.

Chandra and Lil's attention had turned toward them. "Yeah, I've had a week off."

"You said you have two more to go?" Arthur asked.

"Three."

"Seems you'll need more than three weeks at this rate. Pretty soon the station will lose its patience, and you'll lose your job," Evan's father said.

Evan winced internally. His father would never get it. "I'm not going to lose my job."

Mic drew back from the car long enough to reach for his bottle of water. "I think Evan did the right thing."

Arthur snorted a laugh. "A right thing going on administrative leave voluntarily, or being a firefighter?"

Heat spread up Evan's face, and he felt Lil watching him. He glanced over and her concerned gaze caught and held his. He felt her curiosity mixed with worry, and humiliation worked its way through his psyche like a newly acquired wound.

If Evan tended toward violence, he'd have pitched his wrench at his father already. "What happened had nothing to do with firefighting."

"If Mic's father hadn't known Lani's father through firefighting, then you wouldn't have met her. Right?" Arthur asked.

Evan had to bite his tongue to keep from cursing loud and long. "That's a roundabout route to get to why I took leave."

"Lani's family wanted her to marry a firefighter. You were convenient. Besides, she was a groupie."

Evan started to take off his tool belt. "No, she wasn't."

"Have it your way. You always did anyway." Arthur's tone became louder.

Lil stared at their exchange, and Evan knew once they returned to their apartment complex, he'd have to explain the intricacies of the conversation.

Evan kept a straight face. "Can we not do this now, Dad?"

His father shook his head. "It always comes back to your job, Evan. Firefighting is dangerous and it robbed you of a safe life—"

"Life isn't fucking safe anywhere, Dad." Evan glared at his father and returned to work, no longer giving a shit that he'd cursed at his parent.

Lil watched the exchange between Evan and his father with concern. While she didn't understand what Evan's old girlfriend had to do with his need for his extensive vacation time, she decided she wouldn't ask him about the situation. If he wanted to tell her, he would. Pressing him wouldn't be wise.

A few seconds later, dozens of sparrows in the huge tree near the garage took flight, and dogs up and down the street started to bark.

Apprehension wound deep into her stomach. "Something strange is happening." Before she could blink, a sharp headache throbbed in Lil's head. "Oh, great. Here it comes."

She said it loud enough the men turned to look her way.

"What?" Mic asked.

"Earthquake," Lil said.

Chandra's eyes widened as she echoed Mic's earlier statement. "What?"

Lil caught Evan's gaze, and his eyes narrowed.

"Not another one," Evan said.

"I'm afraid—" Lil started.

The ground rumbled, the groan rising on an ominous throaty sound.

The timber-constructed garage let out a creak. A tingling started in Lil's body like an electric current as her head hurt with a relentless pressure. She flinched as the ground vibrated harder. She put her hands to her temples.

"Lil?" Evan's concerned voice echoed above the earthquake's noises.

"Get the hell outta here," Mic said to the other men, pushing them out of the doorway and following close behind.

Chandra stood, her face panic-stricken. "Arthur!"

Arthur lagged a little behind the others, tripped on a rock and went facedown. Hard.

Chapter Seven

ဢ

Earth rumbled under Evan's feet. Lil stood up, her eyes widening in alarm and he heard Chandra call out his father's name. Evan swung around. Mic crouched down beside his father. Alarm hit Evan in the gut the same time the relatively mild tremor came to an abrupt halt.

"Dad!" Evan rushed to his father's side, his heart beating a frantic tattoo against his ribs. "You okay, Dad?"

"I'm fine," his father said as he stood with help from Mic and Evan.

"There's blood on your nose." Chandra put her hand on Arthur's chest, her eyes worried.

His dad patted her hand. Then he wiped his nose. "I think I met the dirt, but it's certainly not broken. It's no big deal."

Evan saw the distress in Chandra's expression and realized he'd never seen a woman respond to his father quite like this. Skepticism shoved aside the thought as fast as it came. Nothing indicated his dad had found the woman of his dreams. Nothing. Love could be elusive, no guarantees. He knew that as well as anyone.

Relieved his father hadn't suffered injury, Evan released his arm. "That quake was as strong as the other one at the pool yesterday and the one before that."

Lil's voice came from the chair. "You're right. Maybe a little stronger."

Evan strode toward Lil. "How's the head?"

As he squatted down beside her chair, Lil appeared wary, her gaze darting to the others.

Mic walked purposefully to her side and stood over them. "Her head? What's wrong?"

Lil's mouth compressed into a stubborn line. "It's nothing."

Stubborn as usual, Mic squatted on the other side of her chair, his glower razor-sharp. "Did you hit your head?"

Lil rolled her gaze to the sky, then groaned. "No, I didn't hit my head. I haven't moved from this chair the entire time."

She tried to make it sound light, but Mic gave her a strange look. Evan didn't blame him. Mic's paramedic training attuned easily to people's distress. He probably saw the strain in her eyes, and the way her lips went tight with pain.

"I don't buy it." Mic glanced at Evan, his gaze sharp and searching. "She's in pain. What's going on?"

Lil's expression went rock-cold. "I'm great. I think we'd better check your house for damage, Mic."

Good sidestep, honey.

Mic nodded as he stood. "You're the seismologist."

She shook her head. "Not really."

Evan gave him a pointed glare. "Go take a look at the house."

Mic held on to his stubborn expression. "But—"

"I need to talk with Evan about something," Lil said with a firm tone allowing no argument.

Chandra and Evan's dad stood away from their little grouping, attention riveted to the drama.

"Come on. I'll help you," Evan's father said to Mic.

Chandra winked at Lil and followed. Once they'd left, Evan kneeled next to her chair again. "Okay, what's up? I know you've got a headache, and there's sweat along your brow line. You've got that weird fever."

She gave him a sarcastic smile. Tension rolled off her, her dismay palpable. "Thanks for your concern, Evan, but I don't want anyone to find out about my headaches, okay?"

"Why do you want to hide it?"

Anger flashed in her eyes. "Why? You saw the way everyone looked at me."

Perplexed, he shook his head. "No, I didn't. Other than Mic turning on his paramedic mode, I didn't see anyone looking at you strangely."

She let out a puff of air, her eyes troubled. "It leads to questions, then disbelief, then people start to treat me differently. I don't want that."

"You trusted me with your secret almost from the moment you met me. Why?"

Confusion filled those pretty eyes. He wanted to lean over and kiss away her anxiety. Instead, different words found their way out. "Lil, you're being paranoid."

Her gaze went from disturbed to anger. "Paranoid? Thanks so much."

Bravo, sport. You've really done it now. "I mean—"

"Never mind." She waved one hand. "It's not important."

"It is important. I may not have known you a very long time, but you're driving me nuts."

"Glad I could liven up your life," she said with a hint of mockery.

He raked one hand over his face, exasperated with himself and with her. "Let's talk this out."

"There's nothing to talk about, Evan. I don't want other people to know."

"So you just let me know on accident? Why was I different?"

She shrugged, her eyes cool and detached.

"That's it? Is that what you want to do? Hide from who you are?" he asked.

"Maybe you're hiding the way you are." Her gaze tangled with his.

"What do you mean?"

"I heard a good chunk of the conversation you had with your father earlier. It sounds like he was giving you hell for being a firefighter in the first place. And then there's Lani. Did she hurt you?"

"Yeah. She hurt me. The worst way you can imagine."

"It's acceptable for me to air my baggage with strangers, but not you?"

She had a point, damn her. Damn her beautiful, infuriating hide. He felt used up, ensnared in complicated emotions.

Lil covered the hand he'd placed on her armrest. Warmth replaced the chill in her eyes. "How did she hurt you?"

He couldn't breathe, the chaos of the last few minutes taking up all the space in his lungs. He stood slowly, breaking her grip.

"I can't talk about it right now." He turned away and walked into the house.

* * * * *

The day had turned weird, laced with undertones Lil wanted to understand but feared. After lunch, Arthur and Chandra left and then Evan and Lil decided it was time for them to depart.

Before she climbed into Evan's car, Mic kissed her on the cheek.

She blushed. "What was that for?"

"For being so damned nice." Mic gestured at Evan, a mischievous grin crooking his mouth. "And for putting up with this guy."

She turned her attention onto Evan. His short hair stuck up in a couple of places and his T-shirt clung to the delectable angles of his body. Pure desire rushed through her in a yearning wave. But what if this disagreement today was the start of more misunderstanding?

Evan smirked at Mic. "Yeah, well, keep your paws off my woman, Mic."

She laughed. "Your woman?"

He grunted. "Let's go."

"I guess he thinks the primitive caveman thing is the way to a woman's heart," Mic said. "Me, I personally think wine, song and—"

"Yeah, yeah, yeah," Evan said with a crooked smile. He climbed into the car, slammed the door and started the engine. "Later."

With a wave and a laugh, Mic let them go. As they drove away, she felt the sizzling awareness between her and Evan rise into the stratosphere. She drew in a deep breath and caught his masculine scent, a little sweat mixed with his unique musk. A tingle built in her belly. She couldn't believe it. How could she find this man so irresistible when their future could implode right before her eyes today?

Not far down the road, Evan broke the silence. "How does a man win your heart?"

Startled, she couldn't answer.

A minute later, he elaborated. "Did I ruin my chances with you when we argued earlier?"

"I was...hasty. You had no way of knowing I didn't want you to mention the headaches and earthquake prediction."

"You've faced ridicule over the years. Makes sense that you'd be sensitive."

Mortified that she'd caused such a stink earlier, she twisted the handle on her denim purse between nervous fingers. "I need to get over it."

"Yes, you do." He grinned.

Surprised again by his about-face, she smiled with him. "What are you saying?"

"You have tremendous confidence and bravery, but you're a coward when it comes to letting people know who you really are. You have nothing to be ashamed of, Lil."

Revelation opened inside her like a bright dawn or a fiery sunset. An epiphany had never come to so easily. A door opened wide, and he'd reached inside to see her secret heart.

She let her handbag drop to the floorboards with a thud. "You mean my inability to reveal what I can do. That I can predict earthquakes."

"Yes. I think you shouldn't hide it. It's who you are."

She nodded. "Maybe you're right." She glanced over at his hard profile. "I'll think about it."

Lil wondered if a couple of days away from each other would return perspective. Most people had baggage…everyone, really. Like anyone else, they could navigate their way through treacherous personal territory. Time would make it easier, or time would show them they couldn't.

When they reached the apartment and Evan carried her upstairs, she enjoyed the strength of his arms. Lingering discontent couldn't remove how she felt about him.

How did she feel?

Growing affection. Wild sexual yearnings.

Oh, yes. There was that.

A physical relationship didn't guarantee they could build anything else together. Disconcerted, she decided she'd given in to idealist thinking from the moment she'd met him. She'd composed an image of him, a hero and maybe a lover. She knew on instinct that she could trust him with her life, if not her heart.

He set her on her feet next to her doorway. "Long day."

She conjured a smile, realizing it didn't quite cut it as genuine. "Yes."

To her surprise, he caressed her hair, then her cheek. He leaned in and pressed a sweet kiss to her forehead.

"I'm a little beat," he said.

"I don't blame you." She added a sunny smile. "I'm a little beat myself. Watching three gorgeous men get all sweaty takes a lot out of a woman."

He laughed, his eyes twinkling. His animation diminished as he sobered. "Hanging with my father can sometimes wear me down. I'm sorry you had to see that exchange between him and me."

"Do you want to talk about it?"

He shook his head. "It's an old story and it isn't going away. We can talk about it later."

Resigned to a quiet evening, she unlocked her door and opened it. As she turned back toward him, he slipped his fingers through her hair and stared deep into her eyes. Before she could blink, he kissed her. Heat engulfed her as his bold kiss took her mouth. With ardent passion, he brought out her response. She slipped her arms around his neck and leaned into the heat of his body. Potent need raged inside her. Stroke after stroke, his tongue loved her with rich attention. She quaked against his strong body as bliss shimmered across her skin. He cradled her, his hands coasting across her back and riding low on her hips. He drew away slowly. Dazed by the potency behind their kiss, she wondered if this would turn out to be a dream. Fierce happiness mated with hunger.

"Damn," he whispered, his voice smoky, his breath ragged. His nostrils flared.

She tightened her grip around his neck. "I'll say."

Sexual awareness crackled inside her and filled her with extraordinary longing. She wanted that connection to continue.

She drew back slowly. "We'll talk tomorrow."

Resignation eased into his eyes. "Tomorrow. Take it easy on that ankle, okay?"

"Of course, I will."

He gave her a dubious look before he turned away and headed to his apartment. "I mean it."

"Okay, bossy." She laughed and entered her apartment.

Chapter Eight

෨

"We have no idea when the big one will break," Michael Hedge said to Lil the next morning.

She'd finished breakfast when her associate had called. Understanding dawned on her in a flash. "Wait. You wouldn't have called me unless there was something else happening beyond the ordinary."

Michael snorted. "I wanted to tell you what was happening, but your boss had other motives."

She groaned. "Oh, no. What?"

"Well, with all the recent seismic activity, the department is hopping. There's a ton of work come in and—"

"Don't tell me." She sighed in major frustration. "Dr. Trosky wants me to come into the office."

Michael gave a shaky laugh. "Yep."

She closed her eyes as budding resentment swelled. "I don't suppose he's considered asking Kirstin to take up the slack?"

"Of course not. You know how it is."

"Yes, I know how it is. When does he want me in?" She inhaled deeply, wanting to grind her teeth in frustration.

"As soon as you can get here."

"I'll have to get a ride. I can't drive."

"Why?"

"Because on the first day of my vacation, one of the quakes hit and I sprained my ankle."

"Ouch. I'd say tell Trosky, but I know that won't make a difference."

"I'll be there in about an hour."

When she hung up, she almost screamed. Her fingers clamped on her coffee mug and she brought the beverage up for a long drink. She didn't want to call Evan for a ride. She couldn't assume he'd have time.

"Damn you, Trosky." She wanted to punch the arrogant head of the department, but wouldn't.

Irritation sent her limping across the kitchen to the cordless phone. She hoped Evan wouldn't mind giving her a ride to her office. She punched his number into the phone and walked back to the kitchen table.

One ring went by before he picked it up. "Hello?"

He sounded sleepy. Oh, crud. She'd probably woken him up. "Evan? I hope I didn't wake you?"

"Hey." His sexy, deep rumble made shivers of longing tingle in her stomach. "I was lying here trying to get my ass out of bed. I didn't sleep well last night."

She really did feel guilty now. "I'm so sorry. Is everything okay?"

"Yeah. Guess I wasn't tired, and I was thinking about a lot of things."

"I woke up a few times last night dreaming we were having another earthquake, but we weren't."

"How's your head?"

"It's fine. Sleeplessness can be an aftereffect of the headaches."

"That means you aren't getting much sleep since there has been an earthquake every day."

"You could say that."

"Hell, that's not good."

She yawned then laughed. "No, it isn't. Listen, I have another favor to ask. If you don't want to help, I'll understand."

She heard sheets rustling, and an erotic image passed through her overheated imagination. Evan, his gorgeous body completely naked, spread out on the bed. Wide chest, strong and sculpted arms akimbo. Legs wide apart to display heavy balls and long, thick, cock ready to thrust deep inside her. She swallowed hard as superheated arousal stirred low in her loins.

"Lil?"

"Um…sorry. My boss called me in to work and I need a ride."

"You're kidding? You're on vacation."

"Tell me about it. Dr. Trosky is the head of the department and if I don't go in, he'll have a fit."

"When do you have to be there?"

"As soon as I can."

"Give me thirty minutes and I'll pick you up."

Relief mixed with apprehension inside her. "Thank you. Evan?"

"Yes?"

"I wouldn't ask you but all my friends are already at work—"

"Don't worry about it." Velvet-rich, his voice brought to mind a forbidden night wrapped in his arms. "I'm glad you called. Besides, *I'm* one of your friends. You can call on me."

Shame-faced, she said, "Right. Thanks again."

When they hung up, relief wended through her. He didn't sound bothered by her call.

She changed into a red sundress with a jacket that covered her shoulders. Evan arrived at her door exactly thirty minutes later, his hair damp. Evan's emerald green T-shirt with two wolves on it hugged his upper arms and chest. A pair of jeans contoured his hips and thighs. Damn, if he didn't look scrumptious. He smelled so good, she took a deep breath and luxuriated in the scent. She grabbed her purse.

"Thanks so much. I appreciate you helping me out again." She balanced on the crutches and took two experimental steps. "I practiced a little last night."

A disarming smile came over his mouth. "I can see that. You're doing well." He crossed his arms. "I take it this means you don't need me to carry you any longer?"

How could she ignore how wonderful it felt to have him carry her? "I figured if I was going to work there was no way I could have you around all day carrying me from place to place."

"Good point. I can't believe you're going to work with a hurt ankle."

She advanced another cautious step with the crutches. "Dr. Elias Trosky is a geek with no social skills. He lives and breathes science and has no other life. He thinks everyone who works for him should be the same."

He pressed her shoulder. "What did your office say about these weird quakes?"

"Before he told me the bad news about having to come into work, Michael said Dr. Trosky isn't trying to predict what's next. His associates don't have any idea what's going on."

"Scary."

"I'm not worried. But I wish if the big one was going to come, that my headaches would give us more warning."

"Not much chance of that, is there?"

He carried her down to the car, not wanting to use the elevators.

When they arrived at the university satellite campus, he shut off the car engine. "Remember, no elevator and don't try to go down stairs on those crutches."

She patted him on the arm. "Okay, bossy. Since I can't take the elevator to the second floor, are you carrying me up to the office?"

"You betcha. Look, we need to talk tonight after you get off work."

She drew in a deep breath. "That sounds ominous."

"Don't worry. I'm not dropping any sort of bomb."

He did carry her, and when Michael and the rest of the staff of three saw her mode of transportation, they gawked.

She smiled and tried to ignore the awkwardness. Michael sobered up quickly and shook Evan's hand. Kirstin, who considered herself Dr. Trosky's assistant, slinked up to Evan and said hello. Lil noted that Evan was polite to Kirstin but the attractive brunette didn't seem to affect him.

Evan then shook Dr. Trosky's hand. "Pleased to meet you."

"Um…you're…" Dr. Trosky probed even after Lil introduced them.

"A very good friend of Lil's," Evan said, grinning down at Lil where she perched on her small office chair.

Trosky's mustache quivered as he held back a smirk. He sat on the edge of the nearest desk and let his leg swing back and forth. He twisted a number two pencil between the fingers of his right hand. "I suppose Lillian has told you about her so-called earthquake headaches?"

A jolt of surprise rocked Lil. Embarrassed and angry, she wanted to scalp him.

"She didn't just tell me. I've seen it work," Evan said.

Lil smiled as Evan's support warmed her heart.

Trosky grunted and looked at his colleagues. "Earth Science is a lot more complex than tension headaches. Don't be fooled."

A cold watchfulness came into Evan's eyes. "I'm rarely fooled by anyone or anything. What's your theory on what's happening with these quakes, Dr. Trosky?"

Trosky's foot stopped swinging, but the pencil still whirled back and forth in his fingers. "We're baffled at this point."

"Induced seismicity," Lil said suddenly, unable to stop her need to explain.

Michael grinned widely, looking pleased with Lil's statement.

Trosky's smug smile showed contempt. "Induced seismicity does occur, but we sincerely doubt that's the reason."

"It happened in Colorado back in the 1960s," Lil said. "Why couldn't it be happening now?"

"What is induced seismicity?" Evan asked.

Lil spoke before Trosky could take over the show. "Earthquakes triggered by manmade disturbances of the crust. Things like reservoir loading or unloading, oil extraction, injection wells and large mining operations."

"Yes, but those are only small quakes," Trosky said, his voice holding contempt.

"It's been argued that magnitude five or more quakes have been caused by human activity. That's pretty damned disturbing," she said.

She didn't say, even though she wanted to, that Trosky didn't have the balls to inquire about manmade rock and roll.

Trosky's deep frown said she skirted the edge. For some reason, Evan's presence emboldened her.

"Let's get to work, shall we?" Trosky asked.

Evan smiled nonchalantly. "Call me when you're ready to come home, Lil."

After Evan left, Kirstin sauntered up and glowered at Lil. "A firefighter, eh? What a hunk. Is he your boyfriend?"

Lil decided to answer truthfully. "He's an intimate friend. I'm fond of him."

Kirstin sat on the edge of Lil's desk. Michael made a face over Kirstin's shoulder and Lil almost laughed.

Kirstin's cool, burnished copper eyes glittered with her usual low-burn contempt. "Thanks for coming in to work. I know it's hard to miss your vacation."

Lil didn't take the bait. With a dry intonation, she said, "Devastating."

As per usual, Kirstin didn't do her share of the work, and Lil took up the slack. She'd always been well armored when it came to Kirstin's snide comments and attempts to take credit. Lil also recognized she needed to change her work environment soon. Allowing Trosky to abuse her work ethic this way had to stop. When she got home tonight, she needed to think of what she wanted to do.

Evan picked her up at six o'clock. She'd caught him doing some grocery shopping.

"Have dinner with me tonight," he said as he carried her into her apartment. "Have you ever tried Frederick's?"

As he set her on her feet, she smiled. "Fredrick's is one of the most expensive restaurants in the city."

He slipped his hands into her hair and drew her close. She put her hands on his chest, enjoying the movement of strong muscles under her fingers.

"Don't worry, it's on me. I already got reservations in case you said yes," he said.

"How can I refuse? I'd love to try it."

His eyelids dipped, his gaze filled with heat. Any walls she could have put up in defense dissolved like a whirlpool. As his lips came down on hers in a bold kiss, she melted. His tongue dipped inside her mouth with a deep, continuous stroke. She met his lavish kiss with all her heart.

He broke away. "I'll see you in a couple of hours."

After he left, and dazed from the powerful kiss, she sat on the couch a full ten minutes. She contemplated what dress to wear and settled on a simple copper and emerald green swirl halter dress featuring a built-in bra. She rushed through a shower and applied lilac-scented body lotion. She added the one thing she'd never contemplated wearing on a date before. A skimpy black thong. She didn't consider thongs comfortable and rarely wore them, but this one night she wanted to feel sexy. After sliding the silky stretch dress over her head, she shivered delicately. Material hugged her curves, and the sensation on her vulnerable buttocks drove a sharp spike of arousal into her loins.

Dressed to kill, Lil.

She'd like to wear thigh-high stockings, but they wouldn't fit over the elastic bandage, and she couldn't wear high heels. She settled on black flats.

"If this doesn't knock him on his ass, nothing will." She could admit it now. Looking sexy and feeling sexy mattered to her. Cushion cut green CZ earrings and a matching necklace almost completed the outfit. She slipped an emerald cut green stone ring on her right hand.

Evan rang the doorbell right on time. When she opened it, she couldn't help the broad smile that spilled over her mouth. "You look terrific, Evan."

A dark grey suit, matched with a grey shirt and bold red tie, made him look wealthy and sophisticated.

His gaze devoured with an eager expression that rocked her down to her shoes. His attention slid down over her breasts, and her nipples tightened. Warmth heated her face as his gaze moved over her hips and down her legs.

He drew her near, his hands slipping around to the bare skin on her back. Hot and possessive, his touch caused a ripple to move over her skin.

"Mmm…God you smell nice." His voice purred against her ear. "And you're beautiful."

"Thank you. You aren't so bad yourself, sir."

He kissed her hungrily. She moaned against his eager onslaught. When his palm slid down to cup her ass, she jolted in his embrace.

He drew back from the kiss and frowned. "Something wrong?"

A little embarrassed at her strong reaction, she said, "No. You startled me."

"I got carried away." His voice dripped with nuances, a sin and sex sound that made tension curl along her skin and plunge into her stomach.

Once they reached the restaurant, she used her crutches. Everything about Frederick's spelled luxury. From the beginning, it had been a hotel and restaurant. Located in downtown Denver, the old brownstone occupied a corner where it had stood since 1889. She'd eaten here once, long ago, with her family. A central five-story atrium featured a beautiful Grecian design fountain. A man in a tuxedo played a piano nearby.

"I'd forgotten how beautiful this is," she murmured as they walked up to the restaurant located on one side of the atrium.

"Gorgeous." Husky and deep, his voice stirred her senses.

She glanced his way, caught the fiery look in his eyes. A few more looks like that and she might melt into a puddle.

Evening flowed into one seamless delight after the other, and Lil wanted it to never end. Sequestered in an intimate booth in a corner with Evan, she felt intoxicated by the night. Sumptuous red velvet, gilt, and dark wood gave the restaurant old-world ambiance. Their wait help treated them like gold, the meal of steak and lobster delicious. She helped Evan polish off a death-by-chocolate piece of cake so rich she thought she'd go into sugar shock.

Had she landed in a dream world? Life presented a glorious challenge in the form of a wonderful man, and she wanted more of his attention, wanted to learn more about the man who'd come into her life a short time ago. She could live in this illusionary state all night, maybe. She sighed, soaking in the pleasure for as long as she could.

He reached over and touched her fingertips, and a bolt of longing astounded her. She sank into the smoky depths of his eyes.

"You look worried," he said.

She found her voice. "Do I? I didn't realize."

"You know, I've got to be honest with you."

His fingers caressed hers, and she swallowed hard as an electric sensation sizzled up her arm.

When he did nothing more than search her face, she cleared her throat delicately. She touched the base of her wineglass with her other hand. "What did you want to say?"

"I'm sorry I pushed you so hard yesterday."

"It's all right. You already said you were sorry."

"While I was lying awake the other night I could have kicked myself for pushing you too hard, too fast. I shouldn't have assumed you wanted anyone else to know about your headaches."

She nodded. "I shouldn't have overacted. Being genuine should be one of my goals. I've betrayed myself for so long being...afraid."

"Afraid of what?"

"It's complicated."

"And you don't want to tell me?" He looked disappointed, his voice pitched low.

"I do want to tell you." Warmth in his eyes held her breath suspended. She didn't wish this night to end on a low note. "Maybe another time?"

"Of course."

She didn't mind the quiet as they drove home, with occasional forays into conversation about the excellent dinner and beautiful hotel.

"I wish we could have danced," she said.

"We can try in a couple of weeks if your ankle is up to it."

A couple of weeks. Happiness surged inside her. Excitement wended through her when they reached the apartment complex.

"Want to come to my apartment and listen to music?" he asked as he carried her up the stairs.

"Absolutely. You have a better sound system."

"And better smooth jazz."

"Think so?"

"I know so."

"We'll see about that."

They retrieved CDs from her place and went to his apartment. Once inside, Lil moved to the big picture window showing a glittering diamond point presentation of the city. The wine she'd consumed buzzed through her veins on pleasant wings, not too much or too little.

He put on a smooth jazz CD, a favorite throbbing with steamy sex and ultimate sin. Lil gasped softly when he slipped his arms around her from behind.

"Something wrong?" he asked.

She placed her hands over his and sank into his protective embrace. "No. You just startled me. And you're so warm."

He nuzzled aside her hair. "That's a good thing, I hope. Did you enjoy dinner?"

"It was delicious. Thanks again. I owe you."

"Yes, you do."

She chuckled and looked at his reflection in the glass against a darkening skyline. "Really?"

"Yeah. A kiss. Maybe two."

"I think I can manage that."

His sigh against her temple sent soft tingles racing along her skin. "Good."

He let her go. "I'm getting this tie off. It's killin' me."

He left for the bedroom, returned a few moments later *sans* tie and jacket, and with his shirt unbuttoned halfway. As he stalked toward her, her breath caught. His masculine grace made her heart beat staccato. She still stood by the window, and he walked up beside her.

He drew her left hand into his right. As he lifted her hand to his lips, she almost held her breath. Music wended around them. Lil's heartbeat quickened as his tongue dipped between her index and middle finger. He turned her hand over and kissed her palm. A lightning bolt of pleasure whipped through her arm.

"Trosky is damned sure of himself," Evan said out of the blue.

"He's always been that way."

"Dismissive, too. I don't like how he talks to you."

She smiled, secretly pleased. "I've been putting up with it for years. I think I can manage a few more. If I didn't want job security I probably would have told him where to stuff it a long time ago."

"You're damned good at keeping the peace."

"That's me. Little Miss Peacemaker."

"Ever get tired of it?"

"Oh, yes."

He paused before speaking again. "So you believe these quakes are being caused by something manmade?"

She nodded. "It has to be. There's nothing seismically that makes sense otherwise."

"You said there have been quakes in Denver before."

"The largest recorded in Colorado was near Rocky Mountain National Park and was back in 1882. Reports estimate it was about a magnitude six-point-two. At least that's the closest guess from damage reports. Large earthquakes are possible anywhere. Denver definitely has a history of activity."

He sighed and went silent. Slowly he slipped behind her and pulled her back against him. His hands moved up over her stomach, pressing her back into his hardening loins. He wanted her. She couldn't doubt that. He groaned and softly nuzzled her ear. Hot longing shivered through her as he kissed the side of her neck. Slowly, with a possessiveness that sent sparks of heat deep between her legs, he palmed her hips, her waist and then cupped the sides of her breasts. She quivered as she chased his hands, cupping over them as he moved. Somehow, it felt more sensuous following his torturously measured progress.

Lightning-quick responses warmed deep inside her belly and spread through her entire body.

"You're driving me crazy," she whispered in a special kind of agony.

"Good." He sounded smug. "At least I think that's good."

Evan turned her in his arms until she faced him. She'd never experienced yearning as staggering as this, as all-consuming. Breathless, trembling on the edge of awareness so acute, her senses called for a finalization to the heady chemistry raging between them.

With feathery strokes, he plied her with kisses along her neck, then down her shoulder. She moaned softly, willing to banish her defenses under his careful touch. Heated caress followed heated kiss. His mouth found hers and tasted with long, deep kisses, his tongue caressing in a carnal tribute that created shameless desire. Evan undid the neck of her halter dress and slowly eased the bodice down to her waist. Sweet affection drew her deeply into the moment, drawing her toward an adventure she wanted with all her heart. No doubts threatened. She'd take this trip wherever it led her.

His big hands cupped her shoulders, and he looked down at her bare breasts without hesitation, his gaze admiring and hot. When his eyes returned to hers, they smoldered with promises. Tonight she'd know a passion she'd never experienced quite the same way before. She felt like a virgin under his tutoring touch, as his hands encompassed her breasts, and his mouth searched out hers. Drugging and deep, his kiss demanded completion. His fingers brushed around her breasts, testing the small mounds before his fingertips clasped each nipple and tugged. She gasped into his mouth and his tongue thrust, tangling and twisting in a frantic dance with hers. Passion reared as she pushed her fingers into his hair and drew him closer. Her bare nipples ached, longed for more. He flicked them with his thumbs, and she gasped. Quivering with excitement, she held on to the feeling, this first blush of new lovemaking. What she felt with him transcended mere lust and blended seamlessly.

His head dipped and his mouth enveloped one nipple. With soft, slow licks, he tortured her flesh. Every indolent brush of wet tongue over her hardened nipples sent shockwaves raging through her body. She wriggled, writhed in his grip as soft cries of pleasure escaped her. Lil melted under his demands, her body alight with a need. She never wanted this breathless excitement to vanish.

He alternated licking and sucking her nipples, torturing with tender flicks and deep pulls. Her hips circled, instinctively seeking more contact. He inched up her dress until his hands cupped her ass. He dragged his gaze up to hers. His eyes burned with need.

"Damn." His voice lowered, hard with desire and rusty with emotion. "A thong."

She laughed softly, glad she'd worn the flimsy scrap.

She toed out of her shoes, and eased out of the thong. As her thong fell around her ankles, she stepped out of it. It had always been her fantasy to make love half-dressed.

He fingered the crevice of her ass, and she shivered as the forbidden sensation sent tingles straight to her clit. He reached between her legs from behind and touched the gathering wetness between her legs. She gasped into his mouth. Oh, my. One stroke over her hot folds, and she shimmied and ached.

Her touch searched over his broad shoulders, wanting him naked for her caresses. She unbuttoned his shirt to his waist and tested the springy hair on his chest that covered hard, defined muscles. One of his fingers brushed with delicate finesse over her clit, and she moaned. *Oh, man. Yes.* One finger sank deep between her wet, tight folds, and she gasped at the exquisite feeling. She ached for explicit and forbidden touches she'd read about but never experienced.

They couldn't turn back.

Chapter Nine

❧

As Evan's finger probed and tested, Lil's clit pebbled into a hard, aching nub. His erection pressed against her stomach, a ruthless reminder of his masculine power. Her need to feel him thrusting inside her came without mercy.

Seconds blended into minutes as his kisses plundered her mouth and his fingers tormented her wet sex with deep strokes and soft brushes. She writhed in his arms, her moans of pleasure coming faster with her gasps for breath. With a combination of touches, he drew her tight as a bow. He pinched her nipple with a featherlight touch and tweaked her clit. Muscles tightened and released, shivering on the edge of completion. All her thoughts disappeared as sensation overwhelmed. Releasing her worries, her inhibitions, she plunged into the erotic moment. Higher and higher, the pleasure rose, a consuming invader she couldn't avoid, didn't want to forget. It rose, it beat, it came at her from all sides. She moaned as it diminished the slightest bit. She whimpered.

"Take it, honey," he said softly against her ear. "Don't be afraid to let go."

She shuddered as ecstasy slammed into her unexpectedly. She tore her mouth from his as she reached for breath.

"Yes," Evan said hoarsely. "Take it, baby."

He pushed two fingers deep into her sex, and flames of pleasure pulsed deep inside her. Startled by the intensity, she gasped loudly.

She writhed and cried out, filled with a sweet, burning ecstasy that rocked her body and mind. He thrust his fingers in and out and kept his gentle plucking motion going on her nipple. Prolonged pleasure rolled through her body.

He gathered her close. "God, you're beautiful when you come."

Heat flushed her cheeks, and she buried her face against his throat.

"What you did to me…"

He laughed softly. "What did I do?"

"I've never felt… That was fantastic."

He cupped her ass, stroking and kneading. His chest moved up and down with his quicker breathing, his cock a hard reminder of his unmet needs. His hungry gaze captured hers.

"Mmmm." He grinned mischievously. "Good. Would you like another one?"

"Are you kidding? Yes."

He kissed her ear, then worked his way to the maddening spot on her neck that made her want to shiver in delight. "You know what I want to do with you?"

"Please tell me." She sighed as he nibbled her collarbone, and his fingers brushed over her nipples once more.

Melodious and deep, his voice seduced her. "I want to lick your pussy until I hear you scream, I want to suck your nipples, and then I want to take you so hard and deep you'll never forget me as long as you live."

The unvarnished truth in his words melted all defenses. She moaned and kissed him. She pushed her fingers through his hair, glorying in the silky texture. She wanted to drown in everything Evan, his scent, his touch, his strength. Cuddled against him, wrapped in his care, she cherished each second like a new beginning.

He kissed her nose, her chin. "I've got to get protection, honey."

"I'm on the Pill, and I'm healthy."

He smiled gently. "I'm healthy, too. Do you trust me?"

It didn't take a second to acknowledge intellectually what she knew in her heart. "I'd trust you with my life."

She sighed, happiness flowing over her in a sweet, wild ache. He pulled her slinky dress up over her head and walked over to place it on the couch. When he returned to her, his gaze devoured. A warm glow covered her. She stood before him naked. Her heart thumped with a madness born of primal fear. The man in front of her bristled with masculine power and intensity. He must have sensed her mild apprehension, for he gathered her close.

He caressed her back with long strokes and murmured into her hair, "Are you all right?"

She tested the muscles in his broad back, enjoying the heat of his body. "It's been a long time."

"How long?"

"I've only made love once since I divorced my husband back in college and the guy seemed to lose interest in me right after. My ex-husband Doug was...he was sort of indifferent to sex. Told me I wasn't sexy, that sort of thing." Time to confess. Let him know. "It wasn't a good situation...the sex wasn't great. I couldn't climax the few times we did make love."

Evan frowned deeply. "He tried to blame his lack of libido on you? Honey, you're the sexiest woman I've ever seen. He must have been nuts."

She smiled as gratification filled her. "Thank you. Doug was a bit of a prig. I think he actually thought making love was dirty and inconvenient."

"Christ, the guy was an idiot." He kissed her cheek. "You're so damned sexy, I want to make love to you for hours." He held her gaze, seriousness heavy in his eyes. "If you still want this."

"Oh, yes."

Hot and feral, his eyes toured from her breasts down to the dark thatch of hair at her pussy. Her belly fluttered with anticipation, her senses aching for another glorious completion. He picked her up in his arms and carried her to his bedroom. Dim light filtered in from the hallway. He allowed her to slide down the powerful length of his body. He backed away and started to strip. She watched with hunger. He drew off his clothes piece by piece. Her breathing grew faster as she watched each glorious inch of him revealed. In the dim golden glow of a bedside lamp, his chest looked broader than she remembered, his sinew and strength evident. She perused him without apology, loving it as he removed shoes and socks and then paused at the waistband of his pants. Her attention riveted to the large bulge pressing against his fly. Like a virgin, she feared and wanted. When she looked into his eyes, she didn't see cockiness or conceit. Instead, his eyes burned with stark craving. He undid his pants and drew them down with his briefs along the length of well-honed legs. Oh, yes. She'd never seen a more gorgeous man. Erect, long and thick, his cock intimidated. She knew that physically she could accommodate him, but the thought of that hard, driving heat pushing up inside her…

He strode toward her, and when he pressed his nakedness along hers, she tilted her head back and sighed. "You feel so good."

She palmed his shoulders, his arms, excited by the feel of strong biceps and crisp hair over strong forearms. She pressed her hands to his pectorals and gloried as his nipples tightened as she teased them. She smiled. His heartbeat against her fingers thrilled her on the deepest level and everything seemed more right, more real in that moment than in any other she'd known.

"We'll go slow. Easy," he said, a special huskiness in his tone.

He kissed his way down her body, pausing at her breasts to tease and suckle. He settled in to lick and torment, his fingers crimping and tugging, his mouth loving the aching tips. Shaky breaths escaped them both as he journeyed to her stomach. His hands pressed her hips. He urged her legs apart, and she knew what he wanted. He used his thumbs to open her swollen folds and reveal her clit. She closed her eyes and plunged her fingers into his hair. His tongue invaded, drawing her moisture into him as he stroked with long, lavish licks.

She twitched under the maddening feeling. He plied, massaging with his lips and tongue until her clit throbbed. She could beg him to touch her. As if he'd read her mind, he worried her clit with a teasing exploration. She jumped in his grip, another gasp coming from her throat. She groaned as he fastened his mouth over her clit and sucked hard. *Oh, shit. Oh, God.* With steady pressure, he thrust two fingers deep into her wet channel. More soft cries slipped from her throat. Back and forth, he thrust, mimicking the push and pull of cock into pussy. He sucked on her clit relentlessly.

"Evan." She moaned the word.

Her hips began a rhythm against his mouth, urging her feelings to a writhing pinnacle. Her moans filled the air as she panted and quaked, reaching ever higher. Climax teased her, rushing up from her pussy through the rest of her body. She sobbed with pleasure, her heart beating so hard she thought she'd never catch her breath.

He tipped her backwards onto the bed and came down beside her. As he looked down on her, she knew she didn't want to wait any longer to know him in the most intimate way a woman can know a man.

He petted her sopping folds, spreading her cream around her sensitive clit. Her breath hissed through her teeth.

"So swollen and tight," he said, his eyes hot.

"I don't want to wait any longer," she said on a shaky breath.

He smiled, the slumberous look in his eyes arousing her once more. "I'm at your command, Lil."

He took her hand and placed it around his cock. She met his eyes and watched his reaction with fascination. Steel-hard, his cock swelled even more under her caresses. He was as big as she'd thought, his length and thickness sure to reach her deepest pleasure spots. She rolled him onto his back and kissed him. He drew her on top of him and arched his hips into hers. She broke the kiss to trail her lips over his neck, pressing gentle affection down to his torso. She licked his nipples, eager to give him some of the pleasure he'd bestowed upon her.

As her lips caressed his nipples, and she licked and sucked, he shuddered and a breath hissed from his throat. "Lil."

She smiled and proceeded downward until she reached his erection. She clasped him in one hand, then enveloped his cock in her mouth with one plunge.

His hips jerked upward as a soft moan left his hips. "Yeah."

With relentless fervor, she took their breathless intimacy and built upon it. She worked his cock, sliding both mouth and hand up and down to an intoxicating rhythm. His fingers tightened in her hair, his breath coming fast and tight. With a low growl, he pulled her away from his cock and rolled her onto her back. As he rose above her, his strong legs parted her thighs. Passion-glazed, his eyes burned with fire for her. He kissed her and lowered his hips. His cock tested her folds, and bliss mixed with anticipation.

He feels so good. So hot and hard.

Bracing himself on his arms, he slowly pressed inside her. She clutched at his back and lifted her hips.

"Oh, shit, honey. You're so tight and hot. You feel so good," he whispered.

With steady pressure, he eased slowly and deeply inside until he pressed to the hilt. She shivered as fine tremors of delight rippled through her. Hard, thick cock, balls-deep, speared her to the hilt.

Heady joy mixed with physical pleasure as his hips started to move. Insistent friction, steady and slow, brought tingles of searing pleasure. She writhed, moved against him until their hips danced together in a scorching give and take. His thrusts stayed gentle and slow, tormenting her to the edge of reason.

"Oh, God," she whimpered as she neared the top, the joy drawing her toward paradise.

His breath rasped with hers as her heartbeat thundered in her ears. She wavered on the abyss. Her groans escalated, her abandon and surrender complete.

Yes. Yes. Oh, yes.

She exploded as fierce, scalding pleasure rocketed through her pussy and flooded the rest of her body.

Evan saw Lil's pleasure as her mouth parted and a scream of utter joy crashed over her. Blind to anything but their mutual pleasure, he thrust harder, deeper. Her silky heat gripped him so tightly he struggled to keep from exploding like an overeager teenager.

No. He would fuck her into another orgasm if it killed him. Her passion-laced cries fired his libido, and so did the way her pussy tightened and released over his cock. He pounded into her and reached for the goal. He wanted more than life to give her whatever she needed, to pleasure her until she lay exhausted and happy in his arms.

Lil's breath caught as she realized Evan hadn't reached his peak, and his steady motion kept the pleasure ebbing and flowing inside her. When he withdrew from her, she whimpered slightly in disappointment.

"Roll over on your hands and knees," he asked quietly.

She did as requested, propped on her forearms so her hips elevated high. His fingers caressed her pussy, then his thumb sank deep and withdrew. He spread her juices up to her tight rosette. She shivered at his forbidden touch, more excited than she would have imagined. No man had ever touched her this way before. His cock touched her folds, then pressed deep within. She cried out. The position felt even better. Deeper. When she felt his thumb teasing her back entrance, she gasped in delight. An itching need urged her to wriggle her hips. His thumb pushed into her tightness, and with a smooth movement, he slid all the way inside. A soft moan slipped from her at the tantalizing realization she was impaled in both entrances. She shuddered as he immediately took her, his thrusts unrelenting, his thumb a mind-blowing counterpoint. She didn't think she could come again, but as his plunging hips accelerated, she discovered each pounding thrust created renewed excitement. His cock head found a special place inside her and the friction jolted and dissolved her. Fierce, rapidly growing sensation made her reach for another pinnacle. His hips jackhammered, and she arched and bucked into the movements, chasing the rising heat. He reached under her to find her clit, and as he plucked and fondled she gasped out a plea.

"Please. God, please."

She trembled violently as the building pleasure headed for a fierce crest. Every ruthless thrust brought her closer to the edge. Ecstatic tension coiled in her violently. Her breath came in short, choppy pants. His thick hardness created a pleasure so intense she couldn't bear it.

"Come for me. Come," he rasped.

His words shattered her. She knew nothing else, reduced to a purely physical being. Orgasm came in a savage burst. She cried out, her harsh scream echoing.

"Yeah," he growled out his satisfaction.

Without mercy, he hurled her toward yet another summit.

Evan glided back and forth inside Lil, the pace of his thrusts picking up. He liked this position. Seeing his thumb buried in her beautiful ass, watching his cock tunneling her hard and deep, all of it turned him on so much he couldn't take it any longer. Her slick channel hugged him, and fine tendrils of ecstasy beckoned. Within her creamy wet embrace, his cock hardened and thickened even more. His hips pistoned between her thighs. He couldn't hold back. As she shook with need, she gasped out another orgasm. Everything inside him tightened as his body demanded a finish. Unable to resist the lure of her body rippling around his cock, he growled out his climax. He shook, he panted, he moaned as pleasure rocked him down to the foundation and yet made him whole.

* * * * *

Lil woke some time later, wide-awake in an instant. She sat straight up in bed. The room was semi-dark, light from the street outside and the partially open curtains. Instantly, she noted Evan didn't lie beside her any longer. Cool air brushed across her body. He must have turned on the air conditioning. Tangled in the sheets, she kicked them aside and allowed the refreshing air to cool her fevered flesh. She smiled, feeling fevered. Amazed.

Face it, Lil. You've been fucked out of your mind. Her body wanted more, even though their one encounter had forced three explosive orgasms from her. Insecurity stepped up and voiced worry. Where had Evan gone? She didn't hear a sound.

She glanced at the digital clock. Five o'clock in the morning.

Disturbed and restless, she left the bed. She turned on the bedside lamp, and pulled the dress over her head. She could rummage in his chest of drawers or his closet for a T-shirt and wear it like a mantle of possession. But, no. She wouldn't take that step. Not quite yet.

She left the bedroom and wandered in bare feet down the semi-dark hallway until she saw a dim light coming from the living room. Evan stood at the big window overlooking the city lights. He wore only a pair of navy shorts, which rode low on his hips. Golden light from the lamp spilled over his broad back and brought a blue-black sheen to his dark hair. Stalwart and gorgeous. God, her good fortune surprised her yet again. Her heart thudded in painful longing. If she didn't watch out, she could fall hard for him.

He turned slightly as she entered the room. A gentle smile parted his lips. "Hey. Did I wake you?"

"I don't think so. How long have you been up?"

"A half hour. I woke up and couldn't fall back to sleep."

She walked up to him, and he slipped an arm about her shoulder. She looked out at the city with him as her arm went around his waist. It felt so wonderful to share a quiet moment. If all went well, she could share hundreds more moments like this with Evan.

"Watching the city lights again?" she asked.

"Yeah. But there's something else. See that weird glow on the horizon? Maybe it's the backwash from the sun coming up, but it should be darker on the opposite horizon."

He was right. A golden and red glow, almost undetectable, rose above the distant horizon and the natural illumination caused by the electric lights.

She frowned. "That is strange. Shouldn't be northern lights. It's coming from the wrong direction."

"Yep. Couldn't be that."

"A fire?"

"Maybe."

They went silent for several moments, then she turned in his arms to look up at him. She slid her fingers up over his chest. "Evan?"

With slumberous heat simmering in his eyes, he looked down on her. "Yeah?"

"I care about you a lot. I wanted you to know that you're a special guy. What I felt last night was…"

"Incredible?"

"Yes."

He grinned. "It's never been that good with another woman. Ever."

She laughed softly. "You know, there aren't that many men as…what am I trying to say? As in touch with their feelings as you are."

He grinned, his smile cocky. "Don't tell the guys at the station that. They think I'm a real hard-ass."

"Well, I'll admit your ass is mighty hard and fine."

He smirked. "Thank you. But I meant they think I work too hard, play too little."

"So maybe you need a steady diet of relentless sex to loosen you up."

He caressed her lips with a gentle kiss. "You want to help me with that?"

His sincere words sent renewed warmth straight to her heart. He reached up and slid his fingers over her face in a tribute, his mouth mere inches from hers. She reached up and threaded her fingers through his hair, then pulled him the final inch. Their lips touched, hot and searching. A simple kiss turned scorching as he crushed her against him. Moaning softly, she accepted his tongue, taking him with heady desire. She needed him like water, like breath. Anticipation drew her closer, deeper into heady longing. She wanted the raw connection that burned between them to continue forever. The kiss grew urgent and heavy as she devoured him and he took her. She stroked his naked torso without hesitation. Kiss rolled into kiss, each caress leading to one end.

"Now. I've got to have you now," he said, his voice rasping.

His hands rucked up her dress, and found her naked ass. He moved one hand between them and gently tested her folds. "Damn, honey. You're wet."

"Sit on the couch," she said.

"Yes, ma'am."

He sat on the couch, and she straddled him. He clasped her waist, and as she slid down on him, he pumped his hips up to help her make the completion.

Her head tilted back. "Oh, Evan. God, you're so big. It feels so good."

"Good."

She'd left on her dress. The curtain of silky material around them, hiding the act, somehow made it all more sensuous. He reached up and plucked her nipples through the dress, then drew her top down so he could lean in and suckle. She arched and moaned, beginning to slide up and down on the steel-hard length buried so high up inside her.

"That's it," he whispered, his voice hoarse with sex.

She closed her eyes and clasped his shoulders, rising and falling with steady hip movements. She felt every hot inch caressing her inner walls, the torment reaching higher with each downward plunge.

Evan's hips wouldn't stay still. Her snug, sopping pussy welcomed him in a mind-melting embrace. Abandoning thought, he concentrated on the explosive feelings as he worked his cock deeply inside Lil. He braced his feet on the floor and urged her into a faster pace. Her breath came in labored pants. She strained, whimpering, and he knew she needed help this time to go over.

Tightening his grip on her waist, he thrust his hips upward hard, jamming high, encouraging her gyrations.

A moan of excitement escaped her throat. "Evan."

"That's it, honey. Fuck me. Fuck me hard."

His blatant plea set her off. Her hips moved faster, her grip on his shoulders tightened. Her hair tossed around her shoulders, a wild creature enjoying their fuck with everything she had in her. God, he loved it.

He thrust even harder.

Lil thought the searing torment would never end. She was so excited, the peak stayed out of reach. She wanted it. Needed it. Couldn't—

"Come on. Fuck me." Evan demanded, his voice harsh with sex.

His cock hit right where she needed it, his hips hammering faster.

It would only take a little more. Just a little more—

One more thrust. Two. Three.

Orgasm slammed her, a bomb of melting pleasure deep within her pussy. She screamed out her bliss, continuing to ride him to prolong the delight. She shook, her body quivering in throes of ecstasy so star-bright she gasped and sobbed for breath. Clenching and releasing in the rhythms of climax, her body milked his cock.

She felt his body bow, his hands on her waist tight, then a roar left his throat as he quivered and shook with release.

* * * * *

"I'll go back over to my apartment and get a shower and change," Lil said, wrapped in Evan's arms as they sat on the couch.

She didn't want to leave his arms, but the day wore on while they stayed in this idyllic sexual cocoon.

"I'll get cleaned up, too." She met his eyes and he smiled. "Lillian O'Hara, you are one damned sexy woman."

"I've always had a sex fiend in my body. I just needed a release for it."

His smile slipped away, replaced by a far more serious expression. "Is there more than sex between us, Lil?"

Did he mean she shouldn't be too wrapped up in him?

The damage is done. Whether I want to or not, I'm falling for him. If he means to make a tear in my heart, he'd better do it right now.

"I couldn't have been like this...this unrestrained with a man I didn't care for very much."

He caressed her cheek, the tenderness in his eyes bringing warmth to her soul. "This wasn't just a one-night thing for me."

They launched into another kiss, which fell into another and soon he laid her back on the couch and treated her to special loving. He sucked and played with her nipples for so long, Lil thought she'd come unglued. Then he settled between her legs and tongue-fucked her into another orgasm.

She lay panting, exhausted when he said, "Let's get cleaned up and then figure out what we've got planned for the day."

She sighed. "Sounds wonderful."

She returned to apartment and showered. Lil took extra time. Dressed in a body-skimming sleeveless peach top and khaki shorts, she stepped into the living room. She sat on the couch to rewind the elastic bandage around her ankle and put on her athletic shoes.

Her mind buzzed with an electric nervousness she attributed to happiness and the thought she'd spend another day with the most wonderful man she'd ever met.

A headache slammed her right between the eyebrows. She gasped and held her head.

"No. No. Not another one." She cursed as pain knifed through her temples. She gasped.

A low-grade rumble, almost like a train making slow progress through a station, started beneath her feet. Foreboding filled her.

No time between the headache and the quake this time. Not a few minutes, not a minute, not a second.

The floor vibrated, a steady building movement. Without thinking, she stood up.

She lurched to the left as the entire building seemed to move to the left. She stumbled, then righted. Tenderness in her ankle slowed her movements, but she skittered toward the coffee table. Another pitch, this one to the right, threw her to her side. She grunted with pain, her head barely missing the coffee table. Lil heard the creaking and snapping as the building gave way to tremendous pressures. *Shit, shit, shit.*

She perceived other sounds, each one more terrifying than the last. Glass shattered, the bookcases near the television set swayed and moved away from the wall with two staggering shifts. A thunderous explosion cracked the air.

Transformer outside must have blown.

She crawled toward the coffee table on her belly like a soldier under fire. She covered her head.

Another jolt hit, this one stronger and longer then the first. She lost all sense of time. Whether the shaking lasted five seconds or five minutes, she couldn't say.

A single thought repeated in her head.

Please, oh, please. Let Evan be safe.

The noise and vibration started to abate. Roaring and crashing diminished. For a few shivering, icy seconds, she registered the insane pounding of her heart. Suddenly she heard another sound, equally insistent. The clamorous cacophony of car alarms blaring. Dozens of car alarms.

Other than that, all stayed silent.

No screams, no footsteps running.

She took a gasping breath.

She'd survived.

She opened her eyes and peeked out from under the table. One bookcase had crashed against the television set and sent the television onto the floor, shattered. Books littered the area.

She inched out from under the table, her whole body trembling. She stood and bumped into the couch. Dizziness made her sway and she landed on her ass on the cushions. Fear rolled through her. God, this one had been sizable.

Evan.

She had to get to Evan's apartment.

She started to stand and heard a loud cracking.

Before she could take one step, the bottom dropped out of her world, and she screamed.

Chapter Ten

ဆ

A scream echoed loud in Lil's head, and she jerked from unconsciousness with a gasp. Her eyes snapped open as pain lacerated her skull. Icy water dripped onto her face and ran in rivulets down her body in several places. She quivered.

Had she screamed? No. This sounded like it came from outside.

Her breath hissed through her teeth as she waited for pinpoints of pain to subside. With a startled flash of recognition, she noticed her surroundings. Something hard and unforgiving poked her in the back, and she realized she rested on a cold, stone-hard surface. She lay in semi-darkness among chaotic destruction. Light speared down from a gap in the tangled building remnants. Boards crisscrossed over her vision, blocking much of the blessed light. Water dripped from the hole, but she heard it trickling from somewhere else, too. Sirens wailed in the distance, and she thought she heard crying, shouting.

Then, as if her brain had been shocked into realizing the truth, a great fear rose up inside.

Collapse. The exterior walls looked intact, but obviously, the interior had fallen.

She'd survived.

How?

Evan. Oh, God. Evan.

She opened her mouth to cry out, but sound emerged as a whimper, a dry rasp of incomprehensible fear.

She had to move. Had to get out of there. Had to find Evan.

The throb in her skull dulled. An ache burned her throat. She moved her arms and legs in experimentation. No pain.

Glass gritted beneath her fingers. Broken masonry, plaster, bricks and boards littered her space. She glanced around the walls and it came to her in a flash. She stood, her legs unsteady.

"Holy shit," she whispered. "It's the basement."

"Lil?" A hoarse male voice reached her ears.

"Evan?" She barely managed a croak. "Evan!"

"Lil!"

She heard creaking and shifting high above and glanced skyward.

"Easy. Just stay right there," Evan said, his voice echoing.

She trembled, then took a steadying breath. She looked to the right, squinting into the gloom. A dark form materialized.

"Evan?" She sounded raspy, foreign in her ears. "Where are you?"

His solid body appeared from the shadows, turning from a formless shape to strength. He crawled over boards, then between two slabs of flooring.

Eyes wide with either disbelief or relief, he stalked toward her, tottering as he climbed over debris. His mouth twisted with either pain or strong emotion.

"Thank God, Lil."

He pulled her into his arms. A single, wretched sob left her throat as she threw her arms around his neck. His bear hug told her everything she needed to know. His hands smoothed up and down her back, the caresses reassuring. She buried her face in his shoulder, and his fingers laced into her hair. Absorbing his warmth, she tried to still the dizzying pace. Her heart skittered wildly and her body shivered. Despite the heat outside, the basement was dank and cold. Water spilled in slowly around their feet.

The dried blood on his forehead reminded Lil how serious their fall had been, and how miraculous their survival. "We should be dead."

He cupped her face. "Honey, tell me you're not hurt."

"I'm not hurt." She managed a wobbly grin.

His thumbs caressed her cheeks, his touch so comforting. "You're not just saying that to be brave?"

"No. I'm fine."

Lil shivered as reaction quivered through her body. She didn't want to give in to more fear. When she smelled smoke, she gazed up at him with concern.

"Is that smoke I smell?"

"Yeah." He sounded grave, obviously unwilling to deny what could be a serious problem.

A horrifying thought came to her. "God, I hope someone has shut off the gas. If they can. Do you think everyone besides us is…"

"Dead?" he asked softly.

"Yes."

"There are only twelve apartments in this building. There's a good chance most people left for work already. Let's keep a good thought."

She nodded, hoping he was right.

He released her only enough to hold her by the shoulders. "We've got one thing going for us."

"What?"

"I saw the maintenance man the other day and asked him whether the building had an emergency gas shut-off valve and he said yes."

"Thank God for small favors."

She hugged him fiercely for a few frantic seconds, then pulled back. Blood dripped from a cut on his forehead, and dirt and blood marred his shirt. His expression worried her.

"Do I look that bad?" Her voice warbled as tears surged into her eyes.

A crooked, heartfelt grin covered his mouth. "You're the most beautiful thing I've ever seen. When I woke up a few minutes ago, all I could think about was getting to you. And when we get out of here—hey, it's all right…"

Tears escaped, and she didn't try to stop them. She brushed away a trickle of blood drying on his cheek. "We survived something we shouldn't have. We fell into the basement."

"Yeah. Fucking miraculous. But right now I want to concentrate on how we can get out of here." He glanced at the opening above. "That's a long way up."

She shivered, and he drew her close. "Have you seen anyone else?"

He nodded, expression grave. "Cynthia. She's… I saw her in a corner over there. She's dead, Lil."

A heavy ache settled in her heart. "No."

He slipped his fingers into the hair at the back of her neck. "It was quick." His gaze intensified. "Are you sure you're not hurt?"

She shook her head rapidly. "I'm all right."

"Adrenaline can mask injury."

"I'm fine. What about you?"

He drew her closer and hugged her. He buried his face in her hair. "I'll be perfect when we get out of here."

A headache blossomed in her already aching temples. "No, oh damn. Evan, it's going to happen again—"

The aftershock rumbled and the wreckage far above them trembled precariously. He edged her away from the hole and covered her head with his arms. The shaking lasted a couple of seconds, and she heard the rattle of a couple of bricks as they fell into the opening and landed on the basement floor. All she could hear was their rasping breaths and the steady pounding of her heart.

She looked up and frowned. "Evan…we can't climb out of here."

He nodded. "You're right. We can't. The stairway up is blocked with bricks."

"There's the entrance that comes out at street level."

"I'll take a look around and see if it's obstructed. Stay here."

She shivered as she waited for him to search. In the semi-gloom, she saw him look back. "The door is unblocked on this side."

"Should we try and open it?"

"If I try and open it, it might cause more debris to come down. But we need to get out of here as soon as possible."

She heard the door squeak open part of the way. "Be careful."

"I've got it open."

She moved forward eagerly. "That's great."

"But it won't open all the way. There must be something holding it partway shut. It's not big enough for either one of us to get through."

"Damn it."

"Hey! Can anybody hear us? We're trapped in the basement! Hey!" His shouts echoed in the basement.

She joined him at the doorway, drinking in the blessed smell of fresh air. At the same time, she smelled something that frightened her to the core. "Oh, God. Is that smoke I smell?"

"Yeah." He looked through the small crack. "I can just see smoke coming from a building down the street. We're not on fire. But the fire should draw Station One." Hope sounded in his voice. "They'll get to us."

They resumed yelling, and within less then five minutes, a man appeared at the top of the half blocked stairs leading up from the basement door. "Hey there!"

"Can you let 911 know we're trapped in here?" Evan asked.

"No problem! The fire department is on the way for the building down the street. Things are a royal freaking mess. I didn't think anybody was alive under here. No one else has come out of the building."

"We're lucky to be alive," Evan said.

The man left with promises to alert authorities.

Evan slipped his arm around her shoulders and they sank down on a clear spot near the doorway. "All we can do is wait for help now."

"God, I can't believe this is happening."

His gaze warmed, filled with desperate emotion. "I don't want to alarm you, but there's still a chance this building could fall the rest of the way."

Fear sizzled up her spine. "I guessed that. It's a miracle we both made it. It doesn't sound like anyone else in the complex did."

He kissed her forehead. "It'll be all right."

He tilted her chin up and looked into her eyes. He searched through her hair with both hands.

"What are you doing?" she asked.

"Looking for a head injury. We both were knocked out." He finished his cursory examination. "You seem okay. Any double vision? Dizziness?"

"No. My head doesn't even hurt anymore. In fact, I'm so wired I could about come out of my skin."

"I know the feeling." He paused and the silence drew out. "Damn it. I can't fucking believe this is happening."

She put her index finger over his lip. "Shhh. Like you said, we're getting out of here."

His gaze, when it came back to her, held a fierce determination. "There are things you need to know."

Concerned by his expression, she said, "All right. I'll make it fair. After you do your confessional, I'll do mine."

"It's a deal. I'll tell you anything you want to know."

She took the plunge. "What happened with Lani?"

"We met two years ago at a picnic the fire department designed as a fundraiser for our firefighters' fund. If a family is burned out, the fund helps them."

"That's wonderful."

"Fire departments around the country use them. Lani's father is prosecutor for the county, and influential. He comes from old money. Lani had finished her Masters in Criminal Justice and planned to work for the county, too. She was smart and funny and beautiful."

"And you dated for a year?"

"A year and two months. We both liked to spend time outdoors, but I also like my quiet time. We were like oil and water, her on the go all the time, me wanting to slow down. The contrasts kept it interesting, until I started to see the real Lani. She called me selfish whenever I wanted some chill time to read or listen to music. She insisted on partying."

Lil winced. "I had that same problem with some friends a long time ago until I put my foot down."

He slipped a hand onto her upper back, his hot palm against her bare skin. His fingers massaged in a sensual contrast to his words. "That's what I did. One night we were coming back from a party. She told me she wanted to go to another party. I was tired as hell. I'd just gotten off three long days of work. Even though she hadn't been drinking, she drove fast. I told her to slow down, but she sped up and told me to stop bossing her around. The road was slick as hell from rain. We were on Old Canal Road in the mountains."

Lil sensed tragedy coming up in his words, but she stayed quiet.

"Lani was so busy ranting she didn't pay attention to the road. She drifted into the other lane. A semi barreled toward us and when—" He stopped, his hand tightening on hers. "She corrected, but she hit a patch of water and we careened right through the guardrail."

"Oh no," Lil murmured.

"We hit the reservoir going about sixty."

Anguish played over Evan's features as he replayed that night.

"The car stayed upright in the water, but Lani was unconscious, and I'd hit my head pretty hard. I had trouble staying conscious," Evan said, his gaze pinned to hers. "I unbuckled her seatbelt just before we sank like a stone."

Sharp horror mixed with his pain. She placed one hand on his thigh. "Oh, my God."

He closed his eyes, as if doing so would remove the picture forming in his mind. "I pulled her out of the car and to shore, but by that time…"

Warm, hard heat pressed her fingers as he laid his hand over hers.

"She had a skull fracture. She'd died before she could drown," he said.

She edged around, reaching up to palm his hair-roughened jaw as she murmured sympathy. "I can't imagine what you went through."

She allowed her hand to trail over his jaw, and he grasped her hand and kissed her fingers. When he released her, she saw his gaze held remorse so deep she wondered if he'd ever vanquish the pain raging inside.

"Another passerby called 911. When the emergency vehicles arrived, I felt like hell. I was almost hypothermic and had cracked some ribs. Then to top off the humiliation and horror, I passed out. Fell right on my face."

"You were hurt and you'd lost someone you cared about."

He nodded. "Being a paramedic, I sometimes feel I don't have the right to be sick or hurt. Weird, eh?"

"Not so weird. That's how I sometimes feel. It's almost embarrassing when you're on the receiving end of medical attention. Like you're supposed to be invincible."

His gaze lightened with appreciation. "That's exactly it."

Well-bottled emotions flickered in his eyes, tempting her to probe deeper. "The accident was a year ago?"

"Yes."

"And the month-long leave is because of the accident, right?"

Darkness haunted his soulful, turbulent gaze as he looked at her. "I went back to work without taking advantage of the post-traumatic stress counseling. That was one of my first mistakes."

"Were people pressing you to get over the grief?"

His fingers rubbed hers as gently as if he comforted her. "No. That's just it. I didn't feel grief. I felt regret, anger at her for getting us into the accident. I got along great with Lani's parents until then. They'd always said how much they liked me. I think they knew Lani was interested in me because I was a firefighter."

She caressed his back. "And because you're good-looking."

He flicked a half smile her way. "Yeah, right."

He sounded doubtful.

"You are. So you didn't get along with her parents anymore?"

"They blamed me for the entire thing."

She scowled. "You're not serious."

"As serious as I can be."

She sighed in disgust. "How could they blame you?"

"Maybe grief. They coddled her. As an only child, she had them tied around her little finger. They really believed she could do no wrong."

"Did you agree?"

He snorted. "No. She was…hot. Gorgeous blonde with long legs and seductive. She was smart, funny and worked hard at her job at the police department. It took a bit of time to come to grips with her deceit, and her self-esteem sucked. She came off as confident because she compensated in other ways. Deep down she didn't think she was worth it. She started playing with me...dangling other men in front of me to make me jealous when she thought I wasn't paying enough attention to her." He turned his gaze on Lil. "I don't know. Maybe I wasn't paying as much attention because I'd lost interest."

"Once you discovered the real Lani."

He sat up straight, his eyes deep with consternation. "That was one of the things I hated the most. I let myself be sucked into a relationship that wasn't good for me or her."

She wanted to comfort him, to bring to life the warmth and hunger she'd seen in his eyes for her. "You never would have guessed her parents would treat you the way they did."

His attention riveted on her, curiosity in his face. "It came as a nasty surprise. They won't speak to me to this day."

The desire to comfort him rose inside her. "I can imagine it hurts you."

"It did, but I'm over that. I took extra leave because it hit me one day I'd stressed out over things that never used to bother me. I need this time to see if I can ever return to firefighting again."

Hurt deepened inside. "Your confidence was shattered by the accident?"

"Yes. I should have dealt with my feelings from the beginning. I didn't, and now I'm paying for it."

"You'll get through it."

"Will I? Somehow the accident and taking to heart what Lani's parents said hurt me more than I realized."

"You can't believe that they were right?"

"At first I did. It took a good week of talking to my friends to get me through the guilt. But there's still a little part of me that doesn't quite want to give myself slack. I have to find my way back...or give it up for something else."

She couldn't say a word, knowing whatever she said wouldn't bring his confidence back. Only Evan could resurrect his love for firefighting.

Another thought came to mind. "You're already finding your way out. There's nothing stopping you from healing and finding your way back to firefighting if it's what you truly want."

Concern flashed in the dark depths of his eyes. "My father doesn't help the situation."

She shook her head. "I couldn't believe he was talking to you that way in front of us. In my family we disagreed almost politely."

He laughed softly. "I'd like to see that."

She sighed. "No. You can't see it. I can't see it ever again."

She didn't want to sound pitiful, but her words formed that way.

Silence dominated until he ventured to speak again. "I'm spilling my guts out here, but I know you have secrets."

She craved to tell him more, to allow her past freedom by exposing it. "Mine is far less serious. I don't believe in navel gazing forever."

He brushed hair away from her eyes. "Is that what you think we're doing now? Wallowing in self-pity?"

"I don't see you as that kind of man. You're telling me what happened to you. Sharing yourself with me. Facing up to demons is hard work, isn't it?"

"Hardest thing I've done."

"There's part of you that wants control, that believes you can change events you have no control over."

He looked startled, but not that she'd dared say it. But as if an epiphany hit him with the force of a rocket explosion. Her mouth opened, but nothing came out at first. Then...

"You wonder how I knew. How I can connect with you so closely...that I can tell what you're thinking?" she asked.

He reached out and gathered her hands in his. "When you said the words, I understood they were true. I've been holding on too damn hard. Wanting to fix what can't be fixed, repair relationships that can't be resurrected."

She cherished the callused clasp of his fingers over hers. Tenderness filled his eyes, and she quivered deep inside with longing.

His voice came softer, lower than she expected after a revelation. "Do you know so much about this type of thing from seeing other's problems, or is it your own sorrow that makes it so easy to see in someone else?"

He brushed his thumb repeatedly over the back of her hand.

"Both," Lil said. "I've been trying to change but nothing so far set me off. You know how people sometimes don't make personal improvements until a nasty situation comes along and forces them to do it? That's me right now. So yes, I can, as the cliché says, feel your pain. Literally and figuratively. The earthquake headaches have a byproduct. Whenever I'm in a zone where there is seismic activity, I get flashes of extra-strength intuition. I often feel things stronger. I can get too sensitive and allow things to bother me."

His fingers caressed her palm and the light flick of skin against skin caused her breath to catch. They could be knee-deep in heavy conversation and disaster and this man fired up her libido faster than a hummingbird's heartbeat.

Outside the shriek of sirens grew loud, and she heard the sound of fire trucks and police cars coming to a halt down the street. "It sounds like they're near."

He stood and looked out the crack. "I can barely see them down the street, but that man who said he'd help us is running toward them." He sighed. "We'll give them a chance to work on the fire."

"I hope no one is trapped in that old building," she said.

He sat down beside her again, but didn't speak for a good half minute. "You never explained why you didn't pursue seismology as a career. Did an inner demon take your dream away?"

"I've fought the demon for years. I haven't found a way around it yet."

She took comfort in his body near hers and pretended in a flash of fantasy that they would always remain this way. Nice thought, if unrealistic.

"Have you talked about it?" he asked.

"What's holding me back?"

"Yes."

God, she so wanted to believe in something beyond the tedium of daily life. "I was always a cautious kid, which doesn't make much sense. My parents took me with them to volcano sites when I was a teen, but not before. They knew if anything went wrong and the volcano decided to wake up…well, you get the picture. They never pressured me to take up science. In fact, they discouraged me in a subtle way. Mom was overprotective, which I always thought was odd considering the risks she took on her job. They did go hiking and fishing and even rock climbing with me after I put up a big fuss that I wanted to experience the outdoors." Her voice rose with passion. "I've always had this inherent excitement inside me for completing a huge challenge, but I've had so few. My dad once told me taking a big step to see whether we survive or fail is important. At least once in my life I want to rise to the bar and limbo right under it."

"Mmm. Good analogy," he said as he pressed a kiss to her hair and slid both arms around her so she pressed against his side. "You told me that as a kid you failed at things. Is that why you believe you're not good enough to be a geologist or a seismologist?"

Acknowledging shortcomings came easily to her, but she didn't like the sound of them now. "I'm sure that's part of it."

She laughed without humor. "The other part is…what happened to my parents."

She heard his indrawn breath, like a man fearing the answer, awaiting a tragedy he knew would come but couldn't avert. "When I was in business school playing it safe, my parents were killed by a volcano in South America. A pyroclastic flow came through and incinerated their equipment, their vehicle, and them."

An ache gathered at the back of her throat.

"Is that when you lost your desire to be a scientist?" His body nestled closer, his hard muscles cradling her with care. "Are you sure you want to give up on your dream that quickly?"

She shifted, but he didn't loosen his embrace. "Not anymore. I think what I've found with you…what's happened today has changed my mind."

"We've made it this far." He cupped her face and plied her with his soul-melting eyes. "If you don't want to stay involved with a guy who has too much baggage, then I'll understand."

"You don't have too much baggage." She scoffed. "You're human and courageous. You're fighting through a horrible event and it took you time to find your way. Most of us are like that. And here we are…surviving something else. Tragedy scarred us, but we're healing. We're moving on."

"There you go," he said gently, his mouth persuasive as he kissed her forehead. "What about your ex-husband? It sounds like he messed with your head."

She nodded. "I was only twenty when we married, and he was twenty-seven. A perpetual student in geology. I worshipped his knowledge. I think he thought he was marrying a shrinking violet." She laughed softly. "Little did he know. I might have been immature and lacking experience, but I wasn't stupid. He ridiculed my high sex drive, he ridiculed my wishes. He didn't encourage me to continue my studies in seismology. It was an all-around mess. Since then I've been a little bit wary of starting up anything serious with another man. I guess I've been broadcasting a message that says stay away."

He smiled. "Not to me you weren't." He kissed her. "I'm going to wipe away every memory you have of that creep."

She laughed. "I think you're well on your way already."

"Denver Fire Department!" A gruff voice bellowed from outside. "Are you in there, Murdoch?"

Evan recognized the voice, and energy spiked through him. "Hey, Jerry!"

"Evan! We're going to get you out of there, buddy. Just hang on."

"We're outta here," he said with triumph in his voice. "We're going to be fine."

And as more firefighters from Station One gathered at the door, serious and yet joking with their buddy, she knew he was right.

Epilogue

"Do you think you could do that again?" Lil asked. "A little higher this time. Oh, God. Yeah. That feels good. Oh, wow. More."

"Mmm," Evan's deep voice said. "You can do that to me next."

Lil smiled, amazed that after several hours of stress and chaos, they'd escaped Denver for sanctuary. Darkness long ago settled over the Pueblo area, and within the quiet of Evan's father's house, they enjoyed a little bit of peace.

Once the firefighters extracted them from the basement and they'd been checked for injuries, Evan and Lil knew they could do little else to help. They discovered no one other than Cynthia had lost their lives in the collapse. There had been a couple of serious injuries, but most people rode out the shaker at work or other parts of the city. The magnitude of the quake came in at around six-point-two. Damage and injuries were widespread around the city, but Lil knew it could have been much worse. They'd suffered numerous aftershocks and resulting damage from those compounded the problem. A few of the brick buildings and Victorian homes in other parts of the city also suffered collapse damage, many brick chimneys had fallen.

Lil was gratified by the way people hung together. Trosky had expressed extreme relief when he heard from her, and Evan's father and Chandra had been beside themselves when they finally heard from Evan. Later in the afternoon, they'd taken their cars through snarled traffic and eventually arrived in Pueblo. Lil cried when Arthur and Chandra embraced her and Evan with enthusiastic hugs. Despite bumps, strained muscles and numerous bruises, she felt on top of the world. A litany ran through her head, bringing her to a peak experience she would never have expected after a traumatic event.

I'm alive, and I'm here.

Evan and Lil now lay on the king-size bed in the guest room suite, and Lil allowed her lips to linger in sensitive areas over his skin.

"Damn, that feels good," Evan said as Lil kissed her way down Evan's freshly showered body. "I thought I would fall over and sleep when we got here, but you're giving me ideas."

She gave him a wicked grin. "I hope so."

His cock, hard and ready, tantalized her beyond bearing. She wanted to show him her growing affection and love in the most elemental way a woman could.

He drew her close until she lay on top of him. "This is crazy, and I don't want to scare you, but I've got to tell you something."

"I don't think after today anything could scare me again."

He plunged his fingers into her hair, his gaze intent. "I feel the same way. We've been given a new chance, a fresh slate. Our apartments are trashed, most of our belongings are destroyed."

Tears sprung to her eyes. "I regret losing things like my family photographs, but I've decided there's a way I can keep their memory alive and sacred."

He smiled gently. "How's that?"

"I'm going to stop denying who I am and become what I'm supposed to be. I'm not going to hide my headaches. I'm returning to college, get my degree, and become a seismologist so I have the credentials to do what I want."

A fervent glow entered his eyes. "That's wonderful." He kissed her, his mouth treasuring with the most exquisite kiss. When he released her, he said, "Being with you made me think about where I want my life to go. At the end of the next three weeks, I'm going back to firefighting. When we made it out of the building, I could barely restrain myself. The hunger to get in there and help, to assist putting out the fire down the street—hell—it was all there. And I know that what I've got with you is more than I ever had with Lani. I've let her and the guilt go. I want to be with you."

Happy tears spilled from her eyes. "What should be one of the worst days of my life is also one of the happiest."

"Come here."

His hoarse demand, added to the heated expression in his eyes, fired her libido. Aches and anxiety aside, she needed this connection, the passion and caring she saw within his eyes.

He turned her so that he spooned behind her. With one solid, determined thrust, he pushed each large, solid inch of cock deep inside Lil. She groaned as his heat spread her walls, caressing as he started a rhythm. He rubbed her clit and with his other hand, he tugged her nipples into hard, desperately aroused points. She gasped and wriggled, impaling herself more deeply on his cock. Her body contracted over him, massaging and squeezing as a climax threatened to erupt. Evan's touch tormented her nipples, his light touch on her clit driving Lil into a frenzy of arousal.

As his slow pumping drew her to the top, the excitement became unbearable. She heard their panting breaths and felt the bunching and flexing of muscles working to bring them to a finish.

Evan couldn't think, his heart pounding madly, his body working to give her the most pleasure. He pulled and tugged on her nipples and worked her sensitive clit. His cock, encased in her liquid, tight heat, throbbed with impatience. He couldn't take it any longer. As her panting, sobbing breaths came stronger, his arousal spiraled out of control.

With a cry of surprise and delight, she climaxed hard, and her pleasure made him happier than anything he could imagine.

Lightning sizzled through her as deep, rippling contractions clenched and released over his thrusting cock.

He shoved hard and with a low growl, he stiffened and shuddered in release.

And as they stayed nested together, Lil knew it would be for a lifetime.

They'd celebrated life in the truest way a man and woman ever could.

The End

Also by Denise A Agnew

୫

By Honor Bound *(anthology)*
Dangerous Intentions
Deep is the Night: Dark Fire
Deep is the Night: Haunted Souls
Deep is the Night: Night Watch
Ellora's Cavemen: Dreams of the Oasis II *(anthology)*
Ellora's Cavemen: Tales From the Temple IV *(anthology)*
Meant to Be *(Cerridwen Press)*
Special Investigations Agency: Hideaway
Special Investigations Agency: Impetuous
Special Investigations Agency: Jungle Fever
Special Investigations Agency: Over the Line
Special Investigations Agency: Primordial
Special Investigations Agency: Shadows and Ruins
Special Investigations Agency: Sins and Secrets
Special Investigations Agency: Special Agent Santa
The Dare
Treacherous Wishes
Winter Warriors *(anthology)*

About the Author

೮౿

Suspenseful, erotic, edgy, thrilling, romantic, adventurous. All these words are used to describe award-winning, best-selling novelist Denise A. Agnew's novels. Romantic Times Magazine called her romantic suspense novels *Dangerous Intentions* and *Treacherous Wishes* "top-notch romantic suspense." With paranormal, time travel, romantic comedy, contemporary, historical, erotica, and romantic suspense novels under her belt, she proves her gift for writing about a diverse range of subjects. (Writing tales that scare the reader is her ultimate thrill.)

Denise's inspiration for her novels comes from innumerable sources, but the fact she has lived in Colorado, Hawaii, and the United Kingdom has given her a lifetime of ideas. Her experiences with archaeology have crept into her work, as well as numerous travels throughout England, Ireland, Scotland, and Wales. Denise currently lives in Arizona with her real life hero, her husband.

Denise welcomes comments from readers. You can find her website and email address on her author bio page at www.ellorascave.com.

Trademarks Acknowledgement

The author acknowledges the trademarked status and trademark owners of the following wordmarks mentioned in this work of fiction:

Barbie: Mattel, Inc.

Battleship: Hasbro, Inc.

Clue: Hasbro, Inc.

Ford Taurus: Ford Motor Company

Monopoly: Hasbro, Inc.

MAKE THAT MAN MINE

Shelley Munro

ॐ

Chapter One

ဆာ

"Good morning, George Taniwha & Co." Emma forced a bright smile and hoped her despondency didn't crawl down the telephone line. Twenty-five years old today. *Twenty-five!* And she still hadn't plucked up the courage to approach Jack Sullivan and ask him out on a date—despite this being the age of equal opportunity. The man in question sauntered past her desk and strode into George Taniwha's office, shutting the door firmly without giving her a second glance. A man to die for…

Emma sighed and stared at the bronze nameplate on the door in frustration. So, she wasn't the most beautiful woman in New Zealand. She was built with the word generous in mind. A large ass and a chest made to house her big heart. Or at least that's what her high school boyfriend had informed her. He'd also told her she had a nice smile and that he enjoyed being with her because she didn't stress about her size. Yep, she was a normal, healthy woman—kind to animals and small children. Most people liked her, yet the wretched man of her dreams didn't acknowledge her existence.

"Are you there, young lady?"

The querulous voice jerked Emma from her grievances about a lack of sex life back to her phone call. "I'm sorry. I had to sign for a courier parcel," she fibbed. "How can I help you?"

"My name is Elisa Denning. I need the services of a private investigator. Someone is stealing my prize rose blooms. Right before the flower show, too."

"Let me take some details, then I'll arrange for an investigator to come and see you," Emma said. "Address? Telephone number?" She jotted the woman's particulars down, an imp inside her laughing as she imagined George assigning this case. None of the men would appreciate chasing a rose thief. George Taniwha's operatives preferred the dangerous stuff that challenged them and proved they were men.

Her humor died, replaced by a frown that drew her brows together. That was another thing she wanted to change. She'd passed all her private investigator exams. George had promised her she would be able to take on cases. Soon. Perhaps she could start with this case. Never let it be said that Emma Montrose didn't have ambition.

"When can I expect someone?" the elderly lady questioned. "I'm sure it's Mrs. Gibb's grandson, but the police won't do anything."

"An investigator will contact you tomorrow morning, Mrs. Denning."

"Excellent. Tomorrow is my baking day. I'll make them a cup of tea when they arrive."

Emma couldn't restrain a grin as a vision of one of George's tough he-man investigators drinking tea from a bone china cup popped into her mind. "I'm sure they'll enjoy a cup of tea. Thanks, Mrs. Denning." She disconnected the phone and typed up two letters while she waited for Jack to leave George's office. She was smitten enough to want to gaze her fill as he left since the man had a truly fine butt. The hands of the clock moved slowly, and still Jack didn't appear. Reluctantly, Emma stood and packed up for the day. She picked up her bag and couldn't prevent a glance toward the closed door, looking for the tall, dark-haired man of her dreams. Oh, yeah. No doubt about it. She was a sad, sad woman.

* * * * *

"I have a case for you," George said.

Something about his boss's tone made Jack cautious. "Yeah?"

"Sports-enhancing drugs. Rumor says there's a ring operating out of the Mahoney Resort on Waiheke Island in the Hauraki Gulf. I want you check it out."

"And?" Jack's gut told him there was more to the story. The glint of humor in George's eyes confirmed it.

"I've assigned you a partner."

Jack straightened from his casual sprawl against the wall, his eyes narrowing on George. "I work alone. I don't work with a partner." His last partner had died. Horribly. And he lived with that guilt. He wasn't damn well having another partner he might come to like.

"You can't do this job alone."

"Why not?" Jack demanded. "I've managed every other job on my own."

George leaned back in his chair, steepling his fingers and looking over the top in a thoughtful manner. "This one might be a little difficult. Reuben J. Mahoney is a slippery character." The chair squeaked a protest each time he shifted his weight.

"I can handle anything he throws at me."

George glanced at the calendar pinned on the wall then cast his attention back to Jack. "There's a blue moon coming up. It might fall before the mission is completed."

Jack filled in the blanks. The blue moon would erode his powers and make it difficult to remain in human form. Without constant sexual stimulation, he'd shift into a taniwha, the legendary monster from Maori mythology. Jack snorted at the thought of being trapped in taniwha form in the middle of a mission. It had happened to other shifters on George Taniwha's staff but not to him. He imagined the pandemonium if a change occurred in the middle of the bustling resort. His lips curled in disdain.

Little did New Zealanders know, but the species taniwha survived and lived among them. Jack didn't intend to be the first taniwha to make headlines in the *New Zealand Herald*. No way.

No how. If he had to find a woman to keep the monster at bay, then that's what he'd do.

"Okay," he conceded. "I guess a partner might help. Who's available? Hone? Billy?"

George made a choking sound, merriment dancing across his lined face as he stuck his feet up on his desk.

"What's so goddamned amusing?" Jack ground out. Another chortle exploded from George.

Jack bounded upright and paced the length of the room trying to work off the agitation that thrummed through his body. He paused to stare out the window, his mind taking in the yachts that zigzagged across blue waters of Auckland Harbor. Jack turned away from the window and stalked across the room to drop into the chair opposite George. He kept his expression neutral despite the amusement that still simmered across his boss's face. "You'd better let me in on the joke."

"You can partner up with Hone or Billy, if you want," George said. "But you might want to consider the special circumstances."

"What circumstances?" Jack bit out. Man, he had a hot date with Melissa tonight. Good, hot, sweaty, no-strings sex. He didn't have time for this crap. "Either Hone or Billy. I'm not fussy."

"Reuben J. Mahoney runs a couples only resort. I'm assigning you a female partner."

"A female— *No.*"

"I guess you can take Hone. Or Billy," George mused. "Of course, you'd have to share a room. And a bed." He shook his grizzled head. "Two taniwha in the same room. Add in a blue moon and things might get a mite ugly."

Fuck. Jack sent a hard glare at his boss. Trapped as neat as an eel in a net. Jack shuffled through the range of possibilities and came up blank. "Who is she?" he gritted out.

"A new operative."

Great. *Just bloody great.* Not only was he being forced to take a female partner, he was getting a raw beginner. Jack didn't trust himself to speak so he firmed his mouth, folded his arms across his chest and scowled his displeasure.

"I'm teaming you with Emma Montrose."

"Your secretary?" Jack heard disbelief in his voice but thought he managed to keep his panic to himself. What the hell did a secretary know about investigating a case? What about the danger? To both of them. They would have to share a room for God's sake. Jack refused to let his mind dwell on Emma's sexy legs…or the rest of her body.

"Emma's capable of assisting you on this case."

"Assign me another case." Spending time alone with Emma was enough to give a man ideas. Jack wasn't interested in anything but sex. No relationships for him. Been there. Done that. Chucked away the T-shirt.

Nope. It was best he kept well away from the very curvy, brown-haired Emma Montrose. Every time he came into the office, her big blue eyes trailed after him like some pet dog. Except instinct told him, she had more in mind than stroking or petting. That was part of what made him so edgy whenever he was in the same room. A woman like Emma wanted happily-ever-after. Jack didn't want that. Not anymore. Some of the taniwha, like George, were happily married, but finding a woman comfortable with her man turning into a water monster wasn't easy. It was a rare female who could cope with the idea that her children might carry the taniwha gene. Or might not, depending on fate. The peculiarities of the taniwha species had rattled his ex-lover. She hadn't been able to cope with his ugly appearance and had run despite his assurances that she would always remain human. He hadn't even reached the part about taniwha living longer—about thirty years longer—than the average human before she'd run.

"Did you say share a room?" Jack ignored the interested twitch from his cock.

"And a bed," George said without inflection. "But if you don't think you can act as part of a couple with Emma, I'll send Hone. He's due off assignment tomorrow."

Jack thought about that for all of two seconds. He'd seen the way Hone looked at Emma. "I'll do it," he said, even though deep down in his gut, he knew he'd come to regret this decision. "Give me the details."

* * * * *

Emma marched into the offices of George Taniwha & Co. the next morning, a woman with a mission. After spending her twenty-fifth birthday with her girlfriends and not one man in sight, she'd come up with a resolution. With the help of her tipsy friends, she'd decided to go for it.

Get Jack Sullivan to notice her or bust.

A smile—was that too much to ask for? No, dammit, it wasn't. And that would be just the start. She intended to progress from there—from a smile and good morning to down and dirty sex. Her breasts tingled at the thought and a swooping sensation spiraled through her lower belly. Of course, she wouldn't go as far as stalking the man, but she wasn't going to be a shy little wallflower either. Emma Montrose was coming out of the shade and going after the man she wanted. She was going to act like the fictional taniwha on George Taniwha & Co.'s letterhead—formidable and determined, ready to scare Jack into thinking her way. By the time she was finished, he was going to know she was interested. Then he could take the next step.

She drew herself up. *No.* That wasn't right. She wasn't letting him slide out of her sights without a fight. She'd take the second and third steps and as many other steps as the situation required.

Emma pushed aside several possible scenarios, concentrating on and visualizing the one she wanted. A secret smile curled across her lips as she fluffed her short curly hair.

Two lovers.

Emma and Jack.

Horizontal dancing.

Heat seeped into her face at the thought. Emma yanked out her office wheelie chair, plonked her butt on it then grabbed up a pile of envelopes off the desk to fan her face. This brave new Emma might embarrass her a little, but she'd try to keep up.

The front door of the office opened, and Emma straightened abruptly, her backbone hitting the back of the chair. *Well.* No time like the present to put her plan into action.

Emma put her best receptionist manner into practice and flashed a smile. "Good morning, Jack."

The man froze like a possum in headlights, giving Emma the opportunity to look her fill. He was tall and built like a rower with powerful shoulders, slim hips and a butt that she'd really like to get her hands on. His hair was shiny black, halfway between short and long and in need of a cut, making her fingers itch to smooth the messy strands away from his face. A dreamy sigh squeezed past her lips. The man was blessed with sun-kissed skin, no matter what the season. She often wondered what he looked like beneath the layers of clothing. Did the gorgeous olive tones that were a legacy from his Maori ancestors extend all over his body? Hopefully she'd be in a position of knowledge soon.

"Morning."

The word came out as a grunt, but it was a definite improvement on being treated as part of the office furniture. Emma forced away the sudden surge of nerves and looked him straight in the eye. "Are you here to see George?"

"Yeah."

"Okay." Emma's breath caught, her lungs filling with his seductive scent—something that reminded her of the mystical Orient with hints of orange and patchouli and a healthy dose of masculine musk. Emma found herself staring. Holding his gaze felt like poking her finger into a hot fire. Dangerous. Crazy. A challenge. Sorta made a girl wonder what it would feel like to have him thrust deep in her womb. A sensuous shiver swept through her body and arousal soaked her panties without warning.

Emma gulped and licked lips that were suddenly dry. All that from merely passing pleasantries. What would happen if they were naked? Together? *Get a grip*, she thought sternly as her hormones went haywire. A cough cleared her throat. "I'll let him know you're here."

Hmmm. Not bad for the first time. She'd do better with the next meeting.

"I don't mind waiting."

Emma felt her eyes grow round and her mouth fall open. Huh? What was wrong with this picture?

Jack closed the distance between them and used his forefinger to tap her under the chin. Her heart stuttered in a mad tattoo. She gasped, jerking away from his touch in outright shock.

The door from the street burst open, and George bounded inside followed by his son Hone. "Ah, you're here, Jack. I thought you might change your mind."

"No," Jack snapped, glaring at Hone.

Hone ignored Jack's scowl and sauntered across the office to stop beside Emma. "Hello, sweetheart." He hauled her from her chair and wrapped her in a bear hug that stole her breath.

"Put her down," Jack growled.

"But I haven't seen her for a week." Hone nuzzled her neck and made Emma laugh. "She's my girl."

"Don't you have a case to solve?" Jack looked as though he wanted to hit his mate.

Not in the least perturbed about his friend's bad temper, Hone parked his butt on the corner of her desk and flashed her a sexy grin. Emma sighed inwardly as she stared through lowered lashes at Jack's surly face. Why couldn't she fall for Hone instead of grumpy Jack? It was a mystery all right. Although Hone made her smile and was easy on the eye, he didn't affect her heart rate in the slightest.

Not like Jack did.

George shook his head. "Hone, I want you to check into a case that came in yesterday. Mrs. Denning has a thief she needs to flush out. Emma can give you the details. Jack, I want to go over a few details about the case we discussed yesterday." He strode toward his office but paused in the doorway. "Emma, I need to see you in my office when you're finished with Hone."

Bother. She'd hoped George might let her gain some practical experience with Mrs. Denning's case. Obviously not. Emma scowled and decided it was time to remind George of his promise. Five minutes later, Emma knocked lightly on George's door and entered. She carried a pad and pen to take notes. Jack was sprawled in a chair near the window. He bounded to his feet when Emma came in.

"Ah, good." George checked his watch then stood. "I have a golf date. I'll leave you in Jack's capable hands."

George's words echoed through her mind for long drawn-out seconds afterward. She heard the click of the door as George left but couldn't seem to concentrate on anything other than capable hands. A vision popped into her mind, aided by fertile imagination. Masculine hands on her naked breasts, fingers plucking at her sensitive nipples.

Oh, my. Emma subsided into a chair before her legs gave out. Suddenly, her cotton blouse felt several sizes too small and her face hot enough to cook a batch of small pancakes. She fanned her cheeks vigorously with her notepad.

"Are you feeling all right?" Emma's head snapped up to find Jack's enigmatic gaze settled on her. "You'll be as useful as a war canoe without a warrior to paddle if you fall sick."

"What…what do you mean?" Emma knew what she wanted him to mean but she didn't dare hope.

"George wants you to help me with my case."

Emma jumped to her feet and pumped her fist in the air. "Yes!" She did an impromptu jig before noticing his gaze on her bouncing breasts. Emma froze then dropped into her chair, striving to keep embarrassment from crawling across her face. She *must* work on maintaining her cool.

"Don't get too excited," Jack growled. "You're along on a trial basis only. You help out with the grunt work. Do what I say, when I say with no questions asked. Is that clear?"

"No problem," Emma said, restraining a celebratory grin and the need to give him a cheeky salute. *Hot damn.* She was going to be a private dick. "What's the case?"

"We're investigating at the Mahoney Resort over on Waiheke Island. We think there's a drug ring running out of the resort. Sports-enhancing drugs."

"Sounds great. Are we going for the day? When are we going?" Emma wanted to jump and dance around the room in celebration. She was finding it difficult to sit still. Her first case and closer contact with Jack all in one hit. Life couldn't get much better than this.

Jack scowled, a fierce frown, no doubt in an attempt to burst her bubble of enthusiasm. "We're going for a week. You'll need to pack tonight since we leave for Waiheke tomorrow. Here's the file. Read through it carefully and let me know if you have any questions."

Emma nodded eagerly and accepted the file. Their hands brushed during the transfer and a frisson of pleasure zapped down her arm. Surprised, she jerked away, almost dropping the file in her haste. "I'll read it," she promised trying to ignore the way her stomach swooped and plunged like a jumper on a bungee cord. She hurried into speech. "What time do we leave?"

"The ferry leaves at ten tomorrow morning. I'll pick you up from home at nine-thirty."

"I live at—"

"I know where you live. Don't be late."

Chapter Two

ଛଠ

Excitement heated her cheeks and danced through her stomach like a swarm of giddy butterflies as they joined the queue to board the ferry to Mahoney's island resort. It was happening. She was actually taking part in an investigation. Emma shuffled from foot to foot, picking up her bag then putting it back down while she tried to take in everything and quell her impatience to get started. She glanced at Jack. Calm. Uninterested even. How could he act so unaffected when everyone else was so excited?

Loud, animated chatter filled the covered walkway where they waited to board. A hostess dressed in black shorts and a tight pale blue T-shirt emblazoned with the word, Mahoney's in navy blue over her left breast, checked people off on her list then allowed them to board. Couples of all ages and sizes lined up, shuffling hand luggage and making friends with the strangers in the queue.

No one talked to them.

Not that Emma could blame them. Jack could look scary to the uninitiated with his unruly dark hair and the serpent tattoo that wound around his left biceps.

Of course, there were some who saw past the tough guy disguise. Emma knew that he gave up his time to help out at a local foster home. She knew there was gentleness beneath the grumpy outer exterior. But he kept it well hidden.

Deep in thought, she leapt in fright when a masculine arm curved around her waist.

"You're gonna have to cure the jumpiness around me. We're meant to be lovers."

Emma's gaze shot up to meet dark chocolate brown eyes. *Sinful eyes*, she thought with an inward sigh. Those eyes could certainly lead her into sin.

Anytime.

"Sure, honey," Emma said, miffed for almost giving them away. Yet she was angry with Jack, too, because she thought he was doing his best to show her up. He'd certainly tried hard enough to talk her out of the assignment. Emma wanted to glare but it wasn't loverlike. Most of all she wanted to needle him. Yes, she felt like poking the man with a sharp stick to see if she could rattle him.

"How long before we get to our room?" she cooed, fluttering her lashes at him. "I need your cock inside me." Part of Emma was shocked at her words, but the couple standing in front of them grinned at her in sympathy.

"Have you seen the contents of those goody bags the hostess is giving out?" the young woman said. A theatrical shiver jiggled her pert, braless breasts.

"No, what?" Emma asked, her fertile imagination creating all sorts of pictures. Handcuffs? Powerful aphrodisiacs? Torturous sex toys?

The woman leaned closer to whisper, "A pair of edible undies."

"Both his and hers," her partner added with a grin.

"No!" Emma breathed. *Good grief.* It would probably be like trying to choke down pills. She'd gag and throw up all over the man's groin. All over Jack's groin. "I hope they're chocolate," Emma said, waggling her brows.

"Oh, you're terrible," the woman said with a giggle.

So terrible that Jack's arm tightened around her in silent warning, his fingers digging into the sensitive flesh at her waist. Emma smothered a grin. Perhaps if she kept needling him, she'd forget her nervousness.

"I'm looking forward to this week," Emma confided to the young woman. "My honey works so hard. He's exhausted when he gets home and most nights just falls asleep." Emma peeked through lowered lashes to gauge Jack's reaction. Her stomach flipped anxiously when she noticed the tic in his shadowed jaw. He looked as though he might burst while the arm around her waist tensed until it felt like a shackle. But not enough to make her stop goading him. "Too tired for good sex, if you know what I mean."

A low growl vibrated through his chest. Emma stilled and the hair on her forearms stood to attention. Slowly, her gaze rose from his broad chest, and traveled up his neck, across his rigid jaw and collided with eyes the color of onyx.

"We intend to make up for that, don't we, sweetheart?" His flashing eyes promised retribution when they were alone. "Can't have you saying I can't get it up often enough to keep you satisfied. Wouldn't want you to wander to greener pastures."

Oops. Perhaps she'd pushed a little hard.

The line moved, and Emma nudged her bag forward with her foot. She was very conscious of Jack standing close behind.

"Hello. Names, please," the hostess said.

"Jack Sullivan and Emma Montrose." Jack stepped up beside her, taking control and smiling at the hostess.

"Ah, yes. Here we go. Here are your goody bags." The hostess handed one bag to each of them. "Your room assignment and everything you need to know about the resort is in there along with a few surprises."

"Thanks," Emma murmured accepting the bag. Her hand shook. It was like stepping over an invisible line. A gateway into sin. She glanced at Jack to find him watching her with the inscrutable expression that gave nothing away. Emma's mouth firmed with determination, and her chin shot up into the air. She could do this. She would do this despite Jack's silent censure. She intended to complete this assignment to the best of her ability. And if she managed to make Jack notice her as a female, a hot sexual being, then so much the better.

The woman was going to drive him to drink. In her short red shorts, and her figure-hugging shirt, she was a menace to clear thinking. Jack glared at her back as she sashayed down the gangplank to board the ferry. His gaze drifted down to her curvy butt, encased in the tight shorts. With the enhanced hearing all taniwhas had, he could hear the rapid beat of her heart. She wanted him. Suddenly, he had a hard-on to beat all. Deep inside his mind, the serpent clawed for release.

Sweat beaded on his forehead. His head started to swim in an alarming manner. Hell, he couldn't shift here. Not now, in front of all these people. The demand of the serpent pounded him until he trembled with the desire to change to taniwha form or to fuck a woman. Any woman. In the serpent's mind, these were the only two alternatives.

Jack knew better.

Desperation made his fists bunch and his chest heave as he tried to force oxygen into starved lungs. Concentrate. Focus on something else. *Block.*

In his mind, he pictured his cat—the scrawny stray that should have known better than to seek refuge with a taniwha who wasn't a vegetarian. The cat had kept coming round anyway. Though damned if he knew when the arrogant black tom had become his cat. Jack snorted under his breath, cursing the taniwha that struggled for dominance. He concentrated hard, forcing his mind to change track. The cat had probably won him over about the time he'd presented Jack with a huge eel in the middle of the night. A gift of the highest magnitude. That had been the defining moment. Jack focused on the scruffy black cat he'd pictured, fighting the serpent that writhed through his body. The serpent roared in displeasure, the sound echoing through his mind. He ached to feel the cool waters of the harbor. Or the explosive release of sex.

You can't damn well have sex, Jack shouted silently. *Behave, dammit.* Shit, no wonder he had a headache.

"Are you all right?" A slender hand with pale pink nails touched his forearm. Jack started, his nostrils flaring as her clean floral scent washed over him. The serpent fought briefly then retreated with a snarl.

"I'm fine. Thinking about the case." Jack didn't relax an iota. How could he when he was reminded of innocence every time he set eyes on Emma's voluptuous body? The scent of lavender and roses backed the innocence up along with the baby pink nail polish she'd painted on her finger and toenails. His gaze drifted up to meet her eyes.

Whoa, baby. No way was her avid gaze innocent. She puckered her pink lips then her tongue slid out to moisten the plump curves of her mouth. The serpent roared approval, and his cock stirred again with definite interest. *Well, hell!*

Emma's intriguing mix of innocence and pure sex appeal knocked all confidence in his ability to remain detached. This assignment could be the death of him. And the serpent wasn't about to let him forget her willingness. Perhaps he should have brought the damn cat with him because he was going to be thinking about the furry creature a lot.

Jack drew Emma up to the bow of the boat. It was crowded at the moment, but when they pulled out of the sheltered harbor and into the Gulf, the cool sea air and brisk wind would send the passengers scurrying for the warmth of the lounge and bar area. He edged her toward the railing and caged her in place with his arms.

Emma jumped like a nervous schoolgirl.

"Quit that," he muttered, speaking close to her ear. "Remember you're playing the part of my partner."

"I hate that word," Emma muttered, looking over her shoulder at him. "What does that mean? When someone refers to their partner."

He crowded her from behind, gritting his teeth as his cock brushed her ass. "Would you prefer lover?" He felt her shiver, and satisfaction filled him as she tried to edge away. "Take care. We don't want people to think we're arguing."

The number of passengers boarding slowed to a trickle then stopped. Finally, the deckhands released the moorings and the ferry slipped from the berth. Excited chatter filled the deck area where they stood. Jack scanned faces and bodies. Despite the breeze, most of the women were dressed in a similar manner to Emma — shorts and skimpy T-shirts or thin cotton shirts. Shouldn't be long before they beat a retreat inside out of the wind.

"I thought the weather forecast said fine and sunny." Emma tried to move. "Can we go inside? It's cold."

"I want to discuss the case before we arrive. Work out a plan of attack." Jack pulled her against his chest and wrapped his arms around her. The taniwha stirred, sighing in pleasure. Jack ruthlessly erected a barrier in his mind, forcing the beast back. Then Jack sighed, too, pushing away the hum of pleasure as her scent filled his senses. No doubt about it. Emma fit his arms perfectly.

"Okay, so talk."

"Ground rules. This is a job, and that's all. Don't get any romantic ideas just because we're posing as a couple. I'm not interested in anything but getting the job done." Emma froze in his arms, and he wished he could see her face. Instead, she stared directly ahead at the dormant volcanic island of Rangitoto.

"Of course, I understand." Her voice was clear but stiff.

"Good." Jack should have experienced relief, but instead he felt like a jerk. However, he'd achieved what he'd set out to do. She wouldn't suffer from a single romantic illusion about them becoming a real couple.

* * * * *

An hour later, the hostess led them from the resort reception area to their room. She pushed the door open and stood back to let them enter.

"There's only one bed," Emma blurted.

The hostess stared at her in bemusement, making Emma realize she'd stumbled at the first hurdle. Of course, they'd be expected to share a bed. This was a week for couples and sex. After all, her mind dwelt on sex.

"He snores dreadfully," she muttered to the hostess, taking petty revenge for the hurt he'd inflicted on her earlier. *Just a job. No romantic ideas*, she mocked silently as she detoured around the bags the porter had deposited in the middle of the floor. She didn't have any romantic ideas. All she wanted was sex. "I suppose I can always pull out the earplugs as a last resort."

"I do not—"

Emma stepped up close to Jack and gave into the temptation to run her fingers through his hair. The dark locks slithered through her fingers like a piece of fine silk. The strands felt as soft as they looked. "Of course you do, but that's part of your charm. Too many good points and I'd get bored. I mean you're good at sex. Very good. Great stamina. What more could I ask of a lover?"

Jack made a choking sound deep in his throat as she trailed a hand across his broad chest. Her fingers tingled while her pulse leapt at her daring.

"Can I help you with anything before I leave?" the hostess asked, amusement coloring her voice. "Remember, the welcome party starts promptly at midday. We would like you to make an appearance for a short time so we can outline the activities for the week. After that, you're free for the rest of the afternoon to partake in all the facilities we have here at the resort. We want you to be rested for our gala dinner tonight."

"Thanks," Emma murmured, carrying on with her exploration while she had Jack captive and within touching distance. "We have everything we need."

The door swung shut with a soft click.

"That's enough," Jack growled. "She's gone now."

Emma drew a sharp breath, gathering up her courage. "You need to kiss me."

"What?"

Was that panic she saw in his dark eyes? "We're meant to be a couple," she explained, starting to enjoy herself. "We'll have to kiss at some stage to make sure we look the part. I think we should practice. We don't want to give ourselves away." Her heart thundered loudly and blood heated every inch of skin on her body. She was hyperaware of his strength and masculinity.

Jack glanced at her mouth and immediately her lips tingled as though he'd touched them. His chest rose as he sucked in an audible breath. Yep, she'd definitely put the fear of God into him. His mouth worked, but no words came out, then before she could take another breath, he grabbed her. Their lips smashed together and parted just as quickly. Jack jerked away from her, and they stared at each other, both breathing hard.

"That was not a kiss," Emma said breaking the pregnant silence. Frustration washed through her, leaving her feeling totally cheated. The mission she'd set for herself was going to be trickier than she'd first envisaged.

Jack scowled. Emma supposed he meant to frighten her like he scared everyone else he came into contact with. It wouldn't work. She was on to him. "Come here. I want to show you how we should kiss in public."

When he didn't move, she closed the distance between them. She placed her hands on his shoulders. They were tense. Like touching blocks of cold rock except for the dragon tattoo. For some reason that was hot. "You're very cold."

"Get it over with." Jack's eyes flashed with enough temper that she knew not to push him any longer.

She stood on tiptoes and gingerly pressed her lips against his. He didn't move but he didn't cooperate either. Time to move this experiment along. Emma opened her mouth and brushed her tongue across the seam of his mouth. A groan rumbled deep in his chest. *Oh, yeah!* Score one for the home team. Working on pure instinct, Emma moved her lips persuasively against his. She nibbled his bottom lip, then soothed the nips she'd inflicted on him with a swathe of her tongue. Jack's arms came around her without warning, tugging her off-balance so his muscular chest flattened her breasts. He tipped her head back and moved his lips over hers with an expertise that made her toes curl. She gasped taking in his masculine taste, a hint of mint and the tang of the sea. He tasted so good — better than she'd ever imagined. Then his tongue slid inside her mouth, and she was addicted. Her breasts peaked against her bra as their tongues slid together in a sensuous dance. Jack pressed her closer and to her delight, she found he was interested. *A hard-on.* With a subtle twitch of her hips, Emma pressed against his sizeable erection. Her eyes fluttered shut to savor both the sensation and her triumph. Emma Montrose had turned on big, bad Jack Sullivan.

Jack pulled away as abruptly as he'd grabbed her. They stared at each other for a long drawn-out moment. Emma's tongue snaked out to lick her lips and his dark eyes followed the movement. Game, set and match, bad boy.

"Right." He straightened and took a giant step away from her. "We've established we can manage a kiss without looking as though we've never done it before." He glared at her, obviously in an attempt to regain control. Emma wasn't about to let her advantage go, no matter how much he glowered. His body was interested in sex. Sex with her. All she needed to do was push harder until he crumpled. Doubt flittered briefly through her mind. Could she act with sexual aggression? She quashed the negative thought. Nah, men were easy. And damned if she would turn twenty-six without knowing sexual pleasure with Jack.

Jack glanced at the diver's watch on his wrist. "We'd better go to this blasted meeting we've all been summoned to. While we're there, I want you to take note of the faces. If there's anyone you think is familiar or is mentioned in the file take note and tell me later."

Emma nodded. "I'll just change before we go. I thought I'd check out the pool after the meeting."

Jack watched the sway of her hips as she walked over to her bag and rummaged through the packed contents. She fished out something small enough to hide in her fisted hand, then sashayed into the en suite and closed the door behind her. The taniwha released a low growl of need.

"Fuck," he muttered with real feeling. He rubbed the heels of his hands over his eyes and dragged in a huge breath. He was in trouble here and was man—taniwha—enough to admit it. What the hell had happened to the brown sparrow from the office?

The creak of the door jerked him upright. He turned and experienced an instant roar of approval from the taniwha. This was no brown sparrow standing proudly in front of him. Emma Montrose was one curvy, confident, sexy woman and she scared the shit out of him. Her breasts were poured into an itty-bitty red top that barely contained them. Then there were acres of smooth, pale skin before his gaze hit the brief bikini panties shielding her femininity. She reminded him of the curvy film stars of the fifties with her Marilyn Monroe figure. Add in a little more height and you got Emma Montrose—a luscious armful of femininity.

"Is that all you're wearing?"

"I have a sarong." She grabbed a square of brightly patterned material from her bag and wrapped it around her hips then tied it with a knot. "I'd like to buy another from the gift store to take home as a souvenir."

"What about a thing for the top? A towel?" He gestured at her breasts in their itty-bitty top. Anything to screen her lush curves from his sight.

Emma tossed her head. "I'll get a towel at the pool."

"Won't you get cold?"

This time, Emma shrugged and her breasts jiggled enough to distract him. "The sun has come out and it looks as though the wind has died down. Besides, the brochure says there's nude bathing—"

Jack ripped his gaze from her cleavage to stare at her in shock. "Over my dead body." Emma was going to be difficult. He could tell by the way her chin lifted. How had he missed her stubbornness? She'd always scuttled out of his way like a frightened bird.

This Emma was no sparrow.

Jack jerked the door open then stood back. "Let's go."

She sashayed through the door, the pert wiggle of her hips drawing his eye. Sweat coated his body while his cock jumped to high alert. Jack didn't know whether to curse a blue streak or laugh hysterically. One thing was for sure. They couldn't share a room without the simmering attraction between them boiling over. *Oh, yeah.* No wonder George had laughed like a bloody loon. His boss had probably noticed Emma's crush, too. The joke was well and truly on him. Jack followed her down the brightly lit corridor and outside.

The sea, pungent and briny, called its siren song trying to entice him to shift and slip into the cool waters. He forced himself to concentrate. Instead of facing temptation tonight, he'd wait for Emma to fall asleep, then leave to do some investigating. With luck, he'd be able to check out Mahoney's office and find something to further their investigation. Or blow the whole case wide open and save his taniwha butt so he could hightail it home to safety and his scruffy tom cat.

Emma paused by a garden full of colorful blooms. She trailed a hand over the lavender border. "Do you prefer to swim in a pool or the sea?"

"The sea," he said without thinking.

"You live by the sea, don't you?"

"Yeah."

She made a small huffing sound. "Do you live by yourself?"

"Yeah."

"No pets?"

"I have a cat. What's with all the questions?"

"I'm your significant other. I should know these things. I live by myself but have loads of friends. I hate swimming in the sea—long story, but I almost drowned. I'll tell you one day. I'm twenty-five years old and my favorite food is hokey pokey ice cream. Oh, and chocolate. I love chocolate."

"Looks like this is where the meeting's being held," Jack muttered. He opened the door and ushered her through, relieved to be done with the twenty questions. There was only one thing worth knowing about a woman and that was how easy she was. As a taniwha, he needed that type of information. He did not need to know her personal likes and dislikes.

The large meeting room was packed to capacity and most of the women were dressed in similar outfits to Emma's. In fact, Jack felt distinctly overdressed in his shirt and shorts.

Jack directed her toward two empty chairs and settled at Emma's side. He scanned the men and women sitting either side of him. Damn, crowds made him antsy. And they were so bloody happy. Shit, make that horny. He could hear their rapid heartbeats and their naughty whispering. The majority of them looked as though they needed a bedroom. He glanced at Emma, and saw the sexy flush on her cheeks, the kiss-swollen lips. Damn, he didn't need this crap. Jack forced his mind back to the job. Given the opportunity tonight, he'd scour the island, and check out the private marina and wharf area.

"Good afternoon!" A young woman walked up to a microphone followed by several others. All of them but one—a man—were dressed in uniform. Black shorts and blue T-shirts.

Well, damn, Jack thought, sitting up straighter. Rueben J. Mahoney himself. Interesting. The owner wasn't always at the resort. His presence could mean a deal was going down.

"Welcome to Mahoney Resort. We have a great week planned with lots of naughty fun especially for couples!" A roar of approval greeted Mahoney's words. "Now I'll hand you over to Lissa."

"Welcome! Sounds like you're ready to party." With a laugh, she held up her right hand in a bid for silence. "To start off the fun, I want you to look under your chairs. Two lucky people should find a red heart sticker."

A buzz of chatter filled the room again as everyone stood to peer under their chairs.

"I've got one!" Emma shrieked.

Jack winced. "That figures."

"Could the two lucky winners come up here to collect their prizes? We have a bag full of sex toys and games for you to spice up your week."

Emma bounded up to the stage with the red sticker clutched in her hand. A man in his fifties followed hot on her heels.

Jack swallowed a groan when one of hostesses on the stage presented Emma with her prize. Reuben J. Mahoney kissed her on the cheek and tossed her a joking remark. Jack gritted his teeth as he heard the drawl of the man's voice but not the actual words. The desire to swear a blue streak and shock the hell out of the little old lady and her bright-eyed husband sitting beside him rode Jack hard. Contrarily, the serpent roared with excitement and anticipation. Bit by bit his strength and determination to stay the heck out of Emma's panties was being eroded away. Jack sighed and finally accepted the truth.

He was a dead man, but at least he was gonna die happy.

Chapter Three

❧

"It wasn't my fault I won the spot prize," Emma said. Jack could tell she wasn't the slightest bit sorry. The twinkle in her blue eyes gave it away. "What are we going to do now?"

"I am going to do a reconnaissance of the resort," Jack muttered. "I thought you were going to the pool."

Her bright smile dimmed then suddenly burst into life again. The sight made his stomach flip with foreboding. What the hell was she up to now? "I think I'll go to the beach instead of the pool." She lifted the large package she'd won and waved it in front of him. "Not to swim. I can sunbathe and check out my loot."

Jack froze then slowly nodded. She couldn't come to much harm on the beach.

One hour later, Jack finished his quick whistle-stop tour of the resort. He'd checked out the gym, the swimming pool with the spa pools and sauna facilities. There was a health spa he'd poked his head in, then promptly retreated but not quite fast enough. He'd ended up making an appointment for Emma for a massage and something to do with seaweed before he could escape.

He'd checked out the golf course, the archery area and the petanque pit, where guests played the French version of outdoor bowls. Then, he'd hit one of the walking tracks that skirted the property and led to Stoney Batter—the World War II gun placements and connecting tunnels—if the walker was willing to walk for two hours. There were several other walking tracks of various lengths along with tennis and numerous water sports available to entertain the guests. The private beach stretched the length of the resort golf course. At the end of the beach, a river mouth emptied into the sea, the sand changing to thick river mud. Hundreds of mangrove trees grew in the oozing mud. They were full of bird life but not very hospitable for humans.

The resort was big and more spread out than Jack was happy with. It would be very easy for a drug ring to operate without detection. He made a mental note to check about day guests.

Jack turned toward the beach to check if Emma was still there. The sand crunched under his sandals when he stepped off the footpath onto the beach. The surge and retreat of the waves lulled him as he searched for Emma. Halfway along the beach, he saw four males crowding around a beach towel. He caught the low drone as one of them spoke and the answering feminine laugh.

Emma.

Jealousy hit him hard and without warning. His steps lengthened, and the taniwha growled ready to kick some butt.

"Emma, there you are." He kept his voice low and even—or tried to. The taniwha let loose with a roar that squeezed past his control before he could blink.

The four men visibly backed away from Emma.

She sent him a chiding look and pursed her rosebud pink lips before saying, "Darling, this is Carlos, Daniel, Justin and Doug. They wanted to know what I'd won in my prize."

Jack made a concerted effort to contain his displeasure, but it couldn't have been that good. The four men jumped to their feet.

"We'd better get back to the bar. The girls should have finished in the spa by now," one of them said after they'd exchanged glances.

"Nice to meet you," Emma said. "And thanks for the hints. I'm sure they'll come in handy."

"See you round," another of the men said.

Jack managed a brief nod of acknowledgment and waited in broody silence until they left. He yanked his shirt over his head then dropped onto the sand beside Emma. All it took was one look and he almost drooled. She smelled of coconut lotion and her skin gleamed, drawing his eyes to the itty-bitty red top and her breasts.

"You could have been a bit more polite."

"Why? What hints?" If she wanted hints, she should ask him.

"About the best way to use some of the sex toys I won. Do you have some hints for me?"

Jack went from pissed to boiling hot in seconds flat. The woman had a smart mouth and he was just the man to cure her of the malady. He sprang, pushing her down until she lay full length on her towel. A small "oomph" escaped her as he covered her body, squashing her breasts against his bare chest. He thrust his thigh between her legs to hold her in place, ignoring the surprise in her big blue eyes. She opened her mouth, probably to complain, but he didn't give her a chance to form the words. He sealed them inside by covering her mouth with his and plundered, sliding his tongue into the moist cavern beyond, just as the taniwha demanded. She froze at the contact, then softened beneath him, her hands coming around his shoulders to hold him closer. Her hands slid across his back then lower to cup his ass.

Jack ripped his mouth away from hers. "What the devil are you doing?"

"I've wanted to cop a feel of your butt for ages," she confessed a trifle breathlessly. "It's...ah...very nice."

The sensation of her hands sliding over his ass, even though he wore shorts, sent his libido soaring into overdrive. His cock hardened with painful intensity until it felt as though his shorts were several sizes too small. A groan formed deep in his chest and without direction, his hands started doing a little exploration of their own.

Smooth skin greeted his touch. He trailed a hand across her rib cage then higher to cup one breast. The hands on his butt stilled and when their gazes met, he saw her eyes were wide and held a trace of shock. Jack traced the edge of her itty-bitty top with a forefinger then dipped beneath the tight fabric to the smooth flesh beneath. Maintaining her gaze, he leaned down and let his tongue trace the same path as his finger. Her scent filled his nostrils—the same lavender and roses he'd noticed earlier plus coconut from her suntan lotion—as he licked a path down the slope of one breast. *Not enough*, Jack thought. Not nearly enough. He peeled the red material away from her breasts, revealing taut pink nipples to the afternoon sun and his gaze. Proud and full breasts, that enticed and enthralled him.

She made a tiny sound. Jack couldn't decide whether it was shock or to urge him on.

Then her lips parted and white teeth flashed in a grin full of challenge. "You gonna stop there?" She rolled slightly, reached behind her back, and Jack heard the faint click of her bikini top closure. The red fabric fell down her arms. A shrug made the top fall completely away leaving her topless and vulnerable to his gaze.

A breath hissed through his teeth. He couldn't have stopped to save himself. His heart thundered and the taniwha stretched and stirred, prodding him to continue. Slowly, he lowered his head to take one pink nipple in his mouth. Jack closed his mouth around the taut peak, the need to do everything all at once riding him hard. Like a man who hadn't eaten for days, he feasted. Savoring the taste of her—the texture. Gently biting. Tasting her and tormenting himself.

Dicing with danger.

Emma cradled his head, her fingers entwining in his hair, urging him on. He drew hard on her nipple and she bucked beneath him, brushing against his groin.

"Harder," she murmured in a dreamy voice. "That feels so good." Emma had no pretense in her. She was innocence and honesty all wrapped up in a bow.

And he wanted to take this to a conclusion. Jack pulled away far enough that he could see her face. Her eyes were closed and her lips were curled up in a dreamy smile. That smile jerked him back to reality.

Jack rolled away, trying to ignore the gleam of her nipples, still wet from his mouth. He wasn't interested in anything more than a roll in the sack. Getting his rocks off.

"We'd better go." He stood and handed his shirt to her so she could cover up. "We have a job to do. Mucking about on the beach isn't getting it done. Besides, we've got this dinner thing."

* * * * *

"I can't believe it," Jack muttered, glancing at the huge box Emma carried. He rolled his eyes while the taniwha inside danced a Maori war dance and combined it with a few exuberant high kicks by the feel of his bouncing gut. A year's supply of condoms. "I've never met anyone with such dumb luck."

"I can't help it," Emma said cheerfully without a trace of remorse or embarrassment.

Hell, no. He'd been the one who'd caught the flack. Lots of jokes and pats on the back—all with the same message. He was going to need to eat lots to keep his strength up. Sure, it was all in good fun, but it wore thin after a while. But worst of all, Emma's win had called attention to them. Everyone in the whole damn resort would recognize their faces. It was going to be difficult to skulk around trying to investigate when everyone was busy snickering.

"What are you going to do with a year's supply of condoms anyway?"

"Use them," Emma said sweetly.

Jack's fists clenched at his sides, and he felt as if someone had kicked him in the gut. The thought of Emma using the condoms with another man fueled his temper. But using them with him wasn't a much better proposition. This afternoon had been a mistake. He wasn't going to touch her again. She was commitment through and through. He was free and easy—a different species of fish altogether.

Jack opened the door for Emma and stood back as she sashayed through into the night air in her short black dress that showed far too much skin for his liking. Gritting his teeth, he stalked after her. Colored lights lit both sides of the path that wound through lush plantings of native ferns and trees and strategically placed rock carvings.

In the bush on the far side of the resort, a lone morepork cried. Its mournful call echoed through the still night. Jack heard the rustle of small creatures scurrying for cover from the owl. Waves rolled into the shore interspersed by laughing and shouting from the couples still celebrating in the bar after the gala dinner.

Even though it was almost one in the morning, he'd have to go back to the room with Emma to give everyone time to settle in for the night. It was either that or hit the bar. He shot a glance at Emma who walked down the path in front of him. Temptation shot through him, fast and hard. He wanted her. Perhaps a drink would be the better option.

"Emma, wait up."

She paused and turned slowly to look at him. That bloody box of condoms taunted him without mercy. "I'm going to the bar to check out who's there. I want to see if the staff will talk to me."

"Should I come?"

Yes, please. Preferably with me inside your tight pussy. "No!" he snapped, appalled at his wayward thoughts. Bloody hell, he couldn't blame his serpent. That's the last thing he needed—to smell her flowery scent and hear each hitch of her breath. He needed sex tonight. That was the only way he could exert control over the serpent and continue to work closely with Emma. "I'll see you back to the room then head back to the bar."

"I could help."

"I thought you'd agreed to do what I said whenever I said it?"

She had the audacity to raise one shapely eyebrow and let the corners of her mouth drift upward in the beginnings of a smile. "Hmmm."

Jack grabbed her by the elbow and hurried her toward their room. Two minutes later, he pulled a keycard out of his pocket and slid it into the door. He slipped the keycard into the wall socket and a single light came on, spotlighting the bed. The rich burgundy cover gleamed, looking decadent and suggestive of sex.

Jack froze. If he were a superstitious man, he'd think someone was trying to tell him something.

Condoms.

Bed.

Emma.

The ingredients were all there. All he needed to do was stop fighting and go with the flow.

Then he heard a scraping noise, soft and totally out of place. He prowled into the center of the room trying to isolate where the noise vibration had originated.

Emma sat on the corner of the bed and bent to slip off her strappy black shoes. The soft sigh she made when she wriggled her toes pulled his cock tight and tented his black trousers.

Surreptitiously, Jack searched the room, looking for anything out of place or remotely suspicious. Feet shuffled and it sounded as though someone fidgeted. Jack cocked his head, listening for the slightest vibration but couldn't pinpoint the sound with accuracy. It came from near the bar. Nothing seemed disturbed yet the back of his neck prickled insistently. He snarled beneath his breath, allowing his taniwha senses free rein or as much as he could with a human in the same room. Gradually, he filtered out the small sounds made by Emma as she removed her jacket and kicked her shoes out of the way. He sauntered over to the minibar.

"Would you like a drink?" Jack continued to scan the area, his gaze skimming a large mirror that hung on the wall near the bar. Standing this close to the mirror, two dark shapes were discernable within. Behind. Jack tensed then forced himself to relax. A two-way mirror directly in line with the bed.

"No, drink for me, thanks. I thought you were going to the bar."

"Soon." The distinct crackle of wrapping paper momentarily shifted his attention. "What are you doing?" To his critical ear, his voice sounded harsh and a touch defensive. Damn, he was losing his grip on this assignment and he didn't like it one bit. All he could think of was sex. He winged a glare at the mirror. Now a bloody two-way mirror to complicate their case. Aware his famed control was starting to unravel, he took a deep breath and fixed himself a whiskey. He tipped back his head and let the alcohol slide down his throat. Although the peaty flavor of the whiskey tasted good, it didn't do a thing to soothe his irritation.

The two watchers remained, and Jack couldn't decide whether they'd lucked out and scored a room specially set up for voyeurs, or if their cover was blown and they were under surveillance for more sinister reasons.

He poured another finger of whiskey and stared into the amber depths in broody silence.

"There are six different types of condoms in here along with two types of lubricant," Emma said. She sounded breathless as if she expected him to react.

And dammit all—he wanted to react.

Perhaps that was the solution. They could reassure the voyeurs by having hot, sweaty sex. Just one bout, he told himself. He glanced at Emma and found her exploring the contents of the package she'd won at dinner. She'd tried to do it before but he hadn't given her the opportunity. His mind grouped sex and Emma in the same sentence too often as it was without looking at visual props.

"Ohhh." Her small breathy sigh snared his attention, mainly because it reminded him of sex. But then, everything reminded him of sex when Emma was around.

"Do people really use these?" she asked, extending something in her palm for him to see.

Two pastel-colored hearts lay in her palm. Each bore a suggestion.

Lick my pussy. Suck my cock.

Both temptation and the taniwha roared at him to grab her up quickly and hammer into her body until they were both satisfied. Jack glanced away to study the dregs of whiskey in his glass. Sex with Emma. He flirted with the idea and the possible repercussions. The taniwha clawed for sexual appeasement, and Jack knew he'd have to give in or shift and scare the living daylights out of Emma and their silent watchers. George Taniwha & Co. couldn't afford the publicity—that was for sure. The hand holding the glass started to itch insistently. When he glanced down, Jack saw the sheen of forming scales. That settled it.

They'd have sex.

He was a professional. He could do this—remain detached and get the job done. Sex was only an exchange of bodily fluids.

Decision made, he swallowed the last mouthful of whiskey and placed the glass on the bar top with a decisive click. His hands went to the buttons on his shirt. He unfastened them rapidly then shrugged from the blue cotton shirt and tossed it aside. He stepped out of his black trousers and chucked them in the direction of his shirt.

"What are you doing?"

She didn't sound scared. A good thing, but he didn't intend to force her. He'd show her the goods and gauge her reaction. Then, he'd give her one last chance to say no.

Jack slid his fingers under the elastic band of his black silk boxers. A growl of excitement escaped the taniwha. Emma's eyes widened at the low, rumbling growl. Jack pushed the boxers over his fully erect shaft. Her mouth dropped open as she continued to stare at his groin. But at least she hadn't screamed and run from the room.

Jack sauntered closer to the bed. "What does it look like I'm doing?" The entire room throbbed with silence. Even the two watchers had stopped their fidgeting to concentrate on the action in the bedroom. Jack hoped they were enjoying the view of his bare ass.

Emma licked her lips. "Ah, getting ready for bed?"

"Full marks for the lady," he said in a husky voice. Damned if this strip tease wasn't winding him tighter than a spring. Turning him on. "Thought we might use some of those condoms you won," he added casually.

"Condoms?" Emma cast a nervous glance at his erect cock then at the box full of condoms. She plucked a bright orange packet from the box and waved it in the air. "Do they make them big enough to cover you?"

"It will fit with no problem," he said coming to a stop right in front of her.

She eyed his cock with misgiving, staring so hard he twitched. "But will you fit?" she blurted.

For the first time in longer than he could remember, Jack wanted to laugh about sex. Grinning, he leaned over and cupped her face in his hands. "I promise that by the time I've finished with you we'll fit perfectly."

Emma had no idea what had made Jack change his mind about sex. She'd been pretty sure he didn't want her after he'd refused her advances earlier on. But she wasn't about to object now that he was naked and sporting an impressive hard-on. She'd fantasized about this moment for months. Heck, longer than months.

Emma stood ready to unzip her dress and shimmy out of it before he changed his mind. Then she'd jump him.

"Wait."

Emma froze. Wait, as in stop, he didn't want to do this? She lifted her head, trying to read his expression. Yeah, right. A book with blank pages contained more information.

"I want to undress you."

"Oh." Emma nibbled her bottom lip while she thought about it then gave a decisive nod. He might as well see all of her straight off. Her body wasn't catwalk model material, but with her height she'd look stupid with tiny bones and no padding. Emma didn't believe in pretense. "All right."

"With the light on," he added with distinct challenge.

In answer, Emma turned her back on him to present the zipper of her little black dress. Her heart raced while she waited for the first step in her master plan to take off. She wanted to grab. She wanted to touch the serpent tattoo on his biceps and see if it was still hot to the touch. And kiss. Fondle. But she did none of these things because she didn't want him to change his mind.

The zipper whined downward. No fumbling or cursing, just masculine competence that boded well for the actual act. The material slithered downward and caught on her hips until he maneuvered the fabric safely over the obstruction. Before Emma could move, he swung her off her feet and dropped her on top of the mattress. She hadn't even stopped bouncing when he was on her, pressing her body into the mattress.

"You need to wear more clothes," he muttered, running his hands around her naked breasts.

"Frightened I'll catch cold?" God, his hands felt so good on her bare skin.

"I'm going to wonder each time I see you." He plucked at one nipple, hard enough that it should have hurt. Instead, the sensation traveled straight to her achy clit. Emma arched her back, silently pleading for him to do it again. "Think about your underwear," he muttered.

Instead of repeating the nipple tweak, he kissed a trail across her rib cage, pausing to circle his tongue around her belly button. Emma groaned, her body a sudden mass of writhing nerves. He could do whatever he wanted to her. It all felt good. She'd exert her rights to explore him later.

"No bra," he whispered, his warmth breath feathering across her lower belly. "Panties that are so brief I don't know why you bothered." His tongue darted out to trace along the lacy elastic band that held her panties in place. Along her lower abdomen then from her hip to inner thigh. "And then there's the stockings. Man, they make me hot."

"I like them," Emma murmured. She was dying here, so close to losing her cool. She stirred restlessly, the urge to beg him to rip off her panties and lick her, trembling on the tip of her tongue.

As if he'd read her mind, Jack tugged her panties down her legs, but left the thigh-high stockings where they were. His fingers felt calloused on her legs and feet, even through the sheer stockings, as he edged the lacy material away. He reared up to a kneeling position beside her, parted her legs and looked his fill.

"Yeah," he murmured. "Stay just like that. So pretty." He skimmed a finger across her labia.

Emma felt the flush of arousal that swept the length of her body. She felt wanton. She felt beautiful and feminine. And she wanted him desperately.

He grabbed a fistful of condoms from the box that still lay on the corner of the bed and dumped them on the wooden bedside cabinet before dropping the rest on the floor at the foot of the bed. The plastic wrapping crackled as he opened the packet. Emma watched with fascination as he rolled the bright orange condom onto his penis. Anticipation danced through her stomach and moisture gathered between her legs. He hadn't done much more than finger her and she was a quivering mass of desire.

Jack's hand slid in a long, luxurious stroke down her body. He combed his fingers through her pubic hair then drew a finger along her dew-slick cleft. Emma started, the zing of excitement almost too much to bear. Jeesh. She wondered if there was such a thing as female premature orgasm. Because if she wasn't careful, it was going to happen to her. What was the man dithering for? Did he want a diagram? A schedule of instructions?

"You're wet for me," he murmured.

Well, that was pretty obvious. No point denying she wanted him. "Yes."

He parted her legs even farther and moved into the space between. "But not wet enough. Can't wait any longer," he muttered almost to himself. Taking his cock in one hand, he rubbed it across the mouth of her pussy, coating the tip of his penis in her juices. Another surge of excitement swept through Emma. Reaching over her, he grabbed up a container of lubricant. He broke the seal and pumped the bottle several times before a colorless gel squirted into the palm of his hand. With a soft grunt, he smoothed the gel in rough strokes along her cleft. Coolness hit her first, tickling and bringing laughter then warmth, intense and pleasurable as the lubricant coated her clitoris and pussy. Jack smoothed the rest of the gel along his erection. He probed her cleft, sliding one finger into her cunt. Emma groaned as he withdrew his finger then slowly pumped two fingers inside her vagina, stretching and preparing her for his entry.

"Better," he muttered as he pushed his fingers inside her for a third time and slowly withdrew them. He replaced his fingers with the thick head of his cock and thrust inside her. His groan echoed in the silent room.

Emma bit her lip, wanting to groan, too. Desire kicked hard as he pushed his cock deeper into her womb. She felt stretched, and still Jack kept up the pressure, thrusting then retreating until he was fully seated.

"You okay?" Jack's glower was downright scary.

Too bad. She was enjoying the experience, Emma thought dreamily, fit to bursting with happiness. It could only get better with an orgasm. "Yeah," she murmured in understatement. "I'm fine."

"Good." He upped the pace, thrusting and withdrawing in a steady, powerful rhythm that made the bed creak.

So good. Her mind hazed with pleasure as she rose to meet each thrust. Her pussy was on fire. *So close to exploding.* His hands traveled up her body to cup her breasts, then he flicked his thumbs over sensitive nipples. Emma moaned. He squeezed one distended nipple between finger and thumb, timing the pinch to coincide with a slow thrust of his cock into her pussy. The sharp nip sent frissons of excitement skipping through her veins.

"Jack," she murmured in a thick voice she scarcely recognized. The sensation built higher and higher. She clung to his broad shoulders, arching her back and meeting each hard thrust with a swivel of her hips.

Deep shudders shook the strong shoulders beneath her clinging hands. Each successive thrust moved Emma up the bed until her head banged on the padded headboard. Jack withdrew again and slammed home. She burned for fulfillment. Burned. Then the next thrust sent her over the edge into a world where sensation ruled. Jack thrust once more and froze. Deep inside, Emma felt the pulse of his cock as semen jetted from him. His arms wrapped around her tight, tucking her firmly against his chest.

He sighed loudly, right near her ear. "You okay?"

"Oh, yeah." Emma brushed a lock of hair off his forehead, then gave into temptation and traced his mouth with the tip of one finger. "What's next?"

Jack snorted a sound that might have been a laugh. Emma wasn't sure since she had trouble reading him, which was a damned shame since he was a mystery she was desperate to solve.

Chapter Four

හ

Like any good private dick, Emma started her investigation of Jack in small increments and proceeded with caution. She wriggled from beneath him then took him by surprise and pushed him back on the bed. She wanted to explore every inch of his body then she intended to entice him into play. Emma didn't expect to leave Mahoney Resort without trying out some of the toys and sex games she'd won.

Jack removed the condom and discarded it. He opened his mouth and looked as though he was going to tell her to stop. That wasn't going to happen. Distraction. She needed one now!

Emma bent and grazed her teeth over one flat, masculine nipple. She plucked at his other one with her fingers exactly the way she liked him to do it to her. Emma slid her mouth across his flesh, tasting salt and smelling a hint of soap. Heady. Addicting. Very yummy. Her busy hands cupped his shoulders then explored further afield, delighting in each new discovery— firm abs, bulging biceps, the mysterious dragon, flat belly and an erection that leapt beneath her questing fingers.

A huge, pulsing erection. She ran her fingers along the silky skin, feeling the inherent strength beneath. Jack was like that, she thought. An iceberg. The man kept a tight lid on his emotions, never letting anyone close enough to get a glimpse of what he really thought. A man like Jack was a challenge. He made a girl want to explore, to discover what made him tick. Emma strummed her fingers along the underside of his cock. For the first time in her life, she wanted to try oral sex. She wanted to hold him in her mouth. Taste him.

A growl rumbled through his chest, but instead of alarm or fear, exhilaration swept through Emma. She lowered her head, the desire to taste and explore, a siren dance through her veins. She cupped his balls in her hands, squeezing gently then licked the length of his cock from base to tip. Jack groaned a dark, needy sound, his hands tangling in her hair. Encouraged, Emma opened her mouth and took the very tip of him between her lips. She swiped her tongue over the slit at the end and a salty taste exploded in her mouth. His hips jerked at her touch, thrusting upward, and an incredible sensation of power filled Emma. He liked what she was doing to him. With renewed confidence, she relaxed her jaw, opened her mouth wider and took more of his erection inside. Jack thrust again, slowly and with more control this time. Emma swirled her tongue then sucked, drawing on his cock and treating him like a sweet—something delectable and delicious to savor.

"You can be a bit rougher," he murmured in a husky voice. "But don't bite," he added hastily when she opened her mouth wider still and introduced the slightest scrape of teeth.

Emma smirked as much as she could with a mouthful of cock. Pleasure coursed through her body as he massaged her head with his big hands. He set up an easy surge and withdrawal, each successive thrust going deeper into her mouth. His cock had been big before but now it filled her mouth and she loved it. Her breasts felt swollen and needy. A simmering sensation, half pain and half pleasure tortured Emma. Juices surged between her legs. So wet. So desperately needy for his cock to fill the emptiness.

He pulled from her mouth without warning, taking her by surprise. "Did I do something wrong?"

Jack barked a laugh. "Hell no! Anymore right now and I'd come. I'd rather come inside your pussy." He levered up on his elbows then leaned over to grab a condom off the bedside cabinet.

"I want to put it on." Emma held out her hand.

"I'll put it on." He ripped the packet open with his teeth and rapidly rolled the condom onto his member. "Ride me," he murmured, his dark eyes glowing with promise.

"Oh, a challenge, huh?" Emma straddled his hips and grasped his cock in her right hand. She couldn't resist stroking his length and feeling the power of him.

"Don't torture me, Emma. Or else I'll take matters into my own hands."

Humor surfaced inside Emma. She was tempted to tease, but his hands locked around her forearms in a silent bid for obedience. She placed his cock at the mouth of her cunt and eased down, closing her eyes to savor the stretching of internal muscles, the slide of their bodies as they joined and he pushed deep.

"Move faster," he directed.

Emma's eyes shot open as she snorted and executed a smart salute. "My ride. My way." She maintained her easy pace, enjoying the sparks of pleasure igniting her body.

He reached up to cup her breasts and tweaked one nipple. Emma gasped, catching her bottom lip between her teeth as sensation raced through her sensitized body. After this afternoon he knew how much she liked that, how hot it made her. Then he reached up to where their bodies joined and slid a teasing finger around her swollen clitoris. His touch was firm, but not enough to push her over into orgasm.

"Please," Emma pleaded. "Do that again. A fraction harder. Now."

Jack grunted as she rose then lowered herself slowly on his cock. Excruciatingly slow, so he massaged her right where she needed it. "You want to give instruction but not to take it?"

"Ohhhh," Emma moaned. She swayed above him, feeling powerful yet needy, feeling as though she could do anything. The first tremors of orgasm shimmered through her, radiating outward until fiery flames licked through her lower body. Her eyes drifted closed so she could savor the experience. The rise and the slow return. The sense of fullness. The slide of their bodies, the intimacy of it. The shimmer deepened. Emma sucked in a pained breath as she balanced on the precipice, unsure of whether to move again and push over or to remain poised in anticipation. Then she felt Jack's fingers, nimble and clever, rubbing her in just the right place, just the right way. A cry escaped. Her body jerked, and she shattered. Her pussy clenched tight around Jack's cock. Emma's head tipped back as she rode out the exquisite sensations then her whole body relaxed.

"My turn, princess," Jack whispered, and he gripped her hips and lifted her off him. Before she could blink, he'd placed her face down on the bed and raised her ass in the air. His big hands cupped her buttocks, making Emma shiver with renewed awareness. He could have as many turns as he wanted. She wasn't finished with him yet.

Jack palmed her ass then ran a finger down the crevice between her butt cheeks. A shiver racked her body and he hesitated. He'd hate to frighten her. When she didn't voice any objections, he took it a little further. Gripping his cock in one hand, he positioned himself at the mouth of her pussy. He pushed inside until her heat enveloped him. She was wet—her juices coated his cock and made his surge and retreat easy and incredibly arousing. But he needed a little more for what he intended. Jack reached for the lubrication again. Half of him expected questions, but they didn't come. Instead, she made a sexy little moan that tightened his balls and made his blood run hotter. Who'd have guessed that the little sparrow was such a sexual creature?

Jack pumped a generous amount of lube on his palm and smeared it from where they were joined all the way up to the puckered rosette of her anus.

The serpent inside him roared. Sex. Now. Jack held the beast back by setting up a lazy surge and retreat. In and out of her pussy. His cock swelled as the pleasure rolled through his body.

"What are you doing to me?" she whispered, her words throaty. Sexy.

Jack rubbed his finger back and forth over her rosette, delicately probing while continuing the steady strokes of his cock into her pussy. "Don't you like it? Tell me if you don't like anything I do to you."

"It feels different," Emma said finally. "But good. I like it."

Jack made a mental note to check out the sex toys she'd won. If she liked this and wanted to try more, he was ready.

The single light that shone over the bed highlighted her creamy skin. Being able to see his cock slide in and out of her cunt was an incredible turn-on. His darker skin against her pale, creamy curves. Jack hastened the pace, removing his finger from her anus so he could grip her hips and hold her steady for each stroke. He felt her quiver deep inside, clasping and clenching at his cock. He jerked his hips, ramming his cock home, flesh slapping against flesh until he erupted, spurting his seed deep and hard with a loud groan.

Gradually, Jack eased away from Emma, separating their bodies. A sharp intake of breath made him still. The noise came from behind the mirror. Fuck, he'd forgotten about their watchers. He'd forgotten everything except Emma and how it felt to pound into her body. Admitting that fact, even to himself, scared the shit out of him.

* * * * *

"We need to check out all the different activities more closely," Jack said the next morning, trying to avoid looking at Emma's cleavage and force away memories of what they'd done to each other throughout the night. The serpent wasn't cooperating. Jack's cock leapt with enough vigor to fuck a netball team—the whole seven plus reserves. Bloody blue moon was really pushing his libido.

Emma dropped her hairbrush into her pink canvas bag and rose from the stool that sat in front of the dressing table. "Good. Where do we go first?"

Jack ripped his gaze away from Emma and glared at the mirror above the bar. That was another thing. He couldn't be sure if a sound system went along with the two-way mirror. They'd have to watch what they said in case it was recorded.

He risked another glance at Emma. Her smile was so bright it almost blinded him. Damn. Now she had expectations. He'd have to make it clear his lone status wasn't going to change. He was going to hurt her, and despite the necessity, he regretted it. Emma was a likeable girl. Easy to be with. Tempting. But after Rachel, he didn't want to put himself through an emotional wringer again. Admitting to the whole taniwha monster thing, and all the garbage that came along with the truth. About him. About George Taniwha & Co., and the team of taniwhas who worked as private investigators. Nah, he'd skip the emotional crap. Better she was hurt a little now, than come face to face with monsters later.

"I think we should split up."

"Oh." She wrinkled her nose. "I thought we'd spend time together like all the other couples."

"We only have the week." Jack scowled at the time constraint reminder. It was tighter than Emma realized. With the blue moon coming up on Saturday, he'd need to have plentiful sex or shift to avoid excruciating pain. He'd hoped to have this case wrapped up quickly and be back home in time for the fall of the blue moon. It was bloody inconvenient, but once he shifted, he was stuck in his taniwha form for twenty-four hours. Suffering through a full moon was bad enough but a blue moon... Jack forced away the dire thoughts to concentrate on Emma. "I forgot to tell you. I made an appointment for you at the spa for this afternoon." He pulled a small card from his pocket and handed it to her.

"Wow! Thank you," Emma said.

"It's not all luxury. You need to ask questions and check out the spa area without being obvious. Think you can do that?"

Emma gave a decisive nod. "I've trained for it. Which areas do you want me to check out this morning? Will we meet up for lunch? It might look a bit strange if we don't."

"Let's go," Jack said. "We'll talk on the way."

The early morning sun peeked over the stand of native trees, warming the clearing and petanque pit not far from the entrance to their apartment block.

Jack took Emma's arm and set a brisk pace. "We'll walk along the beach."

Emma flashed a smile and tucked her hand into his as soon as the path widened enough for them to walk side by side. Jack froze momentarily before resuming his long strides toward the beach. Her floral scent swam through his senses, making it difficult for him to concentrate. Why did she have to touch him all the time? If she stroked her hand across his serpent tattoo one more time…

"We need to watch what we say while we're in our room." Jack couldn't make up his mind whether to snatch his hand from her grasp or not. Her touch burned like a brand, bringing every one of his senses to life. He heard her soft breathing, the waves rushing to shore and a gull wheeling overhead, felt the soft texture of her hand and bare arm. Man, he had to get a grip. *Concentrate.* "It's possible our room is bugged."

"Someone listening in on us? I don't— Someone's watching us right now! No, don't look." Emma's eyes widened then she leaned closer and twined her arms around his neck. "Kiss me."

It was an order, and Jack found himself in a lip-lock with Emma before he could ask questions. Her lips were soft, and smooth and moist and distracting. She slipped her tongue between his lips, and Jack was a goner. Taste and sensation kicked him in the gut, combining with the feel of her curvy breasts plastered against his chest. The taniwha gave a sleepy yawn then woke rapidly with a demanding growl. Jack took over the kiss, plunging his tongue into her mouth and withdrawing in a facsimile of the sexual act. Suddenly, he wanted to rip her clothes off and plunge into her hot pussy. He didn't care about an audience or the public location. He just wanted to fuck her senseless. But what he wanted and what he got were two different things. Jack struggled to hold onto the semblance of sanity that remained. Her fingers curled into his shoulders, her nails digging into his flesh through the thin shirt he wore. The small pain jerked his cock tight enough to cause him discomfort. Emma wriggled even closer, rubbing against his chest and groin and making a sound that resembled a purr. Dammit if the serpent didn't purr in tandem.

Jack tore his mouth away from Emma's. Panic roared through him as the taniwha clamored inside his head, demanding he take what Emma offered. The ever-present guilt surfaced, bringing uneasiness. He was using her, and he had to stop because he didn't intend to follow through and give her what she needed. Jack removed his hands from Emma and took a giant step away. She needed a man who could commit wholly to her. Jack Sullivan wasn't that man.

"I'm not doing that again," he muttered. "What's our watcher doing?"

"Nothing. I made it up," Emma said, lifting her chin up in the air with hauteur. "There isn't anyone watching. And I can't believe that our room is bugged either. This is a low-level investigation. George said so."

"Dammit, Emma! Our room is bugged," Jack roared. Frustration rode him hard. If she'd been male, he could have smacked her. He should damn well tell her about the two-way mirror. If he could trust her to maintain natural behavior, he would have told her about the voyeurs. He stared at the thin gold chain that hung around her neck, his hands fisting. Taking a deep breath for calm, he said, "This is the plan for this morning. I'm going to check out the gym since this is the most logical place for drugs. I'd like you to check out the pool area and this afternoon the spa. Talk to people. Mahoney has to shift the drugs somehow."

Thankfully, Emma must have realized she'd pushed him hard enough and merely nodded agreement.

"We'll meet up for lunch and compare notes. And you can keep your hands to yourself. We're not having sex again. Last night was a mistake." Jack turned away from her wounded expression and stomped off without looking back.

* * * * *

Emma didn't understand Jack. He ran hot then cold like a water tap on a hot day. It was difficult to keep up. One minute, he seemed to enjoy kissing her and then there was the sex. She squeezed her eyes shut and conjured up the memory of their bodies sliding together in the many different ways they'd tried the night before. The way his muscular body felt beneath her hands. And his sexy serpent tatt. A tingle sprang to life between her legs and she stirred restlessly on the sheet-covered couch inside the spa. The idea of never making love with Jack again sent a touch of panic swirling through her mind. She had to get him to change his mind. And if he didn't, she'd try again. They were good together, and one time didn't qualify as a win in the bet with her girlfriends.

The slap of soft soles on the tiled floor heralded the return of the spa attendant. Emma opened her eyes and lifted her head. Eek, that green stuff looked a bit nasty. Didn't smell much better, either. Emma wondered if Jack had intended this spa visit as punishment.

The attendant smeared green paste all over her back, from shoulders to toes and bade her lie still to let the stuff dry for five minutes. Then, Emma had to turn over for the woman to smear the paste on her front. When she looked like the original green alien, she was left in solitary splendor to dry and absorb the goodness from the paste. Mood music slipped stealthily into the room from concealed speakers, while the green glop did its work.

Emma must have fallen asleep. An hour later, the woman shook her awake and directed her to the shower. Feminine chatter hit her the moment she opened the door into the huge shower block. In the outer area, large mirrors covered the wall. A line of padded stools stood ready for women to attend to makeup and hair. A vase of pink roses and white gypsophila fragranced the air. Emma moved through into the steam-filled shower area. Several women, with varying shades of paste covering their bodies, were waiting for showers.

Time for some questions, Emma thought, remembering Jack's terse instructions. "Your paste doesn't smell much better than my seaweed," she said.

The other woman laughed. "Ah, but I'm a prettier color."

"That's debatable," Emma said studying the bright yellow decorating the other woman.

"Oh, look. The communal shower's emptying. Let's grab it. We'll be waiting for ages for these ones."

Emma shrugged. Suited her. She grabbed the canvas bag the spa had provided for her clothes and hurried over to the communal shower with her new friend close on her heels. Three other women bounded over. Emma blinked. Each of them was a different color, covered head to toe with a similar thick paste to her.

"I don't know which of us looks worst," she said, glancing from woman to woman with a critical eye.

"I hope they don't have security cameras getting shots of my naked ass," a dark-haired woman said.

"Do you think anyone will recognize it in purple?" Emma said.

They glanced from one to the other then burst into shrieks of laughter.

"Last one to wash off is a rotten egg," one said.

"You already look like a rotten egg," Emma quipped.

As one, they made for the shower door with good-natured pushing, breasts and butts jostling, and lots of laughter.

Ten minutes later, they were clean and ready to go back for the next part of their treatments.

"How about we meet up at the bar afterward?" the ex-purple woman suggested.

"Good idea," Emma said. It would give her a chance to ask questions. "I'd like to see how we all turn out," she added with a conspiratorial grin.

"Make it the poolside bar," another said, "and we can watch the sunset."

Two hours later, Emma walked into the poolside bar. She had no trouble spotting the women she'd come to meet. Raising her hand in greeting, she ambled over to the bar and waited for the barman to finish with his current customer.

Her gaze wandered the bar before settling back on the barman. With his blond surfer-boy looks, he was easy on the eye. His blue resort shirt stretched over muscular shoulders, the tight sleeves highlighting a set of well-developed biceps. Emma frowned.

"Would you like me to suggest a cocktail?" the barman asked in a husky voice. "Can't have a pretty lady getting frown lines."

Emma started and gave a self-conscious laugh. "I was miles away. What would you suggest?"

"How about the house special cocktail? Good for what ever ails you. Tastes good, too."

"Sure." Emma watched his deft movements as he sliced an orange. "What's it like working here? Are you allowed to use the facilities on your days off?"

"I use the gym a lot," the barman said as he competently measured and mixed a cocktail for her. "The job suits me. Everyone's happy. Lots of people wanting fun." Woman throwing themselves at him, Emma translated as she intercepted the avid gaze of an attractive brunette at the other end of the bar.

"Maybe you can give me some quick advice—if you do weights that is."

"I enter Ironman contests," he said. "I've lifted my share of weights."

"What's your name? Have you placed in any of the local competitions?"

"I came second in the Taupo Ironman," he said.

Emma oohed and ahhed and fluttered her lashes. She leaned over the bar to stroke her hand across his forearm. "Wonderful. If I wanted to train for a bodybuilding contest, who should I talk to at the gym? Just for some initial pointers. I've been thinking about it for a long time now. No time like the present."

"Max is the one you need to see," the barman said without hesitation. "He's an ex-bodybuilder and knows everything that's worth knowing."

"Thanks! I'll check it out first thing tomorrow morning. Nice to chat with you." She paid for her cocktail then wandered over to the group of women by the pool.

"Hello." Emma pulled out a chair and sat down.

"We're going to play strip poker. Would you like to play?"

Emma hesitated before deciding it would be a good opportunity to get to know the women. It was possible that one of them had info or had seen something that would help her and Jack in their investigation. She'd just have to slip her questions into the general conversation. "Okay," she said. "But you'll have to show me how to play."

"Oh, good." One of the women rubbed her hands together and grinned wickedly. "A rookie to fleece. Deal up."

* * * * *

Jack checked their room, but Emma wasn't there. Since he couldn't hear any vibrations from behind the mirror, he took the opportunity to search the room. If there were hidden cameras, his search would alert those who had rigged their room, but he decided to risk it. Instinct told him the cameras were activated whenever the voyeurs were present so they wouldn't need to search through hours of meaningless film. They were probably able to guess when the occupants of the room were present since most guests would attend the gala dinners and special nights. Either that, or they had resort staff alert them when guests were in their rooms. He moved in a systematic manner around the room, searching every conceivable hiding place for audio and listening devices.

"Nothing," he muttered, checking his watch. Perhaps it was as he'd thought—they'd lucked out scoring a room that voyeurs could access, making the addition of sound unnecessary. Or, they'd decided it would be easier to add a soundtrack later, something that would appeal more to their audiences than the words the innocent actors might say. Jack grimaced. Nah, it couldn't be that simple. Surely, they'd want sound? Jack crossed over to the bed and sat while he considered the problem. Where the hell could they hide sound equipment? Enlightenment hit, along with a feral grin of triumph. Under the bloody bed.

Bingo, he thought less than a minute after his brainwave. He tugged at the wiring in such a way that it appeared as though the resort staff had damaged it while vacuuming under the bed. He'd check each time he returned to the room. It should be simple enough now he knew what to look for.

He wandered over to the window and stared out, wondered if he should worry about Emma's absence.

Outside, the sun was starting to set. Ribbons of fiery red and orange spread across the horizon as the sun sank lower. Over on the mainland, people started to switch on their lights and they twinkled in pockets of illuminations along the coast.

Jack paced the length of the bedroom and back. Time for a drink. Tension thrummed through him, and he didn't have to think too hard to analyze the cause. *Emma.* Jack checked his watch again before deciding to shower and change for the themed pirate dinner the resort was hosting.

Half an hour later, Jack was ready, dressed in tight black trousers and a loose white shirt that made him feel like a sissy.

Tight black leather boots encased his feet and calves. He caught a glimpse of his reflection in the mirror and snorted. He'd be glad when this assignment was over and his life got back to normal. He was *really* looking forward to the tarts and vicars night later in the week.

What the devil was Emma doing? Although they hadn't agreed on a time to meet back at the room, it had been implied it would be before dinner. In his mind at least. He grabbed up the keycard, thrust it inside his back trouser pocket and slammed from the room. If something had happened to her, he'd never forgive himself. And if she didn't have a good reason for not showing up and worrying him, he was going to wring her bloody neck.

The bar near the restaurant was hopping, full of pirates ready to plunder and party the night away. Emma wasn't there. A few people had drifted into the restaurant and the reception area, but no sign of Emma. The pool bar wasn't as busy but there was a cluster of people, mainly men at the far end of the outdoor balcony. Despite the warmth of the evening, a gas heater burned above the table where the group sat. Roars of laughter filled the air followed by the odd groan.

"Come on, Emma," a male voice chided loudly. "Concentrate."

Jack's gut tightened as he strode up to the massed group.

"Forget what he said, love." The voice was low and slurred. "Don't concentrate. Get your gear off. Show us your pussy."

Jack scowled and elbowed his way through the men crowding around the table.

"What do you think you're doing?" a man snapped.

Jack cast him a ferocious glare and the man backed up to let him through. Jack took one look and cursed.

Fuck, he was gonna wring her scrawny neck. His hands flexed at the pleasurable thought as he scanned her flushed face. The woman was tipsy, giggling fit to wake the dead and practically naked. His gaze tracked over her butt, and he corrected himself. She was naked. Those panties didn't cover enough to call her clothed.

He stepped up behind her naked back and bent to breathe in her ear. "What are you doing?"

Emma whirled around so quickly her naked breasts bobbed up and down. "Losing," she warbled.

Alcoholic fumes hit him in the face. "I can see that," Jack said with a calm he didn't feel.

The other four women sitting around the table were in various stages of undress but they were all more fully clothed than Emma. Jack wanted to grab a towel, a tablecloth, anything to cover her beautiful naked breasts. All of a sudden, he felt possessive. He didn't want the others to see the tiny mole on the curve of her left breast. And if the guy behind him didn't stop pushing so he could cop an eyeful of Emma and her semi-clothed friends, Jack was going to rearrange his nose for him. The beefy male could have fries with the rearranged nose if he wanted—Jack wasn't fussy.

Emma turned around and beckoned him closer. She wrapped her arms around his neck and whispered in his ear. "I don't want to lose. I hate to lose, but I don't know what to do with my hand. Can you help me?"

"Yeah, okay. What have you got in your hand?"

Emma fanned out her cards so he could see. Feeling the weight of a stare, Jack glanced up. Every one of the four women sitting at the table was staring at him. Suddenly Jack felt like a lump of beef being chucked to the dogs. He turned away to concentrate on Emma's cards. She had a pair of sixes and that was it. Jack maintained an impassive face. With that hand, she was stuffed. Unless she bluffed. Jack leaned closer to whisper instructions in her ear. She turned to him and winked.

Surprise kicked him in the ribs. Emma wasn't as drunk as she seemed.

"Are you in?" the dark-haired woman who was dealing asked.

Emma's body language screamed confident, and pride grew in Jack. "I'm in."

"Cards?" the dealer asked.

Emma didn't bother to look at her cards before she shook her head.

"I'll take two," one woman said.

The men crowding the table were silent as they watch the ending stages of the game. Jack scanned the faces, ready to lash out if anyone tried to help out by letting the others know that Emma was bluffing.

"I fold."

"Me too."

"I'm out." The cards slapped face down on the table.

The last woman studied Emma then laid her cards down. "I'm out."

"Take it off! Take it off!" The chant started with one man then others joined in as the four women removed a garment each.

Jack noticed gooseflesh forming on Emma and decided to take action. "Sorry to be a spoil sport, but I need Emma to come with me. Maybe you can finish the game tomorrow?" *Over his dead body*.

"Good," said the slim blonde sitting on Emma's right. "I'm getting cold, and I'm also chicken." She laughed, gesturing at her pale pink panties. They were the only item of clothing she wore. "I have a premonition that I'm going to be the first naked body. I'm going to quit while I'm ahead."

Jack relaxed as the men started to drift away. "Ladies." He inclined his head and turned to Emma. "Ready?"

Emma knew he wasn't pleased with her. It was in the set of his shoulders and the grim line of his mouth. Well, he could just deal with it. She had flushed out a few leads to check out tomorrow, and she wasn't going to apologize for her methods. Besides, she wasn't the only one to bare her breasts tonight.

"It won't take me long to get ready. I'll meet you back here if you like."

Jack handed Emma her T-shirt, his dark eyes glinting dangerously. "I don't think so."

Damn, he was going to be difficult.

Emma pulled the shirt over her head then yanked on her denim shorts. She picked up her shoes, dropped them inside the canvas bag the spa had allowed her to keep and stalked off. She heard Jack fall into step behind her.

The walk back to their room took forever. Emma was very conscious of Jack walking behind. She could practically feel his glare between her shoulder blades but that didn't stop her adding an extra little sway to her hips. Her nipples were already pulled tight from the chill of the night air, but now they tingled insistently. She sucked in a hasty breath and hastened her pace. The path changed from pavement to gravel. Emma winced at the sharp stones beneath the soles of her feet.

"What's wrong?" The tone was sharp enough to tell her this was a man on the edge. She'd pushed him hard enough.

"Bare feet," she muttered.

Without warning, he swept her off her feet and dangled her over his shoulder. Her butt poked up into the air and the blood rushed to her head. Her canvas bag hit his ass with each step.

"What are you doing?" she shrieked, kicking out ineffectually with her feet. "My brains will fall out."

"Close your mouth and you won't lose them," he snapped, tightening his grip on her flailing legs. He continued to stride along the graveled path without difficulty or labored breathing.

Emma took a deep breath ready to harangue him when she glanced down toward the ground. Her gaze lit on his butt. It was tightly encased in black trousers that gave her a spectacular view. Emma wanted to bite. Really badly. She licked her lips and suddenly being so close to Jack wasn't an undignified punishment. It was a gift. Her heart pounded as he strode through the automatic doors at the entrance to their block of rooms. Between her legs moistened with the carnal thoughts, truly wicked thoughts that circled her mind like a bird of prey after an evening meal.

"Quit that," Jack barked as he paused outside their room and plucked the keycard from his pocket. He shouldered open the door and negotiated the doorway without hurting Emma. Then, he let her slide back over his shoulder until her feet hit the ground. The brush of her unbound breasts against his shoulder and hard chest made her gasp. The intimate touch of his hand on her ass as he helped her stand made her gulp.

"Quit what," she whispered.

"Those little sighs," he muttered moving away from her as if she'd scalded him. His dark eyes were wary as they moved over her face then flickered down her body.

Emma barely suppressed her shiver of desire.

Jack could smell her arousal, and it had woken the taniwha inside, the part he was desperately trying to keep in a locked compartment. The beast roared his need for sex. Hot, sweaty, no holds barred sex. Then, she walked toward him, her hips swaying with a pert wiggle that made his throat tighten along with every appendage on his body. When he felt the wall at his back, he realized he'd been in a steady retreat. With the wall behind him, the only way to avoid Emma was to move her out of the way. Which would involve touching.

She touched him first, and he couldn't restrain a flinch. Her fingers were hot, the heat searing through his thin shirt and into his skin beneath.

"You like my sighs?" Her voice was low. Breathy. And made him think of sex even more. His cock was painfully tight, nudging against the placket of his trousers.

"No." Damn, the one night had been bad enough. But another night… His conscience groaned then spoke sternly to him. *Don't. Do. It.*

"You're trembling."

Him? He didn't...shit! He was shaking like a tree in a storm. "Hadn't you better get ready for the pirate dinner?" *Feeble, Jack. Real feeble. Exert yourself, man. Act like you're her boss instead of a victim.* He watched mesmerized as she licked her lips until they gleamed in the moonlit room.

"Suddenly, I don't feel like going to the dinner. I'm tired." He caught her glance at the bed with a sense of alarm. With that come-hither look in her blue eyes, no way did she want to go to bed to sleep!

Chapter Five

ɞ

The woman was undressing him with her eyes. Jack felt the situation escalating from his control and with the taniwha's roars pounding inside his head, his grip was tenuous at best. Then, she raised a hand and traced the V of flesh visible at his neck. Jack lost it. He grabbed her by the shoulders and yanked her against his chest. Man, she felt good, her soft curves pillowed against him. She leaned all her weight against him, brushing her belly against his sensitive cock. His cursed trousers were so tight Jack thought he'd lose circulation to his groin if he didn't get them off soon. The thought faded when their lips collided, greedy and ravenous for a taste of each other. He explored the moist cavern of her mouth, the contrasting hardness of her teeth and the softness inside her cheek. She tasted of limes and salt. Emma. It was damned addictive. When they finally pulled apart, they were both breathing hard.

Her blue eyes glittered and a soft smile played on her lips. "Did you want to go to the dinner?"

"No." But he didn't want to do this either. Another night of horizontal dancing with Emma smacked of heading down Commitment Road. Just a hop, skip and a dance away from Wedding Row.

His hands tightened around her shoulders. Nope, he didn't want this. He was going to push her away. Push her away—

Liar.

Jack wanted sex with Emma so badly his hands, his body still trembled. Even the idea of them being watched didn't bother him as much as it did at the start.

Her warm hands burrowed under the fabric of his shirt, and just like that, Jack's willpower toppled and he gave up the fight. "Dammit, woman. You're killing me here. If you're going to undo things, start with the trousers. They're cutting off my circulation."

"Poor baby," she cooed. "Can't have that." She redirected her busy hands to the fly of his trousers and cupped his erection, teasing him some more.

Jack heard her wildly beating pulse and knew she was excited. "I bet your panties are wet. I bet you're wet for me."

A soft blush suffused her cheeks. "Why don't you find out?" she whispered, her lashes drifting down to hide the sleepy expression in her blue eyes.

Holding back a grin, he slid his hands beneath the hem of her T-shirt. Blue. It matched her eyes. His hand skimmed the warm flesh of her belly. She sucked in a rapid breath and her stomach as well. Jack decided to ignore the feminine vanity. To his mind, she was perfect. He didn't get a sore neck when he kissed her, and he didn't feel in danger of flattening her if he took her in a missionary position. Yeah, she was perfect—more's the pity. His fingers traced across her rib cage then a little higher to hold the generous weight of one plump breast. He lifted her T-shirt, exposing her breasts to his gaze.

"Beautiful," he whispered. Jack wet his forefinger in his mouth then traced around the areola of one breast. Her pink nipple puckered, drawing tighter before his fascinated eyes. Leaning closer, he blew, his breath moist. Warm. Emma shuddered and made a tiny sound of encouragement at the back of her throat. Jack had never really taken the time to explore a feminine body. Had never been interested in anything but satiating the taniwha's demands. But now, despite the insistent pain in his groin, he wanted to touch, to explore the mysteries of Emma. He pressed a kiss in the valley between her breasts then licked along the fine web of blue veins beneath the pale surface. Strawberries. Tonight, she smelled of sweet, juicy strawberries.

"Stop teasing me," she said in a thick voice.

"I want to make sure I win my bet. I want you wet—dripping with your juices—so I can pound between your legs the minute I remove your panties."

Another shudder racked Emma's body. Jack smiled against the curve of her breast and placed tiny kisses, tantalizingly brief on the top of her breasts, near her nipple and on the undersides of the plump globes.

Emma tangled her hands in his hair, gripping tightly as she tried to direct his mouth to her nipple. Her fingernails dug into his scalp, and Jack's amusement deepened.

"Hurry up," she muttered with a grumpy edge to her voice.

Instead of giving her the relief she wanted, Jack let his hands drop to the dome snap at the waistband of her shorts. He tugged the snap and it parted with a sharp crack. The zipper slid down allowing the denim material to sag down around her hips. Jack wet his finger again and ran it along the elastic waistband of her panties. He studied the wet trail he'd left and sucked in a deep breath. Man, his cock ached, the pressure for release intense and unrelenting. But if he waited, held off, his orgasm would be mind-blowing. A memory to dig out when he returned to solitary life alone in his seaside home with only his scruffy tomcat for company.

Jack knelt in front of her, sliding the shorts down her long legs. He helped her balance so she could step out and kick them away.

The scent of her arousal hit him—spicy and seductive and with a hint of strawberry. The same fruity aroma that perfumed her skin. He pressed his nose against her lower belly and breathed in her scent so he would remember. His lips moved, and he scraped his teeth against the sensitive flesh, nipping then soothing.

"I'm hot for you now, Jack," she said almost defiantly.

"Let's see, shall we?" But even though his words indicated action, he still dallied, teasing both of them to the point of madness. He palmed her naked buttocks, gripping one cheek in each hand. More than a handful, just the way he liked—a sexy curve to hold onto when he wanted to thrust into her tight pussy. He kneaded the flesh, enjoying the fact she didn't attempt to hide her generous ass or try to move away from his attentions to that area of her body. Jack liked that about Emma—her acceptance of her size.

He loosened his grip on one butt cheek and ran his fingers in the crevice between. Emma jumped in surprise as he followed the G-string down. Then she rocked her hips trying to massage her clit to gain relief.

"Not yet, sweet cheeks." Jack allowed his finger to travel between her legs, just a brief foray. His finger emerged wet. Emma was ready for his possession. Jack tipped back his head to meet her gaze.

"Please," she murmured, moving her weight from foot to foot.

He lifted the damp finger to his mouth and maintaining her gaze, he licked it, savoring the tart taste of her juices. Emma moaned, her blue eyes dark with arousal.

"Would you like my mouth on you? We haven't done that yet."

Her eyes widened a fraction before she nodded.

Jack ran his fingers under the elastic band of her g-string and slowly tugged away her panties.

There were changes from this morning. "What have you done?" he murmured, shaking his head. It seemed the spa had a lot to answer for. "What else did you do in that spa?"

Emma glanced down at her pelvic region. "Don't you like it? I thought my heart looked sexy. And besides, you made the appointment."

Well, he couldn't argue with that. "It's...cute," he said finally staring at the close-clipped heart that shielded her femininity. Jack drew her panties down her legs and then leaned closer to lick around the edge of the heart. She smelled intoxicating, and he gave into the temptation to comb his fingers through the heart then made a quick foray down her naked cleft. "You're not sore?"

"No side effects. Not yet anyway. They gave me some cream in case I have itching. Are you going to take all night?"

"Just drawing out the anticipation." And making himself crazy with lust, but it would be worth it. He glanced down at his hand and saw the glint of scales starting to form on the top of his hand. The shadow of claws had formed beneath his fingernails, ready to pop out into webbed talons. He'd run out of time to play with her. "Turn around," he said. "Put your hands on the wall."

She hesitated, looking uncertain.

"Do it."

Slowly, she turned to face the beige-colored wall but cast another doubtful glance over her shoulder.

"Hands against the wall."

Emma sucked in a breath loud enough for Jack to hear. But she placed her hands, one at the time on the wall, her heart pounding and drawing the taniwha closer to the surface.

Jack ripped at the laces that fastened his shirt at the neck.

"What are you doing?" Emma half turned.

"Look at the wall," he barked. Jack scrambled for an excuse to keep her from seeing him. Iridescent scales shimmered on his chest—pearl gray scales the same color as the inside of a mussel shell. Thank God, his chest always changed before his back. If he hurried, the change would recede. "We're doing a role-play and you're the submissive. That means you follow orders. For a change." *Please let her follow his directions.* Jack eyed her still body with misgiving. He yanked at his belt buckle and peeled the trousers over his swollen cock with care. Seconds later he kicked the trousers out of his way and grabbed a condom. His breathing sounded harsh to his ears, and his hands shook, suddenly clumsy because their dexterity was compromised by the start of his change to taniwha form. He unrolled the condom awkwardly onto his penis, hoping like hell he didn't put a hole in the rubber with the sharp claws that extended from his fingers. The last thing he needed were baby taniwhas running around.

"What does a submissive do?" she whispered, still thankfully looking away from him at the wall.

"Follows orders," he growled. He didn't know what he'd do if Emma decided to disobey. Maybe he should introduce a bit of kink. Keep her busy with new experiences. And definitely a blindfold because if he didn't make haste, it was going to take time for the scales to fade from his body. "A submissive does what they're told when they're told. I'm not sure you could manage."

"Of course I can," she snapped.

Jack grinned at her indignation. A sharp, nagging pain shot through his stomach, making him double over with the pain. Damn, if he didn't hurry, he was going to be in trouble. Jack cast a belligerent gaze toward the window. The moon was almost full, and he could feel its siren pull with every particle of his body. Another sharp pain shot through him. Fuck, he hoped Emma was as ready for his possession as he thought, because he wasn't going to manage gentle tonight.

Jack ambled up to Emma and gingerly ran his finger pads over the silky smooth skin of her back, taking care not to scratch her with his claws.

"Spread your legs farther apart," he whispered, hoping she wouldn't notice the changed timbre of his voice. Generally, his vocal cords changed slowly still allowing him to speak in a growl before he shifted. Once he changed, all he could do was roar.

Emma widened her stance, drawing his attention to the full cheeks of her ass. He stepped up behind her so the fronts of his thighs brushed the backs of her legs.

"You feel hot."

"I am." Jack curled his hand around his cock and brushed the tip across the soft flesh of her backside. The resulting jolt ran the length of his body. He changed the direction, massaging his tip down the crevice between her ass cheeks.

Jack fingered her, skimming his fingers across the sensitive nub nestled in her core.

"Ohhh," she whispered, shifting her body weight slightly and pushing her ass outward.

The soft moan reverberated through the room, and his lips quirked as he leaned closer to nip the sensitive cords of her neck. Emma was so responsive with no pretense. No secrets. Jack's hands snaked around to cup her breasts in his hands. Guilt rose but he shoved it aside. He had a job to do.

"I'm wet for you now," she complained. "You must have noticed. Ohhh! Do that again."

A muscle jumped in his jaw and his cock swelled impossibly tight at her sexy sound. Jack kissed her shoulder again then sucked on her flesh. "You ready for me to fuck you?" he growled.

"Yesss," Emma hissed with a trace of impatience.

Jack felt the absurd need to hold himself in check for longer, but he already balanced on the fine line between pleasure and pain. He pumped his cock with one hand then shoved into her tight cunt. Hot pleasure simmered through his veins at the feel of her. Tight. Clinging. Grasping. Enough to send a man mad or keep a taniwha sane. God, she felt so good. Deep shudders shook him as he stroked, hard and fast.

Thank God, the change had slowed. His claws had retracted a fraction. The closeness with Emma and the charged hormones running through his body had pushed the serpent back to its den. Scales still glinted beneath his skin, but he could explain the phenomena away if he needed to.

"More," Emma gasped. Although she'd been skeptical about being taken against a wall, he'd made her so hot, so quickly she could barely think. All she could do was feel. Jack slid a hand over her belly then lower, to rub her clit. His cock filled her impossibly full, possessing her and stamping ownership. Frissons of excitement swelled to a heady spill of pleasure. Another pass of his finger pushed her over the edge and she shattered. Her breaths came in harsh pants, echoed by a grunt as Jack pumped into her then held still, his cock expelling semen deep inside her. Emma sighed softly as the ripples of pleasure kept coming, gentler now, but still consuming. Already, she wanted another go. The man to die for had her hooked, literally addicted, and she didn't think she'd ever be able to look at another man again.

Jack nuzzled her shoulder, his chest pressed against her back. He pulled out of her, removed the condom and led her over to the bed. They stared at each other for a long moment. Jack looked away first, glancing at the mirror above the bar.

"Interested in trying out some of the toys you've won?" he asked.

"Yes, please," Emma said, feeling suddenly happier. Sometimes, it seemed as if Jack was making love to her against his will. But if he wanted to play with toys, then it must be her imagination. Emma plucked her box of goodies off the bedside table and handed it to Jack. "What would you like to do first?" She took pleasure in watching him as he studied the contents of the box. His face was in the dark, his hair tousled, making him look mysterious and sexy. She leaned closer, brushing her breasts against his serpent tattoo.

Jack plucked two items from the box and handed them to her. A glowing thing that looked a little like a penis but had a sort of handle at the end. Emma read the packaging and felt hot all over. A butt plug. She'd liked it when Jack had touched her there before. Excitement rose inside at the thought of trying something new. The other was a jar of chocolate paste. Emma turned the package over to read the instructions. There were several illustrations of breasts decorated with the paste and made to resemble edible items. A snigger emerged. "Which one are we going to try?"

Jack grinned suddenly, making Emma catch her breath and stare. The man was so sexy when he smiled. "I've always liked

Christmas pudding," he murmured, reclaiming the package from her. He opened it, and the deep, rich scent of chocolate filled the air. Emma watched as he dipped his finger into the jar. He raised it to his lips and licked the paste away.

Desire unfurled in her belly. He pushed her back against the pillows and bent to take a nipple in his mouth. Jack drew hard. And just like that, Emma was wet and ready for his possession. Needy. Desperate. Why play with toys when she had the real thing?

"Jack?"

He glanced up, his dark eyes glowing strangely. *A quirk of the light*, she thought. "I need you inside me," Emma said. "We have all night. We can play with toys later."

Maintaining her gaze, he set the jar aside and reached for a condom. He covered his erection with calm, confident moves. "Just a little chocolate," he murmured. "I want to taste it on your skin."

Emma shivered at the avid note in his voice. No doubt about it—she was gonna die a happy woman.

* * * * *

"You like Thai food, too?" Emma paused in the middle of applying suntan lotion, ready to hit the pool straight after breakfast. "There's a great Thai restaurant near Botany Downs. We should go for dinner when we get back to Auckland."

"We're not a couple." The flat and final tone of his voice made Emma stare.

Shock punched her in the lungs, stealing her breath. "I thought—"

Jack scowled. "It's nothing personal, Emma. I need sex. You're handy and willing. It's as simple as that."

Emma's mouth opened then closed. Her jaw worked but words dammed up in her throat. She swallowed once. Twice. After clearing her throat, she managed to squeeze out a few words. "What you're saying is that our affair comes to an end once we leave the resort?"

Jack rolled his eyes toward the ceiling. "By George, I think she's got it."

"You bastard," Emma hissed. The urge to wrap her hands around his neck and squeeze until he gasped for air was strong. Tempting. But it would be too quick. The man needed to suffer like he was making her suffer. "I have—" She broke off midsentence. No way was she giving him the pleasure of trampling on her feelings any more than he had already. Tears built at the back of her eyes but damned if she'd show the feminine weakness. She straightened her shoulders and forced herself to meet his gaze without flinching. "Fine. At least I know where I stand. I won't force myself on you again." Although she tried to keep her voice even, it was colored by the distinct bite of temper.

Her canvas bag lay beside the bed. Averting her gaze from the ruffled bedcovers and memories of how they'd spent the night, she grabbed it up in her left hand. "I'm going out."

"Where?"

He had no rights where she was concerned. Her hand fisted so hard, the canvas strap of the bag dug into her palm. "I am going down to breakfast. I missed dinner and I'm hungry."

"Wait five minutes, and I'll come with you."

Emma stared at him incredulously. The man was thick as two planks. Did he want her to draw attention to them by having the mother of all temper tantrums in public? Because that was a dead cert—if he didn't quit with the big, bad private investigator act. "I don't think so." Emma terminated the conversation by leaving their room and shutting the door quietly behind her.

She stomped down the passageway to the front entrance. Despite telling Jack she was going to breakfast, this morning she'd skip a meal and head straight for the gym to start some subtle questioning.

The sooner the case was solved, the sooner she could leave and head home to lick her wounds. The thought gave her pause. She'd failed in her mission. Emma glared at the man tending the gardens and stormed down the path to the main part of the resort. Bypassing the restaurant, she carried on to the gym.

A male a few years younger than she manned the reception desk at the entrance. Highly tanned and muscled, he looked as though he belonged in an ad for a gentleman's magazine.

"Morning. Can I help you?"

Emma cast aside her sudden doubts. "I've never been to a gym before," she said. "I thought this week would be a good time to see if I like it before I fork out money for membership. How do I start?" She'd scope out the territory first before she started to ask questions.

"How about a tour of the facilities and a description of the different membership options. How does that sound?" The young man—his name badge read Allen—gave her his whole attention, making her feel important and soothing her wounded spirit. Emma shook free of his charismatic spell and nodded. "That sounds perfect."

Allen picked up a phone and minutes later another young man who could have been Allen's twin joined them.

Emma was introduced to various machines and shown the aerobics area, the weights area, the indoor swimming pool where a vigorous water aerobics session was underway. Once again, the instructor was an Allen clone but with red hair this time.

"You all look very fit." Emma batted her eyelashes at her guide. She paused hoping he'd pick up the conversation batten. If not, she'd play bimbo and ask stupid questions.

"Most of us are in training. Mahoney Resort enters a triathlon team in the Ironman competitions. I made the team," he added with modesty.

"That's awesome." Emma fluttered her lashes and peeked through narrowed eyes to judge the effect. Yes, he was lapping up her bimbo act. She let a tiny gurgle escape and flashed a grin. "What's a triathlon?"

"It's a competition. Competitors swim, they do a bike ride and then they have to run. Have you heard of Martin Hamilton? He won a gold medal at the Olympic games for New Zealand."

"Awesome," Emma cooed, closing the small gap between them. "Have you won a medal?"

"I'm going to one day," he said with confidence.

How? How did he know that? Or was he just psyching himself up? Positive thinking and all that? Emma thought rapidly, unsure of how hard to push. "Have you been training hard?" Her voice was breathless as she ran her fingers along his bulging biceps. The man was gorgeous, a real hottie, yet she didn't feel a thing. He wasn't Jack. Emma's mouth firmed at the thought. Jack didn't deserve her loyalty. And now she understood why he had a procession of babes waltzing through his life. The man didn't want to commit. He was a coward.

Her guide's eyes widened, and Emma realized she was blowing her bimbo act. "Do you?" she prodded.

"I train each day and…" He paused to look over her shoulder. "I have a special diet."

"Ohhh." Emma rubbed her finger back and forward across his tanned upper arm. "It's working." *What special diet?* she wondered with a trace of frustration. Perhaps if she shook him, she'd rattle the answer loose faster. Flirting wasn't helping. "I'd like to muscle up. Is there a fast way to do it?"

"You'd need to train every day for a few hours." His gaze held clear doubt. "Protein shakes might help. And you'd have to diet."

"Diet?" Bloody cheek of the man.

He shrugged and grinned. "The changing rooms and showers are there. Ladies to the left and men to the right. And that's about everything," he said, coming to stop by a row of stationary bikes facing a large video screen.

People drifted into the gym in ones and twos. Emma was pleased to see that there weren't many people in bright-colored spandex, the vision that popped into her head whenever she thought of a gym. Most people wore comfortable shorts and a T-shirt similar to her sleeveless top and stretchy back shorts.

Emma smiled brightly. "Okay. I'm interested. What do I do next?" She didn't intend to leave until she had answers.

"We do a fitness check. Would you like me to see if I can schedule one in for you? I have a personal trainer session in five minutes, otherwise I'd offer to do the check for you."

"Okay." Great. A fitness check. Emma hoped it didn't involve too much. Her muscles were sore from the sexual gymnastics of the night before.

They walked over to the receptionist's desk, and Emma scanned the gym. There were five, no, six beefy young men wearing the resort's uniform. Not a scrawny specimen among them. The two women she saw were also muscled up but it might be a coincidence. Jeesh, how was she going to find out? Perhaps they needed to check out the premises during the middle of the night when no one was around. Maybe the offices and places that were off-limits to guests.

"Jamie can do a fitness test, but she'll be another five minutes since she's with a client."

"That's fine," Emma said.

"Come with me, and I'll show you where to wait."

Emma followed her guide down a narrow corridor she hadn't noticed earlier. They passed two offices then came to a third room. Her guide opened the door and gestured Emma inside.

There were charts on the wall with illustrations depicting people doing different warm-up exercises.

"See if you can follow the diagrams and do a few stretches while you're waiting for Jamie. She won't be long."

"Thanks for the tour," Emma said, smiling and fluttering her lashes, keeping up the image of bimbo to the end.

Her guide left, leaving the door slightly ajar. Emma debated if five minutes would be long enough to explore the offices next door and decided to risk it. She was halfway out the door when she heard several masculine voices in the office closest to the room in which she stood. *Bother.* Emma dithered, wondering what to do.

Raucous laughter suddenly filled the air.

"The couple in room 243?"

Emma stiffened. Shit, were they under investigation? She edged from the testing room, flattening against the beige walls so she wouldn't be seen easily.

"Oh, yeah," a loud voice said. "They go at it like rabbits. All night long."

Emma's mouth dropped. Someone had heard them? How mortifying!

"What do they look like?"

"Both tall. The guy looks dangerous. Not the sort to meet in a blind alley on a dark night."

"What about his partner?"

"A bit big for my tastes."

"What are you talking about, man? Her ass is fuckable. I'd like to ram one right up her."

Emma's jaw sagged so much it was a wonder it didn't hit the ground. These men had not only heard them, they'd watched them as well! But how? Why? Emma groped for understanding.

"What's the take been like for this couple?"

"Through the bloody roof. We've made more in three days than we made for the whole of last week."

People paid to watch her and Jack have sex? That was disgusting. Heat flooded her body followed closely by anger. Making love to Jack was private, dammit. Strictly because that's what Emma was doing—laying out her heart for Jack. The idea of other people watching...

"They're filming tonight and intend to release it as an amateur movie. It should win a prize for sure as well as make a ton of money."

Emma felt her face turn scarlet. Her teeth gritted so hard they were in danger of breaking. A tic burst into life in her jaw.

They were not going to get away with this.

Chapter Six

ജ

Footsteps at the far end of the passage galvanized Emma to action. She whipped back inside the room, easing the door shut behind her. Oh, boy. She had to get a grip. Warming up. That's what she was meant to be doing.

Emma sprinted over to the closest poster on the wall, rapidly read the instructions and attempted to emulate them. The muscles at the back of her thigh groaned in protest, sending a wave of jagged pain the length of her leg. Emma winced and eased up. Cripes if she'd known sex with Jack was going to be so strenuous she would have gone into training first.

"Though why you're worrying when Jack has as good as told you there's not going to be any more sex once we're off the island," she muttered. Thinking of sex brought her back to the main problem.

Movies.

Of her and Jack.

Naked.

The door to the room flew open and a tall redhead stepped inside. "Oh, good. You're warming up already. Excellent."

Oh, she was warming up all right. And busy thinking of payback.

"You look as though you're warm enough. I'll weigh you and take some muscle-to-fat ratios then I'd like to see what your existing level of fitness is. But first, I'll get you to fill in this form about your medical history."

Emma stopped torturing her legs and accepted the form and a pen from the woman.

Three quarters of an hour later, Emma teetered from the room on weak, rubbery legs. Jamie was a sadist.

Emma slowed as she passed the offices, but the men had gone so she had no idea what they looked like. Though she'd recognize their slimy voices if she heard them again. That was for sure!

The thought of putting them in their place reinvigorated Emma and she picked up the pace from a teeter to a stomp. At reception, she stopped to find out when the gym closed. A little recovery time wouldn't go astray. She'd come back later to do her first training session and ask more questions. Right now, she'd find Jack and let him know what was going on.

Jack found her first. As she strode along the beach heading for their room, a hand curled around her upper arm jerking her to a stop. Emma whirled ready to defend herself. "Jack." She straightened, tossing her head as his dark glare hit her. At least, she assumed he was glaring because the line of his mouth was straight and firm. Difficult to tell since he wore sunglasses.

"Where the hell have you been? I've been looking for you everywhere."

"I didn't know you cared," Emma said sweetly. No mistaking her tone for anything but snide and bitchy. Despite looking for him, he wasn't forgiven for blowing hot and cold. Jeesh, that sort of behavior was meant to be on her agenda. Men were supposed to be black and white, not shades of marbled gray.

"I was worried," he snapped. He took a closer look at her face then had the effrontery to stroke a finger across her flushed cheek. "What's wrong?"

Emma jerked from his touch and stalked farther along the beach before dropping onto a clean patch of sand. With legs outstretched, she stared out to sea. She felt rather than saw Jack sit at her side. The man could have put a shirt on, dammit!

"I've been at the gym. I wanted to follow up on something I heard from the bartender and also in the spa yesterday. While I was there, I heard some men talking. Our room is bugged." Emma turned to Jack, feeling the full thrust of anger and indignation and loss of privacy sweep through her body all over again. "We've been filmed having sex. They're going to sell it on the Internet."

The concern faded from Jack's face and he suddenly seemed more alert. Dangerous and in private investigator mode. Emma couldn't tell what he was thinking because of the glasses shielding his eyes. Bother the man and his rigid control. Just for once, she'd like to see him really lose his cool.

"Aren't you going to say anything?" she demanded. "Frankly, I'm pissed. What are we going to do about it?"

"We aren't going to do anything."

"What?" Emma's screech of outrage scared a foraging seagull. It took off into the air with a startled cry. "You knew? Why didn't you tell me?"

"I didn't think you'd be able to keep up the act if you knew we were being watched."

Right. This just kept getting better and better. "You could have given me the benefit of the doubt."

"I wasn't sure if they were onto us or not. It seemed better to ignore them and watch developments."

"And?" Emma didn't bother to hide her testiness.

Jack rolled toward Emma and tugged at a short springy curl just behind her ear. Emma was ready to blast him but he spoke first. "Someone is watching us right now."

Jack watched Emma carefully as he fingered another curl. He'd never seen her like this before—curt, irritable. Plain bitchy. He liked it.

"What are you doing?"

"We're going to give another show for our audience. Let's see how your acting skills shape up." Her blue eyes narrowed, making him want to laugh. "I dare you," he drawled.

She landed on top of him before he could blink, knocking the air from his lungs. Her leg slid between his, her thigh riding up high against his groin. Instantly his cock lengthened, and he knew by the gleam in her eyes she recognized the effect she had on him.

"I was thinking of a kiss." But his body had other ideas.

"Well, what's stopping you? Don't say the audience is putting you off," she mocked.

Jack glanced up and down the beach. Empty, apart from the man over on the far balcony. And he wouldn't see them either if they moved closer to the gnarled pohutukawa tree a few feet away. The sun streamed down from directly overhead, and Jack didn't need to check his watch to confirm the time. Almost midday.

He cupped her face in his hands, savoring the buzz of the waking taniwha simmering beneath his skin. "Nothing stopping me at all." He closed the distance between them so her breasts brushed his naked chest. Surprised she was even talking to him let alone letting him get this close after this morning, Jack wasn't about to back away from her challenge. He covered her lips and kissed her, really kissed her, thrusting his tongue deep into her mouth.

"Get a room, why doncha," a man called. He whistled shrilly.

A feminine giggle followed.

Where the hell had he come from? Jack slowly lifted his head, his gaze touching on her lips. They were pink. Moist. And he enjoyed caressing them more than he should. "Guess we'd better go to lunch. See if the big man has arrived back from the mainland. I heard the receptionist mention it. He was away overnight."

"Have you found anything helpful?"

"Nothing. Just a gut feeling." Jack stroked his finger across her silky cheek. His gut was working overtime, but he couldn't be sure if it was edginess because of the blue moon or instinct about the case.

"All the male employees are big. Muscled."

Difficult not to notice them, then there were the security guards who patrolled the perimeter of the resort. Keeping people in or out. Hard to say. "Did you notice the trophy cabinet when you were over at the gym?"

"Bulging with trophies."

Jack rolled off Emma and climbed to his feet. He extended a hand to her and helped Emma up. "I'm going to search the admin offices tonight."

"What time? How are we going to get around the watcher problem?"

"I'm not taking you with me." Jack didn't want to have to worry about her, but one look at her face told him she was going to argue. "We'll talk about it later."

They walked down the beach together, heading toward the main resort area and the restaurants.

"What are you doing this afternoon? I'm going to do a hike around the far boundary of the resort. I want to check out a couple of boats I saw this morning."

Emma nodded thoughtfully. "That would be a good way to get drugs either on or off the island. This is so frustrating. We haven't learned anything new. We don't know anything more than what we knew before we arrived."

"A lot of investigations are like this," Jack said. And she thought she was frustrated? Try being a taniwha with a blue moon on the horizon. His mind turned to sex. *One-tracked bloody thing.*

"I have a hair appointment. I thought I might be able to worm something out of the hairdresser or at least hear something interesting in the salon."

Jack glanced at her curly brown hair then shrugged. She couldn't get into much mischief at the hairdresser's.

"Okay. I'll meet you on the beach near the pohutukawa tree at six to discuss how we're going to get around our voyeurs."

"Perhaps we could stage a fight," she said. The twist of her lips was mocking. "It wouldn't be difficult shouting at you."

Jack grinned then sobered abruptly. He seemed to do that a lot lately. Smile. And usually it was Emma related.

"Don't laugh," she snapped. "I still haven't forgiven you for this morning. You should know that I'm big on revenge so watch your back. You never know when I might strike."

Jack stilled at the idea of Emma plotting revenge. A fight. His mind immediately went to the part after the fight when two lovers made up... Alarm bells tolled loudly inside his head. Hell. Emma Montrose was wriggling into his head. And it was bloody uncomfortable with her in there. Made him think things—impossible things—involving a future.

They walked into the restaurant, and some of Emma's poker partners waved at them to join them at their table.

Emma waved back and hurried over, giving Jack no option but to follow. She'd changed since they'd arrived. She seemed more confident. More everything. Heads turned when she walked past. Jack intercepted the gaze of another man watching her. Jack speared the guy with a dark scowl. The other man hastily looked away to make a selection from the buffet.

"Is everyone having a good time?" the hostess purred into her microphone at the front of the dining room.

The diners roared back a resounding yes, and she beamed.

As Jack dropped into the seat at Emma's side, he noticed several of the resort hostesses trot onto the stage bearing boxes.

Without warning, his gut churned.

"We have several appropriate gifts of the his and her nature. In this barrel, I have discs bearing the name of each guest. A roaring sound filled his head as she read off the first name. A couple at the table on the far side of the room sprang from their seats. Jack relaxed fractionally when a second name was read out.

"And finally," the hostess said. "Jack Sullivan and Emma Montrose."

Jack and Emma shared a telling glance, and it was obvious to Jack they were thinking the same thing. They were being set up, and it was going to make it difficult to leave the room to do a search of the resort if they were being watched.

Amidst much clapping and ribald shouts, he and Emma made their way up to the front to accept their prizes.

"What have you got?" one of Emma's new friends asked.

He was almost afraid to look. Jack ripped away the pretty steel gray bow and tore the black wrapping paper from the box. He lifted the lid to an array of sex toys. Jack jammed the lid back on.

"Toys," he said.

"Emma?" her friend said.

Emma glanced at Jack, her brows rising in a silent question. He shook his head. She tugged the tape from the pink parcel she'd received and peeked inside.

A soft gasp emerged, and Jack noticed she seemed a bit flushed.

"What is it?" Each of her friends leaned forward to peer inside.

"Ohhh," said one. "That's the newest model vibrator out. Wish I'd won that!"

"Why would she want a vibrator when she's got Jack?" another said.

Emma sneaked a look at Jack and found him staring at her. A flush ran the length of her body. But in truth, the vibrator wasn't such a bad prize to win. When they were finished this assignment, she might need it, because finding someone to fill Jack's place was going to be difficult.

Half an hour later, Emma finished her lunch and checked her watch.

"I'd better go," she said. "My appointment is in ten minutes."

"I'll walk you out," Jack said. He stood and picked up the box she'd been given as well as the one he'd won.

"Where are you two going? Are you off to try out your prizes?"

Emma smiled politely, but the same anger she'd felt earlier in the gym rose up her throat to choke her. They'd probably been set up so that they won—props—to enliven the movie that was being shot with them being the star performers. She wondered what other prizes she and Jack would win during the rest of their stay.

They left the restaurant with neither speaking until they were ensured of privacy.

"We're being set up," Jack said, gesturing at the boxes he carried with a jerk of his chin.

"That's obvious," Emma muttered. "Just what I wanted. My sex life plastered all over the Internet."

"Don't worry. We'll get them," Jack said in a harsh voice.

"That's a promise," Emma snapped, still smarting each time she recalled the males she'd overheard in the gym. "And we'll bust their asses for both drugs and illicit filming."

Jack grinned suddenly. "That's my girl," he said, and he leaned forward to kiss her square on the lips.

Emma's heart somersaulted. If he wasn't interested in her then why was he kissing her like this when they didn't have an audience? Men! She sure as heck didn't understand them. Her lips softened under his, and she pressed into him even though the two boxes he carried dug into her ribs. Every breath she took was full of his scent. A groan built deep in her chest. Her body heated. Her pussy heated, moistening her panties. A perennial situation when she was around Jack. All she needed to do was think of him and her body prepared for his possession.

Their lips slid together. Sipping, nibbling, tasting. Mating. Her stomach swirled.

Jack pulled away with a curse, and they stared at each other for a long moment.

"I'll see you on the beach at six," he said. "Don't be late."

* * * * *

Jack paced the sand beneath the old pohutukawa tree and checked the skyline again. The last rays of sun brightened the horizon, but still Emma didn't come.

A couple paddled in the small waves that rushed to shore, slowly making their way toward the main part of the resort. It was a Middle Eastern night tonight so Jack presumed everyone was preparing for another night of frivolity—drinking, eating and dancing late into the night.

He paced away from the tree and shivered when his body reacted to the pull of the moon. Even though it wasn't visible in the sky yet, edginess assailed him. He glanced down at his tented shorts with a wry twist of lips. Damn, he needed Emma.

The vibrations of approaching footsteps made him turn.

Emma.

Jack found himself smiling—an automatic reaction. He couldn't seem to stop.

His gaze scanned her body from the top of her head, down her curvy body and long legs to her feet. Whoa! His gaze darted back to her hair.

"Hi," she called. Her whole body screamed self-conscious, alerting Jack to the fact that he could hurt her if he didn't say the right words. An opportunity to blow this budding relationship apart. He didn't take it.

"I was starting to worry," he said.

Emma came to a stop right in front of him, so close they were almost touching. The back of his fingers drifted across her smooth cheek then he lifted his hand higher to tug lightly on a fragrant curl. It was the exact color of the sunset—a combination of red and golden brown and orange.

"You've got a sunset in your hair."

Her head jerked up, her blue eyes wide and uncertain at his compliment. "Is that good?"

"You look beautiful. Worth the wait." Jack hesitated awkwardly on hearing his words, but they came from the heart. And that gave him pause. What the hell was happening to him? This investigation was going nowhere. Frustration was his middle name, yet it wasn't the lack of progress that irritated the heck out of his life plan. It wasn't the impending blue moon. It was Emma.

A sensible man who happened to also be a shape-shifting taniwha, would do the job and walk away...

Jack shrugged inwardly and pushed away his insidious fears. Emma wasn't going to die because he was a taniwha. If he had his way, she would never find out.

"Find out anything helpful?" Emma sat on the sand and hugged her knees as she stared out to sea.

Jack dropped down by her side, casting a quick glance at Emma. "Nothing."

"Are you still going out tonight?"

"Yeah." Damn right. It was even more dangerous staying in.

"What do we do? Stuff the bed with pillows and make it look like we're sleeping for a change?" She glanced over at him with an impish grin that made her resemble a mischievous pixie.

Jack stared. "It's so simple, it might work." He kept staring. Damn, she was pretty. He'd never noticed how creamy and touchable her skin appeared. His gaze drifted then lingered on her mouth, and he found himself leaning toward Emma. Their lips collided then clung together, lingering, nuzzling and sucking with the ease of familiarity. A hand—Emma's hand— slid around his neck urging him closer. They kissed until the need for air forced them to stop. Breathless, they drew apart.

"I didn't think we were doing that again," Emma said, toying with the hair at his nape. Each sharp tug and scrape of her fingernails sent a corresponding jolt to his groin.

"We shouldn't be," Jack muttered. But he gave into the temptation to lick the delicate whorls of her ear. His mouth drifted lower to nuzzle and taste the soft skin of her neck. "But I was never big on rules," he added.

"Me neither." Emma ran her hands through his hair, still tugging hard enough to send a pleasurable pain to his cock and keep him in sensual thrall. "Are we going back to our room?"

They stared at each other for a long drawn-out moment. Jack considered everything he should do and immediately did the opposite. "Let's stay here."

Emma's mouth dropped. "Make love here? On the beach?" She glanced up and down the beach then looked back at him and licked her lips. "What if someone sees us?"

"They're going to see us in our room." Just once, he wanted to love her without a paying audience. Jack pushed aside sudden guilt as he scanned the beach. The situation was more complicated than a simple fuck. He shrugged inwardly and concentrated on Emma instead of emotions he didn't want to deal with. Besides, he'd hear the vibrations of footsteps coming in their direction long before they were discovered in a compromising position.

"That's true." She nodded, a slow grin spreading across her luscious lips. "I like the idea of cheating them out of takings and movie rights."

Hell, what had he done to deserve this woman as a partner? Once again, Jack shied away from his thoughts. He'd fuck her since that's what they both wanted.

Jack pushed her gently back onto the sand. "Last chance," he whispered. "We don't have a blanket. We'll probably end up with sand in places that are uncomfortable."

"You trying to change my mind?" Emma's gurgle made him want to grin.

"Never," he breathed, placing a kiss in her fragrant cleavage. "Have I told you how much I like your tits?"

"Yeah?" Her eyes lit up with laughter. "Why don't you show me?"

Jack scanned the beach again. The brilliant colors of the sunset had faded leaving the horizon a dark, inky bluish black. Overhead the pale moon shone, a day short of full.

His cock twitched insistently.

God, he needed her—it was that simple. He unzipped her shorts and tugged them down her legs. Purple panties today. Jack removed them, too, leaving her bare to his gaze. He parted her folds, sliding his fingers down her moist cleft, then Jack cupped her bottom with his hands and lifted her to his mouth.

Emma forgot they were out in public and concentrated on the feel of him. Her eyes closed leaving her adrift in a world of senses. His fingers on her bare flesh, his tongue laving across her sensitive clitoris. Heaven. The sensations built, lifting her higher until she shuddered, slow waves of ecstasy washing over her until a final swirl of his tongue made her convulse in a violent climax.

A soft kiss on her belly jerked her eyes open. A grin spread across her face. "That was wonderful." An understatement.

"Yeah?" Jack glanced down the beach before ripping off his clothes. In the moonlight, he glowed, looking mysterious and magical. And so sexy, she couldn't believe he was with her. Even if it was just for this week. Emma chewed on the unpalatable thought. If she was persistent, she could win him over. *I'm going to make that man mine*, she thought as she watched him roll on a condom. Yeah, she'd win him over or die in the attempt.

Jack leaned over her, burrowing his hands under her shirt. "Are you brave enough to take this off?"

Emma thought for all of a second. "Take it off." Cool air brushed across her breasts, tightening her nipples to hard points. The contrast of warm and cold made her needy. Achy. Ready for Jack's possession.

He parted her legs and filled her with one seamless thrust. Pleasure coursed through her body, and a cry escaped. Jack scored the tender skin along her throat teasing another soft cry free. He filled her, hitting the sweet spot behind her legs, at exactly the right angle, sending her soaring. *Too quick*, she thought with a trace of regret as heat punched through her. Jack thrust into her, hard and fast. Deep shudders shook his large frame then he stilled. Emma felt his heart pumping and rejoiced in the fact that she made him feel. She placed a tentative hand on his shoulder, only relaxing when he rolled off her and tugged her into a close embrace.

Tears burned suddenly at the back of her eyes. She loved this man, but how the devil was she going to make him admit he felt something for her? Sighing, she cuddled closer just enjoying the moment.

They dressed slowly, laughing and snatching nibbles from bare skin before clothing fell into place. Relaxed and limber, Emma was ready to take on anything. Jack reached out to ruffle her hair, the peacefulness on his face snaring another piece of her heart in the process. She'd thought she'd known Jack, but each hour spent with him peeled away another layer of mystery. He was gentle and moody. Bossy and loyal. And she loved him even more than she had at the start of the week. Go figure.

"I've been thinking about how to handle the search."

Disappointment surged briefly through Emma. But at least he was sharing his plans and treating her more like a partner. If she couldn't have his heart, at least she'd have a working relationship. "How?"

Jack took her arm, and they wandered toward their room. He leaned close and whispered his plans. "We'll go back to our room. If our voyeurs are at their post already, we're stuffed. If they're not, we'll stuff the bed with pillows so it looks as though I'm in bed."

"One problem with that," Emma said. "They must have some system of lighting. I mean we don't always make love with the lights on."

"I know. I've thought of that. The only thing I could think of was distraction."

Emma stopped walking. "What sort of a distraction?"

"You and your vibrator."

"They'll film me!" She didn't have to pretend horror.

"Yes," he said simply. "The decision is yours."

Emma was still thinking about her vibrator when Jack unlocked their room and slipped inside.

"Wait there." It was an order.

Emma's breath came out in a hiss. The man was impossible and as for expecting her to do a solo performance for the benefit of the camera... Emma waited for all of two seconds before following.

"All clear," he murmured. "No one there yet."

"How do you know?"

"My hearing is very good."

Was it her imagination or had his whole persona undergone a swift change. He looked awfully grumpy, and his dark eyes flashed with an emotion she had difficulty deciphering. Definitely not the time to argue.

"We'd better sort out the bed then. I think there are some spare pillows in the wardrobe." Emma jerked open the wardrobe as she spoke and grabbed two pillows plus a spare blanket. When she turned, Jack had tugged back the covers on the left hand side of the bed.

"That's my side of the bed," she said.

"It's farther away from the two-way mirror." His mouth tightened. "Housekeeping has been busy while we've been out this afternoon. We have two cameras. There and there." He pointed before accepting the pillows that Emma held out.

Cameras.

Anger built inside until she felt like a volcano ready to blow. They were not going to get away with this while she had breath in her body. One glance at Jack confirmed his fury.

"How are the cameras activated? Not by movement?" Emma glared in the direction that Jack had pointed. She couldn't see obvious signs of a camera, but she believed him. "Are we being filmed now?"

"I don't think so. If the cameras were movement activated, they'd film housekeeping and anyone who came into the room. They'd waste a lot of film. My guess is they film when they see some action. They'd be able to guess from the timing of the dinners and special events when the guests would return to their rooms."

"But they must have had cameras all the time. That's what they implied when I heard them talking."

Jack scowled. "Going for different angles for their film, I'd say. But I think these are new. I haven't noticed them before."

A blush suffused her face. It slowly crept down to heat her breasts. Surely, the way they made love wasn't that different. Not different enough to warrant more cameras.

Jack finished arranging the pillows and dragged the covers back into place. "How does that look?"

Emma tilted her head to study his handiwork. "Like two pillows and a blanket made to look like a body."

Jack's scowl grew darker. "Cut out the smart-ass remarks." He paused.

"I wasn't—"

"Showtime. I'd better go. Turn off the main light. Quick. Once I'm gone, you can turn on the bedside lamp on your side, but see if you can adjust the lamp so it shines away from the bed."

Emma nodded and followed him to the door. "Take care."

He grabbed her in a bear hug and squeezed her tightly before kissing her hard and swift. Then he slid out the door leaving Emma alone with the voyeurs.

Keep them busy.

The words echoed through her head — taunting and a touch repulsive. The idea of knowingly putting on a show for these creeps…

Taking a deep breath, she padded across the room to the edge of the bed. After fumbling in the dark for a few minutes, she managed to swivel the bedside lamp so it pointed away from the bed. Before she switched it on, she allowed her gaze to run over the mirror. If she hadn't known about the mirror, she would never have suspected.

Maybe if she switched on the television. She could bore them into leaving.

Emma strode over to the television and pushed the power button then found the remote and settled back to channel surf.

Eek! Not that channel, she thought as naked bodies writhed on the screen. She hurriedly changed channels. Emma's eyes widened when she saw a mass of bodies on the bed. There were so many bodies it was a wonder they didn't fall off.

The third channel change clued her in. The television was strictly R18 and geared toward couples. She wouldn't find distraction there.

Emma picked up her e-book reader and tried to concentrate on her most current purchase, a book called *Talking Dogs, Aliens and Purple People Eaters*. She chuckled at the antics of the dog and other characters, but then she reached chapter three and the hero and heroine started in on the sex. Emma hit the off button. Perhaps reading wasn't the best distraction at the moment.

The phone rang. Not Jack? Emma's heart pounded as she picked it up.

"It's Caroline, your resort hostess. Is there any way we can make your stay more enjoyable?"

Like what? she thought indignantly. *More cameras in our room?* "Everything is wonderful," Emma said, not bothering to hold back on the irony.

"Have I called at a bad time?"

"I was about to go to bed."

"Oh! Say no more! I understand completely. Just give us a call if we can do anything to make your stay more enjoyable."

Emma slammed the phone down, fury and frustration making her restless. She stomped past the bed and stormed into the bathroom. Perhaps she'd take a shower to ease the tension from her body.

Twenty minutes later, Emma stepped from the shower and grabbed a towel to blot the droplets of water from her body. Someone thumped on the door and kept thumping. At first, Emma thought about ignoring the summons then she realized that the racket should wake up a person who was sleeping. It would seem odd if the pillows didn't react. She wrapped a towel around her body and hurried to answer the door.

"Hello!" The girl's greeting was breezy and her smile bright enough for Emma to see she used a tooth-whitening agent. "You and your partner are the lucky recipients of a mystery prize." She gestured at her laden trolley.

Yeah right. Emma fought the need to scowl in her best Jack manner. The cynic in her suspected the voyeurs wanted action in the bedroom instead of the sound of running water and the scent of perfumed steam.

The girl picked up an apple green bag and dropped several small bottles inside. "Here you go. Some massage oils and some special lubrication. Oh, and these are great. Some nipple jewelry!" She thrust the bag at Emma then with a wave, tottered off pushing her trolley.

Emma clutched the bag and slammed the door shut. These people were unbelievable. All to get a stupid movie. Rage colored her cheeks as she tossed the bag on the dresser with all the other *prizes* she'd received during the week.

So, she'd give them a show.

Emma grabbed up the pink box that contained her vibrator. She pulled it from the protective wrapping and deftly loaded the batteries. *It would come with batteries provided.* The vibrator buzzed when she tested it.

Okay. What other props did she need for her show? After checking the towel was secure, she padded across to her box of toys. Scented massage oils with a hint of the Orient. Oh, yes. Just the thing. Nipple jewelry. Maybe Jack would like to see that later.

Emma sauntered over to her side of the bed and bent over, pretending to kiss the head end of the roll of blankets. Then, she sucked in a deep breath. Showtime.

She settled on the corner of the bed nearest the mirror. After popping the lid off the bottle of oil, she smoothed it across her arms, legs and upper chest. A pulse throbbed at her throat as she stood. With a casual shrug of her shoulders, she loosened the knot holding the towel in place and let it slither to the floor. Emma pictured Jack and imagined it was his hands smoothing the scented oil on her naked breasts, his fingers plucking at her aching nipples. The heady scent of cinnamon and oranges filled the air as she massaged oil down her legs and across her buttocks. With a languid move, she dribbled oil on her belly. Damn, that felt good.

Heat pooled between her legs as her oil-smeared fingers dipped lower, through her clipped pubic hair, to smooth down bare pussy lips. Emma caught her bottom lip between her teeth to bite back a moan. The friction of her damp finger was exquisite. Damn, she was getting off on this. Did that make her sick? The anger had receded, replaced by pure lust and enjoyment in what she was doing. Heat flooded her pussy as her finger did another pass. Her heart pounded. Too much. Too fast, she decided. But Emma couldn't help tracing a slow circle around her engorged clit before she squeezed more oil on her hand. Her breasts, she decided, then the jewelry. Emma smoothed more of the fragrant oil across her breasts with light feathering touches. She tugged at her nipples again and pleasure swamped her. After skimming the instructions, Emma fastened the loops at each end of the jewelry around her nipples then tightened them. A surge of hot sensation jolted her and a groan sounded. Her groan. Red and gold glass beads draped over the curves of her breasts when she was finished, tiny bells sounding with each move she made. Emma breathed deeply, her breasts rising and falling. A jolt of pleasure shot to her clit and shimmered in place like a promise of what was to come.

God, she was so turned on, it wouldn't take much more than a nudge to push her over the edge.

The snick of the door drew her head up.

Jack.

Heck, what about the blankets? Distraction. Emma picked up the vibrator. And turned it on. Widening her stance, she ran the vibrator down her cleft. She was aware of soft sounds behind her but didn't dare look because of their watchers. Ripples of sensation streaked through her body, the tautness of the jewelry at her nipples intensifying the heat, the pleasure.

Suddenly, Jack was behind her, his bare chest hot against her back, his erection pressing insistently, nudging her buttocks. His arms snaked around her middle.

"You make me hot," he whispered. "God, I need to be inside you now."

"Yes," Emma murmured, setting the humming vibrator aside. "Yes."

Jack turned her and bent her over the bed. Gentle fingers probed her slick cunt, filling her momentarily then vanishing. Before she could protest, his cock filled the emptiness. Two hard strokes deep into her womb shoved her into climax. She shattered, her body shuddering with the force of her release. Jack climaxed a stroke later while her womb still convulsed and spasmed.

He rested against her for an instant then pulled free, tugging Emma to her feet and into his arms. His mouth lowered over hers as he plundered, kissing her deeply, driving her desire higher and winding her tight as a spring. Her last thought as they fell onto the bed in a tangle of limbs and tinkling bells was that she could never ever get enough of Jack.

Chapter Seven

ℬ

Emma headed for the gym. With Jack's finds last night — a computer with shipment details — the case was on its way to being wrapped up. Once they found physical proof and tied a few loose ends, it would all be over. Back to the way things were. Pangs of regret pierced Emma. Not exactly the same way because she knew what Jack looked like naked, how it felt when his cock filled her impossibly deep.

A man walked down the corridor in front of Emma. Dressed in a suit, he seemed out of place in the casual atmosphere of the resort. Mahoney. *The creep.* He yanked open the fire door at the end of the corridor then waited, holding the door open for Emma. "Thanks," she said, smiling even though she'd prefer to spit at him.

A smile curved his lips, amusement shining in his eyes. "You're very welcome, my dear."

Emma gasped. He knew who she was. Making love with Jack was private, dammit! Fury lashed Emma without warning and accusations bubbled out before she could think.

"Mr. Mahoney. I want the films back."

The smile broadened. Like the dog that had polished off the last of the cat's dinner, he smirked, his gaze drifting up and down Emma's body. "I have no idea what you are talking about."

Emma shuddered, and it wasn't with the same awareness she experienced when Jack looked at her. Mahoney made her feel dirty. His smirk poked her anger to a higher level.

She glared. "If you don't give me the films you've taken of me and Jack, I will go to the papers. I will tell every single guest that they are being filmed without their knowledge. I will warn them that their images are being peddled on the Internet." Her chest rose and fell with the force of her anger.

"I don't know what you're talking about."

The clear amusement in his brown eyes as she looked up told her he knew exactly what she was talking about. And he'd seen the films. With his gel-slicked hair, his designer aftershave and suit, he appeared self-important. Emma's right fist curled and drew back ready to let rip. His face. His gut. She didn't care what she smacked — anything to prick his smug ego.

"Fine," she snapped, taking a deep, calming breath. "I'm going to ring the police." She marched past, but his hand shot out and fastened around her forearm with the force of a steel manacle.

"I don't think so, my dear."

"I am not *your* dear." Only one man for her, and it wasn't this one.

With his greater height and strength, Mahoney forced her to trot at his side a short distance down the corridor before knocking on a door with his free hand.

Emma fought every step of the way. "Let me go."

The door jerked open and Mahoney pushed her inside a storage room. Shelves were stacked with small brown boxes while a desk and two chairs sat just inside between the door and the shelves. Emma squinted trying to read the labels on the boxes. Her breath hissed through clenched teeth. Bingo. The storage room they'd been searching for.

The man who had opened the door looked alert. "Problem, Mr. Mahoney?"

"Nothing we can't handle," Mahoney said, shoving Emma farther into the room.

Emma was pleased to see her struggles had messed up Mahoney's hair. She jerked from his touch, and this time he let her.

"Keep her here out of trouble. Get a rope. We'll tie her up."

Emma backed up, lashing out with her feet, kicking and biting but the two men overpowered her when they forced her into a corner. Still, she didn't make it painless for them, managing to draw blood with a blow to one man's nose. George would have been proud of her. The arrival of a third man made their job easier and soon she was trussed up tight. They left her sitting on the floor near the shelves.

"You can't keep me here," Emma screeched. Hopefully, someone would hear.

Mahoney scowled as he swept a hand through his dark hair. "If the noise gets too bad, gag her." He glared at her before striding from the room.

Emma stopped mid-shout. Best she saved the shouting for later when she really needed to attract attention.

* * * * *

The magnetic pull of the moon gave testiness a whole new meaning. Jack strode to their room, hoping like hell Emma was there and could be tempted into a quickie. His stomach twisted, pain slicing like a blunt knife. Sex. God, please let Emma be there. He'd never felt the like of this before. He needed to slam into her pussy in the worst possible way. A glance at his hand showed the dark stems of his claws beneath his human fingernails. Another sharp surge of pain almost doubled him over. He fell inside the room. Emma wasn't there. Shit. He was gonna have to jerk-off to stave off both the pain and the taniwha. Along with the thought came a sliver of worry. He hadn't seen her since this morning.

Jack ripped off his clothes before a wave of pain doubled him over. He crawled into the bathroom before pulling to his feet in front of the mirror. His face glinted with the pale gray of taniwha scales. His hands fisted around his cock and he noticed that too glinted a pearl gray color. Emma. He concentrated, visualizing her in his mind. Her ripe curves. Her mouth wrapped around his swollen cock. Jack pumped his erection, stroking with hard, even strokes. Not enough to send him over the edge but sufficient to keep the taniwha at bay. Jack stretched the process out for as long as he could before applying a bit more pressure to his sensitive tip. He came with a rush in his fisted hand. As he cleaned up, Emma filled his mind.

Where the hell was she? She'd said she intended to go to the gym. He'd go there first. If anything had happened to her, he'd never forgive himself.

* * * * *

The guards scarcely paid any attention to her. There were two of them and they looked like clones of the ones who worked in the gym. They argued about who was going to lunch first. Evidently, it was chocolate penis day and the chef had a great recipe for the truffle filling. Finally, they tossed a coin and the winner left jubilant. The other placed a pair of earphones on his head and played his music loud enough that Emma could hear the bass where she was sitting.

Half an hour passed as Emma fought to loosen the length of rope they'd tied her wrists with. The first man returned brandishing his chocolate penis dessert and the second left for lunch.

Emma continued to work toward freedom, her gaze on her minder. He swiped his tongue across the very tip of his chocolate penis dessert and moaned in ecstasy.

Good grief. He was taking eating to a whole new level. Emma stared, not wanting to watch but mesmerized by his performance.

His groan was an animal grunt, and when he pulled the penis away from his mouth, Emma saw he'd nibbled off the tip. A trickle of the filling dribbled from the corner of his mouth.

Eew! She shuddered and looked away. That was so *not* sexy.

Without warning the rope that tied her hands loosened — just a fraction. Emma doubled her efforts and five minutes later, one hand slid free. She drew her legs up in a stealthy fashion and unfastened the rope around her ankles.

A weapon.

Carefully, she turned to scan her surroundings. There was no way she could creep out, not with the penis-sucking man right near the door. But he was so engrossed...

Emma's gaze lit on a large rock near the door. It looked as though it was used as a doorstop when they were bringing in more supplies. She glanced from the rock to the man's head. The rock would make an excellent weapon—if she could grab it before the man worked out what she was up to.

The man continued sucking on the penis. Emma's lips curled in distaste while she worked on freeing her other hand. Then she blinked. Even better! The man was nodding off.

She scanned the room. Perhaps she should take a look in one of the brown boxes? The man looked as though he was asleep. Holding her breath, she tugged open the closest box. It was full of foil packs containing pills. Emma slipped one inside her shorts pocket. A snort sounded. Emma froze, but when she whirled around to look, his eyes remained closed. Her breath eased out and she stood, gliding smoothly forward to scoop up the rock. It was heavier than it looked. And in truth, she wasn't sure she could hit a sleeping man over the head. As she edged closer, she saw his face was smeared with dark chocolate. That settled it—she couldn't hit a man who looked like a defenseless kid. Emma took another two steps and reached for the door, still holding the rock. Her free hand closed around the brass handle and twisted. The door squeaked.

The man jerked awake. "What?"

Emma threw the rock at him and ripped the door fully open. The man cried out. She heard a crash but didn't stop to see the damage. Instead, she hurried toward the main corridor, peeked around the corner. When she saw it was all clear, sprinted in the opposite direction to the restaurant.

Jack.

She had to find Jack.

* * * * *

Jack scanned the bodies in the gym, urgency humming through his tense body. Emma wasn't here. He couldn't smell the girly floral soap she used and he sure as hell couldn't see her.

He stalked through to the restaurant, searching faces, his gut churning insistently the whole time. If anything had happened to her...

Pushing through the queue at the buffet, he ignored the comments about rudeness. She had to be somewhere. Outside, he checked the bar and around the pool. Down on the beach. Worry creased his brow while the pull of the blue moon created havoc with his body. Every bone in his body ached as if he had a fever and sweat glued his shirt to his chest and back. He forced himself to stagger farther down the beach, to push through the pain that made him shiver and shake.

All he could think of was Emma. The way she smiled. The way she pushed him, ignoring his bouts of surliness. The way she gave her all when they made love. Jack snorted. Somewhere along the line, Emma had crept into the empty spaces inside. It was a damned uncomfortable sensation, but he'd come to like her presence.

A flash of red caught his eye as he hurried along the beach. "Emma. Where the hell have you been?" A wave of pain doubled him over. Sex. Shit, now. Jack glanced up and down the beach. He jerked her against his chest, shuddering at the feminine feel of her. Her sunset hair was ruffled and dirt coated one cheek. He lifted a trembling hand, battling nausea and acute stomach pangs to unbutton her shirt. A quickie to take the edge off, to stave the pain and halt the shift to taniwha. He fumbled, his nails well on the way to transformation.

Emma frowned, glancing over her shoulder. "What are you doing? Shit! We've got to go." Her hands and wrists were bloodied when she lifted them to push against his chest.

"What happened?" Damn, his voice was changing. Desperation swelled along with pain. Sex. *Now*.

"Run." Emma grabbed his forearm. "They're after me."

A gunshot punctuated her words. Emma sprinted down the beach toward the river mouth. Jack lumbered after her, trying to focus on moving one foot after the other. Waves of pain engulfed him, sharp and intense. His hands had turned. If the transformation went much further he wouldn't be able to come back—not for twenty-four hours.

The soft sand changed to mud that oozed between his sandaled feet. Jack paused to rip off his shirt and yank off his leather sandals. Pearly scales had already formed on his chest. Jack glanced at Emma in front of him as she darted between two mangrove trees. He lumbered after her, ignoring the grasping branches of the mangrove trees that gouged his limbs.

The pungent scent of the mud and the salty tang of the water called to his taniwha soul. *Emma.* Regret pierced Jack along with sorrow, and in that moment, he realized he cared more for her than he'd ever cared for another woman. And he was going to lose her, if he didn't scare her to death first.

Jack's senses sharpened. The pounding of running feet following them continued, the sound of the men's harsh breathing a signal to hurry.

"Emma," he growled. "Into the water."

Her face whitened noticeably. "No, I can't swim."

But he could since taniwhas were creatures of the water. "Climb on my back." He had to concentrate to get the words out.

Emma hesitated but the crack of a gun firing galvanized her to action.

Jack jerked off his remaining clothes and waded into the water. "Come." His voice was barely recognizable. He glanced back, and from the shock on Emma's face knew that the transformation from man to taniwha had progressed enough to traumatize. Jack wanted to rail at fate but instead he grabbed Emma and tugged her resisting body out into deeper water.

Knowing his options were gone, he focused, picturing the serpent in his mind. Muscles and bones lengthened, his face changed, elongating to fit the sharp teeth and fangs that had developed. His nostrils changed shape, as did his eyes. A long tail formed, making him appear much larger than his normal six foot two. His arms and legs changed into strong, webbed limbs suitable for swimming. Fully shifted, the taniwha resembled a water beast, half dragon, half Loch Ness monster in appearance, capable of inflicting mortal wounds to enemies.

Conscious of Emma clinging to his back, Jack filled his lungs with air then swam just below the surface allowing Emma to breath but hiding as much of her from sight as possible. Jack headed for the mainland, his heart heavy. Things would never be the same with Emma now. Her hands gripped him, but after her initial gasp, she hadn't uttered a word. *Shock*, he thought. She would fear him now, and he hated the idea. Too late, he'd realized he wanted her in his life. He shied away from the word love, but it felt uncomfortably close to the emotion he swore he'd never let into his life again.

* * * * *

Surreal. She was shooting through the water on the back of a beast. And that beast was Jack.

George Taniwha & Co.

Emma's heart pounded in fear but exhilaration, too. The taniwha part of the company name was real. She was riding on the back of a taniwha. Jack was a taniwha, and he stunk. She wrinkled her nose. Could be worse. Emma had glimpsed his teeth. The sharp fangs in children's storybooks were not exaggerated.

A wave slapped her in the face. An undignified screech emerged, and she grabbed the long strands of hair that grew on the taniwha's back, twining her fingers through it and using them like reins. Reality check! She was in the middle of the bloody sea. God, she hated deep water. Instinctively, she clung tighter, curling her fingers into the slimy flesh of the taniwha. Panic rose dangerously close to the surface but a glance over her shoulder at the three men brandishing guns put a realistic spin on the situation. She gripped Jack with her knees and squeezed her eyes shut. How fast did a taniwha swim anyway? Faster than a boat?

Emma concentrated on the mainland, praying they'd get there quick. She wondered about George and his sons. And George's wife Meri. Were they all taniwha? Did they look as ugly as Jack? Another wave slapped her in the face and she gasped, inhaling deeply. A mistake. Did all taniwha smell as bad as Jack?

The taniwha changed direction suddenly, and Emma's eyes flew open. Alarm surfaced until she realized Jack was heading for a part of the coast that was covered in bush. Heck, the moment when she could put her feet on the ground again couldn't come soon enough. The waves became bigger all of a sudden. Emma shrieked when one broke over her head. Panicked, she struggled, one hand loosening its grip on the taniwha's coarse hair to flail to the surface. Air. She needed air now.

A growl filled the air, vibrating through her ears like the boom of distant thunder. Then, her head cleared the water and she gasped a lungful of air. Another wave crashed to shore but this one only came to her shoulders.

The taniwha swam then stood at the water's edge. Emma attempted to scramble off the creature's back but the taniwha roared. She froze, trying not to breathe too deeply. The stench was a combination of day-old fish and swamp mud.

The taniwha lumbered up the beach with Emma on its back. It was a pretty color—a bit like the inside of a mussel shell—pearly gray with hints of pink and green. The color was the only attractive thing about the taniwha. Emma found it hard to believe Jack and the taniwha were one. Jack was a man to die for. The taniwha was plain ugly and grotesque.

They crashed through low scrub and bush until Emma couldn't see or hear the sea. The scrub gave way to larger trees— punga, karaka and manuka. The taniwha continued with its uneven lope, taking a small overgrown path. Ferns brushed against the taniwha and the leaf litter cracked under its feet but Emma couldn't hear a single bird. The taniwha—Jack—never hesitated. Gradually, the shadows gave way and they emerged into a clearing. Jack stopped, and Emma cautiously let go of his hair and slid down his slippery back to the ground. They eyed one another but the taniwha broke contact first. He lumbered over to a punga and stripped several of the branches from the fern tree. After laying them on the ground, the taniwha turned to her and gestured with a clawed arm.

Okay. It appeared they were staying.

"I'm going to find help." Emma turned to leave.

A roar echoed through the clearing. Like a clap of thunder directly overhead, it made Emma leap in fright. She took another step and the taniwha moved.

"All right," she snapped. "I get the picture." Maybe there was something of Jack in the taniwha. They were both bossy.

Emma sat on a fallen log and glared at the beast. Its mouth widened, and she could have sworn the taniwha was smirking.

Day passed to night and the temperature dropped. Emma shivered, fighting the need to sleep.

Suddenly, the taniwha grunted. It ambled over to her side and scooped her off the log before she could scramble away.

"I don't think—"

The taniwha growled and flashed its teeth.

"All right!" she muttered, screwing her nose up at the stench. He needed better dental hygiene.

The taniwha placed her on the fern bed and lay down beside her.

"You smell," Emma stated with a trace of defiance.

The taniwha grunted, and it sounded like a bark of amusement.

Emma rolled away from the taniwha and smiled. If only she could get used to the smell, there might be hope for them.

The twitter of birds woke her at first light the next morning. She rolled over, away from the clammy warmth to see the taniwha studying her warily.

"Morning," she mumbled, self-consciously combing her fingers through her messy curls. "When do you change back? You do change back, right?"

The taniwha grunted. He seemed to do that a lot but Emma was no linguist. Each grunt sounded much the same.

The taniwha walked heavily toward a path the other side of the clearing then stopped to look at Emma.

She sighed. "All right. I'm coming."

They walked for hours through heavy bush, scrambling up and down hills. By late afternoon, Emma was footsore, tired and desperately hungry. When they reached a clearing and a bubbling stream, Emma stopped, refusing to go a step farther without rest. She glared at Jack, half expecting a thunderous protest but he shrugged and strode into the stream, splashing like a playful child. Then, he stepped out of the water and stood before her. His skin glowed in the sunshine. He shimmered.

Emma blinked as the air around him shifted. The length of his jaw changed before her eyes. "He's transforming," she whispered, amazement coloring her voice as his long tail disappeared.

Soon, all that remained of the taniwha was the whiff of fish and mangrove mud that lingered in the air.

Jack took a cautious step toward Emma. She hadn't behaved in the way he'd expected. She hadn't screamed. Much. "Aren't you going to say anything?"

"You make a very ugly taniwha."

Jack scowled. "Is that it?"

A slow grinned danced across her face as she looked him up and down. "You're stark naked."

Reaction set in making his knees wobble. Jack sank to the ground and continued to stare up at Emma. "The last woman who saw me in taniwha form panicked. She fled the scene and was so traumatized she crashed her car and died. It was my fault she died."

"Oh, please," Emma scoffed. "How was it your fault? You made her drive? You made her crash?"

Bemusement filled Jack as she continued to smile at him. He opened his mouth to speak then snapped it shut. Hope bloomed and his cock rose in a silent demand. She looked damned sexy with that snooty superior expression on her face.

"So what do we do now? Have we got enough to fry Mahoney's ass?"

"Don't you care that I change into an ugly serpent when the moon is full?" He'd leave the explanation about sex for later. The whole issue was clouded enough already. No, he'd give her the worst now. "When the full moon approaches, I need constant sex several times a day to help me maintain human form."

"It doesn't have any bearing on our case," Emma said, but her cheeks flushed a bright red. "Can we get Mahoney for running the sports-drug racket and selling illicit movies? We have to do something about that man. He's a creep. Besides, I don't want our images for sale on the net."

And they weren't going to appear on the net. Jack would get them before things went that far. But maybe he'd keep them for private viewing. "I love you," he said.

"You do? About time!" Emma dropped to the ground at his side. She plucked at the white flowers of a manuka tree, before looking up to flash him a blinding smile. "It took you long enough to work it out. And the sex part is fine with me. I like sex."

Was that it? Didn't women get off on this emotion stuff? Jack stared at Emma willing her to tell him she loved him, too. She wasn't a casual girl. She must feel something for him. And they hadn't had sex, dammit. They'd made love.

"So, are we going to charge Mahoney?" She dug deep inside her shorts pocket and pulled out a foil pack of pills. "I took this from the room where they held me."

Jack straightened in alarm. "What did they do to you?" Emma looked all right, but he knew about hidden wounds.

"Tied me up." She shrugged. "I managed to get loose, and I threw a rock at the guy they left to look after me."

Shit, she'd even escaped by herself. Why did she need a big, bad taniwha around when she could rescue herself? "We have enough to make life difficult for Mahoney," Jack said finally.

"Good. Let's go."

"I need clothes."

Emma grinned suddenly. "Does this happen a lot? I mean you look pretty good without clothes but doesn't it get a little cold?"

Jack reached over to stroke her cheek. "Not if I have a willing woman to keep me warm."

"I won't share." Emma's eyes narrowed in warning. "I expect you to concentrate on me. No other women."

Jack didn't mind admitting it—he was having trouble keeping up with Emma today. She wasn't reacting as she should. In other words, she was confusing the shit out of him.

"We are getting married. Right?"

"You haven't told me you love me," Jack muttered. Marriage? With Emma? The idea didn't scare him like it would have a week ago. In fact, the more he thought about it, the better the idea sounded. Marriage and Emma.

"You silly man." Emma's blue eyes were full of laughter and something else. Tenderness. Caring. Her expression made Jack hope for the future, marriage and maybe children. "Jack Sullivan, you're a man to die for. Of course, I love you! Haven't you noticed that women fall over themselves to go out with you? Why wouldn't I want you? Come on. If we don't hurry, we'll have to spend another night outdoors." She stood and held a hand out for him to take. "You need clothes."

"I have a friend who lives not far from here. He'll help us."

"Great. I hope he has food." Emma couldn't believe Jack didn't know how she felt about him. He grasped her hand and tugged until she fell against his naked chest. His eyes glittered as he stared down at her and her heart thudded with sensual awareness. Oh, yeah. She loved him like crazy.

A taniwha.

It didn't matter. She could learn to live with the taniwha smell. And the sex part of the equation didn't worry her either. In fact, it made her hot just thinking about it. Emma grinned as another thought occurred. Was that why George and the rest of his operatives looked really tired at certain times of the month?

"I love you, Jack." Emma pressed a chaste kiss to his lips.

He hugged her tight and deepened the kiss.

Emma smiled against his mouth, feeling so happy she wanted to cry. As far as twenty-fifth birthday presents went, winning Jack's love was a doozey. And now she'd caught the man, she had no intention of letting him go. It might take him a while to get the idea, but she had patience enough for them both...

Also by Shelley Munro

ℰℴ

Curse of Brandon Lupinus

Ellora's Cavemen: Dreams of the Oasis III

Fallen Idol

Middlemarch Mates: Peeping Tom

Middlemarch Mates: Scarlet Woman

Middlemarch Mates: Stray Cat Strut

Talking Dog: Never Send a Dog To Do a Woman's Job

Talking Dog: Romantic Interlude

Sex Idol

Summer in the City of Sails

Talking Dog: Talking Dogs, Aliens, and Purple People Eaters

About the Author

∞

Shelley lives in Auckland, New Zealand, with her husband and a small, bossy dog named Scotty.

Typical New Zealanders, Shelley and her husband left home for their big OE soon after they married (translation of New Zealand-speak: big overseas experience). A year-long adventure lengthened to six years of roaming the world. Enduring memories include being almost sat on by a mountain gorilla in Rwanda, lazing on white sandy beaches in India, whale watching in Alaska, searching for leprechauns in Ireland, and dealing with ghosts in an English pub.

While travel is still a big attraction, these days Shelley is most likely found in front of her computer following another love—that of writing stories of romance and adventure. Other interests include watching rugby and rugby league (strictly for research purposes *grin*), being walked by the dog, and curling up with a good book.

Shelley welcomes comments from readers. You can find her website and email address on her author bio page at www.ellorascave.com.

Why an electronic book?

We live in the Information Age—an exciting time in the history of human civilization, in which technology rules supreme and continues to progress in leaps and bounds every minute of every day. For a multitude of reasons, more and more avid literary fans are opting to purchase e-books instead of paper books. The question from those not yet initiated into the world of electronic reading is simply: *Why?*

1. ***Price.*** An electronic title at Ellora's Cave Publishing and Cerridwen Press runs anywhere from 40% to 75% less than the cover price of the exact same title in paperback format. Why? Basic mathematics and cost. It is less expensive to publish an e-book (no paper and printing, no warehousing and shipping) than it is to publish a paperback, so the savings are passed along to the consumer.

2. ***Space.*** Running out of room in your house for your books? That is one worry you will never have with electronic books. For a low one-time cost, you can purchase a handheld device specifically designed for e-reading. Many e-readers have large, convenient screens for viewing. Better yet, hundreds of titles can be stored within your new library—on a single microchip. There are a variety of e-readers from different manufacturers. You can also read e-books on your PC or laptop computer. (Please note that Ellora's

Cave does not endorse any specific brands. You can check our websites at www.ellorascave.com or www.cerridwenpress.com for information we make available to new consumers.)

3. *Mobility.* Because your new e-library consists of only a microchip within a small, easily transportable e-reader, your entire cache of books can be taken with you wherever you go.

4. ***Personal Viewing Preferences.*** Are the words you are currently reading too small? Too large? Too... ANNOYING? Paperback books cannot be modified according to personal preferences, but e-books can.

5. ***Instant Gratification.*** Is it the middle of the night and all the bookstores near you are closed? Are you tired of waiting days, sometimes weeks, for bookstores to ship the novels you bought? Ellora's Cave Publishing sells instantaneous downloads twenty-four hours a day, seven days a week, every day of the year. Our webstore is never closed. Our e-book delivery system is 100% automated, meaning your order is filled as soon as you pay for it.

Those are a few of the top reasons why electronic books are replacing paperbacks for many avid readers.

As always, Ellora's Cave and Cerridwen Press welcome your questions and comments. We invite you to email us at Comments@ellorascave.com or write to us directly at Ellora's Cave Publishing Inc., 1056 Home Avenue, Akron, OH 44310-3502.

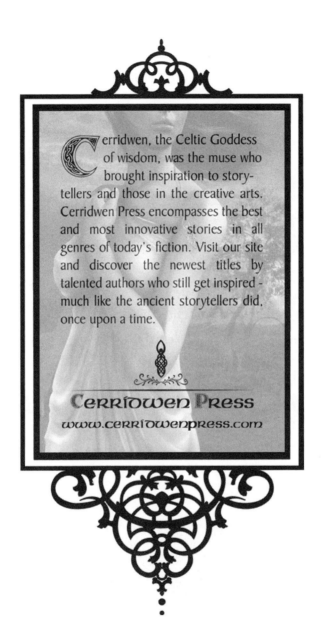

Cerridwen, the Celtic Goddess of wisdom, was the muse who brought inspiration to storytellers and those in the creative arts. Cerridwen Press encompasses the best and most innovative stories in all genres of today's fiction. Visit our site and discover the newest titles by talented authors who still get inspired - much like the ancient storytellers did, once upon a time.

Cerridwen Press

www.cerridwenpress.com